THE BROTHERHOOD OF THE RED NILE

AMERICA RESPONDS

DAN PERKINS

 **FriesenPress**

Suite 300 - 990 Fort St
Victoria, BC, Canada, V8V 3K2
www.friesenpress.com

ISBN
978-1-4602-5100-3 (Hardcover)
978-1-4602-5101-0 (Paperback)
978-1-4602-5102-7 (eBook)

1. Fiction, Action & Adventure

Distributed to the trade by The Ingram Book Company

Thank you Lord, for your inspiration and guidance.

Acknowledgement

There are many people to thank, and the first is my wife for 46 years, Gerri. She is the one person who was with me every day on this adventure. When we were inspired by the Lord to start a foundation to support soldiers, I knew she had to be the President of this new venture. We have a lot of people to help, and with the Lord's guidance it should be a very rewarding journey.

Four people who labored with me in the editing process must be acknowledged. Marty Loftus, who is a long-time friend, business partner, and is now one of the trustees of the Songs and Stories for Soldiers Inc. Foundation. He was the first to take the book apart and ask me questions about the story.

The primary content editor was Dan Pater; he was always finding conflicts and on many occasions the commas would wrestle him to the ground. If something just seemed unrealistic, he would challenge me on the story line.

Bill Rinderknecht was a content reviewer, editor and coordinator between the Publisher and me. He came to me when I desperately needed help and has worked with me on all three books.

The fourth was Linda Kreter who was the final proofer for book three. She has been an avid supporter from book one. She feels, like me, that only God can write a perfect book and I thank her for her passion and her belief in the story.

Last, but not least, is Kathryn Raaker, my manager, who has worked so hard to bring my projects and endeavors to the next level. We both believe that we are doing what the Lord wants us to do. She is focused on the mission and has taken me to places and connected me with people I doubt I would ever have been able to on my own.

Thank you, to all the people who have supported me in the past, and I pray you will continue to support me in the future.

Foreword

This is the third and final book in the Brotherhood series. It is still very hard for me to believe that so much has happened to me in such a short period of time. When I was finishing book one my sister Kathy asked me, "How will you measure your success as a writer?"

I told her that I hadn't thought much about success measurement. In some respects, just finishing the book was a success. She said to me, "Your success will be measured if somebody you don't know buys your book and enjoys it." I have had the opportunity with book signings, radio, and TV appearances and newspaper interviews to meet and talk to millions of people about my books. Some have bought and some have not. I hope that most of the people who bought and enjoyed the first two will also enjoy this third book "America Responds."

The most common comment about this trilogy has been: "It all seemed so real and very plausible, it could really happen." I had several objectives in writing these books. I wanted to give people a great read and based on the many positive reviews, I have accomplished that objective. Another objective was to try and help Americans begin to understand why the terrorists hate us so much and that subject alone could fill many volumes. As a country, we have a long way to go to understand the Muslim religion and why so many followers hate us with such passion.

Many people have asked me, now that the trilogy is finished, what is your next project? I have great attachment to the main players in my story. I created them and they are a part of me. I have decided to use the main players; Ted, Hadar, Megan, Omid and John in the next book. Many people have told me that they feel like they know them and they want to see what happens to them. In the next few books, we will find them again in harrowing adventures. As in the previous books, you will get a sample of what's to come at the end of book three. I know that many of you have loved and enjoyed the adventure of the trilogy. A great many of you have told me how much you enjoyed the people in the story and have asked, "Will we see them again?" Terrorism and terrorists are not going away. In the back of this book is the first chapter of a spinoff where I think you will recognize some old friends.

As in the past, all the technology used in this book is real and available over the Internet, or your neighborhood spy supply store. One final point, many of my readers ask me or send me emails about some of the cliffhangers in both books one and book two. People want to know what happens and they can't wait; it's like a child on Christmas morning having to wait to open a present and it can be very frustrating. Let me assure you that most of the cliffhangers will be answered - notice I said *most*.

One last comment. The sub-title for book three is "America Responds". The story I'm trying to tell in this final book is that we must have a plan to combat terrorism. It would be unrealistic to end the book with the defeat of the terrorists in one fell swoop. We may wear the white hats, but we can't come charging in and save the day in a chapter or two. Like book one, which had a very unusual ending, so is the ending of the trilogy. Some will hate it and others will love it. My hope is that the reader will see the possibilities available to us as a nation should we have the courage to make those difficult choices. I have tried to end the book by talking about a new America; one that has purpose and direction to make America and the world a safer and more peaceful place. I hope this trilogy will stimulate conversation about the real and present dangers with terrorism and what we as a people and nation will do about this threat.

Enjoy the read, remember this is fiction, or it is supposed to be…

Dan Perkins

The Brotherhood of the Red Nile

Prologue

The Brotherhood of the Red Nile is a new terrorist group founded by Mohammad el Sargon in central Syria, with the goal of attacking the United States. Sargon has struck a deal with the Iranian Nuclear Program to rebuild two old Soviet Union suitcase dirty bombs and convert them into nuclear weapons of mass destruction.

The Brotherhood has delivered the bombs to the United States and detonated both, seriously damaging the oil and natural gas infrastructure in Texas and Louisiana and the energy supply from the Gulf of Mexico. The nuclear detonation killed over 60,000 people and affected almost all aspects of American life. In order to protect the American people from riots, President Nathan Jordan has set a curfew from dusk to dawn. Martial law is in effect across the nation. The banks and capital markets are closed, and millions of residents in Texas need to be relocated because they are living on top of radioactively-contaminated oil, natural gas, and refined product in pipelines below their homes, churches, hospitals, supermarkets, and most places of business.

America is slowly recovering from the destruction. Because of the shortage of gas and aviation fuel, travel is restricted, so there are not enough Congressmen and Senators in Washington, DC to have a quorum. The banks and stock markets are closed and cash is king. The food supplies are rapidly dwindling. Millions of people in Texas and Louisiana are homeless, and having to relocate to other parts of the country. The President, Nathan Jordan, is ruling the country by Executive Order.

The Brotherhood is planning an escape from America. The President has appointed a Special Ops group composed of DHS, CIA, military, and Mossad operatives to track them. The Brotherhood is unaware that the elite team is on their trail. The team has a chance to capture them while they are still in America - if the trap they are setting can be sprung in time.

The President has been thinking about how America should respond to this attack that caused such a high loss of life. Jordan believes that he has to stop the terrorists and he is exploring all his options. One option, using nuclear weapons, is on the table.

As the President talks to his advisors, he begins to start formulating his plan, but there is just one problem. Jordan may never get a chance to carry out his plan if he is not elected to a second term as President. Can he get reelected? Will he finally go after the Brotherhood and bring them to justice to pay for their crimes? Who will run against Jordan for President? If he wins reelection will the American people support his plan?

Profoundly provocative in its personification of America's present-day plight of geo-political proportions, *The Brotherhood of the Red Nile, America Responds* is beyond a "must read". Intensely researched and magnetically relentless in its pursuit of me, I could not escape from being drawn into the plot...as if I knew each player personally. Could it be that I found myself in a literary hologram of prophetic proportions? A clairvoyant and visionary, Dan Perkins, once again brings home to us that as Americans 'a Patriot is beyond fiction'.

— Dr. Norman D.E. Raymond, D.O.
Master Faculty Clinical Professor
Ohio University Heritage College of Medicine
Columbus, Ohio

Chapter 1

WHAT SHOULD WE DO?

The Houston DHS team has just returned from a great dinner at Morton's. For most of their stay they have been eating in to not call any attention to themselves. The food has been okay. Omid had volunteered to cook most of the meals and though the rest of the team says he is a good cook, going out to eat is a real treat, especially if the boss is paying. They had walked to the restaurant, located a few blocks from the safe house. When they enter, they notice the restaurant is less than half full. All the tables are set up, but the restaurant seems uninviting and cold.

Megan remarked, "People make the place, and if there aren't many people in the restaurant it's a different place." When you think of Morton's, you customarily think of crowded tables, a busy wait staff and a lot of sound. They sat down at their table and the waiter approached, saying, "We do not have a printed menu because of the various shortages; we are doing the best we can with what we can get. I want to make sure you were informed that we are cash only."

Baker responded, "Yes, we were. Please tell us what you can offer."

The waiter went through the short list and they all decided to have steak in one form or another. The waiter gave Ted the wine list and he ordered a few bottles of wine. As the courses came, they enjoyed the food and each other's company. They finished the meal and all agreed with John when he said, "This is one of the best meals I've had in a long time, no offense to Omid."

He replied, "None taken."

They all stood up, bloated with all the food they had eaten and slowly walked back toward the safe house. Baker motioned to Megan to hang back a little, "When we get back I have $10,000 in cash for food and other supplies; let me know when you need more."

They took the elevator to the 11ᵗʰ floor and slowly stepped into the common hallway. Inside the apartment, Hadar walked down the long hallway from the front door; the hall lights were out. She felt on the wall, found the switch and turned on a light, and continued down the hall to her room.

Hadar went into her room to hang up her jacket in the closet just across from her bed. Just before she turned on the light in her room her eye was drawn to her bedside table. She stopped and stared intently at the bedside table. She had left her cell phone on this table when they went to dinner. As she focused all of her attention, she saw for the very first time since she came to America, a very dim light on the side of her phone blinking slowly. Someone had either sent Hadar an email or a text message. In that single moment, she couldn't imagine who it was. Like a bolt of lightning striking her brain she thought, *it could have come from Mordecai…what should I do?*

Hadar realized that if she had turned on the overhead light she may not have seen the LED light on the phone for hours, perhaps days. *I wonder when he actually called.* She called out in a frightened voice to Ted Baker, "Please come to my room!"

The whole team heard her cry out. They all rushed down the narrow hallway, avoiding bumping into each other, to Hadar's room to see what all the commotion is all about. As they crowded into her room, they could see her sitting on the edge of her bed holding her cell phone in her lap. No lights were turned on, and as their eyes adjusted to the low level of light they could all see the flashing light on the phone in Hadar's hand. Baker told her, "Open it, let's see who it's from."

Hadar slowly opened the phone and on the screen of her flip phone was a text message. She clicked on the message, "No, help me M." They all knew that this was a possible response to the many texts that Hadar has been sending to Mordecai's cell phone, but for now they have no way of knowing if the person responding to her message is truly Mordecai or just one of the Brotherhood using Mordecai's phone to find out who has been texting him.

Baker stepped out of the room and called Williams to tell him about the possible contact from Mordecai. Baker reached Marie at Williams' office. Marie put the call through to Williams, and Baker told him about the response to Hadar's text messages.

Williams responded, "Keep me in the loop."

Baker suggests that they need to figure out something for Hadar to communicate to Mordecai that only the two of them would know. This would be a way of verifying that the other person is in fact Mordecai.

Williams agreed, "Let me know whatever resources you need."

"Sir, I was thinking about that, and it seems to me we have a great untapped resource that we could be using."

"Who is that?"

"The Logistics Office."

"Great idea. Should I call them now and alert them?"

"Sir, let's find out if it is truly is Mordecai on the other end before we marshal our resources."

"Good point; I agree, this could be the break we have been waiting for."

"Yes, sir. Let's hope it pans out; I'll keep you posted."

Baker went back into the room and suggested that they all move to the living room and talk about alternatives for a response to the text message confirming whether it is Mordecai or not. "We don't know for sure if it is Mordecai answering the text message, so we need a way to verify that it. Hadar, I need you to think of something that you could text back to verify it is Mordecai and not one of the other Brotherhood members trying to impersonate Mordecai. It has to be something that only the two of you would know."

Hadar thought about encounters she'd had with Mordecai and things that had transpired between them that only they would know, and yet if it were not Mordecai it would not tip off the Brotherhood. Her mind raced with ideas, *The barn door, or possibly the times he left before they were done eating, the suggestion of where to go to study adobe-building in America, or perhaps the last kiss when he said, 'Can you imagine how great the sex might be?' and her response, 'I was thinking the same thing.'*

Megan offered, "Whatever the question, it has to be seen as non-threatening. Hadar, think of something that can be a one word answer yet something only he would remember."

Hadar suggested, "Do you remember the name of the dessert we had in the café; I can't remember what it was called?"

John said, "Wait a minute, Hadar, you sent a simple message "Are you safe? H." Somebody responds, 'No, help me M.' and you want to talk about dessert? Why not simply ask, 'How? H'. Does it really matter whether it is Mordecai or not? Somebody is asking for help; let's follow the lead and see where it takes us."

Omid responded, "We don't know if this is Mordecai or not and we are not going to let you get in harm's way. This could be a trap set to take a hostage to help them get out of the country. Regardless of what it might be, let's respond to the text message simply and then see what happens."

They all agreed. Hadar took a deep breath and pushed the keys, "How? H", and then closed her eyes and hit the Send button.

Chapter 2

MORDECAI'S CONCERNS

All of the Brotherhood is concerned about the unfortunate death of Adad. Mordecai is concerned that it may not have been a mugging as Ishtar has suggested, but something else. What else it might be is something Mordecai doesn't want to deal with at the moment. He approached Ishtar and asked, "What do you think our chances are of getting out of America?"

"It's hard to say at the moment. Things are still locked down pretty tight with the curfew and martial law. With all the government activity trying to solve the core problems, I would expect things to loosen up in the next month or perhaps a little longer."

Mordecai asked, "Do you have any idea how we could get out of the country should things, as you say, loosen up?"

"I think the Gulf will still be our best bet for escape since there is just too much coastline to patrol. In the next month, I will phone one of my contacts to see about the possibility of getting a ship to pick us up. We will need to charter two; a big ocean going vessel and a second smaller, quicker boat to pick us up and take us to the mother ship. The big ship will have to stay in international waters while the small boat can come close to shore at night. It will cost a lot of money to pull this off."

"How expensive do you think it will be to get out?"

"It may well take all of our cash to get us out of the country. We will have to make sure where we want to go and have money in a local bank before we arrive to get us started on our new life. Once we have made

5

the decision where to go, we will have Oleg contact his uncle to get the money into the bank for us. We will be better off staying here and only go out in the daytime if it is important. The rooftop garden offers some relief for those who want to get some daylight and fresh air and for those who are claustrophobic."

Mordecai asked, "Have you been on the roof, Ishtar?"

"No, how do I get there?"

"As long as the elevators work, take one of them to the penthouse floor. Go through the front door and as you walk in you will see a set of large sliding glass doors on your right. Slide one open and walk out; it's a lovely view of the city and sunrise and sunset."

"What happens if we lose power to the elevators?"

Sargon suggested, "You should take a cell phone with you in case you are in the elevators and the power goes out. Mordecai, if I were you, I would play it safe and use the stairs just in case. It will take longer, but will also be some form of exercise, so the stairs are a great idea. I think we need to let people know where we are going."

Mordecai agreed. "I noticed an eraser white board on the refrigerator that we can use to tell each other where we are going and how long we will be gone. We can then erase it when we return."

"Great idea."

"I'm going to the garden, but I think I'll walk." Mordecai felt in his pocket to make sure he had his cell phone in case he needed to call for help, but he thought: *I don't have any of the cell numbers of the Brotherhood.* Then it came to him; Ishtar's phone number is in his phone.

"Smart idea. Safer, but longer."

Mordecai signed out on the white board that he is headed to the penthouse garden and expects to be gone at least one hour. As he headed toward the door he asked Sargon, "Do you have the cell phone number of all the members? It might be a good idea, just in case we are out and for some reason we get lost, we could call for help."

"I think that is a good idea. In fact we all should have each other's cell numbers programmed into our phones. Where are you headed?"

"Ishtar told me the view from the penthouse is spectacular, so I thought I would go and check it out."

"Here's my number; I'll get you the rest of the phone numbers when you return. What is your number?"

Mordecai walked up to the rooftop garden. As he walked out of their condo on the 17th floor, he looked and saw the exit sign down the hallway to his right and walked toward the sign. Just as he approached the exit door the hallway lights flash off and then back on quickly. *This confirms it; it's the stairs for me.* The door has one of those push bars that run the width of the door, so the door locks when it is shut. He is concerned that the door may lock if it closed behind him, so he looked around for something to prop it open. In the stairwell, he saw a red fire extinguisher hanging on the wall. He held open the door with his foot while he grabbed the extinguisher and wedged it in the door. *I hope nobody sees the fire extinguisher.*

Though the stairwell was dimly lit he could easily see the steps and the floor numbers, but the rest of the area faded from gray to dark. As he approached the landing for the twenty-fifth floor, he felt winded so he decided to sit and rest for a few minutes. He sat on the last step on the stairway before the landing. He was still quite a distance from the stair light. He turned to get up after he rested and he saw what looked like a weak light in his pocket.

Mordecai put his hand in his pocket and pulled out his cell phone. He is reminded of the three text messages from Hadar. "Are you safe? H" and the last message, "How? H". They were the same, from "H" in New Mexico. He remembered, *that is one of the places Hadar was going to study adobe-building before she heads to Africa to teach the people how to build adobe housing.* He is very scared because of the circumstances of Adad's murder. He believes that Ishtar may have killed Adad, but he doesn't know why. He is hoping Hadar can help him disappear.

Mordecai sat down on the landing and thought about the next message he would send, still wondering if it really is Hadar. He is glad he decided to keep it as simple as hers - if in fact it is from her. *What if Sargon is testing me to see if I will betray the Brotherhood?* He could be sending a similar message to all of the remaining brothers as a test.

Trying to convince himself of the positive he thought, *why would anybody else send me that message? Hadar is the only person I spoke to outside the members of the Brotherhood in Syria, so it has to be her. If I'm going to keep this contact secret, I will have to respond to her on the rooftop and only when I'm sure I'm alone. I hope I can see her again.*

Chapter 3

WHAT IS THE PLAN?

The team sat in the living room of the safe house, saying nothing after Hadar sent her reply to Mordecai's message. Baker finally spoke up, "We can't just sit here and wait for a reply; we need a plan in case he answers. We don't know where he is, how many of the Brotherhood are with him and most important, why doesn't he feel safe. We have to be careful we don't spook him and lose him forever. Let's talk about our goals with Mordecai; once we have those down on paper we can figure out how to capture him and hopefully the rest of the Brotherhood."

Hadar responded, "We need to get him to believe it's really me, and that I want to help."

Megan spoke up, "We have to find out where he is and if he is alone."

Omid asked, "Hadar, in your conversations with Mordecai, did he ever mention the Brotherhood, or how many people he was working with at the meeting site?"

"No. As far as I know, he thinks I'm a student who was on a vacation and heading to America."

Megan stepped in, "We have to find out where he is at the moment. Based on the caller ID he thinks you're in New Mexico, so if you're going to talk with him on the phone you have to tell him where you are. Let's say that he is in Houston and you are supposed to be in New Mexico. Then how are you going to get here to help him?

"You can't fly or take a bus, so the only option is to drive. The distance between San Felipe Pueblo, New Mexico and Houston is about 1,000 miles and would take at least two hard days driving to get to Houston, assuming you could get gas."

Omid jumped in, "Wait a minute. We don't know where he is, so why spend the time trying to figure out how long it will take for you to get to him? I think when the time is right you need to ask him where he is currently. Regardless where he is, tell him you'll have to figure out how to get to him, and where the two of you can meet and that you will call him back. We may be able to get a fix on his location based on the phone call."

Baker spoke up, "Hadar, it's most important for you to convey your concern for him. Your first text asked him if he was safe; your response to him asked how to help. You have to continue to show that compassion and concern. The best thing you can do is just ask him simple questions. Let him answer, and based on his answers follow up with additional simple questions."

"Ted, I'm not sure I understand?"

"You told us that there was something there when the two of you kissed. Are you in love with him? Do you think he is in love with you or is it just a physical attraction? If there is something there, how would you talk to him if he was not a terrorist, but somebody you loved?"

"I don't know that I'm in love with him or he is in love with me, but I would say there is a strong physical attraction, or at least at the time there was."

"A lot has happened to both of you since that initial encounter. You have taken the lead to reach out to him and he has responded. What neither of you knows for sure at the moment is what your feelings are now. In addition, neither of you knows for sure who is on the other end of the text messages. In some respect he needs you and you have told him you need him. If we are going to catch him and the rest of the Brotherhood we must develop the need factor."

Megan stepped in. "Wait a minute. We all knew that bringing Hadar to America meant using her as bait to see if we could contact Mordecai, but now you want her to invest emotionally to try to get Mordecai to open up and want to meet her and continue what they started in Syria. I'm not sure it is right or safe for Hadar. Seacrest began, "Megan, I understand your concern, but both you and Hadar need to understand something very important. You are now working in Special Ops in a covert operation against enemies of the United States." With more passion in his voice as if he was warning the women, "You are on mission and your government doesn't care what you do to reach your objectives." Then in a stern voice he said, "This job cannot be a moral dilemma for you. You have to use every asset you have, your brains, your body, your smile, your emotions, everything." John paused for a moment for emphasis. "If you can't make a total commitment, then this job is not for you. The time may come, maybe not on this mission, but on some future mission that you may have to kill someone or more than one someone; are you ready to pull the trigger? Can you have sex with someone to gain their trust in order to obtain information? Can you pull the trigger and kill somebody in the line of duty? If you can't, then get out now." Then, in a voice much like a recruiting sergeant, "Special Ops is very difficult, sometimes physically challenging, and other times mentally draining; not everybody is cut out for it. Right now, today, this minute, you have to decide if you want to do this?"

Baker had been listening and he said to all four of them, "John is right. I agree with him and I need to know right now if the four of you are in this fight all the way or not. What is your answer?"

Chapter 4

WHITE HOUSE LUNCH

Nathan Jordan had Mary Washington, his trusted assistant, call the First Lady's office and tell her he would be in the family quarters in about 30 minutes and could she join him for lunch? Mary spoke to the First Lady and she is excited about seeing her husband and spending some intimate time with him. She thanked Mary, called upstairs to the family quarters and talked with the President's butler George W. Washington, to make arrangements for lunch on the Truman Balcony.

They spent a few moments discussing the menu, and George said, "Mrs. Jordan, I've got it covered; you just come on up, and make yourself as pretty as you can for the President."

"Thank you George, I'll be up shortly."

Nathan and Karen had not seen much of each other since the attack, and Karen was really looking forward to this lunch, just to have some intimate time with her husband. Jordan has spent most nights on the couch in the President's conference room, and so the two of them have not made love or even shared the same bed in quite a while. Karen has always understood that when you are married to the President the country comes first, and the country desperately needed Nathan Jordan right now.

Karen has watched her husband deal with all the challenges thrown at him over the past few months. She is very proud how calm, cool, and self-confident he is in the face of all the significant decisions that need to be made for the country. As she left her office in the East Wing of the White

House, she walked to the East Colonnade, and at the South Portico she walked up the steps to the family quarters. At the top of the steps she saw George. He greeted her. "Mrs. Jordan, everything is under control. As soon as the President arrives, lunch will be served. I will let you know when the President is in the family quarters."

Karen walked down the hallway to her room thinking about what to change into that will help the President focus on her. She knows that the work he is doing is critical, but she isn't wrong thinking she wants some time with her husband even if he is the most powerful person in the world. He is still her husband, the father of her children, and very importantly, her lover.

She swung open the large closet in her changing room looking for something seductive and yet not so much so that the staff serving lunch will be embarrassed. As she rifled through her clothes she found a pink knit dress with black buttons down the front from the neckline to the hem. The dress is very contoured and does real justice to her ample and toned figure. She picked out a pair of black patent leather pumps and laid the dress on her bed. Then she went to her bureau and picked out a nude colored bra and panties. She was thinking when Nathan sees her he will not know for sure if she is naked under the dress, *Not a bad idea to keep him guessing and focused on me if only for an hour or two.*

The First Lady took a quick shower or what she thought was going to be a quick shower. She was startled to hear the shower door open and in walked the naked president. "Need somebody to wash your back?"

"Why yes, and anything else you think needs scrubbing."

Jordan took Karen in his arms and just held her as close as possible to him. "Should we dry off and go to bed or are we doing it here?"

I can't remember the last time we made love in the shower, let's see what happens."

After 30 minutes in the shower, both emerged with a look of satisfaction on their faces. Karen then stopped in the middle of the bathroom and one more time, wrapped her naked body around the president and placed a soft kiss on his lips. On her tiptoes she whispered, "I love you very much Nathan Jordan."

He leans down and whispers to her, "I love you more today than the day we were married, but right now I'm starving." The two of them dressed and went to a late lunch on the balcony.

After lunch Nathan looked at Karen and says, "I have some things I want to talk to you about. I have been giving several issues as much thought as I can, and now I need to bring them to you for your advice and consent," he said with a smile on his face.

"Fire away Mr. President, you have my undivided attention."

"Karen, we have just begun rebuilding America and it will be impossible to complete it before the end of my term. William Wild, the Majority Leader in the Senate, is lining up support to run for president in the next election. I think it would be a mistake, as they say, to change horses' mid-stream.

"I think Senator Wild would be a disaster for the country. With that said, I want to run for a second term as President, of course with your approval."

"I appreciate that you would at least tell me you were asking for my permission, but the reality is you will do what you want to do, and what you think is in the best interest of the country. While I would like to retire, I believe you are what is best for the country and I will happily work as hard as I can to help you get elected with one requirement."

"What is that?"

"I require at least one joint session in my shower per month and more frequently if possible."

Nathan laughed a hearty laugh, "Done. I just have one question, First Lady."

"What is that, Mr. President?"

"Can we use my shower sometimes; it's a little larger."

Chapter 5

MICHAEL'S FEAR

Michael knew that Ishtar was going to kill Adad. He was not thrilled with the idea, but the rationale that Ishtar gave him made sense, or it seemed to at the time Ishtar told him. Now he wasn't so sure. Michael had been working with his twin brother for two years when he was approached to help Ishtar build the bombs. In the very short time the brothers had been working together, they had amassed a significant amount of money. Michael was the junior member and he had $600,000 on deposit at his local bank in Springfield, but Ishtar suggested that he not deposit any more money at the U.S. bank, but start setting up bank accounts in Jordan, London, and the Cayman Islands. In a short time he had built over $1.6 million in these accounts. Michael knew that he would have an enormous amount of money coming from oil trading profits invested by Oleg's uncle. At his young age, he was going to be a very wealthy man.

Ishtar had met his twin in Berkeley, California just as Michael was ready to go to college on a free ride at UC Berkeley. In school back in Texas, he had excelled in science and that earned him the scholarship to UC Berkeley. However, Michael walked away from college for the money and the intrigue of smuggling anything and everything in and out of the United States. He knew that his brother was already a very wealthy young man and in many respects Michael looked up to his brother and what he had accomplished in such a short time, illegal or not. Now the more time he spent with Ishtar, the less he felt he really knew who Ishtar was, and that made him uncomfortable. The murder of Adad, even if it was for a reason, still bothered Michael. The longer time passed, the less trustful he became with Ishtar. This made him very uncomfortable, because he was now questioning his relationship with his flesh and blood; it was even more difficult because this was his identical twin.

The more Michael thought about what they had done, the killing of all those people and the massive destruction of property, he was slowly coming to the fatal conclusion that his life was most likely over. Yes, they would do their best to get out of the country, but the U.S. government would find them and either kill them all on the spot, or put them on trial and then execute them for what they had done. America didn't tolerate being attacked, especially by an American. The time had passed for them to get out of the United States; every day America recovered it would have more and more resources to find the Brotherhood. There was no safe place to escape to and he knew it even if the others held out hope that there was such a place.

Michael had not been home or seen his parents in over three years. To the best of his memory, the last time he spoke with his parents was the day he left for college. He thought to himself, *has it been that long, why didn't I call? Could I call them now just to talk with them and see how they are?* "Sargon, do you think I could use one of the phones in the other apartments to try to reach my parents? I haven't spoken with them in a long time and it would be good to check on them and see how they are getting along in all the turmoil."

Sargon listened to Michael's request. "Let me think about this and I will answer you in a little while."

"What are you concerned about?"

"If you make a call to your parents, could they trace it to us?"

"If I make the call from the 17th floor or whatever floor, their phone ID will not show me calling. Perhaps you're being a little paranoid about this. My parents were not involved in the bombing and how would they possibly know that I was?"

"You make an excellent point; you would just be the good son calling after a long absence checking up on his parents and how they are surviving. Michael, just one question, what are you going to say to your parents when they ask you the question, where are you and why haven't you called?

Remember your phone could show them you are in Houston, Texas, and the area code of 218 will further narrow down where you are calling from. So, if you are in Houston, you are less than three hours from Springfield. They would ask how long have you been there and why haven't you come home?"

Michael weighed the risks in the call. He didn't see any risk for the Brotherhood as long as he controlled his answers; dealing with his mom's questions as to why he hadn't called, now that was another issue.

Sargon came back to Michael and said, "I have been thinking it over and I don't see any risk to the Brotherhood in you making the call, so go ahead."

"I agree and I think I have come up with a solution."

"What's that?"

"I'll use my cell phone from Berkeley. The caller ID will show area code 510."

"Excellent solution." It is 9 PM and Michael believes that his parents will still be up at this time, so he dialed his parent's phone number. It rang seven times. Michael counted all seven rings and then he heard a very strange message that says…

Chapter 6

WILLIAMS' OFFICE

Frank Williams is now out of the loop of the day-to-day activity in the search for the Brotherhood of the Red Nile. His handpicked team in Houston is now running the show. He has told the team that Homeland Security will provide support for the mission. They are now trying to track down the men and possibly women of the Brotherhood of the Red Nile. Rounding up the terrorists is one of the objectives; the other, if possible, is to trace the money that supports the Brotherhood and paid for the old bombs and refurbishment, including the money spent in Iran to fix one of the bombs. The Houston team will have little time to follow the money, but Williams has an idea how he can help find the source of the money. He asked Marie to put in a call to the Attorney General Drew Clinton, as he wants to share an idea.

Marie called Williams back and told him Clinton will be able to meet with him the next day at lunchtime in the Attorney General's office. With that, Williams told Marie, "Have Baker call me as soon as possible using the secure cell connection."

"Right away, sir."

Williams believed the team would have their hands full trying to capture Mordecai and the Brotherhood if they are in the United States. Frank will tell Ted that the team can go wherever in the world they need to go to find the Brotherhood. For the second half of the mission, finding and following the trail of the money, Williams believes he has a solution to the challenge, but he needs to have it vetted before he goes forward.

Baker returned Williams' call and told him of the recent challenge and commitment he has asked from the team. He had not yet received an answer to his question but he hoped that they are all in to the end.

Williams responded, "Keep me posted; by the way you need to tell the team we have a code name for them, Pathfinders."

Baker is excited about the new name for the Houston team. "I like it. I think it will help them feel like a real Special Ops team now that they have a name."

"I want to discuss with you the second part of the mission, namely finding the trail of the money and following it where it leads. Based on the information John Seacrest got for us, the money is coming from Oleg's uncle in Moscow. For now we can't prove it. So, we need to find somebody who can trace the money and link it to Viktor Antipova and his Russian oil empire.

"I was thinking that it should be a person with a great deal of international experience who also has experience in undercover work. It should be a person who is a self-starter and can find a way to get the information we need."

"Sir, it sounds like we need to find out who was doing all the covert work for our Logistics Office. I thought we found out that it wasn't just one person, but the whole Office working on that mission. I don't think we can take over an entire office and have it focus on this mission. They are going to be working with the Pathfinders to locate the Brotherhood if and when we hear from Mordecai."

Williams offered, "I wasn't thinking about the entire Office, I was thinking about one person."

"Sir, you clearly have somebody in mind, but what is the reason for your hesitation in telling me who it is?"

"I have a meeting with the Attorney General at lunch tomorrow and depending on his reaction to my idea, the two of us will have to get the approval of the President. In addition, if the President agrees, then we will need the approval of the person I want. As of right now, I don't know how any of the three will react to my idea."

"Sir, let's suppose that the AG and the President approve; who would have to ask the person you want?"

"I think it could only be the President, but most likely I would have to fill in the detail."

"How soon would this happen and what would be this person's relationship with the activities of my Pathfinders?"

"Ted, I want your Pathfinders to focus all of their time on finding the leadership of the Brotherhood wherever they are and bring them to justice."

"Sir, did you just change the scope of our mission?"

"Ted, I want you and your team to find the Brotherhood wherever they are in the world. I will clear this with the AG and the President, but I don't see a problem. For now, you must assume that unless you hear from me in the next 48 hours, you have your orders."

"Sir, if I may again, who are you going to try to persuade to take the assignment?"

"I don't know if he will take the assignment, but if I'm successful you'll know soon enough, Mr. Baker."

Chapter 7

WHITE HOUSE

Nathan Jordan has just announced to his wife Karen that he needs to run for a second term as President for two reasons. First, he believes that the country really needs him and that he truly believes he has to finish the rebirth of America. Second, the word is that William Wild, the Majority leader of the Senate, is the likely Democratic nominee. Jordan tells Karen, "Wild will screw everything up and put the country further behind in the recovery process. He may well get us attacked again and I don't think we can handle another attack."

Karen already knew that Nathan was going to run and she enjoyed his sales pitch to her. "I believe that you as President would be the best thing for America and you have my vote." Karen noticed Nathan's mood changing; she knew that what he was going to tell her is no small matter. She wondered, "*Have I missed something that is causing this reaction?*"

"Karen, I want to share with you some of my deepest thoughts. These are thoughts I have had since the attack and I have been keeping them to myself, so I guess I have to unload on you."

The First Lady is now getting very worried at what Nathan is going to say. She said, "That is one of the important functions of the First Lady; to be there and listen to the President."

He continued, "In the attack..." Karen moved closer to Nathan and took his hand; she could sense the difficulty Nathan was having expressing his thoughts. "...Over 60,000 Americans, perhaps many more, died as innocent victims in the bombings. I don't consider myself a vindictive person, but while rebuilding America I have to find a way to retaliate. I'm not saying eye for an eye."

Karen squeezed Nathan's hand tighter because she could feel the tension in Nathan as he talked. Karen looked Nathan directly in his eyes and asked, "Are you thinking of using nuclear bombs on the Middle East in response?"

"In all fairness to you, I have considered using bombs, but where do I drop them? Do I drop them in Syria where the group organized and built one of the bombs with no government interference? Do I bomb Iran because they built the other bomb? How about Saudi Arabia? Most likely their oil profits financed part of the activities of the Brotherhood and many other terrorists groups. And what about Russia, because we believe a Russian billionaire provided most of the money for the attack?"

Karen is stunned, she can't believe 30 minutes ago they were making love in the shower and now her husband is talking about using nuclear bombs all over the Middle East and Russia in **revenge**. She wants to respond, but she knows he is not done with his thoughts. Karen keeps a firm grip on Nathan's hand and a steady focus on his face and eyes.

"I feel like we have to do something that breaks the cycle of events and it has to be done in such a way to change the way things are forever. If we don't, the danger of greater destruction of human life will escalate around the world. As much as I would like to do something – not doing anything may well hurt me in the campaign for reelection – I can't do it now. But if I do get reelected, then I will want to spend some serious time planning the 'American Response'".

Karen took a deep breath for just a moment and loosened her grip on Jordan's hand without letting go. "Do you have some kind of response in mind?"

Jordan responded, "I clearly don't have it all worked out but the response has to be a game changer for both them and us."

Karen responded, "I don't understand."

Jordan told Karen, "The core problem is money and the political power money buys, not just in the Middle East but right here in America. The Saudi Family has 5,000 princes that have all made enormous wealth from Saudi oil money. The governments in that area of the world need the revenue from the sale of oil just to keep their people happy, regardless of personal wealth.

"In 1973, things forever changed when OPEC used oil as both an economic and a political weapon while the non-OPEC nations did nothing. We ceded control of the world economies to OPEC, and their interests were not always the same as ours. We thought of ourselves as the policeman of the world, but in reality OPEC had the stick. When terrorists attacked the World Trade Center in 2001, the hijackers were 19 men affiliated with al-Qaeda, and all of them came from Saudi Arabia.

"America spent $2 trillion and thousands of American lives on the war against al-Qaeda and to what end? When Barak Obama took office in 2009, the average price of regular gas was $1.87 a gallon. Over both of his terms the price went as high as $5 a gallon. Did the increase in the price of oil and gas go to the oil companies or to OPEC? It went to OPEC. We have to stop the flow of our wealth out of the country and make America energy independent. That is why the natural gas pipeline structure I want to build is so important. Our program to convert as many new and older cars to natural gas as possible is in our long-term national security interest.

"I believe energy independence for America will change the world and more importantly take the power away from the Middle East."

Karen relaxed and sat back into her chair. She held Nathans hand gently and then asked, "Nathan, is nuclear retaliation as an option in your mind off the table?"

Chapter 8

SAFE HOUSE, COMMITMENT

Baker had stepped out to talk with Williams, leaving the Pathfinders sitting in the living room. Since Baker left the room, nobody has said a word. Brown began, "Were the comments from Baker sexist? Is he more concerned about the potential risk to the two of us girls than he is with you guys? Are we less likely to kill someone and have sex than you?"

Hadar sat up, "When I enlisted in Mossad, I had the same lecture probably for the same reason as Baker's. You need to know that in modern Israel women for the most part are perhaps more equal than women in the United States when it comes to military service. We are expected to go into combat and take the same risks as men.

"The reality is that women are more at risk than men. I'm not saying that men are not raped, but women have a much higher chance of rape, especially if the people we are fighting see women as servants and not equal. Let me be very candid; I need to have a conversation with him to find out if he has concerns because how he might feel about me personally and therefore doesn't want me harmed. I'm a big girl."

Omid said, "Yes, you are."

Hadar stared at him. Then she smiled and responded, "Yes, I am, and I know how to take care of myself most of the time in most situations."

Omid looked at Hadar, "Look, everybody that ever comes in contact with you has to notice you, and it is the fact that you stand out that makes you a target. The bottom line is, will you and your physical attributes jeopardize the mission? That is the only thing Baker is asking. I don't want to leave Megan out because I see her as a woman who is also striking, very attractive and distracting, but in a different way."

Megan looked at Omid and wondered, *is this guy interested in me? I never thought that anybody on the team would be romantically interested in other team members, that could be a real problem and we might have half of the team tied up emotionally.*

Omid continued, "Can we effectively function as a team with, and don't get me wrong, two 'beauties' on the team? If we have to worry about what could happen to you should you or all of us be captured, then the question is, how effective can we be in this mission?"

Seacrest wanted to add his thoughts, "You have only met one of the terrorists and his attraction to you proves one of our points about the power you have at least over Mordecai, but in reality over almost all men that come in contact with you. We know that Mordecai wants to jump your bones and at least one time you wanted him too, just for the pleasure that might happen. But now you are in a covert operation with objectives, and you may have to let him have sex with you with no emotional involvement on your part. The question from Baker and me is, can you allow that to happen if necessary? Can you be uninvolved with him on top of you? Megan, you don't know any of the terrorists. If we send the two of you out to meet Mordecai and his Brotherhood, and one of the members takes a liking to you, what are you prepared to do? This is not about sex - it is about using sex and sexuality as a weapon to gain an advantage."

Megan responded, "Thanks for the backhanded compliment - I'm sorry, I shouldn't have said that. I think we will have to talk about that offline. I know that both Hadar and I are range qualified in many different types of weapons. I have never shot at anyone or killed anyone, but I have trained for a long time and I think I would kill to protect teammates if necessary. If I find myself in a situation that I need to take a life to save mine or yours, I will do it."

Hadar stood up to make her point. "A person's ability to be effective in Special Operations is not dependent on breast size, the shape of her body, or how pretty she is, but rather can she carry out the mission? Can she, or for that matter, can he, rise to the task and do what is necessary? I know I can kick ass and take names and if I have to I can blow the bad guy away.

I have been trained to look at what is in front of me and react, not take time to ponder what I should do. I know the difference between making love and having sex. In the short time I have known Megan I believe I can count on her to protect all of our asses. Any questions?"

Megan stood next to Hadar and turned to Omid and John, "What is your answer?"

Omid spoke first. "Under other circumstances I would have been offended by your question, but I think it is fair for both of you to ask about my ability to do what is necessary. Let me be very straightforward, I have been a Marine for 23 years and I have the ribbons and medals to show the theaters I have served in and the number of times I have been wounded. I'm not proud of the number of human beings that I have killed in many different ways. If we were in danger I can say to you, I will give up my life to protect yours, and if I have to kill, I will."

Seacrest looked at Omid and said, "I'm glad he is on my side."

The ladies echoed the same feelings. Megan thought, *Omid is serious, and he likes me. I better be careful.*

John continued, "I have served for 17 years at the CIA, I'm a graduate of West Point and I have worked in over 200 covert operations in my time with the CIA. I have found myself in positions where I had to defend myself and take human life, not that I'm proud of it, but I did what was necessary. Unlike Omid, I'm a civilian operative, and I have found it necessary to become intimate with someone on the other side in order to gain information to accomplish my objectives. Human emotions are very powerful and sometimes they can add conflict in our minds about what to do or not do. I trust my life in all of your hands. I say we get Baker back in here and get past his concerns and go about the business of catching bad people.

Hadar called to Baker, "Get your ass in here."

Chapter 9

A SECRET MEETING

Karen has asked the President if a nuclear bomb as a response is off the table and she is waiting for Jordan to reply. She is holding her breath while she is waiting because "Yes" is what she wants to hear, but she is not the President. Jordan looks her straight in her beautiful eyes; he knows that she desperately wants him to say yes, yet he knows that using like measures is an option. He knows that many Americas want revenge and they would support him if he should decide to use nuclear bombs.

Nathan has a serious concern whether bombs are the right answer, but for now he does not have a clear picture of his options and that is what he is going to say to Karen. "My dear wife, I know you want me to say to you that I will not use nuclear bombs to even the score. For one thing, right now I don't know whom I would bomb. I will make this promise, that to the best of my ability I will do everything to avoid using nuclear bombs."

Karen slowly took in a deep breath of fresh air. The President has not taken the bombs totally off the table, but he has promised that he will explore all other options first. "As much as I would like to just sit here and look at you, I'll keep thinking about the shower and I won't get much done for the country."

The President left the family quarters and headed down to the war room for a secret meeting. Waiting for the President are the Chairman of the Joint Chiefs, the Secretary of Defense, the National Security Adviser, the Secretary of Energy, and the head of the CIA. As the President entered all the people in the room stood, and the President said, "Please sit down."

The table big enough for the entire cabinet only has six people seated. The President asked the room be cleared of all people, but those at the table. He ordered all recording devises turned off. The TV monitors on the walls were also turned off. "Gentlemen don't take this personally, but put all of your cell phones on the table and make sure they are turned off."

Each of the five was thinking, *doesn't he trust me?* But, he is the President and they all comply.

"Thank you gentlemen; I have to make sure this discussion is between the six of us and for now I want no one to know of this discussion or what is being said. What is said in this room for now stays in this room, does everybody understand?"

All replied, "Yes, Mr. President."

"I have called you here to begin the discussion of how America should respond to the vicious bombing of our country."

Most of the men in the room feel excited that the process of how America will truly respond has begun.

"I want to explore with you some of the options I have been thinking about and I want from you not only your honest reaction to what I propose, but I want your ideas. We will meet on a regular basis and we will refine our options, and then I will pick the one that will be America's response.

"I know that each of you, like me, have given some thought as to what America should do almost from the instant you heard about the attack. For now I want you to put that aside and let's just talk about options. I want you to listen to my thoughts and then react to them in an open and honest way. In the past, the terrorists have attacked and killed in small numbers. Yes, we lost 200 Marines in one attack. The attack on the World Trade Center was the most serious of all the attacks until now. While many thousands of people got out safely, that attack while devastating was nothing compared to the most recent attacks. The terrorists have crossed a line that will cause them to continue to escalate to the point that nuclear bombs may well be used on a regular basis because one group of people doesn't like the way another group thinks, acts, or is trying to dominate the world. In fact, the symbol of the very concept of trade that was supposed to make us all a village and make the world smaller, The World Trade Center, was the principal target for destruction by terrorists.

"I have been thinking about retaliation and the use of our nuclear weapons."

The men were shocked at the words used by the President that nuclear bombs as the means of retaliation were under consideration.

"At the moment I don't know who to bomb, do you? If we don't stop this right now then heaven help the world, so we have to find a way to make the world safe again and at the same time gain America's Revenge."

General Powell spoke up, "Mr. President would you consider an 'Eye for an Eye?'"

Nathan was a little taken aback, so he asked, "What do you mean?"

"Sir, they attacked our energy capacity; we could use nuclear bombs to take out their capacity and make it useless for generations."

The President looked at Powell and asked, "General, I need to ask you one question, whose energy capacity?"

"Mr. President I don't understand your question."

"General, if we don't know for sure who provided the money to buy the bombs, and sold them to the Brotherhood, then do we take out all the oil capacity in the Middle East, Russia, all the nations around the world that have oil and don't like us? **Do we bomb the whole world**?"

Chapter 10

BALCONY "DISCUSSION"

In the safe house, the team was assembled and Baker got the answers to his question. He went down the line asking for their commitment. When he got to Hadar she leaned in and said, "We need to talk." She stepped back and with the same level of conviction of the other three. "I'm in all the way to the end, whatever it takes."

Baker announced, "Now that our commitment has been settled we need to determine Hadar's message to Mordecai. He is asking for help, but how can we help? We don't know where he is and what kind of trouble he is in right now."

Hadar stood up and walked over to Baker, "Can I speak with you on the balcony?"

John made a comment that caused the rest of the team to smile when he said softly as Hadar and Baker walked outside, "somebody is going to the wood shed."

Hadar closed the balcony door after Baker stepped outside. "We have already been through a lot of interesting events. Attempted kidnappings, car crashes, car races, helicopter shooting at cars, jumping from a moving car, and who can forget the airport hangar incident."

Baker asks, "So, what is your point?"

"I'll get to that in a minute. After we tumble down a hill after jumping from a moving car over a guardrail, I find you with your hand firmly planted on my breast. Whenever we are together you take every opportunity to make comments on my body. So here is the question, "Do you have the hots for my body, my brain, or me?"

"That is an unusual question."

"I don't care if it is unusual; do you want me or not?"

Baker felt very uncomfortable. A gorgeous woman wants to know what his feelings are toward her and she is confronting him, and he is flustered.

She pressed on. "Is that too hard a question for you to answer?" She now starts to move in and while she is a few inches shorter than him, at the moment he feels smaller. Hadar reached the point where she is just lightly touching Baker's chest. She could see beads of perspiration on his forehead starting to run down his face. She held her position, not moving, but just in his face. One more time she asked, "Do you want to have sex or make love?" Hadar notices that he is straightening up, and she believes that Baker's shift is a signal that he is about to give her his answer. She knows what she wants to hear, but she wonders if he knows what to say?

He started to move into her and she stood her ground, which pressed more of her against him. He looks down to her and says, "Hadar, from the first time I saw you in that conference room, I knew that you were special. You can go ahead and hit me, but while your body, including you-know-what attracted me, something else did. You are fresh, self-assured, and have a carriage like no other woman I have ever seen. Yes, you have large breasts, and they can be distracting. Go ahead and hit me. But, you carry them as an asset that you use to distract people until you open your mouth and people hear how intelligent you are, how polished, how smart you are. They're not just a rack.

"When I picked you up at the hospital, I knew that I needed to be with you whatever that meant. When Williams kept me in DC and put Megan in charge of the unit, I was disappointed I was not going to be with you. I knew it was the right decision, but I needed to be with and around you. I played and flirted with you about your body to mask my true feelings. That is a long way to get to the answer, but it bought me some time to think about how to answer your question. Lt. Hadar Hassen, I was in love with you at first sight and that has never ever happened to me before, and while I like them, I am in love with you. Do I want to have sex or make love to you? Neither. I want to make love with you."

She asked, "So, what do we do?"

He replied, "You have to tell me if you have any feelings for me or not?"

"Here is where I am at the moment. I had or have a person that I was kind of involved with back home. I have something going on with Mordecai, and now I have you who doesn't want to have sex but wants us to make love. Lots of people want to have sex with me and I can understand that, but I never had anybody say to me that they wanted to make love with me. We can't make love while we are working together on this mission, agreed?"

"Can we fool around; go ahead and hit me."

"I don't think so."

Ted continued his thought, "Hadar, I agree, but after, if we make it through alive, we can talk about it."

"I will have to clear up back home."

"Agreed."

"Ted, I have a favor, before we go back in."

"What is that?"

"You know how you make remarks about my body and I get to hit you for your smart mouth."

"Yes."

"I like that, don't stop, it makes me feel comfortable with you."

"So, does that mean I can look for opportunities, to roll you down a hill, and feel you up?"

Whack!

Chapter 11

MORDECAI WANTS TO TALK

The evening meal is over and Mordecai tells Sargon he is going to the rooftop garden. He is going to walk up and down, so he will be gone about an hour and a half.

"I may join you later," Sargon responded. "I haven't been up there to see the view."

"That would be great; I have never seen the skyline of Houston at night and I would love the company. What time should I expect you?"

"Are you going somewhere?"

Mordecai is concerned that he not act nervous when he responds to Sargon's question, "No, I don't want to be walking down when you are walking up, the view in the stairwell is not worth seeing. If I know what time you're coming then I'll stay on the rooftop and wait for you, then we can walk down together."

"It's 9:15 now. If I'm not there by 10:15, then I won't be coming, is that okay?"

"Yes, that's fine. You should try to make it. Ishtar has said the view is spectacular at night. I saw it during the daytime with him; I think it could be a great view."

Mordecai walked out the front door of the condo. After the door closed he checked to make sure he has his cell phone. He thought about taking the elevator but if the power went out and he got stuck he may never get out, so he took the stairs. His pace up the flights was quick. He used the time to think about a simple text message he could send to whom he believes to be Hadar. He got closer to the landing and as he reached it he decided on the text to send, "I will call tomorrow at 9 PM Mountain Time, M."

He walked out on the platform looked around and could see no one else. He took out his cell phone and checked the signal. He typed in the message and tapped the Send button. He watched it move from the message box to the send box and then he heard the "swoosh" of the text message being sent to Hadar.

Seconds later the cell phone in Hadar's hand vibrated and she dropped it on the floor in surprise. The rest of the Pathfinders saw her startled look and knew something was up. They all crowded around Hadar as she opened the phone to see one new text message. Slowly Hadar pressed the screen to make the message appear. She, along with the rest of her teammates saw the text message from Mordecai, or at least a message from Mordecai's phone.

Baker was on a DHS plane headed back to Washington when Megan called him to tell him of the contact. She had to call Williams' office and ask Marie to patch her through to Baker on the plane. "Do you want Mr. Williams on the call?"

Megan stopped to think about that question. She is currently reporting to Baker and it would be a breach in protocol and the chain of command to speak with Williams before she spoke with Baker. She responded to Marie, "Let's see what Mr. Baker wants to do first."

She heard a click; aware Baker is now on the line. She was standing in the safe house galley kitchen, looking at the stainless steel refrigerator door, when she responded, "Sir, we received a reply to Lt. Hassen's text message. It said he would call her tomorrow night at 9 PM Mountain Time. He has figured out that the area code Hadar's texts messages are coming from are in the Mountain Time zone."

"Have you formulated a response to the message?"

"No, sir, we just received the message a few moments ago."

Baker asked, "Where are you calling me from? Where is the rest of the team?"

"I'm in the kitchen and they are in the living room."

"Take the phone to the living room and put me on speaker."

"Right away, sir." Megan moved out of the kitchen and told the team to sit down. "Baker wants to speak with all of us."

Baker began, "I just asked Ms. Brown whether you have formulated a response."

Hadar spoke up, "This is not rocket science. The answer is just a simple 'OK', and send."

Baker asked the group, "Everybody agrees that simple is better?"

Almost in unison, "Yes, sir."

"Lt. Hassen, send the message and let me know when it's done." Baker and the team waited what seemed like an eternity. In reality, just a few seconds later the confirmation appeared that the text message was "delivered."

Baker came back on the line speaking directly to Megan. "We have to figure out what resources we will need for the call tomorrow regardless of the length. I'm an hour away from DC; I should land about 9:30. I'll call you then and I want your thoughts on what resources we will need and what Hadar is going to say."

"Yes, sir."

A few moments later Mordecai's cell phone buzzed and he saw the message from Hadar, reading, "OK". He stuck his phone back in his pocket, pleased that tomorrow night about the same time he will be hearing from Hadar. His mind wandered to the second time he saw her on that long walk across the village square and that incredible button sweater and those incredible… a whack hit his arm and it was Sargon well ahead of schedule. He was struck with fear, not about the whack on his arm while he was thinking about Hadar's breasts, but the chance that Sargon might come up to the roof tomorrow night when he is trying to speak with Hadar. *Should I text her back and cancel?*

Chapter 12

CLINTON'S OFFICE

Williams sat in the outer office of the Attorney General, Clinton, and thinking about how he was going to tell Clinton his idea. At Williams' request, the Attorney General arranged a meeting for Frank Williams and himself with President Jordan about recruiting someone to trace the money that has been funding the terrorists. First though, Williams and Clinton are going to talk about the idea. Williams has to start moving on the flow of money that has been used to finance the Brotherhood. "Mr. Williams, you may go in now."

"Thank you." Williams walked through the door and he saw Clinton on the phone behind his desk. Drew signaled for Williams to come over and sit down.

The office of the Attorney General is very impressive. Bookshelves line the walls at each end of the office filled with law books. Clinton's desk is made of walnut that he guesses is quite old. Williams is sitting in one of two red leather high back wing chairs. Behind Williams are three large palladium windows that look out on Pennsylvania Avenue, and on a clear day you can see the White House. The chairs are comfortable and Williams could fall asleep, but he knows he can't fall asleep in the AG's office.

Clinton pointed to a silver coffee pot on a sideboard and told Frank to pour himself a cup of coffee. Frank got up to pour a full cup. Just as he finished, Clinton hung up and apologized to Frank for keeping him waiting. "So, you have something important to talk about; if I understand correctly it is about finding and following the money the Brotherhood has been receiving. Am I correct?"

"Mr. Attorney General."

"Please call me Drew."

"Yes, sir. Drew, you know we have a team in Houston that is trying to make contact with Mordecai, one of the terrorist members of the Brotherhood of the Red Nile?"

"Yes, I'm aware."

"Well, we made initial contact by text message and Mordecai intends to call one of our team members. We plan to cultivate a relationship and possibly capture the whole leadership."

"That sounds terrific; I hope it pans out."

"So do we, but I'm not here today to talk about that. I want to try to get the money guy; the person who paid for the bombs and had them rebuilt and transported to the United States.

"I think finding the trail to the source of the money doesn't require a team but one man, if we have the right man. One person can be more agile and can get in and out of a country much easier than a team."

"Do you have somebody in mind for the assignment?"

"Drew, I think I have found the right person, but the only one who has any chance of convincing him to do the job is Nathan Jordan."

"You mean the President, that Nathan Jordan?"

"Yes, sir, the one and only."

"What one person could be so important to finding the money, as you say, that needs to be asked by the President of the United States?"

"Mr. Attorney General, that person is Mike Ridley."

"The same Mike Ridley whose top secret file we spent hours reviewing?"

"Yes, sir."

"Why him?"

"We believe the source of the money is Viktor Antipova, the Russian oil billionaire."

"Okay."

"Mike Ridley met him in Afghanistan when Mike was spying on the Russians. Mike and Mary lived for the last 22 years in a house that Viktor bought and invited Mike and Mary to live in for free. Viktor paid most of the expenses for the house."

"Why do you think Mike would come back from wherever he is and go to work in such a high risk job?"

"Sir, I believe our chance to get him involved is to save his son Michael. You know the asset we had on the ground had no pictures of Michael, but because of the fingerprints we found in the Ridley home we were able to find out that Michael and Ishtar are twin brothers. We believe that Ishtar convinced Michael to join the Brotherhood. We think Michael and Ishtar are with the rest of the Brotherhood. We don't know where they are, but we might be able to strike a deal with Mike. If he helps us, we could make an arrangement for his son Michael.

"You may recall that Michael was given a free ride to UC Berkeley and never showed up for school. We were able to find out that he has in excess of $600,000 in a savings account, yet when we did a Social Security search to find out where he was employed, nothing showed up on his file. He wasn't working legally, but has $600,000 in the bank. We think, based on passport records, his twin brother made contact with him just before he was to start school and convinced him to come and work with him in some form of illegal activity.

"We do not know if Michael has had any contact with his father, so we have no way of knowing if the father knows that his son was involved with the two bombs and the attack on America. The only way to know for sure, assuming Mike will tell us the truth, is if somebody asks him. I don't believe either of us has the power to engage Mike Ridley in this project. If he agrees, then he can report directly to my office and I will keep the President informed.

"Drew, we have to tell the President about the Ridley's son, Michael. The President has to break the news to Mike. The news may force Mike to refuse, but perhaps we could possibly offer Mike protection for his son."

"What do you mean by 'protection'?"

"President Carter cut a deal with Mike, that if he performed certain tasks, some that were clearly dangerous and perhaps illegal, the government would make him disappear – and pardon Michael."

"Are you suggesting the President of the United States cut a deal with a terrorist who was an accomplice in the largest attack on American soil? His actions probably cost the lives of over 60,000 people! Now I see why you wanted to come to me first before going to the President to have him to reach out to Mike."

"We need to stop the flow of money and this may well be the only way. I figured that if I didn't have your support, then trying to go to the President would be a risky proposition at best. With your support we might have a chance. Do I have your support?"

Clinton paused and doesn't answer right away. Williams thought, *"He has a problem. Did I miss something or does he know something I don't know? We both reviewed Mike's file together so how could he know something different than what I know?"*

Clinton finally answered, "I think your idea is sound, but I'm struggling with the approach to the President. I know he wants to bring the terrorists to justice, but he also doesn't want to do anything that would give their lawyers an opportunity to dismiss the case."

"Drew, is it possible that the President could use an Executive Order selecting Mike and giving him total immunity for all actions taken?"

"That has a lot going for it. The President signs the Order, Congress is out of session and they have no power over executive orders."

"Drew, how do we keep his appointment secret so Congress will never know?"

"We make the Executive Order part of Mike Ridley's sealed file, so only a sitting president can order the file opened. We know data was added to Mike's file after it was initially sealed so we could continue the process."

"I like that idea a lot. The President will contract directly with Mike for the work. He gets paid and the results of his work are the property of the government and are sealed in Mike's file."

"Our job is to lay out for the President how this might work and that he has to be the one to approach Mike. We will lay out the terms and conditions for him to present to Mike. The President can approve having Mike report to you, Frank."

"One last thing, how can we offer immunity to his son Michael?"

Chapter 13

HOW CAN I HELP THE TEAM?

Attorney General Clinton and Frank Williams had discussed recruiting Mike Ridley to trace the money that has been used to fund the terrorists and present the idea to the President. Part of the deal would be to arrange a pardon for Mike's son, Michael.

Clinton, concerned about this idea, said, "I don't see the President going for it; the risk is very high."

Williams responded, "You may be right, but we have to make the offer and see how the President reacts, agreed?"

"Agreed."

It was late in the afternoon when the two of them finished. Frank decided to he was going home, so he called Marie to tell her he was leaving.

She responded, "Mr. Williams, I have Ted Baker on the cell phone for you from a plane."

"Put him through."

Ted began, "Sir, I have news. Mordecai - we are assuming its Mordecai - has responded to the latest text from Hadar. They are scheduled to talk tomorrow at 9 PM Mountain Time to see how she, or we, can help. We have scheduled a conference call to talk about resources we will need to deal with whatever comes out of the call. Do you want to be on the call?"

"Give me a moment." Williams plays this out in his head. *I have a team in place that I trust and I think they can handle this situation. On the other hand, the President is looking to me to lead this mission and I need to be able to tell him the latest information.* "Ted, I would like to be a part of the call, but I will just listen and if I see a need that I can help with I will speak up. This is yours and Megan Brown's show, does that work for you?"

"Yes, sir. Where can I reach you in about 30 minutes?"

"Call my office."

Williams hung up, then called Marie and told her about the call and asked her to call Ellen and tell her he would be late.

"Yes, sir."

Williams got in his car and told his driver to take him back to his DHS office. Williams arrived and took the elevator, stopping at his floor. He started to walk down that long hallway but stopped and sat on a bench. *Am I getting to old for this job? This is clearly a younger person's job. For the moment he thinks he can no longer do what needs to be done as an Under Secretary for Homeland Security. On my watch over 60,000 Americans perished. How can I redeem that tragic loss?* Marie was walking from the coffee room and saw Williams sitting on the bench. He was bent over and looked like a man with the weight of the world on his shoulders like the Rodin bronze "The Thinker". She walked over and sat down next to him on the bench. She reached out to Frank, and then quickly pulled her hand back when she remembered she has never touched Williams in the entire time she has worked for him.

She could tell that he needed some encouragement and support, as he looked vulnerable at the moment. Again she extended her hand and simply rested it on his leg. "It has been difficult for a long while; not much time for family or rest and recharging one's soul. I'm so proud to work for you. America has the best and brightest people, people like you, trying to solve tremendous problems. In addition you are trying to make us safe. Do you really have to take this call? Why don't you just go home and be with Ellen for the evening; I'll call Baker and tell him you were called to a meeting."

As she spoke to him his spirits and his body started to rise. "Marie, thank you for caring and for encouraging me, but as much as I would like to be with my beautiful wife, I have to try and make America safer. So call Ellen and tell her I'll be late."

With some disappointment, yet at the same time an element of pride, she stood and said, "Yes, sir."

Chapter 14

THE CONFERENCE CALL

Mordecai is expected to call Hadar tomorrow evening. Williams receives a text message from Baker, now on the ground, with the call-in details for this evening's conference call with Ted and the Pathfinders. Williams follows the procedure, and a recorded voice asks him to state his name and position. He gives his details and is told he is joining the call. On Baker's end a bell and a monotone recorded voice announces Frank Williams. Baker greets him. "Welcome, Mr. Under Secretary."

"Thank you, Ted. Please proceed with the call."

Baker verified those on the line and started the call. "Sir, I have news. Mordecai, we assume, has said he will call Hadar tomorrow at 9 PM Mountain Time. He has requested help, which suggests that something may not be going well in the Brotherhood, wherever they are. Hadar has confirmed she'll be ready to talk."

"I think we need to have a plan with questions for Hadar to capture as much information as possible without scaring him off. We should start with simple questions that could be answered 'Yes' or 'No' and then proceed to more involved questions. If he is asking for help, what does he need?"

Brown responded, "In the initial text Hadar asked, 'Are you safe?' He responded, 'No, help me.' So the first question is, 'Do you still need help?' Next question, 'Can you talk freely?' 'Are you being watched?' 'How can I help?' 'What do you want me to do?' She has to wait for a response. If nothing is forthcoming, what is the next question?"

Hadar responded, "'Do you want to escape from where you are?'"

Brown suggested, "A little too scary; how about, 'Do you need to leave where you are to feel safe?'"

Hadar agreed. "Better message".

Baker suggested, "We need another question, 'Can you get out of wherever you are?' 'Do you need money to get out?' Last question which is not 'Yes' or 'No,' would be 'What can I do to help you?'"

Williams asked, "Ted, if I might ask, are you going to try to track his cell phone signal to see if you can locate him?"

Baker responded, "Sir, we have a communications tracking team on the way from Langley; we expect them to arrive within three hours. We will have them come to the safe house and set up to follow his cell signal through Hadar's phone. The challenge, sir, is that his phone may bounce his signal from towers and satellites around the world; he could be right next-door and we would never know it. The team is hoping and praying we can track the signal but I'm not convinced that they will have much of a chance this time."

Williams asked, "Why did you say this time?"

"Sir, I don't expect him to be on the line that long; he needs to get comfortable with Hadar again and believe she will really try to help him. I expect that subsequent calls will be longer if Hadar uses her wits. I said wits. If she can keep him on the line longer she'll give the tracking team more time to work."

Seacrest cautioned, "We don't want to pry for too much information at one time. If he feels like Hadar is pressuring him, he may hang up and we could lose him forever. I think the concept of simple questions with one-word answers is a great opening, but at some point you have to lighten the conversation. Hadar, is there anything that you could say that would make him have a happy thought about the two of you?"

Hadar thought, *There are several things that could work, knocking him down with the barn door, or his eyes so wide open when he first saw me walk across the square, or the second 'date' with that amazing kiss.* Then she said, "When I came out of the barn, I pushed the barn door open and knocked him to the ground. I was very apologetic and he just laughed."

John said, "That is the first story; do you have more if you need them?"

"Yes, I have a couple more that could fit the bill."

Seacrest told the rest of the Pathfinders, "The communications team will bring a TVSA3 voice stress analyzer that they will hook up to Hadar's phone. As Hadar asks her questions the stress level in Mordecai's voice will appear on a monitor. Hadar, you will want to watch the screen to follow Mordecai's stress level in reaction to your questions. If you see the level increase, then switch to a less stressful question. By the same token, if you start pressing and the stress level doesn't increase, then keep pushing."

Baker asked the Pathfinders, "How far do we want Hadar to go, meaning what are our goals for this call?"

Megan responded, "I would like to find out at least the city where he and the rest of the Brotherhood are located."

Seacrest said, "I would like to find out if he is being held hostage, and whether the rest of the Brotherhood have guns and are confining him."

Omid, who has been very quiet the entire evening, finally spoke. "I think we need to find out why he asked Hadar to help him; has something happened that makes him question his safety? Hadar, as far as Mordecai knows, is just a college student going to Africa to help build mud houses. What is it that she can offer that will save him? Is it possible that he has gotten in over his head and the reality of what he has done is now coming home to roost? So his fear might be, 'Oh my God what have I done? The entire U.S. government is coming after me and I'm going to die!'"

Over the speakerphone, the voice of Frank Williams came through loud and strong, "Omid I think you have hit the nail squarely on the head. When he was working in Syria building the bomb, it was an adventure. Now the reality of what he has done is hitting him like a ton of bricks. Until the bombs went off he was performing a noble act; now he realizes he is a mass murderer. Hadar represents the good from the past and he desperately needs to feel good again."

"I agree, sir. I think Hadar should do everything possible to make him feel good. She should avoid talking about the bombing, but just focus on trying to make Mordecai feel good. I believe it will take more than one call to gain his confidence. Hadar and Megan, I want to make a suggestion and I do not want either of you to be offended. Hadar needs to tease him, take him up to the edge, and then cut him off make him want to call back."

Hadar said, "I'm not offended."

"Nor am I," said Megan. "I think it is a great approach and great insight. Thank you."

Omid responded with a small smile to Megan, "You're welcome."

Megan thought to herself, *is Omid interested in me? This is the second time he has been especially kind to me. I need to find some time to learn what's going on in his brain; he is kind of cute.*

The voice on the phone said, "I think it's an excellent plan; all of you need to work with Hadar so she is ready for tomorrow night. I'm going home. Goodnight."

Baker heard Williams click off and was proud of how the Pathfinders performed.

Megan spoke to the team, "We have to do a lot of coaching, both men and women, so let's get started. Tomorrow may be the day that we make progress in capturing the bastards."

Hadar was struck when she heard Megan call Mordecai a bastard. She realized that perhaps she too had not left behind the time in central Syria when she met a young man whom she thought she really wanted to "hook up with". The term bastard brought her into the reality of today and her heart was a little broken.

Chapter 15

MORDECAI'S FIRST CALL

The communications team has arrived from CIA Langley and has been busy setting up equipment to trace and track Mordecai's phone call. One of the team members showed Hadar how the voice stress system works. "As you talk to Mordecai, the volatility of his voice will appear on the screen in front of you. If you ask him a question that causes him anxiety, the swing in the line will get wider, and as long as the stress is there, it will stay wide. If the questions increase the stress, the swings will get wider and wider. As he calms down, the swing will start to shrink. This is very important. This device works in real-time, however there is a delay in the recording of the reaction. If you ask Mordecai a question that you think might cause him stress, wait a few seconds to see the reaction when he responds. You might want to think about your questions as a bell curve."

"I don't understand."

"You don't want to ask Mordecai all the hard questions one right after another. You may be thinking, why not? The reason is you compound the stress; you may scare the person and not get a true answer. If you use the bell curve, you start with the easy questions, and then as you climb the slope of bell curve, the conversation leads to the most important question at the top of the curve. Once you have asked the primary question, you want to get down the slope as fast as possible by asking non-confrontational questions. By watching the scope you can see changes in tension and then decide if you want to go up another bell curve or make small talk. You will just have to listen and watch for reactions in Mordecai."

"Will the rest of the team be able to hear what is being said, and are you going to record the conversation?"

"The system is designed for three people to listen into the conversation - you, one other person and me. So we need to decide who else should hear the call in real-time. We will be able to hear what both parties are saying, and we will have separate real-time computer access to your notebook screen to ask you questions or send you information. It is important for you to look at your notebook on a regular basis. The challenge for you is to let Mordecai know you are engaged in the conversation, while at the same time reviewing the screen for input.

"I know this is a lot for you to remember on such short notice, but we have several hours until we expect the call. I suggest we have at least one run-through so you become familiar with the equipment. Just one more thing, the messages on the screen can be at times very distracting and cause you to lose focus on the conversation with Mordecai. If you find that happening, just close the notebook and focus all of your attention on the conversation and yes, we will record both the conversation and the stress readings."

Hadar asked, "Will the screen tell me if or when Mordecai might be getting impatient?"

"Yes, if you are having a simple non-intense conversation and you start to see the wave expand, you know that you had better get ready to end the call. Keep in mind we don't know anything about his possible captivity. He may well get impatient because someone might be coming and he doesn't want them to know he is talking with you or anybody. He may also get impatient because he wants to see you. He remembers you from Syria and how he felt and he really wants to see you. Don't be surprised if he cuts you off abruptly and says he will call back later."

On the other side of the room the team set up a signal-tracking device so they can determine where Mordecai and perhaps the rest of the team are hiding out. Omid and Megan watched the screen and prepared to dial Hadar's phone to test the system when her cell phone started to ring. Everybody stopped and looked like they were frozen in place.

Megan told Hadar, "Open the phone and see who is calling."

The phone is on **the third ring**; Hadar has set her phone to go to voice mail after the sixth ring. Hadar opens the phone and looks at the number and she sees it is Mordecai. "What should I do?" **Ring four**.

Megan said, "It is three hours before he said he would call."

Ring five!

Megan shouted, "**Answer the phone**!"

The team is scrambling while Hadar says to Mordecai, "Please hold for just a second - I was in the shower and I'm naked and dripping wet. I need to dry off; can you hold or do you want me to call you back?"

Mordecai thinks about the picture Hadar has just painted in his mind's eye: Hadar naked and dripping wet. The team is in place and has everything turned on and ready when Hadar speaks; Omid is on the third set of headsets listening to the conversation.

"I'm sorry, I wasn't expecting your call for a few more hours and I was filthy from casting adobe bricks so I decided to take a quick shower. I had just gotten in and was covered with soap. So, how are you and how can I help you?"

Chapter 16

WILLIAMS' OFFICE

Frank has returned from his meeting with Drew Clinton and participated in the conference call. Marie let him know that the meeting with the President is set for 10 AM the next day. "I'll leave from home and go to the White House, and then I'll be here as soon as I can. Have you seen Ted Baker?"

"Sir, he was due in at Andrews just over an hour ago."

"Please keep an eye out for him. I need to talk to him about my meeting with the President tomorrow." Frank is trying to figure out what he can say to the President to get him to call Mike Ridley and ask him to come out of hiding and potentially risk his life to get the goods on the Russian.

There was a knock at the door and Ted Baker stuck his head in and says, "Sorry for interrupting your train of thought, but Marie said you needed to see me."

"Come in and sit down. I have a meeting tomorrow with the Attorney General and the President about going after the money that has been funding the Brotherhood while you and the Pathfinders are trying to find Mordecai and the rest of the Brotherhood."

Baker was a little confused. "Sir, don't we know that the money has been coming from Oleg's uncle in Moscow, Viktor Antipova?"

"Yes, we know that, but we need to prove it to the Russian Government."

"Why the Russian government?"

"Ted, they will never allow Viktor Antipova, one of the wealthiest men in Russia, to go on trial for supporting terrorists."

Baker asked, "So, what is the point of going after him if he will never come to trial?"

"Not a public trial, but the Russians will take care of Mr. Antipova in their own way if we give them enough evidence. That is where Mike Ridley comes in. Ted, I hope to convince the President to recruit Mike Ridley to follow the money trail to Antipova and build the case we need to give to the Russians."

"Why would he come out of hiding to do this job for the President?"

Williams responded, "I do not think Mike and Mary know that their son Michael is a terrorist, much less a member of the Brotherhood of the Red Nile who attacked the United States."

"What does he get if he does the job?"

"He gets a pardon for his son Michael and the President spares his life."

"Do you think Mike will make the deal with the President?"

Williams explained, "I'm not sure, but that's what we're planning to pitch. We will lay out the deal and make it strong enough to entice Mike to want to do the job. The President, like many of his predecessors have said, 'America doesn't negotiate with terrorists.' In fact, Mike Ridley will not be doing any negotiating with any terrorist, he will just be gathering evidence for our case."

"So, how do we start building our case for the President?"

"Logistics," was Frank's reply.

Ted asked, "What does Logistics have to do with this?"

"The Logistics Office has been responsible for shielding Mike and Mary Ridley and keeping them out of harm's way for years. For many years there was no problem and then in the last year Mike unwillingly came to the surface in Springfield and the Logistics Office moved him to a new safe location. We need to meet with the Director of the Office today and try and convince him that the President will want to speak with Mike as soon as possible. The hook is Mike's son Michael and his survival. Please go and have Marie call and set up an appointment for me to see the Director of the Logistics Office sometime today."

Baker stepped out and asked Marie to make the call and let him know as soon as she can when they can meet about Mike Ridley.

Marie responded, "Right away, Mr. Baker."

Ted returned to Williams's office and the discussion of the plan. "Sir, it seems to me that this will have to be a two-step process. Someone will have to reach out to Mike and arrange an initial meeting. The objective of the first meeting is to get Mike to agree to a meeting with President Jordan. If he agrees to meet, then we have to brief the President."

"I agree, and I think Logistics can arrange the first meeting; you can work on that today."

"I will get right on it as soon as I hear from the Director. Sir, I just have one more question."

Williams asked, "What is your question?"

"When and who tells Mike Ridley - who has served his nation well - not only that his only son is a terrorist, but that he is a member of the Brotherhood of the Red Nile who is responsible for the nuclear attack on America?"

Chapter 17

MICHAEL CONTACTS FATHER TIM

Michael Ridley has not talked with his parents in several years and now he desperately wants to talk with them. He has convinced Sargon that it will be safe for him to call. He used his cell phone to dial his home phone number. It rang for about ten times and then a recording said the number he is calling has been permanently disconnected. Michael hung up, redialed his parent's number and got the same message.

Why would my parents have their phone permanently disconnected? They were far enough away from the blast that they were not affected. Something has happened to my parents… He hung up and started to think whom he could safely call. Could he call his girlfriend? No. How about his neighbor John Bowman? No. He racked his brain trying to figure out whom he could call and safely talk to, and who would not then report him to the police.

He needs to talk to someone who can't tell anyone what he hears. He visited St. Patrick Church in Springfield many times growing up. One of his few friends was Kevin Fitzpatrick and he belonged to St. Pat's Church. He would get the number for the parish office from the Internet. He'll find out the name of the pastor and his email address and send him an email asking for a time to talk with him over the phone.

He found the web site for the church http://www.spcspringfield.org and the pastor's name, Father Tim O'Leary. Michael called the parish office number and got a young person on the phone. "I have been trying to send an email to Father Tim. I need to get an important message to him, but I must be doing something wrong. Can you check Father Tim's email address for me so I can figure out what I am doing wrong?"

A moment later the person came back on the line and told Michael the email address. Michael said, "I see what I was doing; I put in dot <u>COM</u> instead of dot org; thank you so much for your help." Michael hung up and began to think about the message to Father Tim.

I need to make sure that what I tell him he cannot tell anyone else, so I have to have a conversation - no, a confession - with Father Tim. Then I'll be sure he can't say anything. How much do I need to tell him about what I have done? I think the first thing to say is, Father, I am involved in something that has gone much further than I expected and I'm concerned that something has happened to my parents because of what I have done. Father, it's Michael Ridley; I'm sure you remember me. I have tried to call my parents' house in Springfield, but I get a message that the number is permanently disconnected. Father Tim, do you know anything about what is going on and do you have any information on my parents?

Michael needs to take his thoughts and put them in a short message so he can get a phone appointment with Father Tim. FT@SPCspringfield.org: "I'm writing to you to seek a counseling phone call with you. I currently live in California. I have been trying to get in contact with my parents in Springfield, but I'm not getting an answer when I call. I have done some things that I'm not proud of and now I'm concerned that something I have done has affected my parents. Do you have some time this week when we can talk? Michael."

Michael pushes the enter button and his message to Father Tim is on the way. It will be almost impossible to trace the origin of the message, so Michael feels secure at least until the time comes, to actually talk to Father Tim, if it does. He hopes that Father Tim will honor his vow of secrecy when he calls, if he calls him.

Father Tim walked into his office and sat down at his computer. The screen revealed he has seven emails. Tim thought, *Slow day; let's see who is sending me mail.* He scanned the emails and recognized everybody but a person named Michael. He opened the message and read it and thought, *the only Michael I know is Michael Ridley.* Father Tim knew that a bomb destroyed the Ridley house and Mike and Mary Ridley are missing and presumed dead. *I think I need to call Sheriff Whittles to see what I should do.* He picked up the phone and called the Sheriff's office. "Is Sheriff Whittles in, this is Father Tim O'Leary of St. Patrick Church."

The operator puts him on hold; he is waiting to hopefully hear from Sheriff Whittle. A few moments passed and the operator came back on the line, "Father Tim, the Sheriff is out on a call and he wonders if he can stop by the rectory in about an hour?"

"Tell Sheriff Whittles I'll be here for the next three hours. Ask him to stop by as soon as he can."

"I'll let him know, can I tell the Sheriff what this is about?"

"Tell the Sheriff I think it is about Mike, Mary, and Michael Ridley."

Chapter 18

THE SECRET MEETING CONTINUES

The President has put together a special team made up of cabinet secretaries and special advisors to the President. The Team, at least for the moment is composed of the Chairman of the Joint Chiefs, the Secretary of Defense, the National Security Adviser, the Secretary of Energy and the Director of the CIA. The President has been talking about how America should respond to not only the nuclear attack on America, but also the potential of other attacks on her allies. "We must stop this now, for if we don't, I have grave fears that nuclear terrorism will spread throughout the world."

The President's team has been listening and now he invites them to speak. "Gentlemen, I have been doing all the talking. What do you think, or what questions do you have of me?"

Secretary Findlay from the Department of Energy took the lead, "Sir, you said it's about the money, money that comes from all the oil pumped in the Middle East. The profits run the countries and supply money, in some cases, to the terrorist organizations. I'm not saying it's advisable, but bombing the oil fields with nukes might appeal to some as an eye for an eye. I believe we need some of that oil to run America. With much of America shut down for who knows how long, we may well just have to take our lumps and work on our own to find new sources of crude."

General Powell responded, "Mr. Secretary, are you suggesting that America's response to the mass murder of over 60,000 Americans is to bury the dead and move on?"

Secretary Findlay responded to Powell, "General, when you fight a battle as part of a war, when the battle is over don't you bury your dead soldiers and move on? What I'm saying is, for the most part we don't have bodies to bury, but we can move on. We will find an opportunity to get our revenge later."

President Jordan stepped in, "Wait a moment, Mr. Findlay, I understand your point, but if we wait to respond we may well have nothing left to fight with. How much do we spend on imported oil in America today?"

Findlay replied, "Sir, I don't have that number because the price of crude has skyrocketed, but the last number I saw before the attack was about $700 billion a year."

"Thank you. Now, General, what is the Pentagon's annual budget, all in, for all the branches of the military and to run the Pentagon?"

"Sir, I believe about $500 billion."

"Thank you. Do any of you know what it costs to fund Social Security on an annual basis?" Nobody knows the answer, so President Jordan tells them; "Around $700 billion a year. So, for the cost of what we pay the Middle East and other non-friendly nations, we could pay for Social Security or the Department of Defense for the year.

"Mr. Findlay, let me be clear. I'm not picking on you; you're just the person with most of the important information I need, so I want to ask, what is the GDP of Saudi Arabia?"

"Sir, the last report I saw was about $600 billion."

"And the GDP of the United States?"

"I believe about $16 Trillion."

Jordan concluded, "So the GDP of the United States is 27 times the GDP of Saudi Arabia."

"Yes, Mr. President, but if I may ask, what is your point?"

"I don't have a point yet; I'm trying to get information to make a decision. Let me ask you, if I took out the oil production capacity of Saudi Arabia with a nuclear bomb, and let me point out a bomb that would so contaminate the field and the pipelines rendering them useless for 100 years, what would be the impact in the region? Again, let me point out that I'm not saying that is what I would do, but I'm looking at this as an option at the moment. I would like to hear all of your thoughts."

All the attendees are shocked; speechless. The President of the United States is thinking about destroying an entire nation of 27 million people and making it a wasteland for at least a century.

Finally, General Powell responded. "Mr. President, America doesn't wipe nations off the face of the earth."

The President responds, "Mr. Chairman, if terrorist organizations like the Brotherhood had the money, do you think they would try and wipe America off the face of the earth? This time it was 60,000 people, the next time it could be 60 million.

"I realize it seems impossible that this could happen, but General, I think you have to agree with me that we have to stop this **DEAD IN ITS TRACKS**. Now. If we don't, many millions of Americans will die."

Fred Markel, the National Security Advisor said to the President, "Sir, if I may…"

The President broke in, "Let me stop you for a second. I want all of you to understand, if I have not made myself perfectly clear, I need your best advice, I need to know what you are thinking and nobody has to apologize in advance for what they say, is that understood?"

All agree in strong voices.

"Now Fred, what is your point?"

"Mr. President, the option of bombing Saudi Arabia has some complications that need to be weighed in your deliberation. The population of the Kingdom is about 27 million people, but 80% of the work force in the country is hired workers that are foreign nationals, so an attack on the Kingdom will surely kill millions of people of different nationalities. We may be taking out the Royal Family and the 5,000 princes, but we could also be taking out people whose home countries will be outraged and in turn could call for an all-out attack on America."

"Excellent point, Fred, but let me ask one more question of all of you. Is there any nation that can have a bigger impact on crude oil prices, while supporting terrorists, than Saudi Arabia?"

Robert Hamilton, the Secretary of Defense, looked at the President straight in the eyes and said, "Yes, Mr. President, there is."

Chapter 19

RESPONSE TO MORDECAI'S CALL

The team was stunned that Mordecai called early and they were not ready, but Hadar painted a picture in Mordecai's mind that bought them some time to turn everything on. Hadar was given the signal by Omid, "Go."

When Hadar came back on the line, she started with small talk. "How are you and how can I help?"

Mordecai responded, "I'm good, but I'm not sure how safe it is here for me."

Hadar watched the screen and saw a slight widening of the lines indicating Mordecai was a little uncomfortable. "What makes you feel insecure?" A long pause caused Hadar to ask, "Are you still there?"

"Yes, I'm here. I am trying to help you understand what I'm feeling." *What can I tell her? I don't think I can tell her about my involvement in the bombings, or the murder of Adad. Maybe I should just hang up.* "I'm not sure this was a good idea."

Hadar is watching the screen and she can tell that the tension is rising.

Omid types on the screen in front of Hadar. "He is wrestling with how much he can tell you. Change the subject."

"Do you have time for me to tell you about my project or should we leave that for another time? She waited for Mordecai to respond.

After a pause, Mordecai responds, "So, tell me how you like playing in the mud?" Hadar is concentrating on the screen and sees that the tension is subsiding.

"You know that the mud here is not only great for building bricks, but I'm told that it has great therapeutic value, especially if you roll around in it naked and submerge your whole body. It cleans your pores and detoxes your body. It's very healthy. Have you ever taken a mud bath?"

Mordecai is building a picture in his mind of the two of them rolling around in the mud. His fantasy is interrupted when Hadar asks, "Are you close enough to come here so we could see what it would be like to take a joint mud bath?"

The tension meter is showing a complete relaxation in Mordecai. Omid sends a message to Hadar's screen. Ask Mordecai "Would you like to come here and be with me? Is that possible?"

Now Mordecai doesn't know what to say. *More than anything I would like to see what that body looks like covered with mud, but I can't leave here. How would I ever convince the rest of the Brotherhood to let me go to see her? If I mention it, might I wind up like Adad?*

"Mordecai, are you still there?"

"Yes, I was just thinking about how I could make that happen. As much as I would love to be there with you, I know it is just not possible."

"Well, if you can't come to me, I'm going to have a break in about two weeks and could come see you. Perhaps together we could come up with a plan that works for you?"

Omid sends message, "Excellent, let it rest for a moment and watch for the reaction on the screen."

"I don't know if that is possible."

The meter is rising again. Hadar responds, "That's okay. It was just an idea. I would really like to see you, but perhaps another time." She is trying to give Mordecai the idea that the call is coming to an end and give him an opening to expand the call.

Mordecai has picked up on the signal, "Do you have a moment more?"

Hadar responded, "I'm getting cold with just a towel on so I need to go soon or I'll freeze to death."

Mordecai's mind is spinning with the image of Hadar in just a towel. She is probably having trouble keeping it on.

Mordecai heard the phone drop and then in a moment Hadar came back on the line and said, "I'm sorry that I dropped the phone, but I had to catch my towel as it was falling off. I'm really going to have to hang up soon."

"I wish I was there to help you with that towel."

"When do you think we can talk again? Can I call you?"

Mordecai responded, "I don't know for sure. I'll send you a text. It will always be better for me to call you."

Omid sent a message to the team, "Do we have a fix on where he is?"

The team texted back, "No."

Omid sent a message to Hadar, "It's time to wrap it up. Let's leave him desperate to talk again and more important, to want you to come see him."

Hadar said, "I have to go, so send me a text and let me know when you can call again. I really enjoyed talking with you and I hope we can see each other in the flesh, if you know what I mean. Goodbye, Mordecai…"

"Wait!" but the line went dead.

Chapter 20

SHERIFF WHITTLES GETS INVOLVED

Father Timothy O'Leary has received an email asking for an appointment, which is not strange, but this one seems to show interest in Mike and Mary Ridley. He has not yet responded and has decided to call his friend Sheriff Whittles. He has placed a call to the Sheriff's office and he is expecting Whittles in less than an hour. Tim has not had lunch, so he goes into the kitchen of the rectory to see what he can find to eat. As he walks from his study, the route to the kitchen takes him through the front hall and then down the hallway to the kitchen door. It has been a long time since any remodeling has been done in the rectory. It is clean but very dated. The floors are dark wood and the door trim is as dark as the floor. The boards squeak as he walks down the hallway. The hallway has one wall sconce with a glass cover and there is a 25-watt bulb, which makes the hallway eerie at best.

The house is over 50 years old, and as he goes through the door to the kitchen he throws the light switch and it turns on the single overhead florescent light with a milk-colored round glass cover. The kitchen has all the necessary appliances and they all work, but they look like they could fail any day. On the Formica counter is a white porcelain breadbox, which holds exactly one loaf of bread. Tim sometimes has had trouble getting it to roll back and thinks WD-40 might do the trick, but he just never finds the time to go out into the garage and look for it.

His refrigerator has the type of handle that you pull down on a lever to open it. Tim walked over the linoleum floor and pulled the handle to open the door. Inside are sliced turkey, some mayo, a ripe tomato and some leftover bacon from breakfast. He reaches into painted white cupboards and found a melamine plate and set it on the table. He grabbed the bread and all the fixings to make himself a sandwich or two.

The table is 1960 classic, yellow and white Formica top with chrome legs and a wide chrome band around the edge of the table. The four chairs are a match for the table with the same color seats and the curved chrome legs. Tim started to assemble his sandwich when the doorbell rang. Tim got up from the table and walked out of the kitchen and down the hallway. As he approached the door, the lace curtains made it difficult to see who was at the door. Before he opened the door he looked at his watch and thought, *it's too early for Sheriff Whittles. Who can it be?* When he opened the door nobody was there. He stepped out and to his left and just at the end of the porch, he saw a blur heading toward the back of his house.

Tim heard, "Father Tim, are you okay?" Tim turned to his left and he sees Sheriff Whittles coming up the walk.

"Who was that?"

Sheriff Whittles responded, "I didn't see the face, so I don't know who it was."

"Please come in and have a sandwich and a beer with me."

"I'll have a sandwich but not a beer."

The two walked down the hallway into the kitchen. They made their sandwiches and sat at the table. What they didn't know, at least not yet, was that the person who'd jumped off the porch slowly returned through the back gate and is approaching the window over the sink in the kitchen to try and hear their discussion.

Whittles said, "Father Tim, you called me so what is going on, old friend?"

"Sheriff, I think this is official business. I want you to see something I received in email. Tim opened his laptop and loaded the email and then turned it so the Sherriff read it.

"Have you responded?"

"No, not yet. I wanted to talk to you first before I talk with this person, and he or she binds me under the seal of confession."

"Do you think this person approached you because of the seal?"

"Jim, the way the email is written tells me that whoever wrote it wants to find out what happened to Mike and Mary Ridley. He wants to do so in such a way that he can protect his identity, and keep me from telling anybody who he is and what he wants."

The person listening at the window slipped and made a small cracking noise. Jim heard part of the cracking noise and looked toward the window. The person standing there was casting a shadow on the window glass. Whittles didn't want to alarm Father Tim, but he wanted to get around to the back of the house before whoever it is knows he is coming. In a louder voice Jim asked, "Tim, I need to use the restroom, can you point me in that direction?"

Father Tim told him, "Go down the hallway, and in the front hall turn left and go down past my office. It's the second door on the right."

Jim responded, "I'll be back in a few moments; then we can finish our conversation."

Sheriff Jim went down the hallway and when he got to the front hall instead of turning left he reached for the doorknob and slowly turned it until he felt the door latch open he slowly opened the door. As Jim was trying to open the old heavy door, it started to squeak. Jim stopped at the squeak, and then tried to open the door again and this time it made no noise. He slipped through the door and went down the old crumbly concrete steps, turned to his right and went past the dark green hedge that needed to be trimmed. The height of the hedge gave Jim cover as crossed in front of the house.

When Jim reached the front corner of the house he stood up and pressed his frame into the faded yellow house. Jim stepped back and noticed the yellow and white paint smudged on his dark blue uniform. He peeked around the corner and couldn't see anyone. The green hedge that was across the front of the house continued down the side yard. The difference was that this hedge had not been trimmed in a long time. It was wild and unruly and Jim would have to move away from the hedge, which gave him less cover. Jim stepped out and slowly walked to the rear of the house.

Sheriff Whittles looked around the corner and could see a figure, but he couldn't tell if it was a man or a woman. The distance between the corner of the house and Sheriff Whittles was about twenty-five feet. Jim thought, *I don't know if this is a man or a woman or if they have a weapon or not. I probably should have called for backup before I went out the front door. Well, I can't call now or I'll give away my position. I need to put myself between whoever it is and the back gate – it's the only way out. The side fence is too high to jump, so I'll go out to the center of the yard, swing back and drop on one knee with my gun drawn.*

Sheriff Whittles took off from the corner of the house and went to the spot he had picked out to take his stand. When he was two-thirds of the way there, he saw the person turn toward him; Whittles dove for the ground, rolled and then got to his shooting position. The person came right at Jim. As the person approached, Jim aimed his gun and...

The Brotherhood of the Red Nile

Chapter 21

MEETING WITH THE PRESIDENT

Drew Clinton and Frank Williams are waiting for a meeting with President Jordan in the President's small conference room to discuss Williams' ideas on who should trace the money. The two of them have been talking about how to approach the President. Clinton suggests that he take the conversational lead, but the details of whom and what needs to be done will be Williams' responsibility. They are already twenty minutes behind schedule when Mary Washington, the President's executive assistant, opens the door and tells them, "The President will see you in the Oval Office now."

The two of them got up and walked out the door and then down a narrow hallway made narrower by the presence of an armed Marine guard outside the Oval Office. Mary opened the door and escorted the two men into the President's office. Jordan was sitting in a wing back chair with red, white and blue stripes that was right across from a very long sofa. Between the chair and sofa is a round rug with the seal of the President on it. The President stood, shook hands with both of them and asked if they would like something to drink. Drew requested coffee and Frank asked for cold water. Frank remembered that the first time he met the President he broke out in a major sweat. He has gotten used to being around the President in a small group, but today it is just the three of them and he is sitting directly across and can look the President right in the eye. Frank knows that the subject matter is going to be difficult to discuss and he may be starting another major sweat. He looked down at his pants and he noticed that the suit is dark. He breathed a sigh of relief because if he sweats, in the dark suit it will not be as obvious.

Mary brought in the drinks and closed the door so only the three of them were in the room. Frank took his bottle of cold water and drank almost half in one gulp. Frank then spoke to the President, "Mr. President, before we start I wanted to give you an update on the Pathfinders, our special team in Houston, and their contacts with Mordecai, one of the terrorists. Lt. Hadar Hassen, on loan to us from Mossad, has texted Mordecai several times and they spoke yesterday afternoon for the first time. It was a brief conversation. We were not able to locate his cell phone because too many switches and towers were involved and not enough time spent on the phone. We are expecting him to call back. We just don't know when. We do have a sense from his demeanor on the call that something is not right in the Brotherhood. As we get more information I will update you."

The President responded "Thank you, Frank. Let's hope we can catch a break and get these guys."

"I agree, Mr. President."

Clinton spoke up, "Mr. President, Frank and I believe we need to begin to identify the source of the money that has funded and continues to fund the Brotherhood."

Jordan responded, "I agree we should. How do you suggest we go about finding the source of the money?"

Clinton turned to Williams, "Mr. President, Frank has discussed his idea with me and I think it has a great deal of merit. Go ahead, Frank."

"Sir, we have to have someone who can work on their own and not be associated with our government. If the person is captured while doing his work, we must disavow any knowledge of the person. We have to have a person who understands money and the movement of it around the world. He must know how it is hidden and how it gets to the right person. We need someone who has worked with terrorists. We need someone that can follow the trail and take us directly to the source and prove it to you."

"Does such a person exist, Frank?"

"Yes, Mr. President, I think he does, however, you need to know some background."

"I'm listening."

"The Carter administration needed a spy to infiltrate Iran to get a feel and gain information on what was happening with the Shah and his diminishing power. That person would stay in Iran if the Shah fell. When Americans were taken hostage, that person was asked to stay and was a vital source of intelligence on what was happening to them. This person reported directly to President Carter. He put his life in great danger several times at the request of the President. President Carter agreed that if he returned home, the government would take care of him and his family and keep them in a secure location for the rest of their lives. Should he be discovered, he would immediately be evacuated to another secure location. When Homeland Security was created, all of these special cases were turned over to the Logistics Office. You need two more pieces of information. You gave us permission to review a sealed file on one of those protected spies and we believe that this person would be ideal for the position."

Jordan asked, "Can you tell me who this person is?"

"In a moment, sir. The Attorney General believes that only the President can break the seal and reach out to talk with the protected spy. Under the protection accord only you, Mr. President, can ask for the interview."

Clinton added, "Mr. President you can ask, but the spy is under no obligation to talk with you. He or she can say I have done my job - no more. And there is nothing you could then do."

Williams came back into the conversation and said, "Mr. President, I will identify the person we both think can do the job, but you must hear us out before you speak."

"Frank, are you telling the President of the United States he has to keep his mouth shut until you are finished?"

What have I done? I have told the President of the United States, you listen and I talk. I can feel the sweat starting to run.

"Frank, this must be important, so you tell me when I can react and ask questions. Is that okay?"

"Yes, sir."

"Proceed."

"Mr. President, the retired spy who we think could do the job is Mike Ridley."

Ah! The President keeps his mouth closed and waves his hand for Frank to continue.

"Sir, we believe that one of the terrorists who bombed the United States is Michael Ridley, Mike and Mary's son."

Chapter 22

AFTER MORDECAI'S CALL

Hadar has just hung up on Mordecai and the Pathfinders begin to discuss her action in an open and candid conversation. Megan calls a halt, however, and before they continue Megan asks the communications team from Langley to go to their rooms. She tells them, "When we are ready for you we will call you." The team leaves and the Pathfinders all get something to drink.

Megan started, "Hadar, why did you hang up on Mordecai?"

"I told him I got out of the shower and I was dripping wet and getting cold. I didn't feel like the conversation was going anywhere, so the natural thing was to hang up and hope that he would call back. Let me be perfectly blunt. When I told him that I was wet in a towel, I know what was going through his mind. He was trying to imagine what I looked like and he lost his focus. If I didn't whine about being cold, I would not have lived up to his expectations. He will call back if for nothing more to ask what I'm wearing. I'm not trying to be egotistical, I just understand young Jewish men and I know how they think."

Omid spoke up, "I can understand her reasoning. I watched the screen and Mordecai's reaction to what she was or was not wearing or how wet she was drew higher spikes on the computer stress screen than anything else she said. I have no doubt that he feels that he might not be safe but right now, Hadar is the key. I think we need to send him a text to encourage him to call again."

Seacrest agreed with Omid, "We have to start pushing Mordecai to make him want to come to Hadar or have Hadar come to him. My guess is that they are holed up somewhere and he is not going to be able to convince the Brotherhood to move to see Hadar unless he can come up with a valid reason to move. He knows where Hadar is, so it is a big sell but he will try, and failing that he will most likely try and convince Hadar to come to him."

Omid turned to Megan Brown and asked, "What do you think, chief?"

Brown listened to the other three and agreed that Hadar has to reach out and try and engage Mordecai once again. "He made it clear not to call him; he would call her. So, my guess is that he has some limitations of when and where he can make phone calls. Before we send a text message, I want to call the communications team back into the room because I want to talk to them about an idea. Do we have anything else to talk about before we bring them back? Okay, I'll call them."

In a few moments the team is back in the room and Megan suggested, "We are trying to figure out where the Brotherhood is and the cell phone call is not long enough to learn where the call originates. I read recently about a cell phone laser tracking system. The idea is like the game we played as a child making a telephone out of two tin cans and a piece of string. If you kept the string tight between the two cans the voice frequency would vibrate the string and the sound would move from one can to the other. So, as I understand it, as long as the line is open, the laser is transmitted along the wireless signal to the phone at the other end. Perhaps if we can keep Hadar on the phone long enough we can, in effect, trace the call. Each time Hadar talks with Mordecai we shoot the laser and track its progress. Should Mordecai hang up we know that point. The next time the laser will go to the last point and then start progressing again. If we can get enough calls, we can construct the map to Mordecai."

The team leader responded, "Ms. Brown, you are referring to the RX 27 wireless laser from Data Laser Systems. It is an excellent idea. I don't have one here or in Langley, but I can call the company and get one. I'm not sure how we are going to get one delivered."

Megan replied, "Don't worry about that. I will call Under Secretary Williams and he will arrange a pickup and delivery."

"Ms. Brown, I do need to caution you about one of the shortcomings of the RX 27. What we don't know is whether texting uses the same route to get to Hadar's phone. If he uses a different route every time he sends a text message or a phone call, then the RX 27 will never find him. We may well never be able to trace his call. But it's a great idea and I think we should try. I'll call the company and as soon as I find one, I'll let you know where, and you can call Under Secretary Williams."

"Let me know what you find out. Now what should Hadar's text message be and how soon should we send it?"

Hadar asked, "Will all the electronics remain in place and in operation?"

Megan responded, "Yes, why?"

"Mordecai called three hours early this time. I want to make sure we are operational should he call again unannounced."

Brown replied, "All this equipment from now on is operational 24/7. Now back to the message."

Hadar responded, "How about; 'I was cold; I want to help if I can. H.'"

"Any objections or other ideas? Okay. Send it away."

Omid called to Megan, "Could I speak with you on the porch?" Hadar and John overhear the invitation and wonder, *what is the magic of that porch?*

Omid opened the door and let Megan go through. Then he walked out and stood next to her. They both look over the railing and enjoy the view. Neither of them speaks right away. Finally, Megan asked, "Why did you invite me out here?"

Omid turned toward Megan and she found herself turning toward Omid. She looked at his eyes and could tell that he was nervous. Omid spoke to her in a soft un-Marine voice, "I know that when we finish this mission you want to go to the CIA and work in Special Ops. I have no doubt that you would be good at that, but have you thought of other things?"

"I'm not sure I know what you mean?"

"You are a very attractive woman, you have a great brain and you are in top shape. So, I just wondered if you would have room for a man in your life."

"What do you mean, a man?"

Omid is now getting very nervous. "How about a man like me?"

Megan could see that he was stumbling like a schoolboy who has a crush on a girl. He likes her but he can't think of the right words to tell her so.

"Let me ask you a question, Omid. Do you want to be with me? Do you want to hold me? Do you want to take care of me? Do you want to make love to me?"

Omid has a look of shock on his face and he wants to say something, but all he can think of is, "I think so."

Megan responded, "Do you know all the time we have been together you have never touched me; how about we start with just a hug and see what happens?"

Omid stood and opened his arms allowing Megan to walk right into his welcome and she wrapped her arms around him. Omid slowly brought his arms around Megan and gently brought her close to him. It felt good for both of them.

In a low voice Megan whispers in Omid's ear, "We'll see."

Chapter 23

WILLIAM WILD FOR PRESIDENT

Senator William Wild is the Majority Leader in the United States Senate and has decided to challenge Nathan Jordan for President in the fall election. He has concluded that this campaign may be more difficult than perhaps any other in the history of the nation. With the transportation network short of fuel, it will be difficult for both candidates to fly around the country. Wild needs to find a way to limit the travel of the President to balance the scale between the candidates. If the President can fly on Air Force One at his will, he will have a distinct advantage over Wild or any candidate.

William - he is never called Bill - has scheduled a meeting with the Chairman of the Democratic National Committee, Frank Meyer, to talk about trying to get the Federal Election Commission to limit the fuel consumption of both parties for both the national elections and for office seekers in state-wide elections in all the states. Wild picks up his intercom and his executive assistant Nancy Winkler told him, "Chairman Meyer is here."

Nancy escorted Meyer into Wild's office and then asks, "May I get you something to drink?"

"Coffee, black with two sugars, Ms. Winkler, if you please. Thank you."

Meyer asked, "Senator Wild, how can I help you?"

"You've probably heard that I'm going to run for the Democratic Party nomination for President, and from what I can tell at the moment, it doesn't appear that I will have much competition in the primaries. In order for me to have a chance to win the general election, we have to change the rules to level the playing field."

"How?"

"We don't have a lot fuel to burn shuttling around the nation, but the President has unlimited amounts of fuel which I'm sure he can use to his advantage in the campaign. We need to change the rules for the Presidential election but also limit the fuel consumption in the states for those people who are running for statewide office. We use the state races as the basis to control the consumption of fuel on the federal level."

"Why would the White House agree to limit its travel?"

"If I say that I'm willing to conserve fuel and the state campaigns are willing to conserve fuel then the President has no choice. This campaign will have to be fought on TV and radio, and to a lesser extent in the news-papers. I know the President has a weekly radio address, so if I'm the oppo-sition candidate, I will want equal time on the radio."

"Senator, how are we going to convince the President to agree to our terms?"

"I would like you to visit the Federal Election Commission to see what they think of the idea of the fuel limits in the states. If we can get them to agree, then we move to the Presidential election. We need to use the press to push the idea of preserving important fuel. While it will be limiting travel in this difficult time, we need to have a free and open election, but one that is sensitive to the needs of the people. It will be difficult for the President to disagree without looking selfish."

"Do you think the President will just lay down and do what we want?"

Wild responded, "This will not be what we want but what the people, influenced by what the press, think they want. I also want you to talk to the commission, because of the travel restrictions, about a change in the Presidential Debate format."

Meyer is becoming very impressed with Senator Wild and his ability to lay out a plan and have people implement it for him. "So, how will the format change?"

"We have to keep in mind the short attention span of the electorate. Instead of two-to-three-hour debates, we have a one-hour debate each week. The shows, I mean debates, will be in prime time on same day, same time, each week. The debates will run for five weeks. The night before the election, each candidate will have fifteen minutes by himself to speak to the nation."

"It will be like Reality TV, only it's about the election of the new President."

"I like it. In fact, I like it a lot. This is a great concept, Senator.

"If I may ask a question, why would the Chairman of the Republican National Committee agree to these terms?"

Wild responds, "I don't mean to be degrading, but the leadership of the opposition party doesn't know what it wants to do. The conflict between conservatives and moderate Republicans has so divided the party that they find it difficult to take a stand on anything, so we will divide and conquer. I expect some resistance but I think they will cave rather than fight."

"We will, Mr. Meyer, control the Presidential and the state and local elections into a landslide for my election to the Presidency."

Chapter 24

CONVINCING THE PRESIDENT

Frank Williams and Drew Clinton have just finished presenting their rationale why Mike Ridley is the person to trace the money to its source. They have asked President Jordan to hold his questions until the end. The President asks, "May I speak now?"

Frank responded, "Sir, I am not trying to limit your ability to speak; I just want to get all the facts out first. I will do my best to answer all your questions."

The President asked, "Are you guys' nuts? You want me to bring out of protective custody a man who has not been in the field for 30 years and give him this assignment to follow the terrorist funding - and oh, by the way, his son is a terrorist responsible for using two nuclear bombs against the United States?"

"Sir, if I may? He has spent twenty of the last thirty years working on special assignments for the government. He might be a little rusty, but we believe his contacts are still in place."

"So, why should he come back and work for me and risk his life again?"

"Sir, we have no way of knowing for sure. However, we believe neither Mike Ridley nor his wife knows that their son Michael is a member of the Brotherhood of the Red Nile."

"So?"

"Sir, we think he might work for us if..." Frank took a deep breath and then paused.

The President said, "Spit it out, Frank."

"Sir, we believe that he will work for us if, in exchange for finding the source of the money, we offer amnesty to his son Michael." Frank wants to crawl under the table to avoid the President's reaction.

The President processes all this information. "First, how old is Mike Ridley?"

"Sir, he is 67, but in great shape and has no apparent medical problems."

"Let's suppose we need to convince him come to Washington DC to meet with me, who will go to wherever he is and find out his interest?"

Frank responded, "I will, Sir."

"Do either of you know where Mike is at the moment?"

"No sir, we don't."

"Great, we don't even know where the super spy is located."

Drew suggested, "Sir, Mike and Mary are under the protection of the United States Government; only the President can modify his protection terms."

"So, you think somebody in the government knows where Mike Ridley is at the moment?"

"Yes, sir."

"Who?"

Both men looked at each other and at the same time said, "Logistics, Mr. President."

Frank elaborated. "To be more specific Mr. President, the Logistics Office of the Department of Homeland Security is responsible for the Ridleys' protection."

"Let's say that I'm willing to use Mike. How would it work?"

Frank turns to Drew. "Your turn."

"Mr. President, the Ridley family protection is granted and secured by the Office of the President."

"Not the President himself?"

"No, Sir. Presidents come and go, but the Office is Constitutional. The sitting President signs the order and obligates all future Presidents to fulfill his commitment. So, Mr. President, you would call the Director of the Logistics Office and ask for the person who is in charge of special protection. You will invite that person to meet with you in the Oval Office. At the meeting, you will ask for the contact information on Mike Ridley and for that person to arrange a meeting between Mike and Frank Williams."

"What if Mike doesn't want to meet with Frank?"

"Sir, you will have the contact information and the last choice is for you to call him directly."

"And if he will not talk with me?"

"Well, sir, there would be nothing more we could do."

"Gentlemen, what bothers me most about this whole mess is you want me to give amnesty to a known terrorist."

"Sir, first, amnesty is only possible if Mike finds the source of the money and has indisputable proof of the person's complicity. This is a very difficult assignment regardless of a person's age. While we think Mike is the most likely person to be successful, we are less than 50% sure he can pull it off and survive. Sir, we have one more issue to discuss with you."

"I can't wait to hear this one."

"Mr. President, let us suppose for the moment that Mike is successful and traces the money and he still is alive and gives you the information on who is the source of the money."

Jordan asks, "Okay, make your point."

"What happens if you can't make the facts known to the American people?"

Jordan says, "You mean that we do all these things. People are risking their lives and if or when we have the goods, we can't use it to get the bad guy or guys?"

"Yes, Mr. President."

"Why?"

"Sir, we have an idea who the person is who has been supplying the money, but it is very possible that the individual who is the source of the money will be protected by his government."

"So you believe there is somebody out there who will be protected by his government even if I present all evidence that one of their citizens was responsible for the death of over 60,000 Americans."

"Yes, Mr. President, we do. So, the question is: would you still want to get Mike Ridley to work with us?"

"Before I answer your question, let me ask you a question. If we had all the evidence and we believed beyond a shadow of a doubt that we could prove who it is, then could we take action on our own without going to the head of the government to eliminate that person?"

Williams and Clinton pause and slouch in their chairs, *The President is asking us if we find the evidence, can we take the person out without talking to the head of the country. Is it possible for the United States to murder other people in revenge? The government kills people all the time for potential actions against America.*

Frank began the response. "Mr. President, I can't speak for the Attorney General, but if Mike Ridley could prove the source of the money, I would think taking one life against the 60,000 Americans is worth it and I would do it."

Drew Clinton has listened to Frank's comments. He thinks for a moment. "Mr. President, as the chief law enforcement officer in the United States, I can't opine on activities affecting non-U.S. citizens, but as an American, I agree with Frank's recommendation."

"Thank you both for your counsel. You have done excellent work and you had the courage to show me the options. Drew, on your way out, please tell Mary who I should call."

Frank wondered as he left the Oval Office, *would the President order the killing of the Russian?*

Chapter 25

FATHER TIM'S BACKYARD ARREST

Sheriff Jim Whittles is in the prone position with his Glock 9mm trained on whomever is running toward him and all he can see is a dark gray hoodie. He can see both hands and he doesn't see a weapon in either hand, so he yells, "Stop or I will shoot!" in a loud, commanding voice. The person tries to stop, but the momentum causes him to tumble, fall and land just in front of Sheriff Whittles' gun barrel.

The person said, "Don't shoot, I'm unarmed."

Jim slowly stood up with his gun still trained upon the person and ordered, "Get to your feet slowly and keep your hands where I can see them."

The person stood up slowly and Jim said, "Take one hand and slowly pull back the hood while leaving the other in the air. When the hood was pulled all the way back, Jim was stunned to see that the eavesdropper was none other than Kristen Murphy, Michael Ridley's girlfriend.

Jim spoke, "Please come with me. He put his gun back in its holster and secured it. As they walked back to Father Tim's front porch, he took out his radio and called for a backup team and told them to bring an assistant district attorney with them. Jim kept one hand on Kristen's arm just in case she tried to get away as they walked around to the front of the house. In the front by the grey concrete steps, Whittles told Kristen to sit down, "We will talk when my team arrives."

Kristen asks, "What did I do wrong?"

"I can't and won't answer any of your questions until my support team arrives."

In a more agitated voice she said, "I don't understand; I did nothing wrong and you can't hold me."

As she tried to stand up, Whittles said, "Sit down. Now."

"No, I don't have to, I'm leaving." Whittles blocked her way and grabbed her by the arm, pulling her up the steps. He reached in his pouch on his belt and pulled out a set of handcuffs. He snapped one half on her right wrist and pushed her chest into the pole on the porch. The momentum of being forced into the pole made her left arm swing around the pole. Jim quickly cuffed the left hand. Before she knows what has happened, she is going nowhere.

When Kristen realized she was trapped, she dropped down and started to cry. As much as Jim would like to talk with her to try and figure out what is going on, he couldn't. He must wait for the support team to arrive. If he let her speak, what she says might not be used as evidence against her. Jim turned toward the door and saw Father Tim standing in the doorway with a very serious look on his face. Sheriff Whittles left Kristen and walks over to Father Tim. "Do you know this woman?"

Tim didn't reply immediately and Jim could tell he was thinking. *Can I tell the Sheriff that I know Kristen? If I say yes, then will he ask how I know her? What can I say to him that will not violate my office?* As Tim came out the screen door to the front porch, he looked down and went over to Kristen. He put his hand on her shoulder to comfort her.

She looked up at Tim and stopped crying, "Father Tim, what should I do?"

Just then Jim saw the backup team coming up the walk to the front porch. As soon as they reached the steps, Jim said to Kristen, "Stand up and let's take off the handcuffs and go inside." The Sheriff took out the key and unlocked the cuffs and they all went into the living room and sat down. The last time Jim was in the rectory living room was just before he went off to Marine basic training. As he walked through the screen door and turned right he said to himself, *hasn't changed a bit.*

They all sat down, but Father Tim and Kristen sat on the sofa. The others either sat in any available chair, or stood. They all introduced each other and the assistant DA asked Jim, "Why is this priest here?"

Father Tim cleared his throat and responded for Jim, "I am Kristen's confessor, and I'm here to support her."

The DA responded, "I don't think he can be here while we question Kristen."

The Sheriff responded, "Why not ask Kristen if she has a lawyer?"

"Do you have a lawyer?"

"No. Why? Do I need one?"

The DA responded, "Please excuse us for a moment. Deputy, please stay with Father Tim and Ms. Murphy."

Kristen spoke up, "Excuse me Mr. Willis. That is your name isn't it? I saw your name on your badge."

"Yes, I am the assistant DA for Springfield and my name is Mark Willis"

"I would like to set the record straight, my name is Mrs. Kristen Ridley."

Chapter 26

LOGISTICS AND THE PRESIDENT

The President has a meeting with Albert Noble who is head of the special protection unit of the Department of Homeland Security. Albert isn't quite sure why he is in the President's office; in fact he recalls, *in my 30 years of government service I have never been in the White House or the Oval Office.* He is sitting in an anteroom to the Oval Office waiting to be called to meet the President. He has been waiting for almost 20 minutes when Mary tells him, "It shouldn't be much longer. Can I get you something to drink?"

"A glass of water would be fine." From the moment Albert walked into the West Wing, he was awestruck at being in the Office of the President.

While he was sitting in the chair waiting, his eyes have been flashing hectically; and absorbing his surroundings. He was trying to see as much detail as he could so he could tell his wife Fay about his experience. Albert had not told Fay where he was headed today, but when he gets home, she will be very surprised to hear about his day.

Mary returned with Albert's water and in just a few moments she said, "The President will see you now. You may take your drink with you."

"No, I'll finish it here." Albert set down the glass and followed Mary through the doorway. President Jordan is behind the Kennedy desk; he stood and extended his hand to Albert. *The President has a firm handshake; I like that.*

Nathan said, "Come and sit over on the couch where we'll be more comfortable." They walked over to the couch; the President then sat in the chair and told Albert, "Please sit down. You are probably wondering why I have asked to meet with you."

He has asked to meet with me. How can that be? He is the President! "Well, frankly sir, I mean, Mr. President, I was trying to figure out why you wanted to meet with me."

"Albert, I need your help. As President, I have the power to grant special protections for people who have performed a unique service for the government. I can legally enter into special agreements that are sealed and bind all future Presidents to protect those individuals. Your office is responsible for the protection of those under special agreements for as long as they live. Am I correct, Albert?"

Albert listened very intently to the President and responded, "Yes, Mr. President. That is what I do."

"You have taken an oath to protect the whereabouts of those protected people and the only person you can share that information with is the President of the United States. Is that correct, Albert?"

"Yes, sir."

"Albert, I need your help in locating one of our protected people. I need to speak with him about helping America again."

"Mr. President, how can I help?"

"How long will it take you to find the location of one of those protected persons?"

"Mr. President, that will depend on when they were last moved. May I ask who you are looking for?"

"Albert, I need to speak with Mike Ridley on a matter of National Security. He may well be the only person who can help America."

"Mr. President, I was personally responsible for the recent move of Mike Ridley and his wife Mary."

"How soon before I can get his contact information?"

"Mr. President, I could give it to you now, but the order of protection for Mike Ridley specifically requires us to contact him and notify him that the President wants to speak with him. In Mike's case, the President is the only one who can call him."

"Can I call him now?"

"Sir, I can link to my office computer through my iPad. I could step out and see if I can get his phone number and then you can call him."

"Albert, you sit right there and I'll step out to the restroom, and upon my return perhaps I can call Mike myself."

"You want me to sit in the Oval Office while you go out?"

"Yes."

"Mr. President, I have no way of knowing if he is home."

"Just try Albert; I'll be back shortly." The President left and Albert used his iPad to make the connection and got the phone number of Mike Ridley. He used his secure cell phone to call him. He dialed a 239 area code and the phone rang five times before a male voice answers.

Chapter 27

WHITE HOUSE TWO DAYS LATER

It is 9:30 in the morning and Nathan Jordan has already been at his desk since 7:30 AM. He is hopeful that he will hear from Mike Ridley this morning, or at the latest, before the end of the day. He knows that Mike will be taking a significant risk if he takes the assignment. The President has not slept well since talking with Clinton and Williams about a pardon for young Michael should Mike take on the mission.

Jordan feels conflicted over the possibility of granting Michael a Presidential pardon in exchange for his father's participation. The public policy of every President before Jordan has been to never bargain with terrorists. *What else do I have to offer this brave man other than his son? He doesn't need the money and we have provided him with excellent security. Should I be the one to tell him his son is a member of the Brotherhood of the Red Nile? When do I tell him? If I tell him before we strike a deal, then he might take the job to try and save his son. He may not want to do the job, but has to accept it because of his son. On the other hand, if he wants to do the job and then I tell him about his son, he may change his mind because he won't trust me because I was not truthful with him upfront.*

"Mary, can you get Mrs. Jordan on the phone for me please."

"Mr. President, the First Lady is on the phone."

"Good morning, I love you."

"And I love you too."

"Karen," Nathan said in a very serious voice, "Are you tied up at the moment?"

Karen, sensing something is troubling Nathan, responded, "Nothing I can't postpone if you need me."

"Could you come over to the Oval Office as soon as you can?"

"I'm on my way."

Jordan told Mary on the intercom, "When the First Lady arrives I will not want to be disturbed, with one exception. If Mike Ridley calls, you may interrupt me immediately."

Karen's office is in the East Wing of the White House, while the President's office is in the West Wing. Their offices are not part of the original White House, so Karen has a long way to walk and it's not a straight line. She asked for an escort to get her to the President as quickly as possible and even with that, it took her at a quick pace, almost 12 minutes to arrive at the Oval Office. Karen greeted Mary and asked her to tell the President she has arrived.

Mary buzzed the President. Nathan came out of the door and took Karen by the hand into the Oval Office and closed the door. When they were alone, he took her in his arms and gave her a soft kiss and then just held her for what seems to Karen an unusually long time. "Come sit with me on the couch."

Karen fears the worst. "Has there been another attack?"

"No." He reached out and took her hand to assure her that there has been no new attack. "I need to talk something through with you and then I need your advice."

"I'll do my best."

"I have no doubt." Nathan then told her the details of the meeting with Williams and Clinton and the recommendation that they try and get Mike Ridley to do the job. "Both of them have strongly suggested that if Mike Ridley does the job, I should agree to pardon Michael Ridley, his son. First, we have no idea where Michael is or if he is even alive. Second, we do not believe that Mike currently knows that Michael is part of the Brotherhood of the Red Nile. Lastly, no President to my knowledge has ever struck a deal with a terrorist. It has always been the proverbial line in the sand. When I was inaugurated, I took an oath to protect and defend the Constitution. So here is the dilemma: should I tell Mike about his son and as part of the deal offer to pardon his son Michael? His record will be sealed and nobody would know."

"That's a lot to absorb at one time. So, what is it that you want my advice about concerning this dilemma?"

"I feel that if I put a pardon on the table I have violated my commitments and those of all the Presidents before me. If I make the deal have I demeaned the Office of the President?"

"Nathan, I know that you have strong feelings about protecting the integrity of the Office of the President; you have always respected the Office even when others have not, but it seems to me that you have to make a decision that is best for the country, putting the people's needs above the President's. I don't want to be picky, but it seems to me that you are not making a deal with a terrorist. You are trying to decide if you want to cut a deal with the father of a terrorist.

"Don't make the pardon contingent on the success of the mission. Tell Mike Ridley regardless of the outcome of the mission, if his son is captured you will pardon him. Michael has to surrender to the government and you will arrange that the surrender is done in private and only a few people will know of the surrender."

The intercom buzzed, "Mr. President, Mike Ridley is on the phone."

"Tell him I'll be right there."

"Should I leave?"

"No, please stay here."

"What are you going to say to him?"

"I don't know."

Chapter 28

MORDECAI'S QUANDARY

Hadar has just hung up on Mordecai. She said it was because she was wet and cold. He wants to believe her, but she seemed angry with him and he doesn't know why. *Perhaps she could feel my lack of candor and honesty in the call. She wasn't getting anything of value, so she decided to move on until I was willing to be honest with her.* He feels his phone vibrate that tells him he has a text message. He hopes it is from Hadar. Mordecai opens his phone and he sees the message, "I was cold, I want to help if I can. H." He feels a little better that he hasn't driven her off and she seems sincere that she wants to help. His emotional side wants to text her back right away, but he knows that he may only have one more chance and he needs to spend some time trying to figure out what he wants to say to her first.

Is it possible that she could get here? I can't think of any reason to convince the Brotherhood to move to New Mexico. He was standing at the railing looking at the skyline and the stars when he heard Sargon behind him. Mordecai turned and smiled at Sargon and he smiled back. Sargon asked, "Making wishes?"

Mordecai replied, "In a way, yes, I am. I miss my family back in New York. How long do you think we will have to stay here?"

"I have no idea, all I know is we have to stay here if for no other reason than our protection."

Mordecai analyzed the situation. "We know based on the news that the American government is embarking on two huge pipeline projects to deal with the bombed out infrastructure. They are trying to quickly restore the American economy. In addition to building pipelines, they are also starting a major program that will convert as many vehicles as possible to natural gas. I understand it will take a significant amount of time, perhaps years, to get this up and running. Our goal was to do something that had a long-term negative impact on America. Look at what we have accomplished. We have met all of our goals. I think we would be better off to get out of America as soon as possible. We can't do any more than we have already, so why stay in America?"

"Mordecai, we have talked about leaving and going to an island to start a new life. I'm sure we will have a significant amount of money from our oil trading profits to do that. I have grave concerns about splitting up and each going our own way. We started this journey together and I think we need to finish it together. I have spoken to Ishtar about starting to reach out to his contacts to get us out of America and I have asked him for a plan for us to exit within 30 to 45 days. We must be proud of what we have done and how we have changed America, perhaps forever."

If we are truly going to leave America in the next 45 days, then Hadar has to come here, and soon. If I can convince her to come here, then how can I get her out of the country with me? Mordecai began to think about the text message he wants to send to her that will make her want to come to Houston to see him. He knows that based on Sargon's target departure he is not going to have a lot of time.

If he is going to get her to come to see him, how will he explain that she can't stay with him? He can't make her a hotel reservation and there is probably no chance that they can even have a meal together. Mordecai asked himself, *would I make that 1,000-mile trip under those conditions? If I wouldn't, then why would Hadar?*

If I tell her the truth, would she come here to be with me? Probably not. I have to find a way to let her know that I want to see her, but things are unpredictable. Wait a minute! I could tell her that I'm leaving in the next 30 to 45 days, and after this move I will be leaving the country. Once I'm settled, I want her to come and join me where we will have all the time in the world to get reacquainted. I'm only going to have a few hours to see her before I leave and I must hold her once again. I will give her the money for her transportation to join me, and I'll pay for her trip to and from

Houston. So, what do I text her that will make her want to come and see me even if it is for just a few hours?

Mordecai decided to walk down the stairs. He has done some of his best thinking when he is walking or sitting on the landings. As he took the steps, his thoughts started to come together. His message has to be mysterious and sensuous, and at the same time urgent. "Come here, I need you with me, I'm leaving soon."

Then he decided to change the word order more in line with the way they were when they were together in Syria. As Mordecai thought about their times together, he was always leaving her. He had to cut his time with Hadar short and it was both disappointing and yet very sexual for he couldn't wait to see her again. He pulled out his cell phone and typed in the rearranged message. He looked at the screen and said out loud, "Perfect!" He pushed the Send button and "swoosh", his new message was on its way to Hadar, "I'm leaving soon. I need you. Come here. M."

Chapter 29

WHAT DOES KRISTEN KNOW?

Sheriff Whittles is the only one in the room that is shocked when Kristen announced that she is married to Michael Ridley. Jim turned to Father Tim, "Did you know that she was married to Michael Ridley?"

"Yes, I married them in a civil ceremony."

"How long ago?"

"I think it was about six months ago, is that right Kristen?"

Kristen replied, "I think almost seven months, Father."

"So, you were married to Michael when we were in your bank checking on Mike and Mary Ridley."

"Yes."

"Any reason why you didn't tell us then that you were married to Michael?"

"No, you didn't ask so I figured you were not interested; it seemed you were more interested in Mike and Mary Ridley than me until somebody took a shot at me through Mr. Ford's office window."

Jim asked the group to wait for a minute because he needed to make a phone call. "I'll just step outside on the porch to make the call; I'll be right back." Whittles was walking through the screen door and didn't know who to call first, Frank Williams, Ted Baker or Omid Rahimi. He concluded that if he started at the top it would filter down quickly. He took out his cell phone and called Frank Williams.

The phone rang three times and Marie answered, "Mr. Williams' office. May I help you?"

"Marie, this is Sheriff Jim Whittles of Springfield, Texas. Could I speak with Mr. Williams?"

"One moment, Sheriff." She came back on the line. "I'll put you through to Mr. Williams."

"Jim, how are you and what can I do for you?"

"Mr. Williams."

"Please call me Frank."

Jim continued, "Okay, Frank, I thought you might want to know that I have Kristen Murphy in protective custody. She claims that she is not Kristen Murphy, but Mrs. Michael Ridley. If this is true, then is she married to one of the terrorists? I spoke with Father Tim O'Leary of Saint Patrick's who says he married them about seven months ago just before Michael disappeared and then reappeared in the photos of the Brotherhood in Syria."

"What else have you asked her?"

"As of right now, nothing. I have an assistant DA here, but we have not started to question her."

"I want to send Ted Baker to Springfield to question her. Can you get that local judge we used in the map question to issue a writ retaining her as a material witness in the bombings?"

"I don't think that is an issue."

"Let me know when you have the writ. I will send Ted on military transport within the next three hours. Sheriff, I don't want anyone talking to her. Not even the priest. I know we can't get much out of him, but perhaps Ted can find some ways to allow Father Tim to speak. Let me know when you have the writ."

"Yes, sir, right away."

While Jim was on the phone trying to make contact with the judge, Williams was on his phone trying to reach Ted Baker. While both were now waiting for callbacks, Jim went back into the house and called the ADA to join him outside on the porch. "Mr. Willis, this woman is married to one of the terrorists from the Brotherhood of the Red Nile."

Willis replied, "Isn't that the group that claimed responsibility for the two nuclear bombs that exploded here?"

"Yes. I was just on the phone with the Under Secretary of Homeland Security for Terrorist Activity and he has instructed me to get a writ to hold her as a potential material witness in the bombing attacks. I'm waiting for the judge to call me back, but I feel certain he will give me the writ. Mr. Williams's deputy is on his way here to question her. As soon as I get the writ, I will take her to the jail and put her in an isolated cell. Nobody, and Mr. Williams was very clear on this, nobody is to ask her anything of substance. Nobody, do you understand?"

"Yes, Sheriff. What do we say to her when we take her to jail?"

"For now we say we are taking her to a more secure location for her own protection and nothing more."

Baker called Williams office and Marie answered the phone, "He has been waiting for your call."

"Ted, where are you?"

"I'm at home."

"Pack a bag; you are leaving on a military transport to Springfield, Texas."

"Why Springfield?"

"Ted, I just got off the phone with Sheriff Whittles who tells me that he has Kristen Murphy in handcuffs."

"Isn't that the girl who worked at the bank and was a girlfriend of Michael Ridley?"

"Yes, but she is no longer Michael Ridley's girlfriend."

"What is she?"

"Kristen Murphy is Mrs. Michael Ridley."

Ted asked incredulously, "She is married to the terrorist Michael Ridley!"

"One and the same. I asked Whittles to ask the local judge to issue an order to hold her under a writ."

"Sir, I don't think we have to get a writ. The Sheriff can hold her as a material witness. If it's okay with you, I will call the Sheriff and ask him to check with the DA. The fewer people we have involved the better."

"Agreed."

Baker packed his overnight suitcase and headed to Andrews. On the way, he called Sheriff Whittles and told him to check with the DA about just holding her as material witness. "I want her in an isolated cell and no, absolutely no, phone calls, and nobody talks to her until I get there."

Jim responded, "This could be an important break for us in locating the Brotherhood."

"Jim, let's hope so. We need a break."

Chapter 30

THE MAN ON THE OTHER
END OF THE PHONE

Before President Jordan dials what he has been told is Mike Ridley's phone number, he did a little research. He had White House security match the phone number to a physical location. Mary has placed the requested information on his desk. The sheet says the phone number is associated with the address 1226 Bella Vista Way, Sanibel, Florida. It is in a development called Colony Beach Estates. The President turned to his computer and typed the name of the resort into Google Maps and pulled up a satellite image of the house. Next he used Zillow to learn that the house is a four-bedroom, four-bath house with about 3,800 square feet and estimated to be worth $1.7 million. "Nice house. Karen and I could retire there. We will have to check out Sanibel. Mary, see what you can find about Sanibel, Florida."

Jordan dials 1-239-587-6287. It rang three times, then the phone stopped ringing like it was going to an answering machine, but then a real voice answered, "Yes, Mr. President."

"How did you know it was me?"

"Mr. President, I have a special caller ID, and I also happen to know the phone number of your private line. What can I do for you?"

"Mr. Ridley."

"Mr. President, I would feel more comfortable if you called me Mike."

Jordan responded, "I can do that, Mike. So, Mike, I must tell you that what I want to talk to you about shouldn't be talked about over the phone."

"It must be important."

"Mike, I wish I could tell you how important but I just can't take a chance. I want to send my Under Secretary of Homeland Security for Terrorist Activity, Frank Williams, to come and talk with you. He will explain what is going on and what we think you could do for us. He cannot ask you to do anything, only I can as the sitting President. This provision was part of the agreement you struck with President Carter and I intend to honor that commitment."

"There are a lot of retired FBI and CIA agents in and around Sanibel that I will want to check with to see if Mr. Williams can be trusted."

"I assure you, Mike, he is very trustworthy, but I understand."

"Mr. President, can I get back to you in a couple of days?"

"Time is of the essence, so the quicker the better." Jordan is thinking very hard. Before he hangs up, does he want to tell Mike about his son or not? *This is not a message to give someone over the phone. I'll let Frank deal with that for now.* "I would like a favor if you could, Mike."

"What is that, Sir?"

"Frank and his wife Ellen will be celebrating their 25ᵗʰ wedding anniversary and Frank has told me that Ellen has a keen interest in celebrating it on Sanibel. So, if you have some time, perhaps you could show him around."

Mike replied, "Well, Mr. President, Mary and I have not been on Sanibel very long. We are still exploring the island ourselves, but we'll find somebody to show him around. Mr. President, if I could go back to business for just a moment, why are you considering a 67-year old retired agent for this assignment?"

"Mike, I'm not looking for a swashbuckler, shoot'em up agent. I want somebody who can handle this assignment with his brain and his experience. I have been told that even at 67 years of age you are still the best in the business. Everybody tells me you can handle this assignment. To be perfectly frank with you, Mike, I don't have many options."

"Mr. President, do you want me to call you after I have a talk with Mary, or if I decide that I want to at least listen, should I call Mr. Williams?"

"Mike, I called you and I think you should call me."

"Mr. President, if I might ask, can you tell me anything about this assignment?"

"Mike, you have served your country well and the reason you are on Sanibel is because your security was compromised. I hear that Sanibel is like no other place on earth and I do not want to jeopardize you and Mary. The only thing I can say that would be okay is that we want you to find some money."

"How much money?"

"A lot. Is there anything else you want to ask? I'm not sure I will be able answer."

"Try this, Mr. President, millions or billions?"

"Mike, much more than a billion. I want to thank you for talking to me and I'll understand whatever you decide. Thank you for your past service to our great country."

The President hung up and Mike said, "Much more than a billion…"

Chapter 31

JOHN BOWMAN BACK TO WORK

The Departments of Energy and Interior have the responsibility for building the pipelines in Texas and in the central and northwestern states. In Texas, the Governor has offered to lend John Bowman to the project to verify the welds connecting the pipelines. John suggests in a meeting that we need to keep America abreast of the progress of both pipelines. "I think we should have a mobile camera at each site with a live feed to a website: www.AmericaRebuilds.org, so the American people can see the progress. In addition, I think the website should have a map of the building area and at the bottom, a progress bar that shows how many miles we have built. We have been laying pipe for the last 10 days and we have secured 15 miles of pipeline in Texas and I have heard 25 miles in the northwest. As we lay more and more pipe, I think our website hits will grow everyday as more and more Americans want to see our progress."

Wendell Right, the project manager for the Texas project, responded to Bowman, "John, an excellent idea. I'll get the web designers on it and we will shoot to have it running in seven days or less. Sometime today I will get a note off to the Secretary of Energy with your idea and he can pass it on to the President for his Saturday chat."

Bowman suggested, "I'd be happy to draw a sketch for the designers of what the basic website should look like. We could invite Americans to ask us questions about building the pipeline. This is one of the biggest building projects in the history of America and millions of people will be interested."

When Bowman finished with the head of web design, he walked over to Wendell and asked if they could step outside for a moment. The office is a trailer they got from Homeland Security and they retrofitted it so it is easy to move as the pipeline makes progress.

"John, what do you want to talk about?"

"Wendell, somebody has to make an assessment of Texas City and what needs to be done to isolate it. I was thinking we could take a run down there and see what could be done. My concern is that some point in time we are going to have to get close to Texas City when we lay the pipeline through that area. I don't want to have to stop and lose all our momentum and energy by having to change direction."

"John, I think I agree with you. I have never been close to Texas City and it has been several months since the attack. I can't tell much from the satellite images. I think we should round up some protective gear and go there today. It will most likely be dark by the time we arrive, but that may be a better time than during the day."

"Wendell, I think we should also take a Geiger counter so we can measure the radiation level."

"John, excellent idea. We need to get some food, water and a full tank of gas."

"I agree. I'll get the car, the gas, and food, and meet you here in about an hour."

As Bowman walked to the car he was thinking about what he might see in Texas City. He, like Wendell, has seen the images from space but even as good as they are, the flames are still blocking all the visible destruction. He has been looking at photos every day for the last month and the fire seems as intense as it was a month ago. The closest photos make the landscape appear as a flat area with massive flames shooting hundreds of feet into the sky. The image reminds him of the high fire burners used in a Chinese restaurant to quickly cook stir-fry. The fry cook will step on a foot pedal to dramatically increase the size of the flame and speed up the cooking time. But in the case of Texas City, the pedal is stuck on the floor. John believes that the oil, gas and product in the pipelines are being sucked out of the pipelines by the heat of the fire. He knows that the fire will eventually burn everything in the pipelines, but nobody knows how many years that may take. *If we can suck the oil out of the pipeline and pump it back in the ground into the caves that once held the petroleum reserves, we can starve the fire.*

The Texas Pipeline is now 27 miles long; the natural gas pipeline is 36 miles long.

Chapter 32

HADAR'S PHONE VIBRATES

The Pathfinders are sitting at the dinner table finishing up one of Omid's specials when his phone rings. He looks at the caller ID and it is Ted Baker calling. "Hello, Ted, when are you coming to Houston?"

"I'm on a plane headed to Houston right now, but I'm not coming to see the team. I might need you if you feel like you can get away."

"Can you tell me why you are coming?"

Ted explained, "You remember Mike Ridley's girlfriend?"

"Sure, I think her name was Kristen Murphy."

"Yes, but her name now is Mrs. Michael Ridley; she and Michael were married about seven months ago and at the moment I don't know where, but I know who married them. Williams is sending me to Springfield to question her about Michael to find out what she knows. Do you think you can get away from the team to join me in Springfield?"

Omid replied, "Ted, I would like to, but we could get a phone call or a text message from Mordecai anytime." Just then, Hadar jumped as her phone vibrated with a text message. He finished, "Ted, Hadar's phone is vibrating. Let us see who it is. I'll call you back and then we can decide about Springfield. I would like to go but I've got to see this Mordecai thing through."

The rest of the team waited till Omid got off his phone before Hadar opened her phone. Hadar sat at the dining room table that has been cleared of the dishes, with her phone in her hand.

Megan said, "Open the phone and read us the message."

Hadar slowly opened the phone. The message read: "I'm leaving soon. I need you. Come here. M." She read the message and then passed the phone around for all of the Pathfinders to see. Hadar saw each of the team member's mouths move, as they each read the message.

Megan was the first to say anything. "He wants Hadar to go to him; that means there is a good chance he is in the United States. He says he is leaving, so my guess is the Brotherhood is planning to leave the United States soon. I need to call Williams. While I'm doing that, I want all of you to begin thinking about the message we need to send to Mordecai."

Megan went out to the now-famous balcony and dialed Williams' office. She looked at her phone and realized it is after 7 PM and Williams is at home or en route. She hung up and dialed Williams' cell phone. He answered on the third ring. "Williams here."

"Mr. Under Secretary, we just got a text message that we believe is from Mordecai and he wants Hadar to come to him."

"He wants Hadar to go to him?"

"Yes, sir."

"Do you know where she needs to go?"

"Not yet sir, we are working out a reply to Mordecai. We know that he has told us he is leaving soon, but we don't know where he is leaving from or where he is going."

"Once you craft your message let me know, Megan."

"Yes, sir."

"Ted Baker is on his way to Springfield; he is in the air right now. Do you want him to come to the safe house before he heads to Springfield?"

"Sir, we are going to send a message tonight and we have no way of knowing when he will reply. If you could have him call me once he gets to Springfield, I can brief him up to the moment." Megan rejoined the team to discuss the response.

Hadar started, "Here is what we know: he says he is leaving and it looks like it will be soon, and he wants me to come to him."

Seacrest spoke up, "We need to get him back on the phone. I don't think we can do this with text messages."

Omid agreed with Seacrest.

John continued, "I think it needs to be simple, like 'Call me and we'll make a plan.'"

Megan offered, "I think that sounds too matter of fact. Hadar has told him that she has a break in two weeks, so it might be difficult for her to leave on short notice, so I like, 'Call me and let's try, H.' Hadar has no idea where Mordecai is located so she doesn't know how far she has to go or how she will get to him."

Omid has an alternative, "How about, 'I hope I can, call me. H.'"

Hadar has listened to all three of the team member's suggestions and she has a new alternative, "I want to. Call me, H."

Megan suggested, "I want to, if? H."

Seacrest responded, "I love that, it offers possibilities but no guarantee; he has to call to work it out. Everybody agree?"

"Yes."

Megan told Hadar to send the message. "Swoosh", it's sent.

The Texas Pipeline is now 31 miles long; the natural gas pipeline is 37 miles long.

The Brotherhood of the Red Nile

Chapter 33

TED BAKER MEETS MRS. RIDLEY

Ted has been sent to Springfield, Texas, to interview the new Mrs. Ridley. In so doing, he will be trying to gain some insight into the possible location of Michael Ridley and the rest of the Brotherhood. While he was en route, he talked with Omid Rahimi in Houston to let him know about his interview. Ted would have liked Omid to join him, but Omid wants to stay in Houston and see if Mordecai will respond to Hadar's latest text message with a phone call. Omid would like the opportunity to capture the Brotherhood if possible. Baker understands. He wishes him luck and asks Omid to keep him updated.

Ted's military transport landed at Springfield Regional Airport. The local Homeland Security office sent a car to take him to the Springfield jail and Sheriff Whittles. Baker grabbed his bag and bounded quickly down the steps into the car. When he arrived at the Sheriff's office, he announced himself to the receptionist. She remembered Baker by name and said, "Welcome to Springfield, Mr. Baker. It's good to finally to be able to put a face with a voice. The Sheriff is expecting you; I'll call him and let him know you're here."

"Thank you."

Jim Whittles came through the double door and extended his hand. "I'm glad to see you. I certainly hope your trip has not been wasted."

Ted said, "Well, Sheriff, I hope not either; let's get started. Have any of the local government officials talked to Kristen?"

"No, we have had her isolated; she can't even talk to the other prisoners."

"Do you have an interrogation room with a two-way mirror?"

"Yes, it is just down the hall from her cell."

"I will need a camera setup so we can record all of the conversations we have and I want them digitally duplicated and a set sent to Mr. Williams at the end of each day. I want you to back up every interview on a flash drive and CD and lock it in your safe. When I'm done, I want one copy to take to DHS, and I want you to go to the local bank and secure the files in a safety deposit box."

"Mr. Baker, as to the request for a camera, we have one on the way. We had to rent it from Springfield Camera."

"Sheriff, this is a letter from Frank Williams of Homeland Security declaring Kristen Ridley as a person of interest in crimes against the United States and that she is to be held without legal counsel until stipulated by the Under Secretary of Homeland Security. Questions?"

Jim replied, "No."

"Then, let's get going."

Springfield Camera took another 30 minutes to get the camera set up and tested. Baker wore a wireless microphone; they tested it to make sure it's working. He asked them, "Does this microphone have a battery power level indicator? Also, make sure we have plenty of spare batteries."

It is now 2:30 in the afternoon and Mrs. Ridley is led into the interview room. The Sheriff and Baker are on one side of the table and Kristen is on the other. The room has one door and the glass mirror. The table is gray with a soft top that has been chewed up over the years by people's fingernails digging into the soft top when they are under intense questioning. The three chairs are made of stainless steel and are bolted to the floor so a suspect cannot use them as a weapon to try and escape. The walls are light green and the ceiling has 12-inch square perforated tiles that are now a faded white. The ceiling has four recessed light fixtures. Each is focusing light on the corners of the table whose legs are also bolted to the floor. In the center of the four lights is a ceiling fan spinning slowly.

Baker and Whittles went into the room first and sat in two of the chairs. Baker checked his wireless microphone to make sure his voice is being recorded. Ted has told Whittles that he wants a deputy armed and standing outside the interview room whenever an interview is taking place. There is an intercom on the wall and Jim stands up and pushes the talk button, "Bring in Mrs. Ridley."

The two men waited for a short time and the door opened and in walked Mrs. Ridley with handcuffs on her wrists and ankles.

Baker told the deputy, "Please remove the shackles." The deputy did as instructed and Baker invited Kristen to sit down. "My first question, Kristen, is this: Are you Mrs. Michael Ridley or Mrs. Al Ishtar Hamwi?"

The Texas Pipeline is now 35 miles long; the natural gas pipeline is 37 miles long.

Chapter 34

MORDECAI'S TURN

Mordecai feels his phone vibrate, so he believes that Hadar has responded. He will have to wait until het can get to the rooftop garden to respond. It will be important that he doesn't rush to get to the garden so as not to alarm the rest of the Brotherhood. Sargon has requested a meeting of the Brotherhood after their evening meal to discuss an issue of great importance. The rest of the Brotherhood is guessing at what the subject might be, but all have agreed to wait.

Earlier in the day Mordecai had a discussion with Cyrus about how he was adjusting to such a confined life. Cyrus responded to Mordecai's question, "I find myself at times very depressed. We have a beautiful space, but we can't leave except to go to the rooftop garden. If we have to stay here longer, I want to get out and at least walk around for a change of environment. I can see every day from my window more and more people moving about the city. Not a lot of people, but more than when we came here. I do have a concern that the people who own these condos might at any time just show up and wonder what we are doing in their home."

"I hadn't thought about that, but it is an excellent point; I think we need to find a backup place just in case."

The evening meal finished and the dishes and kitchen cleaned up, they were all sitting at the cleared table waiting for Sargon to talk to them. The conversations between Brotherhood members has declined with the passing of time. Each member has developed, out of the necessity of isolation, his own world. Sargon did not stand. He took a finger and tapped a few times on the table and all focused on him. "My brothers, we have done a great thing. We executed our plan and reached our objectives. I can see that each of you has made great sacrifices for the success of our mission. We have been in this spot for what seems like a long time and I feel we are getting more distant, so we need to talk about your concerns and see if it is possible to address your needs. What I would like to do is go around our table and ask each of you to tell all of us what your concerns are and together we will try to solve the problems.

"Oleg, let's start with you."

"I would like to be able to talk with my uncle to see how much money we are making and to talk to some of my friends. I would like to find out what progress the Americans are making on their pipelines."

"Thank you. Cyrus, you are next."

"My concern is we do not know how long we are going to be staying in this condo. As Americans assess the risk of coming back to Houston, owners of this condo could walk in tomorrow and wonder why we are living in their home and why we put holes in the wall? I think, until we know when we are leaving the United States, we need a backup place to escape to so we can survive."

"Ishtar, you're next."

"I think there is a great deal going on outside of the United States; if you listen to the President's weekly address, America has become totally isolated. They are only focused on their own problems and to hell with the rest of the world. I feel like I'm losing a great opportunity by sitting inside these four walls."

"Michael, your concerns?"

"I haven't seen my family in over three years now and recently I called my parents' home. The phone company said that their phone had been permanently disconnected; I'm trying to find out what happened to them. I also think I want to join my brother Ishtar in taking advantage of opportunities outside the United States. Our goal was to create disruption to the U.S. economy for years. We can see that we have done that, so it is time to move on."

"Mordecai, you're next."

"I was born and raised in America and I thought it was my home. My parents and aunts and uncles and cousins still live here. I'm sure they are supporting the President, but the reason I joined with Sargon was to bring about long-term change in America. I think we may have initiated that change, but I want something different. I think the reward of the investments will give me at least the opportunity to do some of the things I have always wanted to do. I don't know what my options are, but I believe that exploration of my options is impossible under the restrictions the government is imposing on all Americans."

Oleg spoke up, "Sargon, tell us your concerns."

"As I was thinking about having this meeting, I anticipated that question. You see I recruited each of you and my long-time friend, Adad. I had an idea of what could be done if I assembled the right team. We achieved more than I ever thought could be possible. So, to answer your question, regardless of the outcome, I want to leave here and go someplace where I can walk out the front door and go to shops and eat at restaurants. I want to leave America for a better place and as soon as possible. In fact, Ishtar, make it happen **now**."

The energy level explodes and all the Brotherhood asks Ishtar, "How soon?"

Mordecai knows he has to call Hadar. No more text messages. He has to arrange to see her now because Ishtar could make their departure happen very quickly. *I have to get to the garden and call Hadar.*

The Texas Pipeline is now 39 miles long; the natural gas pipeline is 41 miles long.

Chapter 35

HELLO, THIS IS NATHAN JORDAN

Nathan has been talking with Karen about his dilemma of what to say if and when Mike Ridley calls back. Jordan has told the First Lady that Mike is on Sanibel Island in Florida out in the Gulf of Mexico about six miles from Ft. Myers, in southwest Florida. Just then Mary Washington, the President's assistant, uses the intercom, "Mr. President, Mike Ridley returning your call."

Karen asked, "Do you want me to leave?"

Nathan replies, "No. Stay and listen. Hello, this is Nathan Jordan. Mike, have you come to a decision?"

"Mr. President, I have thought about the challenge and I don't want to make a commitment..."

Jordan reacted like the rug was just pulled out from under him. He looked at Karen and she mouths the words, "I'm so sorry."

After a pause Mike continued, "...without a better understanding of the goals of the mission. So, I will be willing to meet your Mr. Williams here on Sanibel to be briefed on the mission and what is expected of me. As we agreed, after my meeting with your representative, I will discuss the mission with Mary. Then, if you and I decide to take the next step, I guess you'll send a plane to Page Field in Ft. Myers and fly me to DC to meet with you."

In a matter of seconds Jordan's gloom turned to hope, and he is elated. "Mike, thank you for agreeing to meet with Under Secretary Williams. Should I have Frank call you on this number? How soon can he call?"

"Mr. President, I don't think you would have called me if it wasn't very important and urgent; please have him call me on this number, the sooner the better."

"Mike, I assure you he will call you within the half hour and thank you. I'll look forward to seeing you in Washington real soon."

"Mr. President, I hope so."

Mike hung up and Karen sprang to her feet and ran to Nathan. He got up and caught her in his arms and gave her a hard kiss, put one hand on her butt and the other on one of her breasts and squeezed both. Karen let out a sound of joy, and Nathan said, "Don't get too excited yet, he hasn't agreed."

Karen replied, "He hasn't said no either. What type of salesman is Frank? Can he do the job?"

"I have no doubt that he can build a compelling case; the question becomes - and it's a big question - who should tell Mike his son is a terrorist and that a pardon could be in play if Mike helps?"

"Mr. President, remember the famous picture of the message sitting on Harry Truman's desk?"

"Yes I do; the famous quote, 'The buck stops here.'"

"Mr. President, I think you already know the answer to your question."

"Mrs. First Lady, I agree with you. So, I want you to run along and finish up your work because the President of the United States has a shower appointment at 12 noon with the First Lady in his shower."

Karen gives him a gentle but sensual kiss on the lips, "I can't wait, but by the way, what is for lunch?"

Jordan said with a smile on his face, "You. Now get out of here. I need to save the country."

As the First Lady went through the curved door to the Oval Office, Mary's phone rang. "Yes, Mr. President."

"Get me Frank Williams of Homeland Security right away."

The intercom rang and Marie, Frank Williams' assistant, told him President Jordan is on the phone.

"Yes, Mr. President."

"Frank, I just spoke with Mike Ridley and he has agreed to meet with you on Sanibel as soon as you can get there. Take down this phone number; it's Mike's. He is expecting a call within the next half hour."

"Mr. President, what about the son and the pardon?"

"Frank, I have given those two questions a great deal of thought; I have concluded that I'm the only one that can have that conversation. If Mike wants to do the job, he will have to come and meet with me and I'll tell him the whole story."

The Texas Pipeline is now 43 miles long; the natural gas pipeline is 44 miles long.

Chapter 36

MORDECAI'S URGENT TEXT

Sargon's after-dinner meeting lifts the spirits of all like a special dessert. Mordecai desperately wants to get to the rooftop garden and reach out to Hadar. The rest of the Brotherhood has left the table and Mordecai signs out for the garden. He indicates that he would be gone for about one hour. He is out the front door and headed for the stairway. He takes the steps slowly so he can think about this last text message to Hadar.

This text, in his mind, was just the setup for a phone call so it needed to be to the point. "I will call in 30 minutes, can you make it?" As he climbed the stairs his pace quickened and he exploded out the stairway door on through the front door of the penthouse and on to the patio. He took out his phone and typed in "I will call in 30 can you talk? M." "Swoosh", the message was sent. He wasn't expecting a return message; he was going to call in 30 minutes, reply or not.

Hadar was sitting on the couch in the living room talking to Megan when her phone vibrated. Both of them stare at the phone for a moment before Megan said, "Tell me what it says?"

Hadar flipped the phone, quickly scanned the message and got everyone's attention, "It's from Mordecai. He wants to call in the next 30 minutes. Can we be ready?"

Omid responded, "I'll get the team. We will be ready. Tell him to go ahead and call."

Hadar texted back one word, "Yes."

Seacrest said to the group, "This could be the call we have been waiting for to find out where the Brotherhood is hiding, so let's talk about the call."

Megan led the way. "You told him that you were going to have a break in about two weeks, so you have about a week to go. You have to find out how urgent his departure might be. I don't think this is the time to be coy with him. He wants to see you, so what you have to determine is, are you going to him or is he coming to you?"

Omid suggested, "He is planning to leave, and soon, so I doubt he is going to have the time to come to you. He will want you to come to him."

Seacrest began to think out loud. "If he wants you to come to him, it would be like handing the Brotherhood to us on a silver platter; almost too easy."

Megan asked, "What are you saying?"

"What I'm concerned about is, why does he want to see her?"

"What are your concerns?"

"He may want one more chance at that body before he leaves, possibly never to see her again, or perhaps he is concerned that he has exposed himself because of his passion for her and now he has to eliminate Hadar."

Omid asks, "John, are you suggesting that Mordecai wants to kill her?"

"Perhaps the rest of the team found out that he has had several contacts with this person, Hadar. None of the others know her. Maybe, because of that contact he has been ordered to get rid of her."

Hadar jumped in, "Okay, now you have me scared. I don't think he would try to kill me."

Megan reminded her, "Mordecai is responsible for the death of 60,000 Americans. I mean, what I'm about to say in all due respect is, you are one gorgeous woman, but you could be just one more added to the list."

Omid said, "Isn't that a little harsh?"

Hadar responded, "It may be harsh, but it is very possible."

Seacrest asked, "How can we protect Hadar?"

Megan offered, "First, we have to put a GPS tracker on her like the one she used on Mordecai, next I go with Hadar as her close friend from school who has a car. I'll bring Hadar to Mordecai. Last, if Hadar agrees to go to Mordecai, she needs to find out how much time they will have, and no hotel rooms. The meeting has to be in the open."

Hadar responded, "You want me to use my assets to keep him off balance."

"Yes, and I want you to put a GPS tracker on him so we can follow him back to the Brotherhood."

Hadar asked a question. "Wouldn't using my assets in bed keep him more off balance?"

Seacrest quickly responded, "Look, if the two of you are naked in bed, you know he really wants to take you, so you let him and when he is satisfied he strangles you. What have we accomplished? We have a naked, dead Mossad operative and no Mordecai and no Brotherhood."

"Okay, I get the picture. I just can't be totally alone with him."

Megan suggested, "If you feel him pressing you for sex tell him, 'Not now. Can I join you when I'm done with my project? Where are you headed and how long will you be there?'"

The Texas Pipeline is now 46 miles long; the natural gas pipeline is 50 miles long.

Chapter 37

PIPELINE NOT FAST ENOUGH

Nathan has a meeting scheduled with his Secretary of Energy, Mike Findley, about the progress on both pipelines. The idea that was adopted is to build two new pipelines: one to carry the contaminated energy in Texas and the other to expand the natural gas supply to the nation. While at the time of the recommendation the enthusiasm for the projects was high as a way to get rid of the contaminated energy, the results have disappointed Mike and the President. Mike Findley knows he has disappointed the President and Mike has asked the President if he can come to the White House to discuss alternatives.

Jordan is disappointed at the speed at which the pipelines are being built. In his own mind, he wants the Texas pipeline to be finished just before Election Day in November. To achieve that, Findley needs to at least double the amount of pipeline laid in a day; perhaps even more.

They are meeting in the President's small conference room just outside the Oval Office. Jordan chooses this place because it is less formal and he thinks Mike will be more open and candid with him. The President hopes that his Secretary has some ideas.

"Mike, I know you're doing your best to get these pipelines built, but my concern is we are not making enough progress and the people can't see the end, so they are becoming disenchanted that these pipelines will ever be finished."

Findley listened but he thought, *The President is really saying, if these pipelines are not close to completion by Election Day, I have no chance of getting re-elected and William Wild is likely to be the next President and both of us will be looking for work.*

"Mr. President, I have been thinking about the challenge, and I have an idea that might work. It will also help boost the economy by hiring several million more people."

"I like that idea already, the more people we put back to work the better it is, all around. So, what is your idea?"

Findlay opened his briefcase and pulled out a large folded piece of paper. He opened it and laid it on the table for the President to see. "Mr. President, the two blue lines represent the proposed path of the Texas and upper Midwest pipelines. The green line next to it is our completion as of last night. As you can see we have a long way to go, even running 24 hours a day.

"Mr. President, here is my idea." Mike took out a pencil and made a mark halfway from where the pipeline is in Texas to the end point. He made another point at the end. "Sir, you remember your American history when the Union Pacific built the railroad to the West Coast, they achieved it with construction crews working from two different starting points and they both met in the middle. I suggest we do even more. We pick a center point and we employ two new crews. One goes toward the crew that is coming from the current construction point. The other crew goes away from the center toward the termination point. Then we employ another crew starting at the termination point, building toward the center. We will have four crews laying pipe; instead of one to two miles a day we are laying four to eight miles a day."

The President responded, "We will hire thousands of new workers to man the crews."

"It's more than that, Mr. President. We use the same approach for the pipelines up north; you would have to issue an Executive Order to wave all restrictions. In addition, you have all the factories that make the materials for the pipelines running 24/7 in order to meet the demand of the building projects. Other businesses that will support the needs of the workers, including housing, food, police, fire, hospitals, and many other kinds of

The Brotherhood of the Red Nile

support services will be needed. All these businesses will need tens of thousands of employees and professional people."

Nathan thought about the plan and said, "Outstanding work. I will have the Attorney General draw up the Executive Order immediately."

"Sir, I met with AG Clinton and I have your Executive Order with me for you to review and sign."

"I have a live radio chat on Saturday, so I will sign it then and tell the American people how we are going to create work opportunities for millions of Americans. Great work, Mr. Secretary."

After Findley left, Nathan just sat for a moment and pondered what has just taken place. *I will be able to put millions of people back to work and give them hope, not only for themselves but also for the country. We have a long way to go, but when people have hope wonderful things can happen, including being reelected President of the United States.*

The President's next meeting would be very different than the one he just had. He will continue his secret talks on how America will respond to the attack. Jordan knows what he wants to do in terms of retaliation. It is so different that many people, when they first hear it, will not understand how powerful the retaliation will truly be, but over time they will see the destruction and slowly understand that America will destroy all terrorists.

Chapter 38

MR. MIKE RIDLEY, PLEASE

Frank Williams has touched base with Homeland Secretary Simons about the Mike Ridley assignment, and asked permission to take his wife Karen with him so that he will not stand out as a single man. In addition, he tells Simons that he and Ellen are thinking about Sanibel for their 25th wedding anniversary and the trip would give them some time together to check out Sanibel. Simons thinks about the request for a moment, "I will approve Ellen joining you, but you have to cover her airfare under the transportation policy."

"Sir, I don't think it will be an issue, but let me check and see what Ellen thinks and I'll let you know tomorrow."

"When are you going to call Mike Ridley?"

"As soon as I hang up with you, sir."

Simons asked, "Frank, do you really think that Mike Ridley can help at his age?"

"Sir, Ronald Reagan was three years older when he became President in his first term. I think Mike Ridley can handle the assignment and besides, we have no one else to do the job."

Frank hung up the phone and stared at the phone number on the note pad. After a while he picked up the phone and dialed the number. The phone rang several times. A voice said, "Hello."

"Mr. Mike Ridley, please."

"This is Mike Ridley, who is calling?"

"Mr. Ridley, this is Frank Williams from Homeland Security. I believe you were just speaking with President Jordan and that you were expecting my call."

"Yes, I did speak with the President and yes, I was expecting your call. If you don't mind from now on could it just be Mike and Frank?"

"That is fine by me, Mike. If it is okay with you, I will be making travel plans to be in Ft Myers in a couple of days. I may be bringing my wife Ellen with me; we will be posing as a couple exploring Sanibel as a place for our 25th wedding anniversary celebration, which happens to be true.

"It appears that a good place to stay as part of our cover is a place called Tween Waters Inn up the road on Captiva Island. Is that a good place to stay?"

"Well, as far as I know, it's not the best place to stay; they probably have more weddings than any other place. It will be fine for the two of you. Do you want me to try to get you a reservation?"

"Mike, I don't want you to do anything that would unduly expose you and Mary. I think I will have the travel agent that Ellen has been working with make the reservation. My guess is we will be arriving late in the afternoon, so is there a place we could have a quiet but good dinner?"

"I know just the place. Mary and I love it. The food is great, they have a good wine list, and they specialize in seafood."

"What is the name of this great place to eat in Paradise?"

"The place is called Jacaranda. It's on Periwinkle Rd on the left about 2 miles from where you get off the Causeway. Your hotel is on SanCap Road about 10 miles from the Causeway. Why don't you call me after you talk to your wife and make your travel plans?"

"Will do."

"Frank, can you give me any information on this assignment?"

"Mike, I would love to. I handpicked you for the assignment. Let me get things set and we can start our discussion and continue it on Sanibel. By the way do you have a secure cell phone?"

"No, but I can get one in less than 24 hours."

"Get one and call me when you have it. In the future, we should have all of our phone conversations over secure phones…here's my secure number…"

"I'll call you tomorrow."

"Thank you, Mike, for giving this assignment serious consideration."

Frank hung up and immediately called Ellen to tell her he is on his way to talk about something important.

Ellen asked, "Can you tell me what it is now?"

"No, just wait. I'll be there in less than 30 minutes."

"Do you have to go back to work or can you stay and..."

"We'll talk about that when I get home. See you soon."

Frank left the office after he gave Marie the outline of his travel plans for her to make the flight arrangements. He told her Ellen would make the hotel reservation. "I'll be back in the office probably tomorrow morning, so let me know tonight what flight arrangements you have made."

Marie offered, "I have heard good things about Sanibel; I'm sure you will have a great time."

Frank is out the door, but his thoughts are far from Sanibel and the food at the Jacaranda restaurant. He is thinking about his discussions about Mike's assignment; Ellen will have to come later.

Frank came through the front door of their house at about three o'clock. Ellen greeted him with a glass of white wine, chilled to perfection. Frank took the glass in one hand and Ellen in his other and pulled her close, gave her a simple kiss and then let her go. "It's a nice day; let's sit on the patio and talk." They walked through the house and out the sliding glass door to the glider on the patio and sat down; just sipping their wine while the glider moved back and forth.

Frank turned to Ellen with a stern look on his face and said, "I'm looking for somebody to work with me on an assignment who can pass herself off as my wife. She has to look fabulous, have a great body, and can take the rigors of an assignment."

Ellen started to frown, *because he wants someone to play me and he is just letting me know so when he tells me who he has picked I will support his choice because it is his job.*

Frank continued, "I was thinking about who I know in the Department that could fill the position and then it came to me that I know the perfect person to play you when I go to Sanibel. **YOU.** So, do you want to be my assistant spy and go with me to Florida?"

"I have nothing to wear."

"I don't think there is a nude beach in Sanibel, but it might be fun to watch you start a trend. I know you will turn heads... I will know in a few hours when we will leave. Your first assignment is to call the Tween Waters Inn and make a reservation as soon as Marie calls and tells us our departure time."

Ellen asked, "Why didn't you have Marie make the reservation?"

"Ellen, this is a real mission, I'm meeting somebody very important there and we want people to believe we are coming to Sanibel to check it out for a possible 25th anniversary celebration site. We, but mostly you, can look around and act like you're sizing it up for a spot for the celebration. You, my dear wife, are cover for me. Are you up to the job?"

She coyly replied, "As the young people say, are you my friend with fringe benefits?"

"Lots of benefits."

Chapter 39

PLANNING THE RETALIATION

The President has assembled his "think tank" to come up with retaliation options for America to use against the terrorists and hopefully break the chain of escalating deadly attacks against the United States and other free and open countries. His meeting today finds all members present including the Chairman of the Joint Chiefs, General Powell, Secretary of Defense Hamilton, National Security Adviser Markel, and Secretary of Energy Findley, with whom he has just finished a very productive meeting a few moments ago, along with Martins, who is the head of the CIA.

The President walked into the room and he gave the order to shut down all recording equipment. When the President saw that the room was clear, he addressed those assembled. "It has come to my attention that perhaps some of you are uncomfortable being in the room and discussing the subject of America's retaliation. If any of you feel that you cannot participate fully and give me your support as Commander in Chief and the protector of the American people, then stand up right now and leave. I will expect your resignation on my desk by the end of the day."

He paused, waiting a reasonable amount of time, and then said, "Let me be clear to all of you. I don't like what I am saying, but if you stay and I hear from anyone that you are working against the country and me, you're gone, and I assure you it will not be pretty. Last chance... Excellent! Let's get down to work."

"Here are some updates you need to know. Most of the things we will talk about are fluid and rapidly changing. First, we are recruiting a former spy whose assignment will be to follow the money being used to fund the activities of the Brotherhood. That person has not yet accepted the assignment. I hope to meet with that person in the next few days. If he doesn't take the job, I don't know what we will do to trace the money. Second, the reason I was late was I got a phone call from Frank Williams from Homeland Security telling me that one of the terrorists will be calling our contact from Mossad and asking her to come and see him. If this happens, she may lead us directly to the Brotherhood of the Red Nile."

Hamilton of Defense asked the President, "Sir, if we can capture the leadership of the Brotherhood, will we announce that we have them, and how will we charge them?"

"It is hard to answer your question because we do not know where they are. My guess is that I would look to Director Martins of CIA for advice. I would think we want them in a place where we can interrogate them with no interference. As to charging them, for the moment I assume that they are foreign nationals and would be charged under the terrorist provision and subject to trial under military court. Would you agree, Secretary Hamilton?"

"Mr. President, my initial thoughts would be regardless of their citizenship, they would be treated as enemies of the United States and tried in a military court. Let me also say, Mr. President, I don't think this has to be a public trial."

"Hamilton, I understand your position, but once we get them, it will be impossible to keep that a secret. Once someone of the opposition press gets wind of the fact that we have them, it will be all over the papers. We don't have to bring them to trial right away. Perhaps we would like to ask them some questions and then take some time to check out the reliability of their statements.

"I will let you know if we make progress on either front. Let's move on. As of right now, we have suspended all foreign aid payments to anybody, friend or foe, outside the United States. I know that is one place we were hurting everyday people. The starving, the oppressed, the freedom fighters are getting nothing from us and that is hard for me to do. On the other hand, we are not sending money to governments in order to buy their cooperation. We know some of the blackmail money had been diverted to support terrorists' organizations that have as a mission the desire to wipe the U.S. and our allies off the face of the earth. So, with that as background, I'm going to issue an Executive Order that will suspend all foreign aid until we can assess the true nature of a country's support of our values and principles."

NSA Director Markel interrupted, "Mr. President, your action will hurt a great many people; are you sure you want America under your term to be remembered as the nation that starved the world?"

"I do not want to be known as the leader of the United States who let his people starve so he could feed the rest of the world. So, in reality, I don't care what the rest of the world thinks. We have a long history of trying to take care of the world and that stops today. If governments have to start focusing on the needs of their people, perhaps they will spend less on weapons and support for terrorist organizations that threaten their existence. Terrorists are blackmailing government leaders. Pay us or you die. It's time to get them to stand up and say no more. Threaten me and you die."

Hamilton listened to President Jordan and thought, *The President seems to be becoming more and more hostile in his discussions with us about his desire to strike back and I'm beginning to wonder how serious he is about considering massive retaliation that could cost millions of lives. Who can I talk to about my concerns where the President might be heading without breaking my commitment to be silent? Are the lives of millions of people more important than keeping a promise to the President?*

Chapter 40

WAITING FOR THE CALL

Mordecai has left a text message that he will call Hadar in 30 minutes, the team is scrambling, and with five minutes to go they are ready. They have spent a little time thinking about the questions and there are only four, when, what time, how long, and where?

Omid agreed, "These are the most important questions. Anything else has to wait until you get the answers, and you must stay focused. You must tell him how excited you are at the possibility of seeing him again and determine that he is equally excited to see you. Tell him how much you remember that last kiss. You ask the first question, 'When', and then wait and let him answer. You pause to give him a chance to focus on the size of your chest. If he doesn't respond, call him by name and then ask 'When' again."

The communications technician told Hadar, "Remember to watch the screen and you will be able to notice the change in tension. Watch that screen when you talk about the last kiss."

Seacrest told her, "I agree with Omid. You have to keep him focused. If he doesn't answer the question of when, then say, 'Mordecai, I need to know when, because I need to arrange time off. I can't just pick up and leave, so you need to give me a date.'"

Megan suggested a follow-up question for what time. "I need to know if the time of day you want to meet is morning, afternoon, or evening." Then she told Hadar, "The 'How long' question is important, for if we only have a few minutes to follow you, we risk not being able to track him because you may not have a chance to attach the GPS."

Hadar responded, "Do you think he will resist these questions coming at him and having my breasts buried deep into his chest so I can get the GPS on him? I think the biggest challenge will be getting him to let go of me."

Megan listened to Hadar and thought, *once she gets in his arms, old feelings may come rushing back and her hormones may get the better of her.* "I think the best way to prevent that from happening is to tell Mordecai that you have to bring your roommate who has the car and she will not let you go alone. When we arrive, you will introduce me to Mordecai and then you will ask me to give you some room to talk. If I see you're locked into an embrace that the two of you are enjoying too much, I'll step in and break it up."

Omid suggested that the last part is the most important. "You have to say you are ready to hang up and then you say, 'I almost forgot; where are we meeting?' You must be very restrained when he answers. You can ask him, 'Do you have any idea how long it will take to drive from San Felipe Pueblo, New Mexico to where you are? I have to find that on a map, figure out a route, and I have to be where, by when, and at what time for how long.' As you progress through the list of things you'll become more frustrated. Say something like this. 'It is too hard. I have no idea where I'm going in this strange country; even with a co-driver, I don't know if I can make it? I really want to see you, but do you think I can do it?'"

Megan looked at Hadar and said, "This guy doesn't stand a chance against you, the more you talk, the more he will want to see you, hold you, and who knows what else. Just use what God gave you and you will do fine."

Omid told everybody, "Just like before, headsets on, no talking, and use the computer screen to speak with each other. We may be on the verge of our biggest break; this may be our only chance to capture the Brotherhood."

Megan thought, *if we can pull this off and capture the entire leadership of the Brotherhood in one fell swoop, it might just be the thing I need to have Williams get me an appointment to the Special Ops of the CIA.* She looked at her watch and it's exactly 2:30 PM, and no call. She and the rest of the team looked at their watches and it is now 2:40 and nothing. Hadar looked at her watch and it is approaching 2:45. She decided to check her phone and noticed it is turned off. She turned it on and she saw a text message several times that she quickly answered, "Yes, I'm here. My phone was off; please call me."

She heard the sound of the "swoosh" of the text transmission and she waited hoping he would call. At 2:50 her phone rang and she answered in a panicked voice, "I thought I had lost you forever. I'm so sorry." She is very apologetic.

Mordecai stopped her, "Calm down, take a deep breath." He can hear her expanding her lungs and wishes he could see that great expansion.

Hadar said, "When can we meet?"

Chapter 41

ARE YOU MRS. MICHAEL RIDLEY?

Ted Baker is interviewing Kristen and he has just asked her, "Are you Mrs. Michael Ridley or Mrs. Al Ishtar Hamwi?"

"I have no idea what you're talking about, I am Mrs. Michael Ridley. I have no idea who this Hamwi person is you're talking about."

Ted responded, "Let me help you, did you know that Michael is an identical twin?"

"No."

"Did you know that Michael's twin is a person named Al Ishtar Hamwi? Did you know that Michael and Ishtar exchanged passports and moved freely in and out of the United States?"

"No."

"Do you remember your interview with Major Rahimi in John Ford's conference room at the bank?"

"Somewhat."

"How about the comment you made about the changes in personality? In the transcript, you said he seemed like a different person. Do you remember making that statement?"

"Yes."

"Then, how do you know who you married?"

"I... I don't know?"

"When you got your marriage license, did Michael show you his birth certificate?"

"I don't remember, but how else could we get a marriage license?"

"If Michael and Ishtar exchanged passports, Ishtar could have used Michael's birth certificate to marry you, couldn't he? Let's move on. Why were you at Father Tim's front door and his kitchen window?"

"Father Tim is a friend to both Michael and me and so we decided to ask him to marry us. The ceremony took place in the rectory; it was very nice, just Father Tim, Michael, one witness who was Father Tim's assistant, and myself. We didn't have time for a honeymoon, so we spent the night in a Motel 6, just outside of town. When I woke up the next morning, Michael was gone with no note, nothing. I have not heard from Michael since then. After a few days, I decided to go and see Father Tim and tell him what has happened. I have been talking with Father Tim every week."

Sheriff Whittles asked, "So, why did you run when I was coming up the sidewalk?"

"I guess I was scared, so I jumped off the porch and went around to the back of the house. I thought that perhaps you might have some news on Michael and I wanted to hear if Father Tim was telling the Sheriff anything about the discussions we had about Michael."

"You say you have not seen Michael since the night of your wedding. Have you had any contact with Michael all this time?"

"No, I have not talked with Michael."

Baker asked, "I didn't ask you if you have talked with Michael, I asked you if you had any contact?"

Kristen seemed to be squirming a little in the chair as if Baker had struck a nerve. Whittles and Baker looked at each other and they both knew they may be on to something. Baker followed up, "Let's talk about what the word contact means. Would a letter be contact?"

"Yes, I guess."

"What do you mean, you guess?"

"If you are asking did I get a letter from Michael, the answer is no."

"How about a voice message on an answering machine?"

"Well."

There was a pause. "Well, did you get any voice messages from Michael?"

"Only once."

Baker pressed, "When, how many, and did you save it?"

"I only received one and it was on my cell phone."

"You said 'Was'?"

"Yes, I erased it."

Baker slammed his table with his fist and yelled, "WHY?"

"I didn't think I needed to keep it."

Whittles asked, "Do you remember what it said?"

"Not exactly."

Baker raised his voice showing his anger, "Do you know exactly what he said?"

Kristen trembled. "I think he said he was sorry he had to leave, but he had to go somewhere and work, but he would contact me as soon as he could."

Whittles asked Kristen, "Would you like something to drink?"

"A Coke would be nice."

"Mr. Baker, could you go out and get our friend a cold Coke?"

Baker looked at Whittles and realized Whittles wanted him to leave, but to go in the room with the camera. With a pretend sarcastic voice, Baker stood and said, "I'll be happy to get our guest a cold Coke." In a huff, he walked out and slammed the door, startling Kristen.

Whittles saw she was scared and in a calm voice asked, "Are you okay?"

"I'll be fine in a moment; I was just scared by the door. Is he always so loud?"

"No, only when he is angry." There is a knock at the door and Jim says, "Come in."

The door opened and one of his deputies brought in a large bottle of Coke and a tall glass of ice. Whittles carried them to the table and slowly filled the glass and handed it to Kristen.

Whittles asked, "Is that better?"

"Much, thank you. Can I ask you a question? How long will I be here?"

Whittles responded, "That depends on how truthful you are in answering our questions."

"I have been truthful, haven't I?"

"I hope so, let's move on."

"Don't we have to wait for Mr. Baker?"

"He'll be back soon. We have been talking about the meaning of the word contact. You said that you had a voice message from Michael; has there been any other contact?"

"Well, I don't know if you would call it contact, but I have been getting strange email messages."

"What do you mean strange?"

"I got an email and I didn't recognize the sender and for a while I never opened them. I just put them in the trash."

"What did the email messages say?"

"I'm going to make a fortune."

"Was it signed?"

"Most of the time."

"Who signed them?"

"I don't know. They were signed M&I and The BRN."

Chapter 42

WHERE ARE YOU?

Hadar was having trouble with her phone and in a panic, answers Mordecai's call. After she calmed down, she asked him, "When can I see you?"

Mordecai answered, "Soon."

"Am I coming to you or are you coming to me?"

"I think you will have to come here."

Everybody's heart stopped. They held their breath, as they all believe they know the next question. It is the most important question and they are waiting for the answer. Hadar asked, "How much time will we have together? Will we be alone?"

The meter detected rapid increases in Mordecai breathing as he listened to Hadar's questions. "I think, depending on how soon we will depart, we may have an hour, maybe an hour and a half. As to will we be alone, perhaps, but my guess would be only a short time."

"Will we be able to hold each other?"

Mordecai's stress level is rising rapidly and his desire to hold that magnificent body next to his is almost overpowering. "I hope so; I will do everything in my power to make that happen."

"I remember our first embrace; what incredible chemistry."

Omid sent Hadar a message on her screen, "Ask him how long it will take to drive from your place to his."

Hadar sent a note back to Omid, "Thanks, and a great transition."

"Mordecai, if I could move on to the practical, how long will it take us to drive there?"

"What do you mean, 'us'?"

"I do not have a car but my roommate Megan does, and she can help with the driving. How far it is? She feels, and I agree, that it will be safer if I have somebody in the car with me."

Mordecai wasn't thinking about two women, but didn't think it would be a problem. "I have looked at the map and my guess is that from San Felipe Pueblo, New Mexico to Houston, it is about 1,000 miles and would take at least two long days of driving, assuming you can get gas."

Megan, John and Omid can hardly keep from yelling the Brotherhood is right in Houston. Hadar continued, "If we change off and drive through the night, how long do you think it would be before I could have my arms around you?"

"Look. Neither of you have driven the roads between here and San Felipe Pueblo. You don't know what gas stations might be open at night with the curfew. So, as much as I want to hold you, it will be safer to take the two days to get here."

"Megan told me she has a GPS and that if we tell it where we are going it will find the shortest route. So, what address should I tell her to program into it? But, just a moment before you give me the address, I need to know when you want me. I have to make arrangements about classes."

"First, let me tell you, now would be a great time to leave because I can't wait to see you again. We had a meeting last night and there was talk about moving to a new place while we were getting ready to leave."

"So, are you telling me that I could leave tomorrow and I might not ever see you again?"

"No, all I'm saying is, I don't know for sure if and when we are moving. Here is what we can do: call me when you have left San Felipe Pueblo. We will keep in phone contact and as you get closer to Houston, I will be able to give you the new address."

"So, I will leave and I will call you to tell you that I have left and then you'll let me know at that time when we'll meet. If you are going to stay where you are now, or if you have moved, you will give me the new address?"

Omid sends a message, "Be careful. Don't push. Take what you can get."

Hadar concluded, "Okay, that sounds good, just one more question. Can I go with you to wherever you are going?"

Mordecai's respiration is off the chart; he doesn't know how to answer her question. He paused and then said, "I can make you this promise, once I get to wherever I'm headed, I will send you the money and the means to join me."

"Thank you for saying that, I hope it happens. Is there anything else we need to discuss?"

"What time do you think you will leave tomorrow?"

"I'm so excited that I'm not sure that I will be able to sleep. I will make the rounds of the people at school in the morning and I hope we can leave by noon. So, expect a call at noon and you'll know that I'm on my way to Houston and points unknown."

"Hadar?"

"Yes."

"I have been thinking about you since our first meeting at the café in the town square when all I could concentrate on was the buttons on your sweater. Now I'm thinking about the whole person."

"Well, I'll see if I have room for that sweater and maybe if you're lucky you can unbutton some of those buttons. I'll talk with you at noon, my time, tomorrow."

Everybody in the room took a deep breath.

Chapter 43

OFF TO SANIBEL CAPTIVA

Frank and Ellen Williams left Andrews in a small jet that was part of the White House fleet. Williams chose this plane instead of a Homeland Security plane, because a White House plane would draw a different kind of attention. They left their home around 9 AM and were at planeside by 10 AM. The flight was scheduled for 10:30 AM, so by the time their bags were checked and they went to their seats, it was almost time to leave.

They were both excited about the trip, but for totally different reasons. Frank was hopeful that he could convince Mike Ridley to meet with the President, and Ellen was glad to get away from DC and be with Frank for whatever time they had together. Ellen knew that she also had an assignment to deflect eyes away from Frank so he could complete his mission... and, she hoped that there would be some intimate time in what she had been told was a very romantic place.

As the plane taxied, Ellen looked out the window to see how much larger the military planes were at Andrews than the small plane they were in. The pilot came on the intercom and said, "We are next for takeoff, please be sure your seatbelts are fastened." The plane turned onto the runway and then, unlike a commercial jet, the takeoff was abrupt and steep. Ellen felt like her stomach was in her mouth. Very quickly the plane leveled off and she felt normal. Their destination was Page Field in Ft. Myers, Florida. After a while the pilot came back on and said, "We should arrive by 1:15, perhaps sooner depending on winds. Sit back and enjoy the flight."

The trip had come upon Ellen and Frank so quickly that they didn't have much time to plan what to do. Frank knew he had to meet with Mike Ridley and he didn't have any idea how much time they would have to explore; Ellen understood her job and she knew she could do it well. Frank stretched his arm and extended his hand to Ellen. She in turn reached out and took his. They knew that this was going to be an adventure for both of them unlike never before.

They had one drink and when they finished, they reclined their seat backs and took a nap. Both were surprised at not only how quickly they went to sleep, but also how long they slept. The sound of the pilot's voice woke both of them. They heard him say that landing would be in 20 minutes. The plane went out over the turquoise blue waters of the Gulf of Mexico, banking to the left so Ellen could see the white sand beaches, and she called to Frank. "Look at the water and the beaches. Aren't they gorgeous?"

A few moments later they landed and taxied toward an Air National Guard hanger. The plane stopped in front of the hanger, the stairway opened and the two of them got off the plane. A black car pulled up next to the plane and the driver got out to help them with their bags. He handed Frank the keys. "The GPS is programmed to get you to the Tween Waters Inn on Captiva, enjoy your stay."

They got in, buckled up and headed down US 41, also known as Tamani Trail. The GPS took them to Gladiolus Road where they turned right; in a short time they saw the sign pointing left to Sanibel and Captiva. They drove for about six miles and came to a tollbooth. Frank paid $6 and they drove over San Carlos Bay and in the distance they could see Sanibel Island. The Causeway had several islands and people were in the water, fishing. As they neared the end of the causeway, they could see the old lighthouse. They came to an intersection, turned right and headed for the Inn ten miles away. On the way, they passed the restaurant Mike Ridley recommended, Jacaranda. It was about four o'clock when they pulled into the Tween Waters Inn parking lot and Frank went inside to register. The clerk welcomed him to the Inn and asked for his name. Frank replied and signed the card. "We have you here for three nights; is that still correct, Mr. Williams?"

"Yes."

"Excellent! We have a deluxe king suite overlooking the water. Will you need help with your bags?"

Frank responded, "No. I can get them."

"Just one other thing, here is a map of the Inn, a brochure of all the places to visit and also a map of the island. Enjoy your stay."

"Thank you. I'm sure we will."

Frank returned to the car, got in and told Ellen, "Room with a view." They drove around to the side and they noticed several different buildings. Frank found their building and got the bags out of the trunk. They were on the second floor; they walked up and Frank carried the bags. He unlocked the door and Ellen went in first. Frank dropped the bags and turned toward Ellen and asked with a big smile on his face, "Can I wash your back?"

Ellen responded, "Absolutely."

Chapter 44

THE CHAIRMEN MEET

William Wild had met with the Chairman of the Democratic National Committee, Frank Meyer, and laid out his plan for the upcoming primaries and the presidential election. The shortage of resources, mostly jet fuel and gasoline, were going to make travel both impractical and cost-prohibitive, so a new method had to be developed quickly with the first primary just a few months off. Meyer saw potential advantages of Wild's plan and contacted his counterpart to set up a meeting to discuss it. The meeting between Meyer and James "Buddy" Smith, Chairman of the Republican National Committee, occurred in Smith's office. The conversation revolved around how they could conduct both the primaries and the general election in such a way that those who want to vote can do so.

Meyer, who had been thinking about the issue much longer than Smith said, "I have been giving this a great deal of thought. As much as I would like to provide for everybody who wants to vote, given the shortage of resources, not everybody will be able to vote. We have to come up with a plan that is as fair as possible, and doesn't, at least on the surface, favor one candidate or party over the other."

Smith responded, "Am I hearing those words from a Democrat's mouth... fair as possible?"

"Yes, that is what I said, as fair as possible."

"Okay, Mr. Meyer, let me hear your idea."

"Every legal voter has one or all of three things, a driver's license, a passport, or a government ID. All three have one thing in common. We set up a national election center over the Internet."

"There's a lot of fraud on the Internet," Smith responded.

"Just hear me out Buddy, okay?"

"Okay."

"So, a potential voter signs on to the Internet voting center and puts in his name, address, zip code, and Social Security number. The computer scans the Social Security file, finds the number and verifies the name and address."

"But..."

"Just wait. Now, the potential voter has to enter the number either from his passport, driver's license, or government ID. The computer scans the record and verifies the address and the Social Security versus the ID number; if it gets a match, then the ballot for their voting district comes up on the computer screen. The voter casts his ballot and when he pushes the vote button, the vote is tabulated and sent to the state board of elections. The process of voting one time locks out the name, address, social security and other ID numbers. They can't be used again. Therefore, we have a safe and secure election and no fraud. So, Buddy what do you think? Will you go with me to the Federal Election Commission and support the idea?"

Buddy responded, "I need to think about it. Can I get back to you? Let's move on to expending resources, namely jet fuel, diesel fuel, and gasoline to run campaigns. Frank, we have resources in some areas, but most of the country is on some form of rationing. I'm thinking about the fairest way for the candidates to get their message out without wasting all of that energy. I think we need to use TV and the Internet. Each state will have a website, as will local elections. Candidates for elective office will have some predetermined amount of time to record a message on the website and the opposing candidates will receive time for rebuttal.

"National candidates, like the presidential candidates, will also have websites where they too can record a message about what they believe. In the last 30 days before the November election, there will be a live broadcast of a debate for three hours broken down into two segments of one and a half hours. Each candidate will ask questions of their opponent. Once the debates are over, the video remains on the websites until the day after the election."

Meyer said, "We could use our voting process on Election Day. Everybody who wants to vote will be able to and will know that his vote will count. No hanging chads or lost ballots."

Smith turned to Meyer and said, "I think that might just work. Can we get it done in time? We have to get to the Election Commission really fast."

Meyer offered, "Let me call them right now and tell them we need an appointment in the next 48 hours."

Smith got up and said, "Let me know as soon as you hear. I will clear my calendar."

"I will, you can bet on it." Meyer thought, *have I just agreed to reduce the number of voters? There has to be a way to get around this; we can't afford to give up our voter advantage. Wait, I have it. Simultaneous registration and voting just might fill the electronic ballot box.*

Chapter 45

BEFORE THE RIDLEY MEETING

Frank and Ellen have finished their protracted shower and a little wet love-making. Now, Frank needs to touch base with Mike Ridley. Frank is drying himself off and as he sits on the bed he can see into the bathroom, and enjoys watching Ellen drying off. He wraps himself in a towel, picks up his cell phone and calls Mike Ridley's phone number. As the phone is ringing, Ellen walks into the room naked and moves toward Frank; when she is close enough she pulls at his towel, but he gives her a stare. The phone is ringing and Ellen finally just sits on his lap and puts his head between her breasts. Frank gets an answering machine and all it says is the number, so Frank leaves a message that they have arrived and to call him on his cell phone when he gets a chance. Frank leaves Mike the cell number.

He put down the phone and Ellen put her arms around Frank to hold him so tightly to her that he couldn't breathe. He let go gasping for breath.

"Are you all right?" Ellen asked.

"I couldn't breathe, and thought I was going to pass out."

"I'm sorry, I just love you so much and I had the chance to hold you. I just wasn't thinking."

"Look if I have to die, then I can't think of a better way than this, but I would like to live a little longer so we can have more chances to make love."

"I agree."

They got dressed and decided to explore Sanibel and Captiva. Frank took his cell phone just in case Mike called. He knew that they were supposed to have dinner with Mike and Mary, but he didn't know when, so he decided to call Jacaranda just to confirm the reservation and time. Frank dialed 239-472-1771. He told the receptionist that he believed there is a reservation for a party of four and it could be under the name of Ridley or Williams. Could she please tell him the time? "One moment please." The receptionist returned to the phone. "Sir, I have it under Mr. Ridley for a party of four at 7:30."

"Thank you, we are looking forward to it."

Frank looked at his watch and saw that it was 5:30. He said to Ellen, "Let's take a quick drive and look around Captiva. I heard of a place near the tip of the island called the 'Mucky Duck' where we can get a drink and sit by the water and talk." They were told to turn left just before the Bubble Room and follow the road to the end and the Duck would be on the right.

The directions were perfect. They found a parking place and walked over to the window to order two drinks. Frank turned around and saw an empty picnic table by the water's edge and said, "Let's grab that one. We can enjoy the breeze and the sound of the ocean." They walked over and sat down. For a while they just sipped their drinks and didn't say anything. Frank was looking at Ellen's profile against the white sandy beach and the turquoise blue water and said to himself, *what a magnificent woman. Why did she marry me? I have to be one of the luckiest men in the world.*

Frank came back to reality and said to Ellen, "We need to talk a little bit about what I want to accomplish and also what you want to get done while you are here. So far I think this is one of the most unusual places I have ever seen and I would love to come back here to celebrate our 25th. You have to understand that the way things are that we may not be able to celebrate our 25th on the actual date? I know for the last 24 years we have always celebrated on the actual day, but things are different now."

"Frank, I know and I understand. We both have no idea when this will let up so that we can have a normal life again. I have resigned myself that we will celebrate when we can."

Frank leaned over and gave Ellen a kiss and simply said, "Thank you for understanding."

She responded, "We have been together for almost 25 years; I don't need a trip to Sanibel from you to prove your love. If we want to come back here when we do celebrate, I would love it, but if we don't, I will not love you any less."

"Ellen, we have not had much time for me to tell you why I'm here. I think you need to know." In almost 25 years of marriage Ellen has learned that when Frank was ready to talk about something no matter how important or classified it is, he would eventually tell her and sometimes ask her for advice. She knew now was one of those times; he was going to tell her something very important.

"I'm here to meet primarily with Mike Ridley to ask him to come out of retirement and work on a special assignment directly for the President of the United States, in tracing the source of funding for the Brotherhood of the Red Nile."

"That is the group that you believed was responsible for the bombings."

"Yes."

"The President wants to meet with Mike to offer him the job, but there is a problem."

"Frank, what is the problem?"

"Ellen, Mike Ridley's son is a member of the Brotherhood of the Red Nile."

"Does Mike know this?"

"We don't think so. The President's dilemma is that Drew Clinton, the Attorney General, has recommended that the President tell Mike and guarantee a Presidential Pardon for his son for doing the job."

"Why would he make such a recommendation?"

Chapter 46

MIKE FINDLEY AND OIL IN THE GULF

A great deal of attention is focused on the new pipeline in Texas and the natural gas pipeline in the upper Midwest to the west, but not much to the thousands of rigs in the Gulf of Mexico. One of the nuclear bombs was exploded in Port Fourchon, Louisiana. The pipeline feeding oil and gas from the Gulf had to be severed because the pressure from the flow was pushing the contaminated product further north. Severing the line had caused millions of gallons of oil to spill into the Gulf of Mexico. It took over a month for all the rigs to be shut down and the flow stopped.

The government mustered the help of other nations to skim the oil as it was coming to the surface. The one thing that helped was that they knew where the pipe was cut so they focus their efforts in containing the spewing oil. Mike Findley has put together a team of oil drilling, pipeline, and tanker shipping experts. They have been meeting almost constantly for the last several months trying to figure out a way to start pumping oil and gas out of the Gulf. The challenge is that with the pipeline cut, they have had to come up with a viable alternative that can be presented to the President.

The pipeline in the Gulf is 60 inches in diameter and they have to determine how to cap the pipe and let the rigs come back online slowly so as not to blow out the connection. The pipe is submerged in 700 feet of water. The manpower required to fix it will have limited working time, so the project will require a large number of divers.

Findley called the meeting to order and asked Jim Michaels, the former head of Exxon Mobile exploration, for his team's recommendation. Jim spoke. "Mr. Secretary, thank you for the opportunity you have given us to be part of Rebuilding America. Our solution is very straightforward. We want to create a filling station in the Gulf. We propose welding a fitting on the end of the pipe that will allow us to extend a pipe to the surface. Once on the surface, we would use a 30-inch diameter oil suction and discharge (OS&D) hose. The OS&D hose will be supported with floats to keep it vertical. Attached to this hose will be another length of hose that can be placed in tanker holds. A valve will be opened and the crude will fill the tanker. When it is full, the next tanker will pull up, hook up, and fill up. That tanker will then disconnect and head to the nearest refinery. From that point on, the oil is processed the same way as if it came through a pipeline."

Findley responded, "Wonderful and creative idea, but what do you do in churning seas with high winds?"

"Sir, we have thought about that and we have a partial solution. If we have a pipeline in place and we have hurricane winds, we shut down the wells and evacuate the crew. Our drilling team has located a new platform that is ready to be tugged out to sea and planted. We propose that the government take possession, sink it and create a docking station for the tankers to be filled. Like a regular platform, if the weather gets bad, we shut it down.

"This is not the most efficient way to pump oil and move it to port, but right now we are getting nothing out of the Gulf. Anything we can get is all to the good of the country. We will not be able to run all 5,000 plus rigs at the same time, but we can rotate and give everybody the opportunity to pump some oil, and most important, in addition to pumping oil we are putting people back to work."

Findley remarked, "I love it, a filling station in the Gulf of Mexico. I want to take this idea to the President at the next cabinet meeting. I realize that some of you have questions and concerns about this approach and I want you to have a chance to express your opinion. I will contact the White House and when the next cabinet meeting is scheduled, I will send an email to all of you and that will be your time to raise your questions. I promise I will read them all as long they are in language I can understand.

I will make the decision as to which of your concerns will be presented at the meeting. Jim, I need a PowerPoint presentation that I can share; you should get started on it immediately, because I don't know when the next meeting will take place and I want to be ready with your team's idea."

Chapter 47

HADAR IS GOING NEXT DOOR

Hadar has just hung up with Mordecai and she needs to go to Houston to meet with him. All four of the members of the Pathfinders have collapsed on the couch. Omid said, "I have to call Ted."

Megan said, "I need to call Mr. Williams and update him."

Omid told Megan, "You call Williams first and then I will call Ted."

Megan dialed Williams' office and got Marie, "I'm sorry, Ms. Brown, he is out of the office and I'm not sure I can reach him."

"Can you try? We have made contact with one of the Brotherhood members and Hadar is going to Houston to meet him."

"But isn't Hadar already in Houston?"

"Yes, but we didn't know that the terrorists were also in Houston. We programmed her phone to look like she was in New Mexico when she talked with him."

"Very clever. I'll try to reach Mr. Williams, but I don't know when I will talk to him."

"Please understand that the meeting is going to take place in two days and we will need a lot of support."

"I'll do my best." Marie dialed Frank's cell phone and it went to voice mail. "Please call, extremely urgent. Brotherhood." Marie thought that she could also send the same message by text, so she did hoping that he would get one or the other.

Frank and Ellen finished their drinks and decided to walk on the beach before heading back to the hotel to get ready for dinner. "Frank, I want to ask you about the pardon because I'm confused. Mike Ridley served his country very well taking risks that perhaps nobody else had the courage to take, all for his country. Now you want him to take on another dangerous assignment in exchange for a pardon for his son Michael's crimes of murder and treason. Are you saying that the pardon will motivate Mike to do the job and without the pardon he will not take on the assignment?"

"Ellen, what I'm saying is that I don't think we have anything else to offer Mike Ridley as an incentive to do the job."

"Frank, are you selling Mike short?"

"I don't understand."

"Is there no other reason why Mike would do the job?"

Frank said, "He doesn't need the money. He has a beautiful place to live here in Sanibel. I have never met his wife, so I have to assume that she has supported him over the years in the things he has done and will again in whatever he decides to do. I felt like I had to come up with a reason. I can't take a chance that he will do the job just because he is a patriot."

"Frank, I know we never had children, but let's suppose for a moment that we did have a son. You have served your government for over 35 years and you have done what you were asked to do, for the most part without question. Many times your life was at serious risk. You have a smart 25-year-old son who is mixed up with terrorists in some way and he, along with the other terrorists, has attacked America. You are called into the Oval Office and the President says he needs your help and if you help your country he will pardon your son. What would you think?"

"I think I would have many different feelings. I would wonder if the President is trying to bribe me to do the job. Does my son's life depend on my performance? What if I do everything I can and I can't get the President what he wants? Does he withhold the pardon because he isn't sure that I did my best? As a father, don't I have the responsibility to try and protect my children from harm? But, on the other hand, isn't my son alone responsible for his actions?"

"It seems to me. Frank, there are a lot of conflicts that you as the father are trying to deal with, when the reality is that your last statement is the truest. Our son would have to be responsible for his actions, not us. I think the President must be dealing with many of the same issues that you have just articulated; remember he has sons."

"So, you think the President, when he meets with Mike, should he even agree to meet with the President, should tell Mike what the assignment is and that his son Michael might have had a hand in the attack with the Brotherhood? The President should tell him that he has no way of knowing for sure, but if he did he must be responsible for his actions."

Ellen said, "No pardon."

Frank agreed, "No pardon."

Chapter 48

MRS. RIDLEY'S INTERVIEW CONCLUDES

Ted Baker was still out of the interrogation room when Omid called and told him the good news that the Brotherhood is in Houston. He told Baker, "Megan called Mr. Williams, but he is out of town and Marie is trying to reach him. He has not returned her call."

Baker responded, "I hope to finish my interrogation of the young Mrs. Ridley in a few hours and then I'll drive up to the safe house. We'll review your plans so I can start mustering the resources you'll need."

"Call me when you leave Springfield."

"Will do."

Baker returned to the room with Jim and Kristen, sat down next to Jim and asked, "Any progress?"

Jim, replied, "Not much."

Baker looked over at Kristen and asked, "This is a real simple question. Since the time you were married to the person you thought was Michael Ridley, have you had any contact from him? Let me be clear, and define what contact is, it includes phone conversations, text messages, letters, post cards, emails, voice messages, and messages from third parties."

Kristen took a few moments to ponder Baker's question.

Baker suggested, "Before you answer, if there is any form of communication I missed that should be added, then consider it added. Do you understand?"

"Yes."

"So, what is the answer to my question?"

"I'm not sure, but Father Tim mentioned he got an email asking about my in-laws, the Ridley's. The person wanted to make an appointment to come and see him in confession. I thought it strange that somebody was inquiring about the Ridley's and their house with Father Tim."

Jim asked, "Why do you think somebody would want to find out information about the Ridley's from Father Tim?"

"I don't know for sure, but if the conversation between Father Tim and whoever is asking for the meeting is in confession, then Father Tim can't tell anybody. I think that is still true, but you should check with Father Tim."

Baker asked, "So your answer is that there has been no contact between you and Michael since the wedding night?"

"Yes."

"Kristen, when Major Rahimi and I visited with you at the bank, you reported to Mr. Ford that Michael Ridley had $600,000 in his money market account. Do you remember?"

"Yes."

"Who now has control of the $600,000?"

"I produced a certified copy of the marriage license. So, as his wife, I get the money if Michael doesn't come and claim it in six months. We were married shortly after you left town. Michael told me to take a certified letter, the deposit book, and our marriage license to Mr. Ford and then wait out the six months. He told me to go back to the bank if he was not back in six months and have the money transferred to an account in my name."

"Have you done that?"

"Yes, it has been more than six months, so the money is in my name."

"After we left, did any additional money come into the account?"

"No."

"We asked you to try and find out where the money was coming from in his account. Were you successful?"

"I believe Mr. Ford notified the local Homeland Security office that they were able to trace the deposit to a bank in Cyprus, but they would not cooperate by giving us anything further information regarding the originating bank. So, neither the bank nor I have any information on the actual source of the funds."

Whittles asked, "With that amount of money you could live very well in Springfield. Are you planning to stay here and work at the bank?"

"Sheriff, I agree that $600,000 is a lot of money, but if I put it in a one year CD it would earn about $2,500. Hardly enough to retire on is it? So, yes, I'm staying put and keeping my job at the bank."

Baker asked two last questions. "If Michael got in contact with you and wanted the money, would you call Sheriff Whittles before you did anything?"

"Yes."

"The last question is, if Michael contacted you and said that he wanted you to join him wherever he might be in the world, would you go?"

"Do I have to tell the Sheriff before I go?"

Chapter 49

HOW DO WE TRACK MORDECAI?

Omid returned from his phone call with Baker and told the team members, "Baker will be here perhaps late tonight and he wants to go over our plan to see what other resources we will need to capture the Brotherhood. So, do you think we need a plan before he gets here?"

Brown responded, "We already have one; we have Hadar attach the small GPS tracking device to Mordecai while she has Mordecai drooling over her chest. They make nice for a while, roommate Brown steps in and says, we have a long drive and it's getting late, we need to find some gas and get on the road." Brown's speech quickens. "They kiss and we depart. We have 1,000 Special Ops people follow the GPS signal and they rush the building and capture the bad guys." Her speech quickens even faster. "All the Brotherhood members are taken to Ft. Hood, Texas where they will be held under extreme security and classified as enemy combatants. The trial is a military trial, no press. They are all convicted of crimes against the United States and sentenced to die by firing squad."

Hadar said, "Megan, take a breath. A thousand Special Ops for five or six people is a little overkill, don't you think?"

Megan replied, "Perhaps a little, but let me ask Omid and John their thoughts."

Hadar spoke up, "Do I get any input? I am the bait, you know."

"Yes, the bait gets a turn. I'm sorry." The two women laugh; the two men have no idea what they are laughing about and don't want to try and figure it out.

Omid asked Megan, "Who should go first?"

"How about John?"

John was somewhat surprised, but began. "I like the idea of Hadar pinning Mordecai in an embrace, but if it is a warm day and all he has on is a shirt, will he feel the GPS? And, just as important, we must be concerned that the other members of the Brotherhood spot the GPS on the shirt or pants? So, what if Hadar doesn't have a chance or a place to put on the GPS? We need a backup plan.

"We can get some Wild Fire, WF30 Lear black light liquid and put a bandage on Hadar's left hand in her palm. We soak the bandage with WF30 clear, and when Hadar reaches around Mordecai left shoulder she touches his shoulder and it marks him. We can use special glasses on the ground and in the air to see the markings on Mordecai's back and follow him to the rest of the Brotherhood."

Megan responded, "What if we can't find Wild Fire WF 30 clear?"

John answered, "That's a problem. I will go right now and find the contact information on the company and call to see if they are open and if they have a dealer in Houston. If they do, I will try to reach the local store on the phone to see if they are open. But if they are not, we need another backup plan."

Omid agreed, "We may well need more than two plans, because whatever we think might work may not work when Hadar and Megan are in the reality of the moment. I agree we need to mark Mordecai, but we must think in terms of marking Hadar and Megan so that Mordecai doesn't get suspicious, and should the two women get taken we can follow them."

Megan reacts, "What do you mean, 'the women get taken?'"

"I understand that Mordecai has been kind and respectful in all the phone calls, but we must remember he is now a terrorist as all of them are and he is capable of anything at any time."

Megan was shaken by Omid's comments; it had never crossed her mind that she could be in real danger. Hadar looked at Megan and could tell for the first time that she is afraid.

Omid commented, "I don't know if we need 1,000 Special Ops people, but we will need some snipers, some people in street clothes, and overhead support. We are somewhat constrained in that we don't know where the meeting is going to take place, so our plans need to be fluid. It is still warm in Houston, so my idea is that we need the youngest looking people we can find and arm them with water balloons. In the water will be an infrared dye that will mark whoever or whatever comes in contact with the water. We have some kids throwing water balloons and they accidently hit the three of you down at the feet, so you are not soaked but you are marked, and the ground team will follow Mordecai back to their hideout. Once we have identified the location, we can surround the building. We find out what floor they are on and land a team on the roof that works its way down. At the same time, we have a team coming up from the ground floor to trap them."

Hadar's turn, "Are you guys' nuts? Water balloons? WF 30 invisible markers? GPS stuck in possible T-shirts? I like Megan's 1,000 SpecOps; we are going to storm the City of Houston. Look, I have not seen this guy in a long time and he has the hots for me. He has asked me to come and see him; he has told me he is leaving shortly for places unknown. I want to keep his memory of me in his mind."

What Hadar doesn't know is that Baker has quietly entered the room and all but Omid have their backs to Baker. Omid sees Baker, but he puts his finger to his mouth and motions to Omid to be quiet.

"So, I need to give him something to remember me, something that will for a long time at least keep me in his memory."

Baker says, "Can I have one of those naked pictures of you for my bedside table?"

Hadar jumped up and saw Baker. She jumped over the couch and almost knocked him down getting her arms around him. "Wow, I should have stayed away longer. Who knows what would have happened. I know…"

Hadar whacked Baker's shoulder, "God I missed those shots. Can I finish my idea?"

Baker responded, "You have something better than naked pictures?"

"Yes," she said. "We need to find a simple men's bracelet. I can have my name engraved on the face, but inside we have a GPS tracking device. We just track him to his building and the GPS will take us directly to the floor where the Brotherhood is hiding out. Once we know their location, then we can send in troops from both top and bottom and trap all of the Brotherhood. So, we need to focus our attention on finding a jeweler who is open and has the bracelet we are looking for. We need to get it back here so the communication team can rig the tracking device."

Baker, after listening to Hadar's idea, said, "I have to admit that is a great idea. So, what do the rest of you think?" All agreed on the need to find that bracelet and quickly.

Hadar reminded the team that it is close to noon in New Mexico and she needs to call Mordecai to tell him they are leaving.

Chapter 50

DINNER, MR. & MRS. MIKE RIDLEY, AND MR. & MRS. FRANK WILLIAMS

Dinner is at 7:30 PM, so Frank and Ellen head back to Tween Waters Inn to change and get ready for dinner at Jacaranda's. They fool around in the shower, nothing serious, get dressed and go to the car. At the car Ellen asks, "How do I look?"

"If we didn't have one of the most important meetings in my life, I would take you back upstairs and order room service."

"I think that is a compliment. At least, if the meal goes badly, you can still have me for dessert," Ellen said with a smile on her face, but thought, *this is the most important meeting in his life and he is taking me to dinner. I hope I don't screw up. What can I talk to them about; not children, we don't have any and their son is a terrorist who bombed America. We could talk about the anniversary and about her impressions of Sanibel. That'll work; let's stay with talking about Sanibel.*

They turned left out of the parking lot and drove down SanCap road. At points on the road, the water from both the Gulf of Mexico and Pine Island Sound are within 100 feet of each other. Some of the homes they pass are enormous. They passed two homes that looked almost exactly alike and both looked like the builder was trying to make full-size replicas of the White House. Frank said to Ellen. "Did you see the size of those houses?"

"Yes, I just can't imagine living in a monstrosity like that." They continued to the end and turned right at Tarpon Bay Road and go to Periwinkle Way where they turn left. They passed a couple of small shopping centers and ahead on the right, Ellen saw the round turquoise and white Jacaranda sign.

They pulled into the gravel parking lot; it was only about half full. Frank looked at his watch - 7:25. They got out of the car and Frank came around to grab Ellen's hand. "I have every reason to believe that Mike and Mary are lovely people and that Mike will at the least want to meet with the President. We may be here for a few days or not, and Mike and I will have to meet alone part of the time. Speak with Mary, invite her to breakfast; no, make that lunch. You'll be busy at breakfast."

"Doing what?"

Frank paused.

Ellen looked at the sheepish grin on his face and said, "Yes, we both will."

They walked through the door and Frank told the receptionist their name and that they are with the Ridley party. She looked at the book and told Frank, "The Ridley couple has already arrived. I'll take you to the table. Please follow me." They followed her as she walked down the hallway and then turned right toward a back corner of the restaurant. Frank saw Mike and waved. Mike stood and greeted Ellen. Frank shook Mary's hand.

Mike said, "Please be seated. Welcome to Sanibel."

Ellen responded to Mike, "We have only been here a few hours. It is a very unique place. Frank and I have been thinking about coming here for our 25th anniversary next year."

Ellen knew that Mike and Mary have not been here long but wants to focus on her job. "This is our first trip to Sanibel and I was wondering, Mary, could we have lunch tomorrow so I could pick your brain about what we should see while we are here? I want to see if you have any suggestions on where to have the party?"

Mary responded, "I think I'm free unless you hear from me, Ellen. Shall we say 12:00 at the Sanibel Café?"

"Fine with me; I'll look forward to it."

Frank asked, "Do you and Mary have a favorite entree here?"

"They make a wonderful wedge salad with blue cheese and crisp bacon. I happen to like the grouper blackened and Mary, what would you recommend?"

"The salad is nice, but the gulf shrimp, ice cold with traditional cocktail sauce is outstanding. I love seafood, so I recommend the mussels; alone they make a meal."

The waiter came over with the menus and asked for their drink order. Mike spoke up. "Give us a minute to look at the menu." All four of them looked at the selections and asked Mike and Mary about other items on the menu.

The waiter returned with fresh baked bread and placed it on the table. Next to the bread, he placed a small plate piled high with grated Parmigiano-Reggiano. With a spoon he created a pocket in the cheese, filled it with olive oil and mixed the cheese and the olive oil. He asked, "Have you decided, ladies?"

Mary went first. "I would like the shrimp cocktail and the mussels in marinara sauce."

Ellen says, "I'll also have the shrimp cocktail and the mussels, but could I have them in a garlic butter and white wine sauce?"

"Excellent. And for you, gentlemen?"

Mike ordered, "I'll have the wedge salad and the grouper blackened, and savory rice."

"And you, sir?"

"I'll have the red snapper grilled and rice as a side order."

The waiter commented, "The snapper was caught this morning out in Pine Island Sound. Now, what about drinks?"

Mary said, "I'll have a glass of chardonnay."

Ellen said, "That sounds good to me as well."

Mike ordered a white zinfandel and Frank said, "I'll have the same as the ladies."

Mike looked at Ellen, "So, you have been married almost 25 years. How has it been?"

"I know it sounds so silly to some people, but I love Frank more today than at any time in our almost 25 years together. How long have you and Mary been married?"

"This year it is 45 years."

Ellen asked, "To what do you attribute that longevity?"

"Some people might call it love, but I prefer to call it loyalty."

Frank saw an opening and asked, "I was wondering about your comment about loyalty – how important is loyalty to you?"

Chapter 51

WILD'S ELECTRONIC CONVENTION

The two leaders of the major political parties went to the head of the Federal Election Commission and presented their case for Internet voting. The Commission listened attentively and said they would respond as quickly as possible. Frank Meyer went back to Wild's office to discuss the upcoming Democratic Convention that was scheduled for Kansas City. For the moment it is on hold. Wild said to Meyer, "We have to get out ahead of the Republicans on this convention issue."

Meyer responded, "What are you thinking; what's your idea?"

Wild responded, "I think we should scrap the Kansas City convention and let the delegates vote over the Internet. Nominating speeches as well as speeches on the issues can also be broadcast over the Internet. Hell, even my acceptance speech will be delivered over the Internet. We will let the Republicans and Jordan scramble to make their own convention changes. What they will not know is that we will secretly cut a deal with all the major networks, so two days before the election, I will get 30 minutes to tell my story. The President will have no chance to get on the networks."

"Senator, how will you keep it a secret?"

"We will use one of the Political Action Committees to front for us. When the program airs, live, I will be speaking on behalf of the PAC. It will be perfectly legal."

Meyer suggested, "We might want to get a legal opinion on your idea."

"Go right ahead, but right now I want to talk about how we get the electronic convention. You will have to go to the rules committee and get them to go along with the changes in how the convention will be conducted. They need to understand that everybody's right to vote will be protected. Challenges and amendments will follow the traditional rules except everything will be electronic. I realize there will be challenges, but we must get the systems right so we can use them for the November election. Internet voting will decide all offices regardless of position. Frank, I really believe we have the security technology in place to protect a fair and honest vote."

"Senator, I have an issue, not about what we have been talking about, but what is happening in the country. The President is going to hire hundreds of thousands of people to speed up the building of both pipelines. I heard through our sources that Energy is about to present a plan to start pumping in the Gulf of Mexico again. There is talk in Justice about curtailing martial law, reducing the hours of curfew and opening the banks and markets a few hours at a time. In other words, Senator, the country is rebuilding. America is rebuilding, and at least for now Jordan is getting all the credit. Hope is growing and Nathan Jordan is riding those coattails, at least for now."

Wild responded, "For now."

A chill went down the spine of Meyer as he thought, *what does Wild mean when he says "for now"? Does he know something that we, or even the government doesn't know is going to happen? Is he planning something that will impact the President's momentum and swing votes to him? What could it be?*

Chapter 52

WAR ROOM, THE PRESIDENT AND HIS "THINK TANK"

The President walked into the room and all present stood; the President motioned for all of them to sit down. "Gentlemen, it has been a week since we last met. Have any of you come up with ideas or suggestions for us to consider?"

Defense Secretary Robert Hamilton spoke up. "Mr. President, if you will allow me to be very blunt?"

"Go right ahead Bob, I will not be offended."

All present leaned forward in their chairs to hear what Hamilton has to say. "I believe the recent attack and its success will embolden other groups to attack and be even more aggressive than the Brotherhood with even bigger, more powerful and destructive weapons."

Jordan said, "I'm sorry for interrupting Bob. I just want to make sure I understand that you think more aggressive attacks are coming?"

"Yes, sir, I do. If I may go on."

"Please proceed."

"Sir, why do you think the Brotherhood attacked us the way they did?"

"Well, Bob, they must have figured that energy was where we were the most vulnerable."

"With all due respect to you, Mr. President, my question was why, not how or where?"

"Okay, Bob, why?"

"Mr. President, I believe we are responsible for the attack."

The room erupts with vocal objections to the idea that we caused the attack. Jordan did not say anything; he just watched the reaction and was not surprised.

The President cautioned, "Gentlemen, please settle down and let Mr. Hamilton make his point."

"Thank you, Mr. President. You see Mr. President, in some ways these men just proved my point. What America and several other Judeo-Christian nations don't understand is the magnitude to which they want to destroy us is based on the conflicts between what we believe and they believe. If you would, Mr. President, the difference between the Bible and the Qur'an divide us. I will not embarrass anybody in the room by asking who of you has read the Qur'an. Not many people in America including most elected leaders have ever read it. The last 60 years of evolution in the United States has seen the highest court upholding abortion. In the time since the court allowed the woman's right to choose, 65 million abortions have been performed.

"The legal right for men to marry men and call it marriage, for women to marry women and call that marriage, flies in the face of the teachings in the Qur'an; at the least it is offensive to many Muslims. The freedoms we have granted women over the years fly in the face of what they believe and how they treat women. Many Muslims believe Sharia Law should replace the Constitution of the United States."

Again the room erupted in protest. The President said to the group, "**STOP RIGHT NOW**! Bob is trying to help us understand his point of view, and I for one want to hear it. So, no more outbursts. Proceed, Bob."

"If our laws conflict with their beliefs, then they feel that it is their responsibility to *save* the world and at the same time *rule* the world. They feel they are right and everybody else is an infidel and must be converted or killed. The conflict between the religions has always been there, but why has it erupted so much in the last 60 years? Sir, I believe the core reason is population. There are more Muslims now than ever before, and because there are more, their strength comes from numbers. So, the question is why has the population swelled so much? Sir, another one word answer, money. And, their money comes from oil.

"Oil and the money it produces has forever changed the life of the Muslim. For many centuries they were a nomadic people. Oil gave the Muslim nomads the ability to change their lives, but as they started to acquire wealth, they felt their religion slipping away, much like what has been happening in America. Churches here are no longer relevant in many people's lives. The Muslim leaders didn't like what was happening to their people, so they turned their focus to the Qur'an for direction. Religious leaders saw the need to return to a faith-based value system and the people began to flock to the mosque to worship and learn the rules of their religion. We, on the other hand, have walked away from our value system and core principals.

"Mr. President, if we don't do something soon, the Muslims will rule the world and we will live under the threat of the total destruction of our country."

"Well, Bob, you have scared me to death. Do you have a solution?"

"In fact, Mr. President, I do. I have several solutions. Remember, I'm being candid, not politically correct."

"I understand. Go ahead."

"We must find a way to return the Muslim people to being nomads. How we do that is to stop the flow of money. The source of all the wealth and power in the Middle East comes from oil. If we can develop our energy resources and teach the rest of world to develop their energy, the world will no longer depend on the whims of OPEC. "All of those massive towers and tall buildings in all the cities in the Middle East will eventually fall like the World Trade Center in New York, without planes crashing into them. These will fall because they don't have the money to keep them up."

Everybody in the room including the President was quiet. All were trying to take in what Hamilton has said, but he wasn't finished.

"Mr. President, I have one more suggestion."

Jordan responded, "I'm not sure my mind can absorb any more, but go ahead."

"Mr. President, every nation has the right to set the rules on who can immigrate. I suggest that immediately the United States insist that all Muslims on temporary visa check-in with immigration and naturalization. They will be politely asked to leave within six months or they will be deported. Within three months they must report their travel plans. That information will be posted so Immigration can track when and how they have indicated they will leave. If they have not left the country within six months, an alert will be issued to local law enforcement agencies. If they are caught, they will be jailed and tried as illegal aliens and may be physically escorted out of the United States to their country of origin or be imprisoned as enemy combatants.

"Effective immediately no emigrant visas of any type will be granted to people of a nation that is deemed by the United States government to be a Muslim state. If we are going to save this great nation from total destruction, we have to make decisions that many in our country will disagree with, as will other nations around the world. Those who don't have the willpower to stand up for their history and culture may well perish.

"But, sir, please let me close by saying, May God – Our God, bless America."

Chapter 53

DINNER IS SERVED

Mike, Mary, Frank and Ellen have been talking about loyalty, and Mike has said that loyalty is very important. He claimed that it is one of the reasons his marriage has lasted as long as it has. In addition Mike said that, "Loyalty affects all areas of our life."

Frank sees an opportunity to ask a pressing question. "Mike, in all of your time working for the government, did you ever have a problem with loyalty?"

Mike responds by looking at Mary and asked her, "Do you recall any time that I had somebody who was disloyal?" Mary shakes her head indicating, no. "Frank, as I'm sure you know, I had some assignments that were very top secret and my life was in grave jeopardy. Because of the risk, I needed to trust people to protect my back. People who are willing to protect your life with theirs have to be very loyal. This is a longwinded answer to your question. Perhaps it was because of the nature of the work and the risks I was asked to take that made loyalty so important to me."

Frank responded, "It wasn't longwinded at all. It was well thought out and I thank you for your perspective."

About that time, the waiter brought their meals. Ellen said. "We didn't have lunch, so we are very hungry; it looks and smells wonderful."

They all enjoyed their meals and talked some about Sanibel being one of the best shelling beaches in the world. Mike told Frank it also has some of the best big game fishing in the world. They finished their dinner and the waiter cleared the dishes and asked if anyone wanted dessert. Frank responded, "What do you have?" When he heard coconut cake in the list, he said, "That's for me."

The waiter asked, "Anybody else want dessert or coffee?"

Everybody said yes to coffee. Frank told the waiter to bring four forks just in case. The waiter brought a very large piece of cake and Ellen immediately took a fork and told Frank, "I'll just have a bite of yours."

Frank responded, "Anybody else want a bite?"

Mary said, "It looks wonderful; perhaps a small bite."

Frank passed the plate. She took a section and passed the plate to Mike. "Well maybe just a small bite."

Mike passed the plate back to Frank. He looked down at what was left, laughed and said, "I'm glad you three weren't hungry."

They finished their coffee and the waiter brought the check. Frank took it and Mike said, "Can I help you with that?"

"No, I've got it, but thanks anyway." Frank paid and then said, "I need to use the restroom; will you excuse me?"

Mike said, "I need to use it, too. I'll join you."

As they got up to go to the men's room, the ladies said, "We'll meet you in the lobby."

Frank and Mike walked down the hall toward the men's room and Frank held the door for Mike. They both walked up to the urinals and Frank said, "Will you have time tomorrow to discuss your possible meeting with the President?"

Mike responded, "I thought we might go back to my house and spend some time tonight talking about what the President would want me to do."

Frank said, "I'll take Ellen back to the hotel and then I'll come to your house."

Mike offered, "Better yet, let's have the receptionist for the restaurant call Sanibel Taxi to take Ellen home and then you can follow me to our house."

"That sounds like a good idea. I wanted to start the discussion sooner rather than later. I'll order the taxi and tell Ellen."

The two men left the rest room and headed down the hallway to the lobby. Frank asked the receptionist to call a cab. "How long will it be?"

"About 10 minutes, sir."

Mike suggested, "I'll send Mary ahead and then after Ellen is in the taxi we can drive to my house so I can show you the way. You can easily get lost since there are no street lights in Sanibel."

"Why no street lights?" Frank asked.

"It's to protect the wildlife."

Frank walked up to Ellen to tell her of the plan. "I don't know how long it will be, so if you get sleepy go, to bed I'll try and be quiet when I come in. Oh, one other thing."

"What's that?"

"Go to bed naked."

Ellen looked at him and smiled and responded with a salute, "Yes, sir."

The cab arrived right on time and Frank put Ellen in the car. As he gave her a gentle kiss he said, "See you soon."

Mary had already left the parking lot. As soon as Ellen's cab pulled out, the two of them walked toward Frank's car and they both got in. Frank asked, "What direction?"

"Go right out of the parking lot and head toward the lighthouse." They drove through the four-way stop intersection and continued toward the lighthouse. Mike asked Frank, "Do you know the assignment the President wants me to consider?"

Frank thought, *I want to answer Mike and give him as much detail as possible, but I don't know that I should tell him much. But, on the other hand, my job is to get Mike to want to fly to Washington and meet with the President. If Mike respects loyalty as much as he says he does, then how can he refuse the assignment, and more importantly, how can you not go to the President when he wants to see you?*

"Frank, I don't know how much you know about the assignment, but before we reach the house let me ask you a very important question. Your answer will be very important to me in making a decision to go forward."

"Okay, what's your question? If I can, I will answer it."

"Frank, I have to assume that the President has unsealed my file for you and whomever else the President wants to see my history."

Frank interjected, "Mike, you need to know only two of us have seen your file - Attorney General Drew Clinton and me."

"I guess that's reassuring...you know some of the things I have done in my career with the government. So, my question is, will the President want me to kill somebody?"

Chapter 54

HOUSTON SAFE HOUSE, TIME IS GETTING SHORT

It is close to noon and Hadar needs to call Mordecai and tell him that she and Megan, her roommate, are leaving now and should be in Houston by late tomorrow afternoon depending on traffic and the availability of gas. The team is meeting in the safe house along with Ted Baker. The question that needs to be asked is, where is Mordecai now? If they can find out today, the team without the women can find the location and scout it out to see what can be done to capture the Brotherhood. Baker asked the team, "What is the least threatening way to ask the question and still get the answer we need?"

Megan was the first to respond, "Hadar, can say that we need to set our GPS so it can show the shortest route to get to you? We have the starting address, can you tell me the end point?"

Baker responded, "Excellent. Do any of you have an alternative?"

All agree that the question is not threatening, but Hadar suggests a modification. "We don't know if the place Megan and I are meeting him is anywhere near where they are living. So, don't we just want to ask him the location where we are meeting him?"

Baker responds as do others, "I agree with her line of thinking; the focus should be where the two of them are to meet. If we are all agreed, then Hadar, make the call."

All the gear is still hooked up to the phone and just as Hadar was ready to dial she stopped. "Should I send him a text and see if he can talk now or, if not now, when?"

Megan tells Hadar, "Send the text and see what happens."

Hadar sends the text and she hears "swoosh" that the text message has gone through. Hadar says, "Now we wait."

Megan suggests, "Let's talk about the ID bracelet with the communications team." Megan told them about their plan and wanted to know what would be the best GPS device to use.

John suggested, "We need to have something that can stand water and still transmit, and the bracelet can't reveal that a tracking device is embedded."

The specialists asked, "What range do you need?"

Megan asked, "What are our options?"

"My guess is that the ID section will be about five-eighths inches wide and about one and a half inches long. The bracelet will fasten in the back, so the device will have to sit inside the back of the bracelet. We could have the jeweler make a saddle that would be the same size as the bracelet and the sides of the saddle would be soldered to the bracelet and then buffed to make the seams disappear. We can fit the GPS with a small lithium battery for power that could run it for years."

Megan asked, "How long will it take to modify the bracelet and insert the GPS?"

"My guess is that it could be done in a few hours. I have the device and the battery, so all we need is to find a jewelry store that is open and see if they have an ID bracelet in stock."

Seacrest responded, "I'm on it. I'm doing a Google search in the area right now. I found a store three blocks from here. Let me call and see if they are open." John dialed the number, but no one answered. "I'll keep trying and let you know if I find one."

Baker asked Omid, "Do you have iMovie on your computer?"

"Yes, why?"

"If Hadar is in a car and on the cell phone, Mordecai will expect moving car sounds in the background. Check and see if you have it, and if so create a sound loop of moving cars and trucks."

"Megan, what is your favorite music?"

"I like country."

"Find two songs you like on iTunes and download them so you can play them when Hadar tells you to turn down the radio so she can hear the person on the phone. You need to hustle. We have to be ready before he calls."

Seacrest shouted, "Got one who is four blocks from here. I'll go and see if he can do what we need; do you have the GPS and the battery?"

The specialist replied, "Give me a minute and I'll be right with you. Mr. Baker, would it be okay for me to go with Mr. Seacrest to get the bracelet made up?"

"Go right ahead."

Megan yelled, "Stop! What does the bracelet say?"

Hadar shouts, "Mordecai/Hadar."

"Got it, thanks."

Baker asked Omid, "Got the sounds ready?"

"Horns and cars passing. I have them on a two minute loop."

"Megan, got your country music?"

"Done."

Everything is in place so they all sat down on the couch, all except Baker and Hadar who headed to the balcony and closed the door.

Chapter 55

THE RIDLEY PORCH, TIME
TO GET SERIOUS

Frank followed the directions from Mike and they turned right. Mike told Frank, "Pull up to the gate and stick this card in the slot. The gate should open." Frank put in the card but nothing happened. Mike said, "This time push it in all the way and quickly remove it and the gate should open." Frank followed the new instructions and heard something click. His headlights illuminated the gate as it started to swing open. After it opened enough, Mike said, "Go through and follow this street for about a half a mile and then you'll turn right." Frank pulled through the gate and as soon as he cleared the gate, it started to close. He followed the road and Mike said, "Turn right here. We are the building close to the water. Park in the underground."

They got out of the car and Mike led the way to the elevator. Mike pushed the Up button and the elevator slowly came to the ground floor and opened. A man and his dog on a leash came out and he said, "Hi, Mike," and walked on.

Mike said, "Retired CIA; a lot of them and FBI on the island." Mike pushed the button marked PH. Mike said to Frank, "The elevators here run at about at the same pace as the speed of life on the island." It stopped and the doors opened to a hallway. "Just to the right. We are unit 307."

Mike led the way down the well-lit hallway. As they walked down the hallway, Frank saw geckos climbing the pink walls; they scattered when

Frank and Mike got close. Mike unlocked the door and they went in. Some of the lights were on, so Frank got some idea how the unit is furnished. He saw paintings of fish and the beach on the walls. Frank thought to himself, *very colorful*. The floors had large sandy looking tiles and the chairs and sofas were a rough textured fabric, one in an ocean blue and the other one covered in a smooth tan fabric. Between the couches was a sand-colored area rug with starfish, seahorses and shells in the pattern. On top of the rug was a large chunk of Florida cedar driftwood. Frank liked the contrast of the colors. To Frank's right, he saw a triple sliding door that was open to a screened porch. Mike suggested they go outside; that way they won't disturb Mary who has already gone to bed. Mike asked, "Would you like a drink?"

"I know it isn't very 'islandish', but do you have a cold beer?"

"Frank, I have several kinds. Come over here to the frig and pick your own. I'll meet you on the porch."

Frank selected a Yuengling, twisted off the cap and walked to the porch. As he went through the doorway, he began to hear the ocean waves hitting the beach below. Frank walked over to the edge of the porch and looked out to see a full moon shining on the water. He thought to himself, *what a beautiful spot. I think Ellen and I could retire here; I wonder how much the government is paying for this condo.* "How are the beaches down here at this end of the island? We spent some time up by the Mucky Duck this afternoon and those beaches were great."

Mike responded, "I think you will find the lighthouse beaches just as impressive as the ones up in Captiva. Come and sit down. I want to ask you a question."

"In the car I asked you if you thought the President wants me to kill somebody. You didn't answer…"

"Mike, to the best of my knowledge, the President does not intend that your mission will be to assassinate a government leader, or for that matter, anybody. However, he realizes that you may find yourself in a position on your assignment that in order to protect your life you may have to takes someone else's. He would want you to do that at your discretion."

"Frank, do you know what the President wants to talk to me about? Should I go to Washington?

"Mike, I would not presume to speak for the President, but I can tell you that I made the recommendation to the President that you were perhaps the best possible person in the United States to do this job."

Mike asks, "Should I take that as a compliment or a death warrant?"

Frank responds, "My hope is that you take it as a compliment to your talent and ability proven over many years of loyal service to this country."

Mike asked, "Specifically, why did you pick me for this assignment?"

"Mike, you know that America was attacked by the Brotherhood of the Red Nile with two reconditioned nuclear bombs. We are getting close to the location of the Brotherhood and we may capture them in the next few days. While they were responsible for rebuilding at least one of the two bombs and made the decisions as to the targets, they didn't have the money to acquire the defective bombs, nor did they have the money to rebuild these bombs and pay all their living expense for months or perhaps years. That money had to come from someone and the President wants to know the source. Your assignment is to trace the money to its source and then get the indisputable evidence to prove under total scrutiny who the person or persons are who supplied it. The President doesn't care how long it takes or how much it costs; just prove it so we can get him or them. He has indicated that this is an assignment that may outlast his presidency, but you will be fully funded and protected as much as we can on this assignment. The solution for the destruction of the terrorists and their funding may well be beyond all of our lifetimes, but the President believes it must start on his watch. I can't tell you much more. Only the President can finish the conversation.

"I would like you to talk it over with Mary tomorrow and see if the two of you agree this is something you want to do for the American people."

"That was a cheap shot about the American people."

"Mike, it was not a cheap shot. It was the truth. If you are successful in your assignment, you may well change the course of history and if you do, almost no one will know you did it. I know, based on your file, that you have done many dangerous assignments on behalf of the United States and even directly for several presidents. I cannot stress enough that this is a very important project."

Mike asked, "You want another beer?"

"One more, then I need to get back to Ellen."

"Bring me one of what you're drinking if you would, please."

Frank returned, handed Mike the beer, and said, "You had another question? I'll try and answer it if I can."

"In my conversation with President Jordan, he indicated that billions of dollars are at stake, why?"

Frank responds, "First, let me tell you that the number he really wanted to tell you and couldn't because it is unbelievable was trillions, not billions."

"How could trillions of dollars be in play?"

Frank answers Mike's question, "First of all, let me say that I found it hard to understand myself, but what we know is that the day before the two bombs went off someone was orchestrating massive purchases of oil futures contracts and options on oil futures. When the bombs went off crippling a significant amount of America's oil producing infrastructure, the price of oil tripled. Granted, the futures that were traded in America were frozen; the SEC has frozen all contracts in place so when the markets open those oil futures will skyrocket in price."

Mike asks, "So, are the other futures and options trading around the rest of the world?"

"Yes, and they continue to rise. You will have full access to all the trading records that have been frozen and they may be helpful in identifying who is behind this attack on America and why."

"You keep referring to a person or persons involved. Do you really think one person could be running all of this?"

Chapter 56

THE SHERIFF AND MRS. RIDLEY JUST TALK

Baker was long gone on his way to Houston, leaving just Jim and Kristen in the interrogation room. There will be no charges filed and Kristen is free to go, but Jim has been thinking about this young woman, perhaps not knowing who she really married and that she may never see that husband again. It is possible that, in either case, she is married to a terrorist. In some ways she seems self-assured, yet he sees in her a deep vulnerability.

Jim looks over at Kristen and said, "Can I buy you dinner?"

She responded, "Why would you want to buy me dinner?"

"I would like to thank you for all your help and for enduring the discomfort you went through today."

Kristen thought, *does he know something that he is not telling me? Does he think I haven't been totally truthful with him? I can't think of anything I haven't told him, so why not get a free meal?* "Sure. What time do you want to go?"

"Are you hungry now?"

"Actually I didn't have lunch, so sure; why not have an early dinner? Do I have to ride in your Sheriff car?"

"No, I have a regular car; we'll use that one. What would you like to eat?"

"I don't eat meat, but I like pasta. How about George's?"

"That works for me. Do you want to use the restroom before we leave?"

"Yes, thank you."

"When you're finished, come to the front lobby and I'll bring up my car."

Kristen went to the ladies room and Jim went to get his car. As Jim walked to his car he was thinking, *this young girl is in for some serious pressure if the government finds the terrorists and Michael is captured alive. She is going to need Father Tim more than ever. I need to call Father Tim and go see him to alert him on the possible trouble this young woman is facing so he can try and help her.*

Jim got in the car and saw Kristen at the front door waiting for him. He started the engine, pulled out of the parking space and stopped at the front door. Kristen opened the door and got in.

"Buckle up."

"Yes, sir," she said with a small smile on her face.

Twelve hundred miles away, Frank Williams is driving along Periwinkle Way on his way to a naked wife in bed, hopefully awake. His phone rang. Ted Baker is on the phone. "Sir, we have a huge break. Mordecai has told Hadar that he is in Houston. We are assuming that the rest of the Brotherhood is with him. Hadar is supposed to meet Mordecai tomorrow afternoon. We are assembling a special ID bracelet for Hadar to give to him that will have a hidden GPS tracking device so we can follow him when Hadar leaves and he goes back to the rest of the Brotherhood. Once we can identify that we have most of them, we will break in with SWAT and capture all of them."

Williams responded, "Outstanding, I need to alert the President of the progress. Do you have all the resources you need?"

"Yes, sir, I believe we do. I will run a check in the morning and if I need more help I will call on the local FBI office."

"I don't know if I can get through to the President tonight, but if I can't, I will call him first thing in the morning. Tell the team, including Megan, that I'm very proud of all of them."

"I will, sir. Goodnight."

"Well done, Ted. Well done."

"Thank you, sir."

Back in Springfield, Jim Whittles was having dinner with Mrs. Kristen Ridley. They were eating their salads and Jim said to Kristen, "It must be difficult to get married and have your husband leave in the middle of the night, and on top of that not hear a word in many months."

"That is why I'm seeing Father Tim. You see, Sheriff, the depression is really bad sometimes. I wonder why I married Mike, and when Mr. Baker told me about Ishtar, I about lost it. Now I don't know who I'm married to. I know what the marriage license says, but just because it says Michael Ridley doesn't mean that it's true. When Mr. Baker said that, I kept asking myself if I might be married to somebody else … and then who is the father of my baby?"

Jim was taking a sip of his Bud and spit it back into the glass. Jim, with shock on his face asked, "Who knows you're pregnant?"

She responded, "You, Father Tim, my doctor, and his nurse."

"You don't look pregnant."

"I have been wearing oversized clothes so people can't tell, and I'm not that large yet."

"How far along are you?"

"About four months."

"Kristen, four months. So, you were married and with Michael literally just before the bombs went off?"

"So?"

"So, Michael or Ishtar was here before they planted the bombs."

"What bombs?"

Jim stopped in his tracks. *She doesn't know that Michael and Ishtar are part of the Brotherhood. She has never been told. Thinking on his feet he has to decide to tell her the truth or lie. He decides to lie.* "We got a report of a bomb going off down the road and initially somebody thought they identified Michael, but if you were being married it couldn't have been him. Do you have any family that can help you with the baby?"

"No, I am on my own."

"Perhaps Father Tim can arrange some help."

"Funny that you mentioned that because that is why I was going to see Father Tim when I was arrested. I'm sure glad you didn't shoot."

"So am I."

"Please finish your meal; you're eating for two and you need to eat well."

★★★

In Captiva, Frank pulled into the parking lot of the Tween Waters Inn and dialed a special phone number directly to the President. It rang several times and a voice message on the line said that the President is unable to answer his call at the moment and to please leave a message. "...The President will return your call as soon as possible."

As the message was playing Frank was trying to think what to say then it came to him. "Mr. President, we have made contact and may be able to execute the capture of some or all of the Brotherhood late tomorrow. Please call as soon as you can. Frank Williams."

Frank was out of the car and up the steps in a rush to share with Ellen the fantastic news. He stopped at the door, quietly opened it, and slipped into the room not wanting to wake Ellen if she was asleep. The light was on in the bathroom and cast a soft light on the bed. He could see the outstretched arms of a naked woman just covered by a sheet.

He said softly, "Give me two minutes."

Chapter 57

THE PRESIDENT'S BEDROOM
HAS A HEAVY PALL OVER IT

The President had his cell phone in his hand. He has listened to Frank Williams' message several times. He decided that he would not call Frank back tonight. Instead, he will call him tomorrow. The President was sitting on the edge of the bed in his silk dressing robe with the Presidential seal on the left breast pocket. Nathan was not dressed for bed; he just liked the feel of the silk robe. It gave him comfort and he has not had much in the months since the attack. Karen is asleep; he will not wake her to discuss the serious problem on his mind. *I know that I have some very important decisions to make and no matter what I decide many people will be upset and angry and they may even call for my impeachment.*

I want to talk with Frank about his meeting with Mike Ridley. I really hope that Mike will be receptive to meeting with me in Washington. Finding the source of the money is critical to stopping terrorism. As if I don't have enough on my mind, I can't get out of my mind the meeting this afternoon and the very pointed comments and suggestions of Bob Hamilton. America is a country that from its founding has been open to immigrants. We have been the land of opportunity, the land of milk and honey. The idea of sending people back to their countries of origin flies in the face of what we have stood for as a nation for almost 240 years.

Nathan got up and walked out into the hallway and paced as he thought. He walked down to the Lincoln Bedroom hoping for some inspiration from that great President. He knew that Lincoln never slept there, but perhaps Lincoln's spirit will give him some inspiration. *I know that things are very different perhaps for the first time since World War II. America is at risk. Yes, more than 60,000 Americans died in the Civil War, but that was a battle of Americans fighting Americans to figure out a direction for the nation.*

The two deadly attacks on America were not by Americans. They were not another nation attacking us, but a handful of men who decided that they were going to change the world and the best way to change would be to knock out the biggest nation, America. What Hamilton was saying about the conflict between the Bible and Qur'an is true. As long as we continue in the direction we are going as it relates to what we will accommodate in our moral fiber we will have conflict, a conflict that will expand as we indirectly attack Islam and the Qur'an. If we implement Bob's suggestions, America will become an isolationist nation. We experienced that prior to World War II and we were pulled into the war because another nation attacked us at Pearl Harbor. The price we may have to pay to secure our country, or at least try to secure it, may be high indeed. I'm not sure we, as a nation, at this moment in time, are up to the challenge. We may well lose trading partners and allies when we recover if we do not start paying financial aid to many governments as we have in the past. I believe current governments will fall and the people will starve. This may create an opportunity for radical Islamists to gain control of those nations, and perhaps the world. Wait a moment; is it possible I'm being too extremist? No.

Our willingness to share an energy policy that takes the power away from OPEC and puts the power to generate energy into more and more hands reduces the volatility in energy prices in the world. In fact, it will create more stability and far less concentration of money and therefore power. The strength of money in a few hands will disappear and perhaps the funding for groups like the Brotherhood of the Red Nile will diminish and eventually stop. With no money they become worthless. As Bob said, if we can stop the funding, we will begin to see the cities fall. The people who are being deported from America will have to find ways to work and support themselves and their families in their homeland. Homelands that will have to focus on their own countries and the needs of their own people if they want to survive.

*I have a little over two years left in my first term as President. All this stuff going on in my brain is forcing me to consider the ultimate decision. Should I **not** run for reelection for President and focus on making the right decisions regardless of the outcome for the nation and perhaps the world? If I take the bold action Bob is recommending, then I stand an excellent chance that William Wild will be the next President of the United States. I believe that Wild will try to undo most of what I* decide to do and as a result, he would, I believe, be terrible for the American people, the nation, and the world. Jordan sought something to eat in the kitchen in the family quarters; all of this thinking made him hungry. He pulled over a cook's stool and sat down at the stainless steel prep table for a moment. His head was swirling. He got up and went over to the frig and got some fruit and milk and sat down at the table. He continued to ponder all of his dilemmas while he ate and sipped his milk.

I have to start making some decisions and laying down some plans to try and make America secure. I really believe that with all that is going on, America can only absorb a certain number of shocks to the system. If I tell them everything, they will not be able to follow all the complexity of what needs to be done. Tomorrow I will call Frank and ask him about Mike and if he is coming to DC. Then, I will tell him what I want the team in Houston to do with the Brotherhood. After that, I need to schedule a meeting with Senator Wild to discuss the limits in the campaign. I will take the risk of sharing with him some of my ideas and see how much I can trust him. I will set a trap, and if the press publishes the story of what I'm planning, then I'll know that Wild has leaked it to them. Tomorrow will be a long and tough day.

Jordan looked up and saw an angel named Karen, "Are you coming to bed? I need a hug."

"Me too… me too."

Chapter 58

SPRINGFIELD, SANIBEL AND HOUSTON HAVE LOTS GOING ON

Sheriff Whittles is shocked at the news that Kristen Ridley is four months pregnant and after today's session with him and Ted Baker, he has serious doubts about who is the father of her child. Jim has suggested that she spend some time with Father Tim to figure out a support option since she has no family in Springfield. As Jim is driving Kristen home he is thinking, *if she is about four months pregnant, then Michael or Ishtar was with her after the bombs went off. It is possible that they may still be in the United States. I need to let Baker know this information. I'll call him after I drop off Kristen.*

The entire ride has been quiet small talk, at best. As Jim pulled up in front of her apartment she unbuckled the seat belt and with tears in her eyes she says, "Sheriff, can I ask you a very personal question?"

"Go right ahead."

"I do not know who the father of my baby is and I may never know. It's possible that I may never see him again. Should I have an abortion? I don't know if I can raise this child on my own."

Jim is shocked at the question and really doesn't know how to answer her. "Kristen, I can't answer that question, only you can. But, I can suggest that you need to spend some serious time thinking about your decision. I would be happy to contact our social service counselors and set up a counseling session for you."

"You would do that for me?"

"I want to help you make the best possible decision, one that you can live with for the rest of your life. Do you want me to call for you tomorrow?"

"Yes, please, and thank you for dinner and your help."

"I'll call first thing in the morning and see what I can do. Give me your home phone number and as soon as I have some information, I will call you."

"Sheriff, this is my home number, but I will be at work tomorrow and I would prefer that you not call me at work, okay?"

"No problem." Jim watched as Kristen got out of the car and walked into her house. *She is in for a difficult time and she is all alone. I hope we can help her make the right decision.*

★★★

Frank Williams undressed and slipped into the open arms of Ellen who has been waiting for his return. As they cuddled, he felt her warm body next to him. He wanted to pull her closer to him; as close as possible without hurting her. Ellen turned over on her side and pressed her back into Frank. She reached around and took one of his hands and placed it on her breast and encouraged him to caress her. They'd made love earlier in the day so there is not the urgency to make love again. The closeness of Ellen's body and the caress of her breast aroused him and Ellen could feel him against her. She said, "Do you want to make love again?"

"Maybe later."

Ellen asked Frank, "How was your meeting?"

"Before I answer that let me tell you how proud I was of you tonight at dinner, you did a fabulous job." Frank gave her breast a firmer squeeze and Ellen wiggled a little bit rubbing her butt on him.

"Thank you. How did the after-dinner meeting go?"

"I don't know. I couldn't get a read on him. We talked a little bit about the assignment and I think he will at least go to DC to meet with the President. I'll know more tomorrow. Oh, I must tell you that I got a call from Ted and he thinks we might have a chance to capture the Brotherhood in the next day or so. I called the President to tell him, but I got his voicemail. Hopefully, he will call me back tomorrow. It would mean so much to me to capture them. I hope it happens. Say, I was thinking, we both had a pretty good day, how about a little love making?"

Ellen responded, "Well, I can see you're up for it."

★★★

The Pathfinders plus one wait for a text message from Mordecai as to when he can call and give Hadar the meeting point. Seacrest found a jeweler who was open and had the ID bracelet in stock. He took the communications team member along with him to the store.

John asked, "By the way, what is your name?"

"Sir, my name is Dan Matthews."

"Dan, do you have the GPS and the battery with you?

Matthew patted his pocket, "Right here, sir."

Back in the safe house, Hadar and Baker were on the balcony at the moment, just sitting in chairs, neither of them saying a word. Hadar spoke first. She knew that Baker was thinking about her and what her reaction will be when she sees Mordecai and puts her arms around him. "Ted, do you remember when you gave us the lecture on our commitment to the mission and that it might mean having sex with somebody just to obtain information, or killing somebody or breaking the law to achieve the mission?"

Ted stood up. "Yes, I do. I thought it needed to be said; it's a fact of life in our kind of work. It doesn't happen every day and for some it never happens, but the reality is, for you, just look at you, who wouldn't want to have sex with you?"

"I understand what you are saying but I want you to know that I want to be with you, and to be honest, for now I don't know what that means. I now know that I want to, after this mission. I want to stay here and be with you. No matter what happens tomorrow or the next day, my heart belongs to you."

Baker responded, "Does the body come with the heart?" Whack! "I deserved that."

"Yes, you did. Get your mind off my body and back on the mission."

"Easy for you to say. You're not sitting here looking at you."

Inside the safe house, Omid and Megan were sitting on the couch together, both watching Hadar's phone, waiting for it to ring. There has been a nervous sexual tension between the two of them for some time and this is the first time the two of them have been alone for any extended period. Omid is not married and has had very few relationships with women. Megan has been with a few men, but nothing serious ever developed; she has been very occupied with her work and her desire to get into CIA Special Ops. Neither of them knows where to start.

Omid thought, *this is crazy. We are both adults. We can sense the attraction but it appears that neither of us has the courage to start. Machine guns, rocket launchers, tanks and even bombers have fired upon me and that all seems easy compared to this. I don't want to lose this opportunity, so I'm going to start.*

Just as Omid opened his mouth to say something to Megan, Hadar's phone buzzed.

Megan called to Hadar, "You have a text message."

Both Omid and Megan reach for the phone and their hands touch. Omid looked up to Megan and handed her the phone, looked in her eyes and softly said, "I want you."

Megan looked back and said, "Me too."

Hadar took the phone from Megan, opened it and saw a text message from Mordecai, "I'll call you in the morning with a location. M"

They all collapsed on the couch showing great disappointment. Ted put his arm around Hadar as if to comfort her in her disappointment and Omid slowly puts his arm around Megan in a similar way. Megan slid herself into Omid's body and they both felt good.

Chapter 59

TWEEN WATERS INN, TIME FOR ELLEN

The President didn't sleep well the night before, even cuddling with Karen. She went back to sleep in his arms and eventually rolled over and stayed asleep. On the other hand, in Sanibel the action last night in room 306 was hot and furious and when it was over both Ellen and Frank were fast asleep. Ellen woke up first and got out of bed. Frank watched her naked body get up out of the bed and his gaze followed it to the bathroom. He noticed that Ellen was walking funny like something was hurting her. "Are you okay?"

"Just a little sore from all the action last night. I'll get a shower and loosen up."

Frank asked, "Want some company in the shower?"

"Only if there is no hanky-panky."

"What fun is a joint shower without it? Okay, I promise, but can I lather you up and hose you down?"

"What, do you think I'm a cow?"

"Perhaps a poor choice of words."

The phone rang. It was Mike Ridley, "I wanted you to know that Mary and I talked about the possible assignment and we both agree I need to go to Washington and meet President Jordan. I'm planning to call him later today and see what his schedule looks like for me to come up."

Frank responds to Mike's concern, "I'm sure the President will make time for you whenever you can get there. I'll call the White House and alert them to your call. I have a plane at Page Field, we could arrange for you to use it to go to DC and back. If it's okay with you, I will ask the President."

"That would be generous of you. Let me know what happens."

"Mike, I'll get back to you as soon as I talk with the President."

Mike hung up and Frank ran into the bathroom and jumped in the shower with Ellen, grabbed her and held her tight, but covered with soap she kept slipping away.

"Stop for a moment. What is going on?"

"That was Mike Ridley. He is going to Washington to meet with the President."

Ellen grabbed Frank, held him close and because of all the soap one of her breasts popped out. They looked at it and both broke out laughing. Frank stopped for a moment, looked into Ellen's eyes and said quietly and seriously, "I love you very much even though you have flying breasts."

Ellen responded, "I'm so proud of what you have done. I hope you and Mike can save American lives." This time they held each other not with passion but with tenderness and the warm shower just flooded both of their bodies with what felt like gentle summer rain.

Back at the Oval Office the President was going over the things on his desk and he was waiting for the right time to call Frank Williams and share with him his decision. Mary Washington, the President's executive assistant, buzzed the President and told him, "Frank Williams is on line one."

"Thank you, Mary; please tell him I'll be right with him."

"Hello, Frank. How is Sanibel?"

"It is a beautiful place, Mr. President. Sir, I may have some great news."

"What is that?"

"Sir, I met with Mike Ridley last night and he called me just a moment ago and has agreed to come to Washington to meet with you. I have, assuming it's okay with you, offered the stand-by plane at Page Field to take him to DC and back."

"Excellent work. Using the plane is a great idea."

"Sir, he said that he would be calling you sometime today to work out a visit based on your schedule."

"I will make time to see him as soon as he can get here."

"Should I call Mike back for you, Mr. President?"

"I think it's best if I wait until he calls me to make the arrangements."

"Yes, Mr. President."

"Frank, I have one other issue to discuss with you concerning the Brotherhood."

"Yes, Mr. President."

"As I understand it your team is working on an ID bracelet that Hadar will put on Mordecai's wrist. Is that correct?"

"Yes, Mr. President."

"Frank, this has been a difficult decision and someday I hope to be able to prove to you it was the right one."

Frank is wondering, *am I being relieved of my position?*

"Frank, I want you to let the Brotherhood go free. I do not want them captured and I do not want to give them any indication that they are being followed or under observation."

Frank can't believe what he has heard. The President of the United States is passing on the opportunity to get the people who were responsible for the bombing of America. "Just let them go?"

"We will deal with them later. We can follow and observe them, but from a significant distance. I believe we will have an opportunity to capture them later, but not now."

"But, Mr. President –"

The President interrupts Frank, "Frank, I know this is hard to swallow, but as of now I have no choice but to let them go, do you understand what I want done?"

"Yes, Mr. President."

"Frank, tell your team immediately."

"Yes, Mr. President."

"Frank, I know they will be disappointed, but it has to be this way. Let me know if Hadar gets the bracelet on Mordecai. For now that bracelet will be our only link to the Brotherhood."

"Thank you, Mr. President.

"Goodbye."

"Goodbye, sir."

Chapter 60

PATHFINDERS HAVE TO STAND DOWN?

The next morning Jim called Omid to tell him about Kristen and the baby and that the Brotherhood might still be around. Jim checked his phone for Omid's cell number, found it and dialed the number. Omid answered, and Jim said, "Hello, I might have something for you."

"What's that?"

"As you know Ted Baker was here yesterday and he was questioning the young Mrs. Ridley. He didn't find anything, so I decided to get her something to eat. At dinner she told me that she is pregnant and now she isn't sure if Michael or Ishtar is the father of her child. She estimated that she must have gotten pregnant her wedding night, but she has not heard from either of them, other than receiving the letter giving her the $600,000 in the bank. Whoever the father is, he was with her after the bomb attack. My guess is that they are still in the country."

"Jim, my old friend, thank you so very much for this information, but we have located the Brotherhood. They are here in Houston."

"Are you sure?"

"Jim, Hadar has been talking and texting Mordecai and they are to meet later today."

"Wow, that's great! So, you should have all of them tonight; that's exciting."

"Not so much..."

"Why?"

"The President has asked us not to capture the Brotherhood but to only observe them from a distance."

"Again, why?"

"Jim, I can't answer that other than to say we were told the President has his reasons."

"WOW, what a bummer."

"So close but not. We have a tracking device that Hadar is going to put on Mordecai today so we should be able to track at least Mordecai around the world. Three of us will stay close to protect Hadar and Megan."

"I'm going to see Father Tim later today and see what, if anything, he can tell me about what is going on with Kristen. If I learn anything more I'll let you know. Good luck today."

"Thanks for calling and giving me the information."

Whittles hung up and dialed Father Tim's rectory number. After a few rings Jim got Father Tim's voice mail and Jim left a message for him to call as soon as possible.

★★★

In Sanibel, Frank Williams finished his call with the team and was ready to get out of the car and go see the one person who can help him through this devastating disappointment. He slowly walked up the stairs at the Tween Waters Inn. He slipped the card key into the lock and opened the door and before him is that angel he saw back in their house. She is dressed in an extremely sheer long flowing gown open from top to bottom and her firm breasts are the only thing adding contour to the shape of the angel. As Frank slowly walked over to her, she could see in his eyes the look of terrible disappointment. Frank approached and Ellen took both of his hands and then split the opening and reached around her until his hands met in the middle of her back. He just stood holding her for what seemed the longest time.

Ellen spoke, "I take it that the phone calls didn't go well; care to fill me in?"

Ellen knows Frank and she can tell when he is ready to talk. She gently pulled his hands from behind her back and took his right hand into hers and led him over to the sofa. She pointed for him to sit, and so as not to distract him she closed her robe and covered up as much as she could in a sheer gown. Ellen said to Frank, "Talk to me, tell me what happened?"

Frank first responded about the call from the President and what has to happen. Ellen leaned back on the couch and put Frank's head in her hands, and then she placed Frank's head on her breast and put her arm around his shoulder. He continued his story about telling the team the President's order. Frank concluded, "I honestly was very surprised at how well Ted took the news. They are not totally out of it; they can watch and follow."

While Ellen held Frank she could feel tension leave his body. At the same time he raised his head to look Ellen in the eyes, his hand reached inside her gown. He caressed a good portion of her breast and said to her, "Thank you for being here and listening."

"Frank, thank you for sharing. Are you hungry?"

"Didn't we make love last night?"

She responded, "No, silly, I meant hungry for food, but now that you mention it we could have lunch at Jacaranda, see a little of Sanibel and come back here for some dessert."

"You mean you would rather have sex than go to the Bubble Room for their famous Red Velvet Cake?"

"Frank, can't we do both?"

"Anything you want."

Back in Springfield Father Tim heard the phone ring but let it go to voice mail because he is trying to have a discussion with Kristen Ridley about her pregnancy. So far she is saying nothing, but he can tell she is thinking about it. *If I tell Father Tim I want an abortion he will freak out. If Ishtar is in fact the father of my baby, then I was raped and should have an abortion. Michael's name is on the marriage certificate, so even if it was Ishtar that had sex with me then a court could nullify the marriage. What do I do with the baby in that case? I don't want to raise this baby alone even if there are social services that can assist me. I'm just not ready to accept the responsibility of raising a child. I want to take the $600,000 and move away from this town. I don't want any baggage.* She heard somebody calling her name. It got louder and louder and then she realizes Father Tim is calling her.

"Kristen, what are you thinking about?" Father Tim asked her.

"Father Tim, I think I want to get rid of the pregnancy."

Tim responded, "An abortion."

"It's my only choice."

"No, you have other choices. Don't make a decision that you will most likely regret the rest of your life."

Kristen stood, walked toward the door, and she turned to Father Tim and said, "If I don't, I don't think I will have a rest of my life."

Chapter 61

MORDECAI CALLS WITH THE TIME AND PLACE

Baker is watching the reaction of the team to Williams's announcement. Ted believes their emotions tell him if they have lost all passion for the project. *If I don't get them refocused, we could be in for a serious problem. A team that is not committed and focused will make mistakes. In this case, a mistake could blow all the work we have done to this point and jeopardize the long-term success of the mission.*

"Are you done with your, 'pity party'? This mission's far from over. The tracking ID bracelet may be the only way we can follow them for now and comply with the President's wishes. So, let me start with Hadar. Do you want to take that beautiful face and great body back to Israel and regret the rest of your life that you didn't finish the job, and turn into an empty shell of self-doubt? Megan, you took this mission for the opportunity to get a position with the CIA. If you quit now, do you think Mr. Williams will write that letter of recommendation for you?

"Omid, as a Marine, have you ever quit when people expected you to complete an assignment? John, do you want to see these bad guys in jail or dead? My point is to all of you that we all started this project together. We never thought the bad guys could win. I'm disappointed that the President has told us to back off for a while. He didn't say fold your tents and go home; he said don't arrest. Observe and keep him posted. Do you all recall that I said the President ordered us to follow the Brotherhood no matter where they went in the world? We still have a great deal of work to do, so you need to stand up and look me in the face and tell me if you're in or out. If you're out, I'll find somebody to replace you.

"Tell me now, Hadar.

"Yes."

"Megan?"

"Yes."

"Omid?"

"Yes."

"John?"

"Yes."

"Alright, let's get to work. We have a terrorist to meet. Hadar what are you going to wear?"

"Megan and I have talked about that very issue. We were thinking a pair of short shorts and tank top that falls down from the shoulder that exposes some cleavage.

Ted asked, "Megan, what are you wearing?"

"I don't think I should distract from Hadar - just kidding Hadar - probably some shorts and a form fitting top so that Mordecai can see I'm a woman, even though I'm not proportioned the way Hadar is. I want the focus on her."

"Okay, we know what the women are doing. What about you guys?"

John said, "I have a camera and I'll be taking pictures of Mordecai and Hadar so we get better images than we now have of Mordecai, and I will be backup protection for the women."

Omid said, "My role is after the meeting is over."

Suddenly Hadar has a shocked look on her face; her phone is vibrating. She looked at the screen and realized it's Mordecai. She answered. The background noise is on so it sounds like she is in the car driving. Hadar said, "Can I pull over? The traffic is noisy and I can't hear you." After a moment she came back on the phone, "How are you?"

Mordecai responded, "I'm fine. I can't wait to see you again."

Hadar responds. "Me too. Where am I going? Let me get a pencil so I can write down the address... okay, tell me where I'm going."

Mordecai said, "Where are you?"

Hadar responded, "We are about 60 miles northwest of Houston on Route 290."

Mordecai told Hadar, "Set your GPS for the Hotel Derek in downtown Houston. The address is 2525 West Loop South; I'll meet you on the corner in front of the Hotel. Please call me when your GPS says you are 15 minutes away. I'll see you probably in about an hour and by the way, what will you be wearing so I can recognize you?"

"Have you forgotten what I look like?"

"Not really. I just wanted to spend some time thinking what you will look like in the warm Houston weather."

"I don't think you'll be disappointed."

What can she be a wearing, a short skirt, low cut top? I can't wait. Mordecai responded, "I hope not; see you soon."

Hadar hung up and looked at the team, "He will be just around the corner. We have walked past their place a dozen times. How is it I have never seen him?"

The team, including Baker, walked out to the balcony to look at the meeting point and plan their positions. Baker suggested to Hadar, "What do you think about driving until you see Mordecai, and then pull up close to him and then asking him if there is a place to park close by?"

"I like that a lot, but I think Megan should be driving as I don't have an international driver's license."

"Good catch. I didn't think about that."

Omid asked Hadar, "How are you going to give Mordecai the ID bracelet?"

"My guess based on the phone conversation is he will spend much of the time until the meeting thinking about what I'm wearing, so I'm guessing he will want to get his hands on me."

Baker isn't thrilled with the idea of Mordecai's hands on Hadar's body, but he bites his lip.

Hadar continued, "After some controlled hugging and squeezing I will gently push him away and pull out the box with the ID bracelet and get him to open it. I will press him to let me put it on him. Once it's on, I will change the subject and ask how much time we have together? I will call over Megan and introduce Mordecai to her and press him again on the time."

Seacrest asked Hadar, "What if he wants to take you inside the hotel out of my visual range?"

"I will have Megan who can step in and tell me that we have to get back to school and we don't want to risk driving after curfew."

Baker asked, "What if he pressures you to go with him?"

Chapter 62

WILLIAMS DELIVERS RIDLEY

Frank Williams picks up Mike Ridley to take him to Page Field in Ft. Myers. On the way to the airport, the causeway from Sanibel is choked with traffic. Frank reached to turn on the car radio when Mike said, "Do you mind not turning that on? I have a few questions I would like to ask you."

"Not a problem." "Frank looked out the windshield and remarked, "Look at the turquoise water; isn't it beautiful?"

"The seclusion, the beaches, and the water are all part of the reasons we chose Sanibel. Frank, if I may, why did you suggest me to the President?

"Mike, initially you were not even on the radar scope; we thought you were dead. From the night you and Mary disappeared nobody could find you; it was like you were hidden behind a smoke screen. Your friends in the Logistics Office gave you great cover. It was actually one of my men, a Marine on assignment to us from the Pentagon that suggested the idea that Homeland Security might have a spy or a mole. The more we looked into what happened, the more we felt like we were being watched. At the time we didn't know that the whole Logistics Office was your cover. When we decided it was not a mole or a spy, we started asking who was being protected and one name came to the top - Mike Ridley."

"We knew that you worked for the government in some way and when we tried to look at your personnel file we were told it was sealed under Presidential order. So, Attorney General Clinton and I met with President

Jordan to get his approval to open it. The President listened to our reasoning and after serious consideration agreed that only the two of us could review the file. No copies of the contents could be made and no notes could be written down. When we were finished, the file was returned to the President and he personally resealed it and had it returned to the vaults."

"Mike, if you don't mind, I have some questions that have nothing directly to do with your file, but deal with the events that happened in your house in Springfield."

"I'll do my best to answer if I can."

"Why was the map on the wall in the basement and why were your son's fingerprints on the map?"

"Michael and I used to play a mind game. You see Michael was very smart and Mary and I were always coming up with ideas to challenge him and his brain. After the attack in 2001 on September 11th, we would look at a map of the United States and try and figure out what cities the terrorists might attack and why. As we talked about the cities, we would circle them and then move on to the next target city. Sometimes a city would be very interesting, so we would download a smaller street map of the city to try and figure out where the soft spot might be in that city."

My God, Mike Ridley was the unwilling developer of some of the target cities in the United States that the Brotherhood used. I have to warn the President before he meets with Mike.

"Mike, I was at your house the night you disappeared, why did you leave and how did you escape?"

"Well, the best I can tell you is that early in the day I got a phone call from one of my protective agents telling me that Mary and I had to leave because the agency had a report that foreign nationals were on the way to Springfield to talk with me about work. They decided that the report was not that good guys were coming but bad guys, and Mary and I had to get out that night. Our escape plan was to use the fire rescue from Texas City to extract us and get us to the most secure airport nearby and out of Springfield."

"So why did you set such a powerful bomb in the house?"

"We had very little time and we always had a destruction plan. You see we left on very short notice. In any place we stayed we had to have the ability to wipe the place clean of any DNA of Mary and myself. I had been wiring the house, but I didn't have time to make all the connections, so I used a simple clock timer, set to go off long after we were out of the house. I'm truly sorry the Deputy Sheriff was killed."

As the traffic began to move off the Sanibel causeway, they went through the tollbooth and headed down Summerlin Rd to Route 41. At the intersection of 41, Frank noticed a Lowes and a Home Depot right across from each other. "Two home stores so close; that is amazing."

"Yes, Frank. In the boom they were, I was told, doing great business but now, not so much." The car turned left and they headed toward Page Field.

As they approached the airfield, Mike asked Frank, "Do you know if President Jordan wants to talk about my son Michael?"

It took all of Frank's willpower not to hit the brakes when Mike raised the question about Michael, but he knew that he had to respond to Mikes question and yet not give Mike any indication of what the President might say. "The best and only answer I can give you is that I have no specific knowledge of what the President wants to talk to you about. I know that he wants to find the source of the money that funds the Brotherhood and other terrorists groups, but beyond that, I just don't know." *I hope he believes me.* "Mike, let me know when you return and I'll get Mary and Ellen and we'll take you to dinner." *What a stupid suggestion; would you want to go to dinner just after you have found out your son is a terrorist and responsible for killing 60,000 Americans?* "Good luck, and I'll see you when you get back."

Chapter 63

DOMESTIC LEND LEASE?

Mike Findley, the Secretary of Energy, is meeting with President Jordan with a report on the progress of expanding the construction of both pipelines. They had agreed crews at both ends would work toward the middle with two additional crews starting at the center and working outward toward the other crews. Jordan wants the pipeline done before the election. He wants to throw a switch that will start the process of sucking all the contaminated oil out of the pipelines.

Findley is ushered into the Oval Office and President Jordan stands and greets him. "Welcome, Mr. Secretary, I hope you have good news for me."

"Sir, I do. All the construction points are running and we are laying pipe in all directions 24/7. I believe that unless we have any major glitches, we will finish both pipelines very close to the election. The filling station in the Gulf of Mexico will be up and running on a limited basis in the next 30 days, again before the election. I think we will be extracting several hundreds of thousands of barrels of crude per day out of the Gulf.

"On the natural gas car conversion program, well sir, that is not going as well as it could. The problem is we have the system manufacturing and building the kits, but because of the shortage of cash and credit available, people can't buy them. I have to admit, Mr. President, I'm stuck for a solution. If we could find a way to start converting, we could build momentum, so any ideas you have would be helpful."

"So, Mr. Secretary, what you are saying is we can and we are building more units every day."

"Yes, sir."

"How many do we have on hand right now?"

"Sir, the government ordered five million units."

Jordan asked, "How many units have been installed?"

"Sir, the last count was just over 250,000."

"So, we have excess conversion kits and they are building more every day?"

"Yes, sir."

"Mike, let me ask you a question."

"Sir, I'll do my best to answer it, what is your question?"

"Will you loan me a dollar?"

"Why of course I would, Mr. President. Let me get out my wallet."

"Mike, stop for a moment; don't get out your wallet yet."

"But sir, I would be happy to lend you a dollar."

"Mr. Secretary, if you lend me a dollar, when would you expect me to pay you back?"

"Mr. President, you don't have to pay me back."

"So, as I understand it, we have millions of units just collecting dust, not really helping our people or the country, is that correct?"

"Yes, Mr. President."

"So, why don't we just give them to the American people for one dollar and they can pay us back when they start saving on fuel costs?"

Findley asked, "You want the government to do what Roosevelt did with military equipment and England before we got into World War II? We lent it to the British with terms of returning the equipment when they were done or paying a nominal amount, Lend Lease. This time we will lease the conversion kits to Americans for a future payment of one dollar.

"Mr. President, we will clear the kits in the warehouses in a week, but there is one problem. As I said before, there is a shortage of cash and credit, so while people will take the kits without being installed, all we have done is moved the inventory out of the government warehouse."

Jordan added, "We will give the companies who install the kits a tax credit; those people who can afford to pay for the installation will get the tax credit dollar for dollar for making the conversion. We add a tax on natural gas of five cents per million cubic foot to pay for the installation for those Americans who can't pay for the install."

"Mr. President, I think these ideas are fantastic, will we need Congress to approve?"

"Excellent question, you see Congress currently doesn't have enough members present to call a quorum, so I will issue an Executive Order to get it done. Congress can ratify my order when they can convene. Mr. Secretary, I want you to say nothing about this until I announce the new program in my address to the nation on Saturday, agreed?"

"Mr. President, not even my wife."

"Mike, thank you for all the progress you have made. I will look forward to seeing those warehouses being emptied in the next two weeks."

"Thank you, Mr. President, for trusting me."

Chapter 64

TIME TO MEET MORDECAI;
PROTECT YOURSELF

Baker has just asked Hadar how she would respond if Mordecai wants her to come with him to the hotel, "What are you going to do?"

Hadar replied, "That depends on where he wants to go in the hotel? If he wants to get something to eat, then I would say we have to feed Megan. If, on the other hand he wants to go to a room, then I have to assume he wants to have the sex we never had a chance to have in Syria."

Baker asked, "Would you go to the room and have sex with him?"

"It seems to me that it wasn't that long ago you were lecturing us about sex and love and in our job sometimes we may have to do things that we may not like, including having sex to get the information we want."

Baker didn't like what he was hearing from Hadar. She was saying that if it advanced the mission, she was willing to have sex with Mordecai. Ted's feelings for her were getting in the way of rationally understanding what she might have to do when he knew the right thing to do. In one respect he was proud of her; that she was willing to sacrifice her body and perhaps some of her spirit to get what the government needed. He knew that she was married before so she was not a virgin, but he was still having trouble with her having somebody else inside of her when he wanted so much, not to have sex, but for the two of them to make love. He wondered if she had sex with Mordecai would he feel differently about her?

Each member of the team had a job except Baker and so the team discussed what he should do. They felt it was best for him to observe the events from the balcony and provide feedback to Omid, John and Megan. They all decided that in the event the two of them went to a room she had to be clean; no wires, but her shoulder bag could be bugged so all could hear. Should she need help she could ask for it by a code word and the word they agreed upon was "buttons".

Megan and Hadar went down to the garage and found the car that looked like it had just come from the deserts of Arizona. As Hadar got into the car Megan noticed that Hadar had taken off her jacket. She was not wearing a bra. She said to her, "You're not wearing a bra. Why?"

"I feel freer without a bra. I want the ability to move."

Megan responded, "You're free alright and so are they, if you're not wearing a bra then neither am I. Megan looked around and could not see anybody so she took off her shirt and unhooked her bra.

She was ready to put her shirt on when Hadar said, "Nice rack."

In her earpiece Megan heard, "I agree."

Megan tried to cover her breasts with her hands while wildly scanning for Omid but not knowing where he was. Then she heard, "Get that shirt on and get out of there. We can talk about those later."

Megan threw her bra in the back seat of the car among the candy wrappers, empty soda cans and several white paper bags that held unfinished sandwiches. The outside of the car was filthy from road dirt. They pulled the car out of the garage and made a series of left hand turns. They had the windows open so their hair would look windblown. When they made the third left turn of four, a terrible stench came into the car but then quickly cleared as they continued.

Megan who was driving asked Hadar, "What was that smell?"

Hadar knew what it was; she had smelled it on the battlefields when she was in the Israeli Army. It was the smell of a human body decaying, one that had been decaying for some time. She responded to Megan, "Probably a dead dog or something."

Megan made the next left and found she was three blocks from the front of the hotel. Hadar's heart was pounding in her chest in anticipation of meeting Mordecai again. The car was about a block away when Hadar screamed, "There he is, pull over by that mailbox and I'll get out."

Megan replied, "That was not the plan; we pull up and ask for a place to park."

"You're right. Let's stay on plan." As they pulled over to the curb, all the passions from Syria reignited in Hadar's brain and parts of her body. Hadar leaned over Megan's chest to speak with Mordecai. "It is so great to see you again, where can we park?"

Mordecai recommended, "If you look one block up on the right you will see a Park 'n Lock. I'll wait here for both of you."

They drove the car and parked it but there was no attendant, so they locked the car and walked toward Mordecai. He could see the two of them coming and it reminded him the first time Hadar walked across the village square, only this time there were no buttons; just four nipples pushing through the snug fitting shirts. As the two of them got closer, Mordecai could see both sets of breasts bouncing, he audibly said to himself, "What a sight." As Hadar got closer, Mordecai decided to run up to her; when he got very close he stopped and took her into his arms and crushed her into him. He had not held or even a touched a woman in many months and having her next to him felt wonderful.

He separated slightly from her and then gave her a very passionate kiss. When they parted, she felt his hand squeezing her breast. He said softly to her, "I missed you." As they slowly came apart, Hadar felt his hand on her, it was almost as if she was detached to the physical things that were going on. She thought, *it's not the same as in Syria. I don't feel the same passion I did when we first met. Nevertheless, I can do whatever is called for to do my job. In the case of Mordecai, I'll do whatever I need to do to capture the Brotherhood.*

Chapter 65

MIKE RIDLEY COMES TO TOWN

The cabin attendant announced, "We will be landing in about one hour. Would you like something to eat or drink?"

Mike responded, "Could I have a J&B on the rocks?"

"Right away, sir." Mike is trying to figure out how he can help the government, but he does not know any detail of the assignment. *All I know for now is that the President wants me to help him find the source of the money that is funding the Brotherhood of the Red Nile and perhaps other terrorist groups, that's it. I liked Frank Williams, and his wife Ellen is a stunner; both would be great assets to Sanibel.* Mike fell asleep, relaxed by the drink.

The attendant lightly touched his shoulder and said, "We will be landing in about ten minutes. Please make sure your seatbelt is buckled; we do need to raise your headrest before landing."

Mike made all the adjustments and a few moments later they were on the ground at Andrews. The plane pulled over in front of hanger 22 and parked. The steps were lowered from inside the plane and Mike walked down the steps to a waiting car. The driver asked, "Are you Mr. Ridley? Do you have ID?"

Mike showed his passport and then asked the driver, "Do you have ID?" The driver pulled out his government ID. Mike looked at it and said, "That's fine, let's go."

The driver opened the door and offered to take Mike's bag, but Mike responded, "Thank you, but I prefer to carry this myself."

As the car sped through Andrews, the sights brought back many memories for Mike. In an effort to make small talk the driver asked, "Do you get to DC very often?"

Mike responds, "I haven't been here in 20 years."

"If you don't mind, I will alert the White House we are on the way."

"Go right ahead, give them a call." After about 30 minutes, the car stopped at the first of two-security gate checkpoints. The guard asked to see both of their IDs and then passed them to the next checkpoint. At this checkpoint, both men were asked to get out of the car and were asked for their IDs. A bomb-sniffing dog was brought in to check the car. One guard used a rather large mirror on the end of a pole to search the bottom of the car for bombs. Everything was declared clean, and the driver was told to follow the driveway to the left where they will be met by Mr. Ridley's escort for meeting the President.

The car proceeded slowly around to the left of the White House and looking ahead, Mike could see somebody waiting at the entrance steps. The car stopped and the person opened the door and asked Mike to step out.

"Would you please show your ID?" Mike pulled out his passport for the third time and presented it to the escort. "Thank you, Mr. Ridley. I will take you to meet the President." The two of them walked into the main lobby of the West Wing. Mike began to think about his first visit to the Oval Office many years ago when Lyndon Johnson hired him. Not much has changed except there are a great many more people than when he first came to the White House. The two men snaked their way through the building and finally come to a door and two fully armed Marines. Simple letters on the door said, Oval Office.

"This is where I leave you. When you are done, Ms. Washington will call for me and I will escort you back to your car."

Mike opened the door and walked into a small waiting room with a guard at the desk. The guard asked his name and wanted to see his ID. When they were finished, he pushed a button and the door unlocked. He was told to go in to the next room. He is now in the office of the first executive assistant to the President, Ms. Mary Washington. "Mr. Ridley, I will let the President know that you're here. Please be seated; he won't be long."

Mike sat down and in just a few moments the door opened and Nathan Jordan, the President of the United States, walked out, extended his hand and asked him to join him in the Oval Office.

Mike let the President lead the way; he invited Mike to sit on the couch across from him. Jordan opened the conversation, "Mr. Ridley, it is my understanding that you have sat on that couch before."

"Sir, if you wouldn't mind, could you call me Mike, and to answer your question I have sat here across from several presidents."

"Would you like something to drink?"

"Water would be fine, Sir." Jordan buzzed Mary and asked her to bring in some bottles of cold water. Mary walked through the door, set two bottles on the table with two glasses of ice. She left two extras on the table and quickly departed.

"Mike, I know we spent some time on the phone, but we didn't discuss a lot of particulars. With technology today, no matter how much you try to protect your conversation a lot of people are trying to listen into what is being said. Let me ask you a question. Are you familiar with a terrorist group known as the Brotherhood of the Red Nile?"

"Sir, I believe they were the group that took credit for using the two nukes against us."

"You are correct. This group like many others around the world has no means of support, so they must depend on governments or other organizations for funding. I want to use proof of the funding of the Brotherhood as a means to force the rest of the world to help us to break the back of those funding organizations, and by doing so destroy terrorism. We believe that the funding for the Brotherhood was not from a nation state but from one person."

"Do you know who that person is Mr. President?"

"Yes, we do, and we think based on past records, you do too."

Chapter 66

ON THE STREETS OF HOUSTON

Hadar and Mordecai were still in each other's arms and neither was paying any attention to Megan. She cleared her throat several times and neither of them looked at her. She finally stepped in and introduced herself to Mordecai. "I'm Megan Brown. I'm Hadar's roommate at school. I did all the driving to get you two together."

Mordecai released Hadar from his grip and extended his hand to welcome her. "Is this your first trip to Houston?"

"It's my first trip to Texas, and I have to tell you I'm a little nervous with all that contaminated oil running under our feet."

Mordecai then focused all of his attention on Megan to try and reassure her that she is safe and that the contaminated oil is hundreds of feet below. Mordecai had been so focused on Hadar he had not noticed what a looker Megan really is. She is built different than Hadar, but she is still striking. Hadar brought the focus back on her by asking Mordecai, "How much time do you have to spend with us today?"

Seacrest was snapping pictures of the hotel and other buildings and planned to snap a picture of the three of them. Finally, he had an idea; he walked over to the three of them and said. "I don't know who you are sir, but you have two of the most striking women I have seen in a long time. Do you mind if I take a few snaps of the three of you? I won't be long."

The two women said, "Can we have a copy of the photos?"

Seacrest asked Mordecai, "Would that be all right with you sir? By the way, what are your names?"

Mordecai asked, "Can we just give you our first names?"

John replied, "Sure, but I'll need an address for somebody to send the prints to."

Hadar spoke up. "I will give you my address at school later."

John asked them to line up near the fountain. He wanted Mordecai to hold each girl around the waist and to pull both girls in to him. He told the girls, "Put your inside arm on his shoulder and turn your bodies slightly into Mordecai so we can get a great shot of those profiles." John took a few snaps and then shot a few focusing on Mordecai's face. "Done and thank you very much."

Hadar asked, "Could we see what you got?"

John has to think quickly, "I'm sorry this is my old camera; it shoots film. You promised to give me an address to send the copies of the photos to, so what is the address?"

Hadar asked, "Do you have something to write on?" He does, so she writes down a fictitious address back in Arizona.

Megan asks, "How long before we will get them?"

"I have no idea with mail service so screwed up, but I will process them tonight. I need to take more shots of the buildings, so thanks for your help and enjoy your stay."

Hadar went back to the question she was asking before Seacrest came over to take pictures. She looked at her watch. "Mordecai how much time do you have?"

Mordecai looked at his watch and he knew that he had to be back at the Brotherhood in less than twenty minutes or they would come looking for him. He responded to Hadar's question, "Just a few minutes."

Hadar pouted, "You are always leaving me. How long before I can see you again?"

"I don't know. I told you I'm leaving America soon."

"How soon?"

"Could be a couple of days or a few weeks, I just don't know."

Hadar reached into her pocket and pulled out a gift box with a crumpled ribbon around it. She handed it to Mordecai and said, "Then wear this and remember me."

Mordecai opened the box and finds the ID bracelet with his name engraved on it and Hadar's just below his. "This is too much; I can't accept this gift."

Hadar responded with a smile on her face, "Unless you know another Mordecai and a Hadar then it is pretty much worthless. You'll just have to wear it. She took it from him and put it on his wrist. "It looks great. Will you promise me that you will wear this until we meet again?"

"Yes, I will." But he is thinking, *how am I going to explain this to the brothers? I know, I'll tell them that I got it from Hadar in Syria and I just remembered I had it in my bag because I took it off while I was working on the bomb, and I decided I needed to put it on to think about her. That will work.*

Mordecai looked into Hadar's eyes. Megan saw that time is running out and she stepped away so the two of them could be alone.

Mordecai lamented, "I wish I had more time. I can't tell you how many times I have thought about making love to you, and I truly hoped that we would have had time at this meeting to explore each other's bodies. But it was not meant to be, which makes it harder to leave."

"We can still keep in contact by phone and text can't we? And, when you get settled, can I come and be with you?"

Mordecai quickly responded, "YES and YES."

Mordecai took Hadar into his arms and held her tight. He gently moved his hand around, gently caressed her breast and at the same time gave her a deep kiss. He increased his hand pressure and then he was gone. Hadar felt like this may be the last time she will see him and this was his strong, final kiss.

Megan asked Omid and Baker, "Do you have him?"

Chapter 67

MIKE AND NATHAN EXCHANGE
DIFFICULT QUESTIONS

"Mike, we think that an old friend of yours, Viktor Antipova, may be the source of the funding for the Brotherhood and other terrorist groups. If my information is correct, your house in Springfield is owned by Antipova."

"Yes. That is true. We met in Afghanistan and struck up a casual relationship."

"Did that relationship blossom?"

"You could say that we became better friends. He knew that I was leaving the country and he had a house in Springfield as a safe house should he have to leave Russia. He offered it to me, so I said, 'A free house, an extended stay, why not?' I took him up on his offer. I never expected that it would be over 20 years and that Viktor would become one of the wealthiest men in the world."

"Mike, do you remember the last time you spoke with Viktor?"

"Sir, to the best of my recollection it was in Afghanistan."

"So, you lived in the same house for 23 years and never heard from the owner?"

"Sir, my guess is with all of his wealth he has probably forgotten about that safe house in Springfield, Texas."

Jordan offered, "The best we can tell, one of his companies has been paying the taxes on the property for the last 23 years. Were you ever contacted by anybody connected with Antipova during that time?"

"No."

"Mike, what if I told you that I need you to prove beyond a shadow of a doubt that Viktor Antipova was the money behind the attack - not only on the United States, but also the funding source for other terrorist groups. Could you do the job?"

"Sir, what resources would be available to me?"

Jordan offered, "You name it, you got it. But let me caution you, the larger your group, the greater the risk of a leak. If Viktor finds out that we are after him, he will just disappear."

"I understand what you are saying, but the Viktor I know will want to stay and challenge anybody who comes after him. He will want to prove he is the best in the world. And I understand your concern about secrecy and I agree. Let me ask: you would you be comfortable if the team operated outside the United States?"

"I must admit I hadn't thought about it; do you think working outside America will improve your ability to catch him?"

"Sir, what I'm thinking about is setting up an operation that will compete with Viktor's companies. It will make inroads with the terrorist organizations Viktor is supporting. Mr. President, this new group will need a lot of money to operate. Can I get it?"

"I can fund it; that should not be a problem."

"What happens, Mr. President, if you are not reelected in November?"

"I can't promise that a new president will continue to fund your group, but if I'm reelected, the funding will continue."

"Mr. President, can you tell me about the Brotherhood of the Red Nile?"

"What do you want to know?"

"Who is the leadership and who are the major members?"

Jordan began to name the players. "The leader is a Syrian named Mohammad el Sargon. There is an Israeli, Mordecai Hagel, who is their nuclear scientist..."

"Wait a moment, sir. Did you say an Israeli?"

"Yes, I did. His expertise in nuclear science; he is an MIT graduate."

"Wow, things have changed... an Israeli working with Arabs."

Jordan continued, "Next we have a Syrian, Adad Al Assad, also an MIT graduate in computer science. Then we have Cyrus Jaiari, an Iranian, who is a London School of Economics graduate. Next we have someone very interesting to you; his name is Oleg Barbolio. He is a graduate petroleum engineer from Stanford and he is the nephew of Viktor Antipova. There are two younger latecomers to the Brotherhood; they are twin brothers, including Al Ishtar Hamwi."

"And the other?"

Jordan stopped short, but he knows that if he is asked he must tell him the other brother's name. Mike asked the name of the other twin. "Mike, before I answer that question you must understand we have not verified that we are correct. We have many resources trying to verify what I'm about to tell you. We believe the other twin's name is Michael Ridley."

"My son?"

"Yes. We believe it is your son."

Mike slumped down on the couch as if he were hit with a massive hammer. "Are you sure?"

"We know that Michael and Ishtar are twins. We checked fingerprints from the map removed from your basement before the house exploded… Mike, do you want to take a break?"

"No, keep going."

"Our research shows that Michael went west to go to the University of California at Berkeley, but never went to class, ever. The best we can determine, he was intercepted by his twin, Ishtar, and was taken into Ishtar's illegal business. We know that he has a bank account in Springfield with over $600,000 which he has signed over to his wife…"

"HIS WIFE!"

"Yes, he was married to Kristen Murphy about four months ago."

"When will this nightmare end?"

"Mike, you must clearly understand that if you take this assignment you may well be signing the death warrant of your son Michael."

Chapter 68

WHAT NEXT FOR THE PATHFINDERS?

Megan looked around for Seacrest and Rahimi, but she couldn't find them; they had not returned her request for contact. As she turned back toward Hadar, she saw her sitting on a bench with her head in her hands; she sounded like she was crying. Megan sat down beside her and put her arm around her as if to comfort her. "Are you okay?"

Hadar responded, "I'm fine, except I'm going to have some very sore breasts in the morning. I let Mordecai fondle me as much as he wanted and he had a very strong grip. I can't be sure if he was more interested in feeling my breasts or was he trying to tell if I was wearing a wire. You may recall there was a lot of me to fondle."

"Yes, that is very true. My guess is he wasn't feeling for a wire, but still, why are you crying?"

"I don't know if the other members of the Brotherhood are around and could be watching me and trying to tell my reaction. If I had feelings for Mordecai and had just driven two days to see him, would I just kiss him goodbye and be on my way?"

"Excellent work; how about we walk back to the car and I will keep my arm around you and you can lean your head on my shoulder as we walk back to the car. When we pull out of the garage you keep your head down but still visible from the car. We want to be careful to check to see if we are being followed; when we think the coast is clear, then you can relax. I did notice a 7-11 near the parking lot; do you want to stop and get some ice for your breasts?"

"Yes. I think a five pound bag of ice and a large bottle of Advil would work."

The two of them started walking, and as instructed, Hadar put her head down on Megan's shoulder. Megan asked Omid and John their location. She told them that they were stopping at the 7-11 and then headed for the car. She asked John to meet them at the safe house. Megan asked Omid, "Do you still have him?"

"Yes, he is several blocks from your position and went into a building number 101. I have a strong signal from the ID bracelet and he has stopped on the fifteenth floor. Before I return, I want to make sure I have a backup and that we can provide 24-hour coverage until they leave. I will let you know when I'm heading back to base."

Megan asked, "Ted are you on the line?"

Baker responded, "I have been monitoring all the traffic. I will contact Williams and request a team that can track Mordecai until he departs. I will call him right away and I hope to have an answer when you return to base."

"John, are you there?" Megan asked several times, but received no response from John. "Omid, did you see what happened to John?"

Omid responded, "The last time I saw him he was turning down a side street and I lost contact with him. I couldn't follow John and Mordecai, and I chose Mordecai. As soon as I get a replacement, I will go look for John and we will both join you at the safe house."

Megan responded, "I'm sending one of the Langley communications teammates to join Omid. Let me know when he arrives and then head on back."

"Roger that."

John Seacrest completed his assignment and must have taken 60 pictures of Mordecai. He started to head back to the safe house when he got a whiff of a strange smell in the air. Like Hadar, he had experienced that smell once before on a battlefield in Iraq. He knew that a body had been decaying for some time and that body was close. John was curious, but he could hear Megan's repeated calls and he thought, *I had better get back to the things at hand and return her call. If I have some time in the next few days I might come back and see whose body is decaying.* "I'm here. I must have been out of range; what do you need?"

Megan replied in a stern voice, "I need your ass and your camera at the safe house right now. Do you read me?"

"Yes, ma'am, right away."

"If you get there before me, I want a series of images of Mordecai given to Baker. He'll send them on to Williams so we can find out more about this guy."

Baker responded, "I'll contact Williams and let him know that the images will be on his computer within the hour."

Chapter 69

MIKE RIDLEY PROCESSES
THE BOMBSHELL

The President has just told Mike Ridley three things he didn't know. His son has a twin brother, Michael may be married, and lastly, Michael may be one of the terrorists that bombed the United States with nuclear bombs. It is almost too much for this seasoned Special Ops operative to accept and deal with. "Mr. President, before we continue, could we take a break and let me try to get my arms around all that you have just told me? Maybe we could recess for about ten minutes?"

Jordan responded, "We can take as much time as you need; I realize this must be overwhelming. Why don't you take a walk around the Rose Garden? Call Mary when you are ready to talk to me again."

"Thank you, Mr. President; I will try to be quick about it."

"Mike, I've laid a lot on you; please take the time you need to process all this information."

"Thank you, sir, for the time and the use of the Rose Garden. I must admit that I have never been in the Rose Garden before; I hear it is beautiful."

"Not a problem, I'll get Mary to escort you there. Take your time and call me one way or the other as soon as you can. Mike, on behalf of a grateful nation, thank you for your great service, and for risking your life for your country. Whatever the outcome, I thank you for all that you have done for your country, now go clear your head and smell those beautiful roses." Nathan got up and escorted Mike to Mary's office and requested that she show Mr. Ridley to the Rose Garden.

Mary responds, "Right away, sir?"

"Yes, Mary. Right now."

Mary and Mike walked down a hallway together and she stopped at a double glass door that led to the colonnade. They walked for a short distance and Mary pointed out a bench were Mike could sit and think. "If you want to make a phone call, the green box on the side of the bench is a secure phone. You might want to use it because the signal from certain cell phones is blocked. When you are ready to talk with the President just dial double zero and it will come straight to me. Is there anything more I can do for you, Mr. Ridley?"

"Not right now. Thank you so much."

Mary Washington left and he watched her go through the door and it closed slowly. Mike waited for it to shut completely and then began to focus on all the information the President has dropped on him in the last hour. His son has a twin brother, his son may be married to a girl back in Springfield, and Michael may be one of the terrorists who used nuclear bombs against the United States. The President wants me to trace the flow of money feeding not only the Brotherhood, but also expose an entire network of money flowing to terrorist groups.

I think I need to call Mary and tell her what I just found out and then I can concentrate on what the President wants me to do. Mike looked down at the end of the green slatted park bench and saw a green box with a latch but no lock. He opened the latch and pulled the box open. He saw the wireless phone and took it out of the box and dialed Mary in Sanibel. After a few rings, Mary answered, "Who is this?" Mary's phone can't see that it is Mike calling – just that the White House is calling.

"Mary, its Mike. I'm calling from the White House Rose Garden.

"I just met with the President and he told me things that I just can't believe." Mike told Mary everything, including the possibility that Michael is one of the terrorists that bombed America.

When Mary got over her shock, she asked, "Does the President want you to find our son?"

"I have to go back and meet with the President in a little while. I will learn the answer to your question, but for now he has not asked me to find any terrorists. He wants me to investigate the flow of money and follow it to the source.

"Mary, did you know anything about a twin brother for Michael?"

"Mike, I was never told that Michael had a twin. Do we know his name? Is he one of the terrorists, too?"

"I don't know. I just find it hard to believe that Michael is in the Brotherhood. What do I do if the President wants me to find the Brotherhood and Michael?"

"You have not made a commitment to the President on this assignment, have you?"

"No, I wanted to talk with you before I go back and meet with the President. Mary, is it possible that for some reason our son may have been in some way responsible for the death of 60,000 innocent Americans? I have to take this assignment, if for no other reason than to learn why he would do such a thing. If possible, I'll look for an opportunity to capture Michael. If I catch him, he must pay the price for what he has done even if he is our son; do you agree?"

After a long pause with the sound of crying coming over the phone Mary responded, "Find him and protect our son."

Chapter 70

FRANK REFOCUSES

Frank has had no contact with the White House or The Pathfinder team in Houston. He had left a voice message with Ted Baker to call, but there was no return call yet. He decided to take Ellen to lunch at what is turning out to be their favorite restaurant, Jacaranda on Periwinkle Rd. Frank called ahead for a reservation.

When they arrived the hostess greeted them by name, "Welcome back, Mr. and Mrs. Williams, are you eating inside or outside?"

Frank responded, "It's a nice day." He turned to Ellen and asked, "How about outside today?"

Ellen agreed with the suggestion and with the hostess in the lead, they moved to the garden room where it is quiet. Not many people are in the restaurant at the moment.

They both studied the menu and decided to have an iceberg wedge salad. Frank ordered a glass of the house chardonnay for both of them. The server brought the wine and they clinked glasses to a beautiful place.

Ellen said, "Sanibel is everything the brochure said and more; I could come back for our 25th."

Frank reached out with his right hand and took Ellen's right hand in his. "Could you retire here on Sanibel?"

Ellen responded, "I don't know. That is a few years away, but it is something to think about."

"But what if it wasn't a few years away, but a matter of months?"

"Frank, are you saying you want to retire now? Can we afford to retire at such a young age? What would you do? For that matter, what would I do?"

Frank responded, "I have been thinking and playing with some numbers. The way I figure it, we both have enough years in to qualify for our pensions. We could sell the house in DC and buy a small house or a condo here on Sanibel."

Ellen tightened her grip on Frank's hand and asked, "Okay, what is going on; we have yet to have a discussion about retirement. I know this is a beautiful place, but are you running away from something back in DC?"

"Ellen, the issue is, I'm here on this beautiful island with the most stunning woman on the island and people who work for me are working without me. I feel like I have outlived my usefulness and I need to move on."

Ellen was stunned at what she heard from Frank and wasn't sure how she should react. *Frank is a young man with an incredible amount of experience and has a great deal to give to the people. I understand he feels like for the first time in this crisis he is out of the loop. I have to find a way to get him refocused. This time sex will not do it; I have to find a different way to snap him out of this funk.*

Ellen pulled on Frank's hand to get his attention. "Look at me Frank. Someday we may well retire to Sanibel, BUT NOT NOW. I have work to finish and so do you. Did the President suggest that if Mike Ridley takes the assignment that he wants Mike to report to you?"

"Yes, he did."

"So, if you walk, who is the President going to assign? Don't give me the crap that no one is irreplaceable, because some people are, and I believe you are the best at what you do. Mike Ridley will have a much better chance of succeeding if he has you and your talent and ability in his corner. So your job is far from finished, and you are not washed up. The President has great confidence in you and if Mike takes the assignment, my guess is that you and Mike will want to spend a great deal of time together before you leave this island."

Frank listened very carefully to what Ellen said to him and the more she talked, the better he felt. It is the first time in almost 25 years of marriage that Ellen has ever chewed him out. He saw in Ellen a passion that he had never seen, a confidence in knowing that she is right, and a concern about him and their relationship. Finally Ellen asks, "Do you have Mike Ridley's phone number?"

"Yes, why?"

"I want you to call him and encourage him to take the assignment from the President. You need to stress to him that you look forward to perhaps the most difficult assignment you, and perhaps he, has ever undertaken, and together if you succeed you can make America, and the world, a safer place."

Frank asked Ellen, "Are you finished? Oh, and by the way did you ever coach football for Ohio State? I never had a pep talk like the one you just gave me! Thank you for your support and encouragement. I'm going to go outside and call Mike right now. When I finish, we are going back to the Tween Waters Inn and I'm going to get 'tween you."

Frank stood up and went to the parking lot to call Mike Ridley on his cell phone. He decided to call Mary Washington to see if the meeting between the President and Mike was still going on and tell her he wants to speak with Mike. He dialed Mary's number and she answered. Mike told her who was calling and he wanted to know if they were still in the meeting.

Mary responded, "They have taken a break and Mike is in the Rose Garden thinking about all that the President has shared with him. In a while they plan to get back together."

"Mary, can you patch me through to Mike on the Rose Garden Phone?"

"I'll try."

Mike heard the phone ringing in the box; he picked it up and answered, "Mike Ridley."

"Mr. Ridley, please stand by for Mr. Frank Williams. Go ahead, Mr. Williams."

"Mike, before you go back into your meeting with the President, let me give you two things to think about. First, I truly believe that you are the best, and in fact the only man, to do this job. Second, I will do everything in my power to make sure that Michael is safe. If we capture him, he will have to pay the consequences of his actions, but I promise you, Michael will not be killed by us."

Mary interrupted, "Excuse me, Mr. Ridley, but the President wants to know when you might be ready to talk?"

"Ms. Washington, tell the President NOW. Thanks, Frank. Together we can do this."

Chapter 71

BACK IN THE SAFE HOUSE...NOW WHAT?

The team, including Baker, assembled in the living room of the safe house awaiting orders for the next step. Ted opened the conversation by asking Hadar how she felt about her encounter with Mordecai.

Hadar responded, "It wasn't anything like I expected it to be. The passion of the moment in Syria wasn't there today, at least on my part. I don't think Mordecai has changed. What he wanted was to get me in bed and that didn't happen. I'm not sure I would have let it happen for the good of the team. In some respects, I felt like I was being mugged the way he attacked my body."

Baker asked, "Is the ice helping?"

"Yes, thank you. My greatest disappointment was that we didn't learn anything about their plans. We don't know when they are leaving or where they are going."

Omid responded to Hadar's comments. "I know he roughed you up a little, but you must remember that you got the ID bracelet on his wrist. It has both of your names on it so it will be very difficult for him to take it off. As long as he is wearing it, he'll be thinking of you and we can track him."

Back at the White House, Frank Williams had just hung up with Mike Ridley and he urgently asked Mary Washington to speak with the President *before* he speaks with Mike Ridley. "Mary, it is very important."

"I will ask the President if he can speak with you."

A moment later Nathan Jordan was on the phone with Williams. "What's your idea?"

"First, Mr. President, thank you so much for taking my call."

"Frank, if you got an idea that will swing Mike Ridley, I'm all ears."

"Mr. President, you asked my Pathfinder team to stand down and not capture the Brotherhood."

"Yes, that's correct."

"I'm sure you have a reason; you do not have to justify it to me or anybody."

"Go on."

"You have assigned Mike Ridley to report to me and indirectly to you; he is going to need resources to assist him on his assignment."

Jordan responded, "I have already told him that I would give him anything he needs to get the job done."

"Sir, I understand your commitment to the project, so my idea is to have my Pathfinders work with and for Mike Ridley. My team knows more about the Brotherhood of the Red Nile than anybody else in the world. I think they would be excellent assets for Mike." Frank waited for a reaction from the President; no sound is coming from the other end. Finally Frank asked, "Mr. President, are you there?"

"Yes, Frank I'm here; I was just thinking about your idea. I think it is a great idea. It may just tip the balance in Mike's mind to take the assignment. I will talk to him about it and I'll let you know so you can notify your team."

"Thank you, Mr. President."

"No, Frank. Let me thank you for such a brilliant idea."

"Good luck, Mr. President."

"Goodbye, Frank. I will be in touch with in the next few hours."

Back in Houston, Megan asked Baker, "We don't need all of us in Houston to follow a signal; can't John's operation in Langley follow it on a computer?"

Before Ted could answer, John jumped in and said, "We can follow Mordecai, but we can't follow the rest of the Brotherhood, and for now we don't know for sure how many others are in the Brotherhood. We can track Mordecai with the signal from the bracelet, but we need bodies on the ground to figure out how many members of the Brotherhood there are in that building. It may not be all of us, but we clearly need observers along with somebody or something monitoring the ID bracelet. Wouldn't you agree, Ted?"

"I agree, John that we need observation teams and signal trackers in Langley, but at the moment I don't know how many bodies we need here in Houston. It seems to me that we have to rotate a lot of people through here. I think we need to get into the building and establish a listening post. Some of those people can pose as returnees, while others have to be transients. We do not want to spook the Brotherhood by constantly having the same people and faces. John, I think we have to keep this building and the Brotherhood under 24/7 surveillance. So that would mean probably six people per shift, three shifts a day, seven days a week. We would have 21 shifts per week, at six people per shift, working five days a week. We need about 126 people and one-third should rotate out every two weeks."

Megan was just sitting there listening to the numbers and people and rotation of personnel. She began to think, *that is a lot of people to manage on a classified basis. We can't put them in this safe house; we have to find a place where we can house and feed them that is secure and continues the talk. The process of building a pool of people that we can trust will take time. Who will screen candidates? As we expand the people necessary to do the job we risk a leak, and a leak could be devastating to the mission and could cost lives. Can we lock it down and keep it locked for a long time, perhaps years? There has to be an alternative. I need to talk with Omid about a few things, including this issue.*

Chapter 72

MIKE AND THE PRESIDENT MEET AGAIN

Mike Ridley has come to a conclusion, but he needs some answers from the President before his final decision. Before Mike leaves the Rose garden, he stops and just looks around at this beautiful place. He can understand why a President might come here to think about serious issues. Mike reaches for the door handle and a Marine opens the door for him.

Once inside the Marine said, "Sir, I'm here to escort you back to the Oval Office. Please follow me." They walked down the hallway with windows that look out on the colonnade and the Rose Garden. They walked farther, and then made a sharp left turn and down another hallway past a series of heavily armed Marines. They stopped just before they arrived at the Oval Office. Mike's Marine escort opened the door to Mary Washington's office and invited Mike to go in and sit on the couch.

Mary told Mike the President would be with him shortly; she asked if Mike would like anything else to drink?

Mike responded, "Thank you, I could use some ice water if you have some."

Mary saw the message light flashing on her desk; it was a signal, a message from the President to send in Mike. "The President will see you now, please go right in."

The President extended his hand to Mike and asked him to sit down.

"Mr. President, I have a few questions if you don't mind. I have had to absorb a great deal in a very short time. I spoke with Mary and to say that she was shocked about Michael would be a gross understatement. So, let me start off by asking you, will part of my job be to capture the Brotherhood, including Michael?"

"Mike, I have wrestled with that question for many hours wondering if I were in your position what would I do, and I would have asked the President the same question. The best I can tell you at the moment is that capturing the Brotherhood is not a primary part of your mission. When the time comes that we want to capture them, I will give you a choice to participate or not."

"You said that you would do everything in your power to help me, but should you not be reelected, you could not bind the incoming President to continue to pursue the money. What would happen to my work and my son?"

"I would meet with the new President and explain the program to him and the need to keep you supported, but it will be his choice to continue or not. As to your son, if I continue to be President, I think at some point he will have to be captured and brought to justice. I can assure you he will get a fair trial, but regardless of the verdict, I cannot issue a pardon. If your son is helpful in the collection of information regarding the other members, then we could talk about a reduced sentence. He may have been complicit in the death of tens of thousands of Americans and he will have to pay for his crime."

"Thank you, Mr. President. I think you have been extremely honest and fair. I wish he was not involved, but if he was and is found guilty, he must be responsible for his actions. Both Mary and I agree that, as hard as it is, he has to be held responsible. If I may, I would like to move on to the money. As I understand it, you believe for some reason that my old friend Viktor Antipova is the source of funding for the Brotherhood and perhaps other terrorists groups as well?"

"Mike, we believe that Viktor is not only the source of funding for the Brotherhood, but many other terrorist groups. He is not alone. We also believe that other oil rich Middle Eastern countries and super wealthy people are funding terrorists groups on a global basis. We don't think there is a network of funding agents, but there may well be such a loosely knit group providing the funding. We just don't know. We need you to find out and bring me the evidence that I can bring to the UN, the press, and other governments all over the world. If you are successful, we can stop the flow of money to the terrorists and in turn make the world a safer place. Mike, I don't want to sound as if I'm giving a Sunday sermon; I just feel so strongly that if we can stop the flow of money we can make real change."

"In some respects, Mr. President, I like your passion and your commitment to bring about real change, but I wonder if I'm the right person to help you?"

Jordan countered, "It is important for you to understand that I don't expect that you will accomplish this mission totally on your own. You are going to need help and I have been thinking about having you report your work to Frank Williams and me. I want you to have as much freedom as you want, but also the resources you will need to get things done.

"We have a special unit in Homeland Security under Frank call the Pathfinders. They have been responsible for tracking down the Brotherhood, and they have found them. I had them stand down on their capture until I had a chance to talk with you. Williams called me while you were in the Rose Garden and suggested that he reassign the Pathfinders to your direct control if you decide to take this mission. I don't know of anyone in the world who knows more about the Brotherhood and I think they can carry out any assignment you can give them."

"Mr. President, if I take the job, how soon before I could meet with them?"

"Mike, if you take the assignment, I will have them on a plane to Ft. Myers in two hours."

"If I may, Mr. President, one more question, perhaps two."

"Shoot."

"How will we be funded?"

"Your operating budget will come from the Logistics Office of Homeland Security; whatever you need you just tell Frank and he will get it for you. What is your last question?"

"Sir, my last question is reporting; what access will I have to you and Mr. Williams?"

"Mike, I expect in the beginning that not much will happen, but when there is progress I want updates. I will give you secure server access so you can send reports directly to my desk computer. If at any time you need to talk with me or you want to see me, you call Ms. Washington and she will arrange the time. If you need me, you've got me, understood?"

"Yes, sir."

"Mike, do we have a deal?"

"Yes, sir, I'll do my best and will try not to disappoint you."

"Mike, your best is more than I can hope for, and on behalf of a grateful nation, thank you."

The President stood up, reached out to Mike and gave him a big hug and whispered in his ear, "Thank you again."

As they walked through the doorway, Nathan said to Mary, "Get me Frank Williams on the phone right away."

"Yes, Mr. President, right away."

Chapter 73

MEGAN AND OMID FINALLY TALK

The meeting in the safe house was breaking up and Megan thought, *now is as good as any time to have a discussion with Omid about what is going on between us.* She got up from the couch and walked over to Omid and said "Are you up for a walk?"

Omid looked at Megan and said, "Anytime."

"How about now?"

"Let's go." The two walked out the front door and nobody seemed to notice that they were leaving. They walked across the hallway and Omid pushed the elevator down button. They stood in front of the door waiting for it to open. Neither said anything.

The bell rang indicating that the elevator arrived; the doors will open shortly. As the doors opened, Omid invited Megan to go into the elevator first. He looked around and saw nobody in the car. Megan pushed the button for the first floor and as soon as her hand pulled back from the button, Omid gently took her hand and turned her to face him. As the doors closed, Omid took her into his arms and gave her a firm kiss. Initially, Megan resisted slightly, but all the pent up, unresolved feelings for Omid came to the surface and she returned his kiss even more passionately.

As the elevator slowly descended toward the main floor the intensity of their passion increased. It was almost as if the falling elevator pushed their passion up to the surface from deep within both of them. Omid opened one eye and looked at the floor indicator that displayed the number of each floor as they passed by. He noticed that the lobby is the next stop. Omid slowly separated himself from Megan and softly said to her, "The lobby is next."

Megan stepped back and checked her appearance in her reflection in the polished elevator doors.

The doors opened and Omid, still with no words, pointed the way out and then followed her out of the elevator. After they cleared the elevator doors, they headed to the exit door out of the building. Megan stopped about halfway to the door and turned to Omid and said, "We have to talk. Before we leave the building, I want to let Ted know we will be away for about an hour; if he needs anything just to call me. Megan types the text message and sent it to Baker.

Omid responded, "I agree. Let's go outside and look for a bench."

With no conversation, the two walked out the front door of the building and onto the sidewalk. Not many people are in Houston, so the sidewalk is mostly empty. They started walking down the main street and came to an intersection. Omid spoke up. "I know this place not too far from here; it has a little park were we can sit and figure things out." At that moment, Omid slid his hand into hers and she grabbed it firmly. When their hands came together, their pace quickened as if they were racing to get to the park bench before anybody would take their spot.

In just a few moments, they turned the corner and there was the park and nobody was in it – at least for the moment. They ran over and staked a claim on one of the benches in the back of the park. Omid and Megan sat down and took a couple of breaths. They turned to look at each other and realized that they had turned at the same time. Megan looked at Omid and asked. "What just happened in the elevator?"

Omid, with a little smile on his face said, "I don't know what would have happened in that elevator if we would have had ten more floors, but I would suspect something very interesting."

He continued, "I think there has been a suppressed physical attraction that has been there for a long while and being alone for the first time just gave both of us the opportunity to release those repressed feelings for each other, does that make sense?"

For a moment Megan didn't say anything; she just sat on the bench with her hand firmly in the grasp of Omid and she knew that she didn't want to let go of him anytime soon.

★★★

Back in the Oval Office, Nathan Jordan was in a phone conversation with Frank Williams and they were discussing the meeting between Mike and the President. "Frank, Mike wants to take the assignment and he also wants to work with you and your Pathfinders. I told him they could be on the way to Sanibel in two hours. Mike has already left for Andrews and should be at Page Field just before the team leaves Houston."

"Mr. President, I will round them up and get them on a plane to Sanibel."

"Frank, I can't tell you how excited I am to have Mike working on this assignment. I don't know how long it will take, but he is the right man to lead the team and get us what we need."

"I agree, sir. Well, I have a lot to do. I'll keep you posted, Mr. President."

★★★

Back in Houston on the park bench, Megan and Omid were still looking and not saying much. Megan asked Omid, "Do you think you are in love with me?"

Omid responded, "Megan, are you in love with me?"

They both looked at each other and said simultaneously, "I don't know." At that moment they both burst out laughing.

Omid looked Megan directly in her eyes and started to say, "I…" Just then Megan's cell phone buzzed with a text message requesting her to come back to the safe house ASAP, and does she know where Omid is?

Megan responded, "On my way, and Omid is with me." Megan turned to Omid. "We have to go. Something is up."

Omid grabbed her hand and pulled her back down to the bench. "Just one moment, I want to answer your question… I want to find out if I'm in love with you."

Megan responded, "Omid, I feel the same way; we have to figure out how we will know if we love each other, but for now we have to get back to the safe house. One thing is for sure. I'm no longer going to hide my feelings for you. Let's just take this one day at a time and see where it goes. Omid, can you do that?"

"Yes, I can."

Chapter 74

BROTHERHOOD MEETING

Sargon wants to have a meeting to discuss their upcoming move. He knows that people are getting nervous about being in one place for a long period of time. From the garden on top of the building, they all have seen an increase of people in the city, but so far they have not seen anybody come back into this building to reclaim their condos. He believes it is just a matter of time before the owners return.

Ishtar has been working on a plan to get the Brotherhood out of the country to a safe place where they can live in comfort and security, and he is ready to tell them his plan. All are assembled around the dining room table and Sargon addresses them, "Brothers, the time has come for our next move and that move will take us out of the United States to a safe and beautiful place. Our brother Ishtar has been making the arrangements and he will give us as much of the detail as he can at the moment. All of the arrangements are not complete, but as more details are determined, we will keep you posted."

Ishtar stood and spoke, "This has been what we have been looking forward to for many months. As it stands at the moment, we will leave here and drive about 90 minutes south to Port Arthur, Texas. From there we will turn south on Jetty Road and take it to its dead end. At that point, we will be met by a small craft that will take us out into the Gulf where we will transfer to a larger ship that will take us to our final destination.

"My goal will be to execute the money transfer within the next 30 days. We will need Oleg to contact his uncle to set up bank accounts for all of us, with deposits of $1,000,000 each as an opener. Oleg, we will need an accounting of how much each of us has earned and what amounts we can expect to be deposited in the accounts, and when."

Oleg responded, "I will make the call right after this meeting and provide Sargon the information."

"We will need two cars to get us all to the pickup point, so I want Michael to go out in a week or so and buy a late model car that runs, but is not fancy. I want you to drive it back here and park it in the covered garage. Don't spend over ten thousand dollars, and tell the dealer it is a cash deal. In about two more weeks, go to a different lot and buy another car and bring it back here and put it in storage. Make sure that both cars are full of gas. Any questions, Michael?"

"No, I'm good."

Mordecai asked, "What time of day will we leave?"

"I'm hopeful that the curfew will be lifted by the time we leave, but if it is not, we will want to leave in time to reach the pickup point on Jetty Road around dark. The road runs alongside the outflow of Sabine Lake into the Gulf of Mexico. I have not seen any houses or buildings on Jetty Road, so we should not be seen in the dark."

Ishtar turned the meeting back to Sargon. He said, "You are all probably wondering where we are headed; for now we continue to explore several islands in the Caribbean. Again, as was said before, as soon as a decision on the exact location is made, we will let you know."

Back at the safe house, the team assembled in the living room. They were waiting for Ted to get off the phone. Nobody knew who Baker was talking to, but he seemed to have a big smile on his face so it must be something positive.

While they were waiting, John Seacrest talked to the group about a surveillance idea he has to cover the Brotherhood. "I have been thinking about the manpower that will be needed to cover the Brotherhood. Every time we add a team, we run the risk of a leak, so why have any teams? We can have Williams contact Langley to reposition a spy satellite that will hover over Texas and lock on to the GPS signal from the ID bracelet and track them to the edge of its scan range and then hand the signal off to another satellite. That way, wherever Mordecai goes we have got him as long as he is wearing or carrying the bracelet."

Megan looked at John and said, "A brilliant idea! Will you please tell Ted when he comes back into the room, if he ever does? Is it me or does it seem like he has been on the phone a long time?"

A moment later, Ted came into the room and said to all of them, "Pack your bags - we are headed to the airport in 20 minutes."

Megan responded quickly, "What about the Brotherhood? John has a great idea how we can cover them."

"I want to hear it. We can talk on the way to the airport, so everyone gets packed. Time is wasting."

Megan asked, "Ted, where are we headed?"

Ted responded, "For now, the airport. Once we are on the plane, I'll brief you on our destination and our next assignment."

They all looked at one another and mouthed the words, "Our next assignment?"

Chapter 75

OVAL OFFICE

Nathan Jordan has scheduled a meeting with Bob Hamilton, the Secretary of Defense to discuss with him his plans for retaliation against terrorism. Mary Washington buzzes the President to tell him that Secretary Hamilton has arrived. "Mary, show him in please." Hamilton walks through the door and extends his hand to the President, "Mr. President, good to see you again. How are you doing?"

"Bob, I'm doing fine, and thanks for coming on such short notice. I wanted to spend some time with you to talk about some of the things I'm considering as a basis for retaliation for the attack, and I have come to believe that you and I may well be on the same page. So, I would like to tell you what is on my mind and just ask you to listen for a while. When I'm finished, I want your impression. Can you do that for me? I want honest opinions."

"Mr. President, I will be happy to react to whatever you put on the table. I will give you my honest opinion."

"Bob, we know where the Brotherhood is right now. We could walk in and capture all of them and I'm sure many Americans would be ecstatic that we have captured the bad guys who killed so many Americans. But, that isn't enough. We have an opportunity to destroy the infrastructure of the terrorist groups if we have the courage to do so."

"Mr. President, can I ask a question or should I wait until you're done?"

"Bob, wait until I'm done, and then ask away. If we truly are going to kill the terrorist movement, we must kill their funding. Without money, the groups can't survive long-term.

"I'm sure there are many people in America who want me to blow up stuff, military bases, training camps, even some cities. The problem I have with that is, in the case of the Brotherhood of the Red Nile, they are not a country. However, the Brotherhood would not have been able to attack us without funding from some nation or individual. If we are going to win, then we must destroy all the OPEC governments. Again, I'm not suggesting we send in warplanes to bomb the capitals of all the OPEC nations. We must find a different way to destroy this cartel in such a way that the money dries up so the terrorists lose their funding and disappear.

"If we flood the world with cheap energy, OPEC will try to compete for a while, but their costs are so high a sustained decline in the price of crude will eventually cause massive unrest in their citizens. Governments will topple like dominos. Governments will spend their reserves to try and keep their power, so they will not have money to fund terrorist groups. With such expenses, their treasuries will be depleted very quickly, and with oil prices so low the income will not be enough to fund the government. I believe the people will rise up and overthrow the governments.

"What we say and do can have a very direct effect on this change. When the pipelines we're building are complete, we can expand the discovery of natural gas exponentially. We will be able to reduce our dependency on foreign energy and thus the demand for OPEC energy. If the world markets think that America is becoming energy independent and that we will start exporting oil and natural gas, the price of energy on the markets will fall like a rock. If we say to the world we have more energy than OPEC and our reserves are growing rapidly and we make our energy available in the markets at the lowest price, we will continue to reduce the price of energy as we increase the quantity of energy we export. OPEC will have to compete, at least for some time, but quickly they will find they are losing a vast amount of market share to the US.

"These governments will not have the money to provide services to their people and all the people we will be deporting back to those countries will put additional pressure on the resources of their governments. Our balance of payments will disappear, for we will no longer be importing foreign energy. The profits from the sale of energy can be used to retire our debt and fully fund those programs to protect the sick and the elderly. With more people working, we will have more tax revenue and the size of government will shrink, creating more surpluses so we could start lowering income taxes on all Americans.

"We must do this with the clear understanding that what we do will create chaos in some parts of the world and people will die as a result of our actions. We will be blamed for the destruction of OPEC and the collapse of many governments, which will be the price we have to pay. I believe in the long run this is the best thing for America and the world. If I'm reelected, I propose to deliver this message on January 20th after my oath of office. So, Bob, thanks for being quiet; what do you think?"

"Mr. President, I don't know where to begin; the destruction of OPEC is a very strong idea. I agree with you that it is not about bombs; it has always been about the money. They didn't bomb the World Trade Center to kill people or bring down buildings. These were means to an end of shutting down the American Capital Markets. They succeeded in their objective for a short time and clearly the nuclear bombings in America represented a ratcheting up of the desire to take America's money. If we don't do something now, the terrorists and their funding sources will be even more emboldened to increase the size and scope of the attacks on us. I think you are on the right track Mr. President - we must take their money. We have no choice but to destroy their economy before they destroy ours.

"One challenge, Mr. President, is this: I think that many Americans will not understand that our retaliation is not with guns, planes, or missiles but with oil and energy. I hate to say it this way, but most Americans can better relate to getting even by blowing something up. When you tell the people, if you get a chance, you will have to figure out a way to tell them your plan so they can understand. I believe that if they understand, they will support you in what you are trying to do for them."

"Excellent point, Bob, and a big challenge. Thank you for listening, and just so there is no mistake, this conversation was just between me and you."

"Yes, sir." As Hamilton left the Oval Office and walked down the hallway he thought to himself, *that was the most amazing idea I have ever heard. The President has nailed both the problem and the best possible solution; for America first and the world second. If he does what he says he will do, then I need to protect him with more security. I will have to coordinate with Homeland and CIA in building some new counter-terrorist special ops teams and expand the rapid deployment forces. If President Jordan pulls the trigger, then we have to be ready to back him up and protect him from the onslaught that will surely follow.*

Chapter 76

PATHFINDERS ON THE PLANE, WONDERING

Ted Baker didn't say much in the car to the airport. He asked John about his idea for following the Brotherhood and thought it was a great idea. "I'll call Under Secretary Williams from the plane and have him call Langley and get it done. You know, the more I think about it, the better I like it. As long as Mordecai has the ID bracelet on or near him, we can follow him and hopefully the rest of the Brotherhood anywhere in the world."

The car pulled into an unmarked hanger and the team rolled out of the car and up the stairs into the plane. Baker was the last on the plane and the door shut immediately. Within seconds, the plane was taxiing for takeoff and in the air and heading for a cruising altitude of 35,000 feet. When the plane leveled off, Baker unbuckled his seat belt and walked back to the rest of the team. He stood in front of them and began to tell them what is going on.

"The President has convinced Mike Ridley to head up a special project to trace the various sources of funding for as many terrorist groups he can, including the Brotherhood of the Red Nile." When Omid heard the name Mike Ridley, he was stunned.

Baker continued, "The President has assigned the Pathfinders - that means all of you - to report to Mike Ridley and act as his support team. We are on our way to Sanibel Island, Florida, and there we will meet with Mike and Under Secretary Williams to begin the plan of attack. John, I have already talked with Under Secretary Williams about your surveillance idea and as we speak, the satellite is being repositioned.

"I want you to know for the foreseeable future our plan will not entail the capture of the Brotherhood. You may recall in reviewing your briefing material on the Brotherhood, that Mike's son Michael is believed to be a member. The President has informed Mike about his son and he knows that when Michael is captured that he will have to stand trial for his crimes. Mike has expressed his sorrow about his son's actions, but is willing to actively work on the mission suggested by the President. We should be in Ft. Myers in about two hours. Mike left Andrews about an hour ago, so if things work out, we should arrive at Page Field within twenty minutes of each other.

"The Homeland Security Logistics office is working on securing rooms for the team members at the same hotel where Under Secretary Williams is staying; we will know when we land where we are staying. Any questions?"

Hadar asked, "Am I included in the team?"

"Williams has cleared it with Nava Dobias, the head of Mossad. You will have to periodically check in with the closest Israeli embassy."

Megan asked, "Do you have any idea how long we will be on this assignment?"

Baker paused for a moment. "I need to be honest with you. All I can tell you is you'll be working on this assignment as long as Jordan is President or until the mission is complete. The new President could abolish your job, if Jordan is not reelected in November. If William Wild is elected, I believe he'll cancel the project as soon as he hears about it."

Megan asked, "Ted, will you be working with us?"

"Megan, this is all happening so fast, I don't know the answer to your question. We will have a better idea of my involvement once we all meet on Sanibel. My guess is that Mike will want to keep the same structure, with me being a liaison with Homeland and you will continue overseeing the team and report directly to Mike."

Omid asked, "I'm on TDY from the Pentagon, and that assignment was due to end in about 90 days. Will I stay on?"

"Let me respond to all of you; I know you all gave up other assignments to work on this taskforce. You all serve at the discretion of the President; he is the boss and any agency that you were working for will follow the orders of the President concerning your assignments, so no more questions on that subject." Baker stopped for a moment and thought, "*I have assumed that they all want to serve even though the President could order them to serve. If they want out, they should have the right to leave, especially since the assignment has changed.*"

"Let me say one more thing to all of you. If for some reason, after you hear the discussion of the assignment tonight or tomorrow, you decide that you don't want to work on this taskforce, let me know right away and I will make arrangements for you to go back to your previous assignment - no questions asked. This is still a free country and you are potentially putting your life at risk. You need to evaluate the risk before you agree. Understood?"

All responded, "Understood."

Chapter 77

TWEEN WATERS INN, SANIBEL

Frank and Ellen Williams went to bed after the exciting phone call with Mike Ridley and the President. Frank awoke with Ellen in his arms. He thought, as he held her, *it is just possible she saved my life with her challenging words. I feel like a new person with a purpose in life and a reason to get up and get started.* Frank had to leave soon to get to Page Field to meet Mike and the team from Houston. He slipped Ellen out of his arms and she stayed asleep. Frank got up quietly and closed the bathroom door behind him. He took a quick shower, dressed and opened the bathroom door slowly to check on Ellen; she was still asleep. He slipped out the door, got into the car and headed for the airport.

Ellen heard the car pull out of the parking lot. She was not asleep, but just pretending so as not to distract Frank. Ellen lay in bed with just the sheet covering her naked body. As she pulled the sheet to cover herself she could smell Frank's scent on the sheets. *I'm so proud of him. I knew he had a great deal more to give to the country. To walk away now with the job unfinished would have haunted him the rest of his life. Sanibel is a beautiful place and perhaps someday we will retire here. It is a place where you can slow down and take on a different pace of life, but I don't think Frank is ready to slow down. It would be a great place to come on a getaway vacation.*

I know that Frank was pleased with the President's reaction to his suggestion of using the Pathfinders to help Mike Ridley, but I wonder how much time Frank will have to devote to helping them. He needs to get back to Washington and lead

250

his unit. He needs to trust Ted to oversee the Pathfinders and get whatever resources Mike and the team will need. I have to figure out a way to help Frank let go and let the people he picked run the show. I know that he was depressed when he felt like he was not involved, but maybe working with Mike will fill the void and motivate him. That's it; he needs to see himself as the big picture guy between Mike and the President. The day-to-day detail belongs to Ted Baker.

As Frank drove down SanCap Road heading toward the causeway, he began to think about how he could give Mike Ridley the room he will need to operate, but at the same time make sure he is in the loop to inform the President. Ted will interface with Megan, so he will get regular reports from Ted on the activities of the Pathfinders. *I will just have a separate meeting with Mike as soon as possible to work out the details.* Frank also thought about where to meet while on Sanibel. He remembered that Jacaranda has a meeting room, so he decided to stop there on his way to the airport.

The restaurant is a mile or so ahead, so he decided to pull in and ask to speak with the manager. As he turned into the parking lot, he noticed there are not many cars, so not many people in the restaurant. Frank walked in the front door and for a moment nobody is at the hostess station, and then Brenda came by and recognized Frank. "Mr. Williams, welcome back; how may I help you?"

"I need to see the manager if he is in."

"I don't know if Mr. Patton is in, but let me check for you." Frank looked down at his watch. He still had plenty of time to get to the airport. Brenda came back with John Patten, the General Manager.

"Mr. Williams, how can I help you?"

"I'm looking for space for a small meeting that might run several days; is your meeting room available for the next three to four days?"

"I will have to check the reservation book; just give me a moment. Mr. Williams, how long during the day will you need the room each day?"

Williams said, "My guess is nine to five each day."

Patton responded. "All day, every day?"

"Yes."

"That could be expensive. Would you want breakfast, lunch and an afternoon snack, plus beverages?"

Williams responded, "Yes"

"How many people?"

"As of right now, I would estimate seven."

Patton excused himself and came back in a short while. "We can handle that for the next three days but I can't promise the fourth right now. I need to check with catering to see if we can make a change in our schedule."

"Excellent; I would like to use it tonight for dinner around seven thirty for a party of nine."

"Not a problem, we will see you tonight."

Williams got back in his car and headed for the causeway. Once he got off-island, he had about 30 minutes to Page Field. He looked at his watch and saw he should make it if Mike's plane is on time. As Frank turned on to US 41, he began to think about how important this new assignment is not only to the country, but also to him. The head of Homeland Security Mark Simons had told Frank that his health is declining and that if Jordan is reelected he will most likely resign. If Frank can pull off this assignment, he might have a shot at Simons' job, and at the end of Jordan's second term, he and Ellen could retire to Sanibel... Sweet.

Chapter 78

MIKE RIDLEY ON THE
PLANE TO FT. MYERS

Mike is in Mary Washington's office waiting for the profiles of the members of Frank Williams' Pathfinder team. President Jordan has suggested that he might want to review them on the plane while he is en route to Ft. Myers. Mary puts the copies of the members' files in plain brown envelopes with no markings on them. All the team members and Ted Baker's profile are included. Mike puts them under his arm and walks out of Ms. Washington's office. The escort who brought him to the Oval Office is waiting to take him back to the waiting car.

In a few moments, they were at the main entrance. The escort walked out with Mike and opened the door in the waiting car. Mike stepped in and thanked the escort and said, "Goodbye." The presidential black SUV slowly left the White House and sped to Andrews and his waiting plane. Mike decided to wait until he is on the plane to look at the files. He wonders; *almost every assignment I have had for the government in my career I have worked alone. Now the President wants me to use these Pathfinders to help me with this very complicated and difficult assignment. I don't know that I can do both. How can this team help me? I know from my discussions with the President, they know more than almost anybody about the Brotherhood, but what do they know about the flow of money that funds them? I suppose I should admit that I don't know much about the flow of money, so perhaps we will all learn together."*

The car pulled up to base security at Andrews and the driver showed an ID but Mike, at least for now, has no government ID and is thinking he should not have any. If they want him to have a security badge, then somebody has to start a new file on him and that means more people will have access to his information. He made a mental note to speak with Williams about an ID. The car cleared security and in a few moments they were in a special hanger. The car pulled up to the plane where Mike got out and went up the ladder into the plane. A few moments later, the pilot said, "We have been cleared for takeoff."

When the plane leveled off, Mike took out all the files and starts reviewing Ted Baker's files first. The steward asked Mike, "The flight to Page Field will take about two and one-half hours; would you like something to drink or eat?"

Mike thought for a minute and realized he'd had nothing since breakfast. "Do you have any sandwiches?"

"Yes, sir, what would you like?"

"Do you have any turkey?"

"Yes, on white or whole wheat?"

"Could I have whole wheat with lettuce and tomato and a little spicy mustard?"

"Not a problem; what would you like to drink?"

"Do you have sweet tea?"

"Yes, and would you like some chips with your sandwich?"

"That would be nice."

"I'll have it for you shortly."

While Mike waited for his sandwich, he continued to look at the files. His first impression was that he had a very diverse pool of talent to work with on this mission. *I could see how at least three of them could fit together nicely. But this Hadar woman, so far she seems to be here because of a flirtatious relationship with one of the terrorists. She has some military experience and based on the photo she is very attractive but there is not much on her skills. I will want to see what she can bring to the table, if anything.*

On another military plane that has already taken off from Houston, the steward told Baker that their flight would take about two hours. Baker decided that now is the time to share the new mission with his Pathfinders. "The President has asked Mike Ridley to trace and prove the source of

funding to the Brotherhood of the Red Nile and as many different terrorist groups as possible."

Baker continued to flesh out the mission according to the best of his
knowledge. "Under Secretary Williams will meet us at the airport along
with Ridley, and we will start meeting immediately to develop a plan with
Mike. I'm assuming Mike will want all of us, but I don't know for sure. I
know that if I were in his shoes, I would want to interview each member
of the team, me included, to try and determine who I can work with or
not. Mike has the final say, so if any of us are not picked, then I'm sure
Williams will find new assignments for any who might not be retained."

Hadar thinks, *all the rest of the team members are government employees; they
can't be fired. I'm just a pretty face and a great body; what else do I have to offer?
I'm gone; maybe I should just tell Ted I want out before I get fired.*

Chapter 79

THE PETROLEUM PLAN

The President has a meeting scheduled with Attorney General Clinton, Secretary of Energy Findley, and Secretary of the Interior Summons. Mary showed the gentlemen into the Oval Office. The President had not yet arrived, and Mary told them, "The President is just upstairs with the First Lady. I expect him momentarily; can I get you something to drink while you are waiting?"

All three respond, "Water will be fine."

Mary was fixing their drinks when the President walked in; all three stood to greet Jordan. "Please sit down. Mary, I could use a drink of cold water; could I have it with some ice please?"

"Right away, Mr. President."

Jordan waited until Mary passed out the drinks and left the room and the door was shut. "Gentlemen, thank you for coming. I have something to speak with you about that will be top secret. I will need you and your staff's full cooperation to pull this off, so make sure you only tell the people necessary to accomplish this mission, understood?"

All respond, "Yes, sir."

"I'm sure you all have heard of the Manhattan Project."

Findley responds, "That was the development of the first atomic bomb that led to the bombing of Japan that brought the Second World War to an end."

"Excellent. Given you were not even born at the time, you must have had an exceptional high school history teacher." Findley smiles that the President is pleased at his response.

"What I want to propose is, for now, as secret as the Manhattan Project. I want to start by putting the AG on the spot; is there a limit to what I can do under my power of Executive Order? Before you answer, let me ask you a concurrent question. Does an Executive Order have to be made public?"

Clinton paused for a moment and then responded, "Mr. President, the power of the Executive Order is very broad, and many Presidents have used them for a wide variety of initiatives and issues. For example, Roosevelt used it in the war to place Japanese-Americans into what were effectively prisoner of war camps. More recently, President Obama used his Executive Order power over one thousand times for many different reasons. If you are not ordering illegal or immoral activity, you can do just about anything. Now to your second question; as to notification, that is a little grayer. If I knew what you wanted to do, I might be able to give you a specific answer."

Findley and Summons looked at each other and wondered why they are here; they are not lawyers. Nathan could see in their expressions they had no idea why they are here, but he is about to get their attention. "Secretary Summons, your department is responsible for granting oil and natural gas leases on Federal land, correct?"

"Yes, Mr. President."

"Secretary Findley, your department is responsible for granting rights of way and monitoring the construction of these pipelines, is that correct?"

"Yes, Mr. President, you may recall my department is responsible for building the two pipelines to move the contaminated energy and increase the flow of natural gas."

"Mr. Clinton, could I issue an Executive Order granting drilling rights on U.S. government land to develop oil and natural gas more quickly than the normal sale of energy leases, and could I do so without an open bid procedure?"

Before Clinton answered, Summons jumped in, "Mr. President, we have a specific protocol on how energy leases are awarded, I don't think…"

Just then Clinton interrupted him, "With all due respect, Secretary Summons, I realize companies who do not get the invitation to drill may be upset in time when they find out. They may well try to bring legal action against the Government and more specifically your department. I will need to study the case law, but I don't immediately recall any Executive Order that has ever been overturned."

Secretary Summons then asked, "Mr. President, if I may ask you a question?"

"Of course you can, what is it?"

"Mr. President, how would you decide who gets the rights to drill?"

"The first thing I would do is ask both of you: who has drilled the most oil and gas wells in the last five years? I would expect the names of the Chairmen of the top twenty drillers and I would personally call them and ask them how many wells they can drill on the government's land in 90 days. I would do the same thing for the natural gas companies."

Findley asked the President, "Let's say that the Attorney General gives you the go ahead; I have two questions. First, why do you want to try to keep it under wraps, and second, how do you propose to keep it under wraps?"

"Excellent questions, Mr. Findley. Let me try to answer both of them. I want to keep this a secret for as long as I can, because I want to jump-start the flow of energy to America and I want to stop importing foreign oil. Second, I want to take my opponent in the presidential campaign by surprise. As to your last question, when I talk with the Chairman of each company, I will let them know that if they leak the story they will find it difficult to get leases in the future and they will certainly be off the favored list. Those companies that don't make the initial ten may find themselves moving up if the companies above them can't meet the demand.

"The last thing, gentlemen. If America can develop its energy assets, we can destroy OPEC by becoming the low-cost provider in the world. If we can destroy OPEC's revenue, we stop the flow of the money going to terrorist organizations. I'm focused on taking away the funding for terrorists forever, and if we can do that, then our country and the world will be a safer place."

Findley asked, "Mr. President, what do want us to do?"

"I want Mr. Clinton to quickly research case law to find if there is any precedent that the President must disclose an Executive Order. I want the two of you to come up with my list of twenty Chairmen's names, and I want it in three days or sooner - any questions?"

"No, sir."

"Then let's get busy and protect and save America."

Chapter 80

MIKE MEETS HIS TEAM ONE BY ONE

Mike has decided that it's time to get to the seclusion of Sanibel, and he instructs the driver from Homeland Security to take Ted, Megan, Omid, and John to their hotel. Frank, Mike, and Hadar will go in Frank's car and they will join them at the Tween Waters later. Hadar swallows hard since she is to be in the car with Frank and Mike. This is the first interview and perhaps her last with Mike. Hadar starts to get into the front seat of the car, but Mike asks Frank to drive and he tells Hadar they will sit in the back seat and talk.

They all got in and Frank pulled out of Page Field, headed for US 41 south toward Sanibel. Mike said to Hadar, "Hadar, I wanted to spend some time with each of the team members to determine as quickly as I can whether each of you can work with me on my project. Under the terms agreed upon by the President, I will work for both the President and Frank. The team's day-to-day activities will be reported to Frank. Based on my working relationship with Frank, I have asked him to sit in on the initial interviews with Pathfinder members.

"I have read your file and it is quite impressive for someone so young. What do you think so far has been the greatest challenge to your success?"

"Mr. Ridley…"

"I do apologize for interrupting you Hadar, but if we are going to work together, then you have to start calling me Mike, okay?"

"Yes, sir; I mean Mike. That is a very interesting question. I don't think I have ever been asked that before, but I think I have a very straightforward answer to your question." Hadar took her hands and extended her index finger on each hand pointing from the top of her head all the way down to her feet. "Mike, I'm not trying to be funny. Many people can't get past my body and my face to believe that I have a brain, and that I can use that brain to accomplish things.

"The assignments I have been given, except for my last, were underwhelming to say the least, not very challenging; but as my report says, I did them well. In some cases the comments were surprisingly complimentary."

"You said, except for your last. What do you mean; are you talking about your current assignment?"

"No, I was referring to my last assignment for Mossad in Syria."

"What made it different?"

"Our unit was split into two groups. I was in charge of the unit in the village to mark any members of the Brotherhood that came into town with GPS tracking devices so we could follow them anywhere they went."

"I understand you marked the one called Mordecai and struck up a relationship with him. Am I correct it was because of your actions that Frank asked your government if he could borrow you to come to America to see if you could assist his people to track down Mordecai and determine if the Brotherhood was still in the country?"

"Yes, Mike."

"Is it fair to say that your contact with Mordecai was enhanced by your body?"

"I think just about any attractive woman could have played him with potentially a similar result."

"How did you get the assignment to lead the team?"

What do I tell him about my relationship with David Oppenheimer? Will he think that if I tell him we were lovers, he will think that I got the assignment because of the sexual relationship? Is that the reason David gave me the assignment? I don't think he would have trusted me with the lives of a dozen people just because I was great in bed. "I believe that I got the opportunity because I proved that I could accomplish my mission and protect the lives of the men and women in my responsibility. In this case, I used my body to gain information from Mordecai, but I believe I have the confidence of both Captain Oppenheimer and the head of Mossad."

"When was the last time you spoke with Mordecai?"

"I met him in Houston just about four hours ago."

"How did you feel about the decision by President Jordan to pull back and not capture the leadership of the Brotherhood at this time?"

"Frankly, Mike, I was pissed. All of us had worked so hard to find them, and then when we had them at the point that we could walk in with a small squad of men and capture the whole bunch, we were told to stand down. Well, I hope you can imagine our disappointment."

"Hadar, what have you learned so far from being involved in the project?"

Hadar paused for a moment before she answered Mike's question. "Mike," feeling more comfortable calling him Mike, "I can only speak for myself. In Israel, the Army is small and Mossad is even smaller, so you have a greater sense of family and mission. Sure, there are some missions that are very secret and are not well known until after they are completed, but you know what is going on. But here in America I don't feel that. I read that at Newark Liberty Airport Homeland Security has over 11,000 employees and that is just one airport.

"I came to the United States at Mr. Williams request to try and help his team catch the Brotherhood. I never thought that the President of the United States would in effect say to us, I don't want them now. Let them go, we'll catch them later. I know it sounds like I'm criticizing the President's decision. Well, being truthful I guess I am, because I don't know the plan. I came here as, like one of my teammates called me, 'The Bait' to attract Mordecai if he was here. I did my job, but not my entire job. These are bad people and they killed a lot of Americans and frankly, Mike, I want them dead, including Mordecai. I'm willing to do whatever is necessary to get the job done. All I ask of you, if you want me to stay on the team, is tell me what the plan is. You see, Mike, the head on top of this body has a very good brain, and I can understand just about anything you can throw at me."

Chapter 81

ISHTAR SAYS IT WILL BE SOON

Mordecai has returned from his secret rendezvous with Hadar and is depressed that he didn't have more time with her. As he thought about the short amount of time he had with her, he became concerned that he hurt her with all his forceful fondling. He has such strong feelings for her, it was impossible for him to resist. He was so excited to see her again that he was probably more aggressive than he should have been groping her breasts. On the other hand, she didn't seem to resist his advances; perhaps she didn't want to disappoint, so she let him do what he wanted. *I wonder if she will respond if I call her again; I should really call her and apologize for my rough behavior.*

As Mordecai walked through the front door of the condo Sargon greeted him, "Where have you been?" The Brotherhood has a rule that when one of them leaves, he needs to sign out so people will know where he are going and when they can expect him back.

"I just went out for a walk. I forgot to sign out; I will try to remember the next time."

Sargon said, "We have a Brotherhood meeting in about 20 minutes and I was concerned that I couldn't find you. I'm glad you are here now; everybody is accounted for, so we can proceed with our meeting. I think everybody will be pleased."

Mordecai knew that he didn't have time to call Hadar now, but he could send her a text message. He proceeded to his room and pulled out his phone, flipped it open and found Hadar's phone number. He typed in, "Got a meeting in 20; something big. Can I call you in about two hours?" and he pushed Send.

While on the plane to London, Hadar could not receive a text while flying. After landing, she forgot to turn on the phone. Now she realizes that her phone is off in the car with Williams and Ridley traveling to Sanibel. During the discussion with Mike, she turned on her phone and saw the text message from Mordecai. Hadar announced in the middle of a question from Mike, "I just got a text message from Mordecai asking me if he can call me in about two hours; that's just about now. What should I do if he calls?"

Mike responded, "We can pull over if the call comes and talk with him."

"What should I say to him?"

Mike responded, "Let's see what he is calling about first; don't commit to anything. Just talk. Tell him you are on your way to Africa and look for an opportunity to see if he will tell you when he is leaving Houston and where he is headed."

Mike thought, *if Mordecai calls then, I will be able to hear how Hadar plays him and what information she is able to get out of him. There is no question that she is one fabulous looking woman, but can she be effective when nobody can see her? Granted Mordecai has seen her several times, so she has that advantage, but without that body in his face, will he be just as willing to share information? Is she good enough to extract it without alarming Mordecai? We will see soon enough.*

Back in Houston, the meeting of the Brotherhood began and Sargon told the team. "We will be leaving soon. Ishtar will tell you when, how and where we are going. Ishtar, you have our attention."

Ishtar stood. At least everybody thought it was Ishtar, but they couldn't be sure if it was Ishtar or Michael. "The election primaries for the Presidential race will be held in three weeks, and in addition to the vote for the party Presidential candidate, the American people will be voting for candidates in every elective office all the way down to dog catcher. This entire primary election cycle for all states will be held across America in one day. The country will be distracted with the election, and that is when we will make our move. Americans will be glued to their TV's and computers watching the results. I have been told that the Federal Election Commission has requested the President suspend the curfew until after midnight. It will take us about three hours to reach our pickup point. Around 6 PM the day of the move, we will leave Houston in two cars and head for Sabine Pass National Park. From there, we will head due east to pick up Jetty Road. At the end of Jetty Road, we will get on our speedboat and quickly move out of American waters and then on our way to independence. The larger ship outside the three-mile limit will take us to our final destination, a small Caribbean island.

"Oleg's uncle has arranged bank accounts for us on the island with one million dollars deposited in each of our accounts. A day or so after we arrive, we will go to the RBC bank and sign for our accounts. We will take up residence in a walled compound of three houses. We will have two swimming pools and each of us will have our own suite of rooms. We will have several servants and two cooks for our meals. I have arranged for each of you to have a Mercedes 550 to use to get around the island. The island is little - about five square miles. It does have an airport, but mostly small planes come and go. The native population is about 1,500 and some 25,000 tourists visit the island annually.

"The government is very favorable, for it is a Dutch colony and both English and Dutch are spoken. They use the U.S. Dollar as their currency and the local banks clear their currency transactions outside the United States. We can fly out and travel, but we must wait awhile until America gives up looking for us. I'm in the process of getting all of us Dutch passports for identification. Any questions?"

Cyrus spoke up, "I would like to know the name of our new home?"

Ishtar was about ready to answer when Sargon spoke, "Ishtar and I have spent a great deal of time trying to find a place to move and while we have a primary target we also have plans for an alternative place just in case something unforeseen happens. Once we are on the big boat, I'll confirm where we are headed, but for now think of white sand beaches, deep blue waters and lovely island girls."

Chapter 82

ON THE WAY TO SANIBEL

The lead car has Omid, Megan, John, and Ted and they are heading to the hotel where they will be staying, but they do not know how long.

Omid asked Ted, "How long do you think we will be here?"

Ted responded, "I don't know, but I do know that if we are going to use Sanibel as a base of operation, we can't do it out of a hotel, we will need a couple of houses."

The driver spoke up, "Sir, it is my understanding that Logistics is looking at a couple of houses that can be rented for an extended period of time."

John asked the driver, "How long is an extended period of time?"

The driver responded, "I don't know sir; that is not my responsibility. I think it depends on how long Mr. Ridley thinks it will take to complete the assignment."

Megan was in the middle of the back seat; Omid and John were on either side of her. All of a sudden, she feels a hand under her right leg and without looking or showing any alarm, she puts her hand on Omid's leg. At that moment they turned their heads and looked into each other's eyes and both knew they needed to spend some time alone to figure out where they are going, if anywhere, in this relationship.

Omid asked the driver, "How much further to the hotel?" And then he asked Ted, "How long after we arrive before we have our first meeting? Will we have time to go to the beach?"

The driver responded, "About 15 minutes until we arrive."

Ted responded, "We have all been cooped up for months, so a little time for fresh air would be good. I'll text Mr. Williams to discuss what time dinner will be and make sure you all have at least one hour."

The idea that she could have an hour with Omid excited Megan and she squeezed her hand on his leg. Omid responded by gently squeezing hers.

In the other car, they were talking about Hadar's response to Mordecai's text. Hadar suggested, "I should send him a text back saying, 'I have been on a plane and I just landed. I have a close connection and not sure I can talk until I land in London early tomorrow morning. Do you want to call me at nine your time or do you want me to call you?' What do you think?"

Mike responded, "Shows interest but time constraints and a desire to talk; any comments Frank?"

"No. I like it; go ahead and send it." Hadar pushed the enter button and sent the message on its way to Mordecai. "Hadar, set your phone to airplane mode just in case he calls; he will get the message you are unable to take calls, but can leave a message. Later this evening, I will want you to see if you have any messages from Mordecai and let me know what he says."

Williams' phone vibrated and he saw a text message from Ted asking, "What time is dinner and can the team have an hour or so just to take in the fresh air?"

Frank told Mike about Ted's message.

Mike said, "Give me his cell number and I'll respond. You're driving and I don't want an accident before we even start our mission." Mike sent a text to Ted, "I'll call the restaurant and push back dinner to 7:30 PM. Tell the team to enjoy the beach, M." Mike then called Jacaranda and moved the reservation. Next, he called Mary and told her of the change and asked her to call Ellen and tell her.

With that done, Mike turned to Hadar and said, "Where were we? We were talking about your qualification to be on the team, so let me start again. How old are you?"

Hadar responded, "What does my age have to do with if I'm qualified or not, and by the way, how old are you?"

Mike heard the fight in her voice and responded, "Right now I ask questions and you answer them, and by the way I'm 66 and I can see your age in my file, but I want to hear you respond."

"I'm 29. Mike, may I ask why age has anything to do with this assignment and my ability to perform the assigned tasks?"

"In my opinion, the people we will be trying to establish connections with will be older, closer to my age than yours. There may be some young people in the money supply chain but a young woman, especially one as attractive as you, could stand out and be very distracting to these people and that could cause problems for you and the project."

"So, what you are saying, my assets, as people call them, could also be a liability to the success of the mission – is that correct?"

Mike responded, "Very much so, especially in the Middle East. No, let me correct that. You could be a disruption anywhere in the world."

"Is that a compliment?" Hadar asks with a smile on her face.

Mike responded, "I suppose it is, but it could be a dangerous one."

"As you can see from my file, I have experience both upfront and in the background. Could there be times where I could be a benefit upfront, no pun intended, and other times I could disappear in the background?"

Mike answered with a question, "You really want to be on this assignment, don't you?"

"Mike, I have never wanted anything more in my life."

"Why?"

"In my country, we live every day in fear of an attack. I have seen fear on the faces of Americans since the nuclear attack; I have seen that fear in many people's faces. I want to eliminate that fear in my own country, America, and the rest of the world, and I believe now is the time to take the stand. I have to be a part of that stand."

"Hadar, I must admit when I saw your file I asked Frank: why this woman is on this team? She is not an American. I had real reservations about taking on the problems of working with a foreign agent, much less one that is as distracting as you are. I need all my team members to be focused on the mission, not on your chest. But with that said, your passion has impressed me. Your desire to rid the world of terrorism is a lofty goal, but the same as our President and mine, and I'm sure the rest of the team. This is a very dangerous and perhaps deadly assignment. I want you on my team."

Hadar responded with a fist pump and the word, "YES!! Let's go get the bastards."

Chapter 83

OMID AND MEGAN COME TO TERMS

The first part of the Pathfinders team arrives at the Tween Waters Inn on Captiva at about four in the afternoon. The dinner has been pushed back to 7:30 PM; they will have to leave the Inn around seven. That leaves about two hours for beach time and other things. After they checked in, Megan and Omid decided to cross the road and go to the Gulf of Mexico Beach where the wind and waves were up, the water was crystal clear and a deep marine blue. As they looked up and down the beach they could see that not many people were on the beach; it was like everybody knew this was an important meeting between the two of them and they all wanted it to happen in private. Neither of them had bathing suits, but they did have shorts, so going into the water would not be a problem. Marine shorts are green olive drab and very unattractive.

Megan asked Omid, "Could I borrow one of your tee shirts to use as a cover-up in case I get cold on the beach?" When Omid gave her the shirt Megan asked him, "Do you own anything that isn't olive drab?" She took it anyway.

As they started walking up the beach toward the tip of the island they saw some unbelievable homes from the beach and they wondered what the people did to be able to afford such magnificent estates. There were homes with guesthouses, three or four car garages, and even a golf cart garage. Many of the estates had giant pools right next to the ocean.

Megan commented, "I have heard that some of these pools are saltwater pools. Can you believe it, right next to an ocean of saltwater?"

Omid pointed toward two beach chairs close to the water's edge and suggested they go and sit for a while.

Megan asked, "Do you think it will be alright to sit in the chairs? They must belong to someone."

Omid responded, "Look, if the owner doesn't want us to use the chairs, he will come and tell us to move on and we will apologize and move on; no harm no foul."

Megan agreed with his logic and the two of them walked to the faded white rigid beach chairs and sat down with the Gulf just a few feet away. The seats of the chairs were faded blue fabric that creaked when they sat down, stretching the fabric.

For a long while nothing was said between the two of them, and finally Omid broke the silence. "I must tell you that I desperately want to make love with you. I have had this desire for a few months, but could not find the nerve to tell you how I feel. I don't want to scare you off, but I felt that if I didn't take the opportunity today, I may never have said anything to you at all."

Megan responded, "I don't understand; if you felt this way, why wait until today?"

"I think there may be a possibility that one or perhaps both of us may not make Mike Ridley's team and we would be separated and I may never see you again."

"That sounds a little onerous, don't you think?"

"I think I have a good understanding of what he is going to try to do and it will be very - I mean very - dangerous. It could be so dangerous that none of the team members, including Mike himself, may survive. I didn't want to miss the opportunity to tell you how I feel and take the outside chance we might make love at least once." Megan has been watching Omid's face the whole time he was speaking, and she could see the blush of embarrassment on his face when he suggested the outside possibility of making love.

Things are quiet between the two of them. All they can hear are the sound of the waves when they roll up on the beach. Omid had opened his heart to Megan; he waited for a response, and when nothing was forthcoming he thought he had made a terrible mistake. He was about to open his mouth to say something when Megan took the first two fingers of her left hand and placed them on Omid's lips indicating that it was her time to speak. Megan looked up and down the beach to see if anybody is coming and sees nobody. After she looked back at Omid she took her left hand, reached out for Omid's right hand and slowly and gently led it to her left breast. She held her hand on top of his and gently pushed his hand, encouraging Omid to caress it firmly. Megan dropped her fingers from his lips and leaned over and placed her warm and wet lips on top of Omid's mouth. Both of them open their mouths and the passion created electricity that ran through both of their bodies. Omid's other hand found its way without any help to Megan's other breast. The embrace lasts for a few moments and then Megan gently pulled away and as she separated, Omid released her breasts from his grasp.

They sat in the chairs quietly for a few moments and then Megan spoke. "Omid, I have to admit I have had some of the same feelings for you and I'm willing to admit that I have often wondered what it would be like to make love with you. I have been reluctant, because as the team leader, I might have to make the decision to send you into harm's way and I don't know if I could live with myself knowing that my decision might be the reason that you are killed. It is for that reason I have suppressed my desire for you.

"But I think things have changed and changed dramatically. I agree that one or both of us may not make the team. Based on what Williams and Baker have said, the President has given the leadership of the team, whatever its makeup, to Mike Ridley. He will make the decisions about how to deploy the human resources, not me. So, on the surface it would seem okay for the two of us to go back to the Tween Waters Inn and make as much love as we can until it is time to get to dinner."

"I hear a 'but' coming."

"Very astute." Megan continued, "But can people who are team members be lovers and for that matter married and still be effective and objective?"

Omid paused. "I understand your concerns and I think they are valid. The military does not ban marriage between two soldiers, but has set limitations that one cannot command the other. You have decided that Mike will be in command of the unit and its activities and in many respects we will be equals. Now unless you have any objections, I think we need to head back and get as much skin-to-skin time as we can before dinner. On a more serious note, I know my feelings are strong right now and I also know that once I'm inside you can expect an explosion from pent-up desire. But, let me say I want to find out if you are the one for me. I'm not looking for a one night stand and no matter how much I want you, I will pass if that is all you want."

"I don't know where this is going, but I too want to find out where it can lead. I'm ready for you to take me. So, do you want to race back to the Inn? She started to take off.

Omid reached out and grabbed her by the arm and gently brought her back to him. He kissed her with real passion and desire and then pushed her to the sand and took off running to the Inn.

Chapter 84

RULES OF ENGAGEMENT

Attorney General Drew Clinton has asked for some time with the President to go over the new rules released from the Federal Election Commission for the primary and general elections. Clinton and other party leaders represented the Republican Party in the negotiations. The President is meeting with Clinton in the small conference room next to the Oval Office. Drew is already in the room when the President walks in and greets him.

"Tell me, Mr. Attorney General, is the news good or bad?"

"Sir, I think it's about even and that is good for the people."

"Can I get the five minute overview before we get to the details?"

"Yes, sir. This is a big challenge that just might change the way elections are held in the future. The primary season is three weeks, with the national primary on the second Tuesday in June. After the primaries, each party will have three days to hold its national convention. There will be a flip of a coin and the winner will have the right to have their convention on the Fourth of July. If things stay the same in terms of process, then the losing party will get the Fourth of July in the next campaign. The opposing party will have its convention one month later, in August. The party primaries should select the candidate before the convention and the acceptance speeches for President and Vice President will be presented on the last night. Each day of the convention will be four hours long and be broadcast on C-SPAN only. No network booths, no floor reporters, just a feed from C-SPAN.

"The first two days will be platform; not pages and pages of bull crap that most people don't even understand. Each party will develop the ten most important things that need to be accomplished. These ten planks are the party platform that will be voted on before the last night's speeches. The candidates will be kept apprised of the development of the platform, and he or she will have the freedom to embrace or reject the platform.

"Labor Day will be the kickoff of the fall campaign. On September 15th, there will be an Internet webinar Presidential debate. This first debate will be on the subject, 'Getting America Back to Greatness'. Each candidate will have 45 minutes to make his or her point as to how he or she would attack the problems facing America. The last 90 minutes will be devoted to questions from the people. The FEC will scan the email submissions and then forward the chosen questions to each candidate. Each candidate will have three minutes to respond to the people. The second debate will follow the same format two weeks later at the end of September; the format will be the same as the first, but the subject will be 'What Should America's Role be in the World?'

"The third and final debate will take place on the Tuesday before Election Day in November. The debate will have two sections. The first section will be each candidate addressing the question, 'How Will You Fight Terrorism?' Each candidate will have ten minutes to respond. The second section will be two hours with questions from Americans, with preference given to members of the military.

"Election Day will be as usual on the first Tuesday after the first Monday in November. This is where it gets really interesting; each major campaign has a fuel allowance of 1,000,000 gallons and when it's gone, no more. No direct mail will be allowed, but there will be unlimited Internet use until the end of the second debate; after that no more email or any type of marketing except unused fuel can be used for campaign appearances.

"The polls will open at 12:01 AM Eastern Time and will remain open to midnight Pacific Time. C-SPAN will post results after that time. The new President and Vice President will be given the oath of office on January 20th as in the past."

Jordan appears excited. "Wow, that was fantastic Drew; seems to me like a radical departure from past election process. Simple, quick, doesn't cost an arm and a leg, no PAC, not one special interest group, just a simple straightforward election process where everybody will have the chance to vote. So, now that I have given you my Pollyanna point of view, tell me what are the risks and challenges?"

"Sir, the one thing that could throw a huge monkey wrench in the plan is what do we do with same day registration? The FEC has a set of criteria on who can vote and the key is a Social Security number. It is possible that the Democrats could challenge the Social Security number issue and request the Ninth Circuit in San Francisco suspend the specific provision on Social Security and in its place allow any acceptable form of ID."

"So, Drew, you could have millions of illegal immigrants voting based on a state driver's license or a state ID?"

"I'm afraid so, Mr. President."

"Is there any way to stop it without tipping our hand to the Democrats?"

"Sir, it could be a little underhanded, but I might just have a way to stop it."

Chapter 85

STANDING AT THE DOOR OF ROOM 101

Megan and Omid arrived at the doors to their rooms; Omid recalled that the rooms interconnect. "You go into your room and I'll go into mine and let's see if we can open the connecting doors; that way we can go back and forth without going outside." They both went into their respective room and Omid tried his side first. A moment later Megan opened her side and saw Omid.

Megan suggested, "Why don't we both take showers and then we can meet in your room Omid?"

Omid responded, "You sure you don't need some help with that hard to reach spot?"

Megan responded, "No, at least not now." They both undressed quickly and jumped into their respective showers.

Megan thought, as the warm water rolled down her body, *what have I got myself into? I do have feelings for Omid, but can I truly give myself to him; how do I know that he won't just walk away in the morning and add me to his list of conquests?*

In the other shower Omid thought, *I have never felt this way before; Megan is more than I deserve in many ways. I have strong feelings for her, but are they enough to last a lifetime?*

After a few minutes they each stepped out of their respective showers and wrapped themselves in large wraparound bath towels. Megan knew that she had to go into Omid's room and as she walked through the door she noticed that Omid had closed the drapes to darken the room, but the afternoon sun is strong and is burning through the light drapes. The whole room has a soft yellow cast that takes all the edges off everything and softens the appearance of both bodies. Megan saw Omid sitting on the side of his bed and she slowly walked over to him. When she is within a few inches of Omid she stopped, let her arms fall to her side and just stood there waiting for Omid to make a move. He reached out and put his hands behind Megan and pulled her a little closer. Megan slowly moved toward Omid, strangely with no fear of what could happen that may well change her life forever. Omid put his ear to Megan's body and through the towel he can hear her rapidly increasing heartbeat.

Omid puts his hands below her towel and then reached up under the towel and caresses her butt cheeks and begins to massage both of them at the same time. He moved up to the small of her back and then down to her upper thigh with long slow caressing movements. As he extended the range of his massage, he moved up again, just passed the small of her back and all of a sudden the towel that has been covering most of Megan's body fell to the floor. Megan didn't move. She stood her ground, looked straight ahead, and Omid found himself looking right into the lower part of her naked breasts. He was surprised at what he sees because of the size and shape of her breasts. He looked up to see her eyes and asks with a smile on his face, "Where did those come from?"

Megan responded with a smile and a laugh, "They have always been there; I have just kept them hidden. I feel that I want to have people appreciate me for my brain not my body."

Omid asked. "Do you mind if I look around? I think you have a magnificent body and I would like to take a look at it. I'm so shocked at what I see I just can't believe it's you. I know you work out three to four days a week; I'm just blown away. I'm not sure I'm good enough to make love to a woman as beautiful as you. Megan, you are way above my pay grade."

Megan responded with a blush on her face of embarrassment, "Nobody has ever talked to me that way before."

Omid responded, "How many people have seen you totally naked before?"

"Good point; have you seen enough for now?"

"Yes, but I know I'm going to want to look again."

At that comment Megan pushed Omid into the bed, but before she pushed him she grabbed his towel. When she pushed him his towel came off and Megan can see that Omid is ready for action. Megan told Omid, "Please move to the center of the bed; it will make more room for me." After Omid slid over, Megan climbed into bed and lifted her right leg over Omid. She straddled Omid on her hands and knees.

As Megan rocked back and forth she felt Omid. She found him and as she started to take him in, she could feel her passion building along with Omid's. Omid looked up at Megan and quietly asks, "Are you okay? Am I hurting you?"

Megan brought her head down close to Omid and gave him a passionate kiss and responds, "No, it is incredible."

They continued for what seemed to be hours, but it was just a few moments. Within seconds of each other they each have perhaps the most exhilarating orgasms ever. They lay next to each other for a few moments when Omid turned to Megan and asked. "Are you up for another round?"

Megan responded, "Bring it on soldier boy."

Omid responded, "But this time I'm on top."

They looked at the clock. They have made love four times, each as satisfying as the first but in a different way. Omid said, "To be continued, but now we have to get ready for dinner."

Megan lay in the bed for a moment and wondered, *Will there really be another time? If not, then this afternoon has been an incredible magical experience.*

Chapter 86

HADAR SENDS A MESSAGE

Hadar is excited about being on the team. *I wonder if Ted will be happy or disappointed?* Mike Ridley has told her that her body may well be a problem, but he thinks she could be a valuable asset on the team. The three of them have agreed upon the message to send to Mordecai, and Hadar is typing it on her phone and reads it back to Mike and Frank before she pushes the Send button. "This is what I have: 'Been on a plane and just landed and I have a close connection and not sure can talk until I land in London early tomorrow morning. Do you want to call me at nine your time or do you want me to call you? H'"

Mike responded, "I think you need just a little hint of sex at the end."

Hadar responded, "How about, 'I miss your touch.'"

Mike responded, "I love it."

Hadar made the addition and pushed the Send button. "I think that change should elicit a response from Mordecai very soon."

The conversation in the car stopped after Hadar sent her message and they remained quiet until they arrived at the Tween Waters Inn. As Frank and Hadar left the car, Frank said, "See you at Jacaranda's 7:30 sharp."

Frank walked Hadar to the front desk to check in. As soon as she got her key, Frank said he would meet her in the lobby at 7:15.

As Frank walked out the door, Hadar asked the desk receptionist, "Can you ring Mr. Ted Baker's room, please?"

The clerk said, "Mr. Baker is in room 321. You can use the house phone over on that desk and call his room directly or I can dial it for you."

Hadar responded, "Can you point me in the direction of room 321?"

"Go out the door, turn to your left and it's the third building on your right, third floor."

Hadar walked out the door and turned left toward building number three.

As she got closer to the building she thought, *what am I going to do or say if I go to his room? What will he be expecting from me? What am I willing to give to him? If the two of us are alone, could it be too intense or even dangerous for both of us?* As her thoughts have raised many questions, her pace slows. She arrived at the stairway and is about ready to take the first step when she heard, "Confucius once said, 'the longest journey starts with the first step.'"

Hadar turned around to see Ted standing behind her. He has on the loudest blue, yellow, and white shirt she has ever seen; it is so loud that it makes her laugh. She has not laughed this hard in many years and found herself so relaxed by the laughter, she fell softly into Ted's arms.

When Hadar stopped laughing, she looked Ted right in the eyes and gave him a warm slow and passionate kiss. Baker was so taken aback by Hadar's actions, he didn't respond. When he realized she was serious, he then responded with an equally passionate kiss. After a little while, Ted reached up and placed his right hand on her left breast. Hadar didn't initially respond. They continued to kiss and Ted caressed more firmly, but still no pulling away by Hadar. Hadar reached up and grabbed the zipper on her jacket and pulled it down. Hadar's movement opened the jacket and Baker slowly moved his hand inside her flight jacket. To Baker's surprise, Hadar did not resist. Baker took as much of Hadar's breast in his hand as he can grab. Her breast was very firm and Baker moved confidently to firmly squeeze her. Baker thought, *As much as I would love to make love to her, and based on her reaction she seems to want to also make love, we need to talk this out.*

Baker released her breast and separates their lips and while very close he says to Hadar, "We need to talk before we go any further."

Hadar was shocked that Baker, who seemed to have had the hots for her since they met, wanted to back away. *This is the first time in my adult life I have had a man pull away from me.* In some respects, her ego was hurt. Every man she has ever met wanted her body, and now somebody she really likes is pulling away from her.

Ted put his arm around her shoulder and said, "I think we need to talk before we take another step toward my room. Let's just sit here on this first step and talk this out. You know that if we are going to make love, I couldn't get us to my room fast enough. You also know that I have an attraction to you and I have the bruises on my arm to prove it. In some respects, I think there is something in me that attracts me to you. As much as any man worth his salt would die for the chance to make love with you, I want to know where this is going. You see Hadar; I'm not looking for a hookup. I want something more. So, I'm sticking out my bruised arm so you can hit me for screwing up your life."

Baker closes his eyes waiting for the strike but nothing happens. He feels Hadar move and when he opens his eyes he sees her standing in front of him with her flight jacket unzipped and open exposing most of both of her breasts. Baker looked at her face and then her breasts in confusion and he found himself switching back and forth between both and then he finally said, "What the hell is going on here? And by the way, zip up your jacket before somebody sees and wants a closer look; wait can I see those one more time?" Hadar quickly opened the flight jacket all the way fully exposing both breasts to Baker.

Hadar zipped the jacket up halfway and then leaned down and gave Ted a gentle kiss on the lips and a said, "Thanks for respecting me, I agree we need to talk about this with our clothes on, because I too want to know where this is going. Should we go to your room or mine?"

Ted responded, "How about we go to the dock on the bay side and see if we can find a place to talk?" All of a sudden he felt a slight tap on his shoulder and responded, "What was that for?"

Chapter 87

DINNER IS SERVED

The Pathfinders with Ted Baker assembled in the lobby along with Frank and Ellen Williams. Frank introduced Ellen to the members of the Pathfinders and they got into the cars and headed to Jacaranda. Frank took Omid and Megan in his car, and based on the expressions on both of their faces he suspects something took place this afternoon. Frank asked Omid, "So, what did you do with your free time this afternoon?"

Somewhat startled by the question Omid quickly turns to Megan as if to ask, what did we do? What should I say? Omid finally responded, "Megan and I went for a walk on the Gulf side beach and found a couple of chairs and sat enjoyed the sights and sounds of the beach."

Frank looked at Megan in the rear view mirror and asks, "Anything else?"

"We spent some quiet time together."

Omid was thinking, *I don't know how quiet we were.* A smile came to both Omid's and Megan's face when Megan told Frank about their quiet time.

Ellen spoke up, "Frank, leave them alone. It's none of your business what they did or didn't do on their own time. Sanibel is a beautiful and romantic island; anyone with half a brain can see that these two have feelings for each other, so just butt out."

"Ellen, you're right." Frank said to them, "Make the most of your time together; figure out what the two of you want to do and then do it, never look back with regret. Never find yourself saying, if only."

The cars pulled into the parking lot at Jacaranda's and they all walked in together. John Seacrest looked around and found he is the only single person in the group. Mike and Mary Ridley met all of them just inside the door and escorted them to the private room where they will eat and work over the next few days.

John was the last to head toward the private room and says to Mike, "I'm going to the men's room. I'll be along shortly." Having not been in the restaurant before, he is unsure where the men's room is located.

Over his shoulder he heard a voice say. "May I help you?" John turned around and met Anna Walters who is in charge of reception. John is somewhat dumbfounded by the appearance of Anna. She is tall, in fact taller than him; slender, yet well defined, so there is no mistaking the fact the she is all woman. Her sun bleached blond hair complemented her deep blue eyes. John just looked at her and thought, *a natural blue-eyed blond.*

Anna has John in a trance as she tells him, "The men's room is down this hall, the second door on the left."

John snapped out of his Anna-induced daze and said, "Thank you," and walked down the hallway. As he walked toward the men's room, he said to himself, *"Maybe I'm not going to be alone after all."* When John walked out of the men's room, he saw Anna and walked over to her and said, "I'm sure you have heard this line before… I'm here for a dinner meeting and I was wondering could we talk after my meeting?"

Anna responded because she has felt a spark that is new and different for her. "I get off at 11:00 PM. If you're still around, we could talk then."

John responded with excitement, "I'll look forward to it."

Anna replied, "Me too."

"Can you show me to the meeting room?"

Anna responded, "Just follow me."

John thought to himself, *"I can't wait to watch her movements."* Anna has a great gait; her hips move back and forth with a fine rhythm and John is watching, albeit at a short distance, all the movement.

"Here is your room, and will I see you at 11?"

"You can count on it."

John entered the room where he heard from Mike, "I thought you were lost; we were just about to send out the Marines to find you."

"I'm sorry, I was distracted. Did I miss anything?"

Mike responded, "I just introduced my wife Mary, who is part of our team. Ted suggested that we order a J&B Scotch for you, so come in and sit down so we can get started." The waitress came by and took all the orders and left the room.

Mike spoke, "We have a few moments alone, so let me brief you on some housekeeping issues. We will eat all of our meals in this room. I expect us to meet most of the day in this room for the next three days. I will finish up my interviews over that time and when we meet on the last day the team will be formed. Homeland Security has arranged to get us a house that has a wall all around and a front gate. Each of you will have your own room and bath, and when you move into the house, it will be our meeting site. Sanibel seems to be the home of many retired FBI, Secret Service, and CIA; Homeland has contracted with several individuals to provide perimeter security."

Just then the waitress came through the door with salads and bread for everybody. Baker got a smile on his face when he heard Hadar say quietly, "I'm starving."

While John ate his salad, he couldn't seem to get the image of Anna out of his mind. He could never remember a time when one woman had such a dramatic impact on him at the first meeting. John would find out later that she is from Cleveland and has a brother named Will who is a charter boat captain. Their parents, Mark and Helen Walters, came to Sanibel forty years ago. Mark left the Ford plant and Helen was an elementary school teacher. They bought a house on Sanibel and sold it to the kids and moved to the Shell Point retirement community, which is located just before the causeway leading to Sanibel. Anna and Will are Sanibel natives, and neither has found a soul mate, so they live in the family home in the Gumbo Limbo section of Sanibel. They enjoy their work and try to enjoy life to the fullest. Little does John know that Anna was shocked at her reaction when she first met John and he doesn't know that right now she too is thinking some of the very same thoughts as John. *Could a complete stranger be the right one for me?*

Chapter 88

THE PLAN

The waitress brought coffee and dessert and left the room, and Mike told them, "We have some time, so let me tell you the mission. The President wants to start a two-pronged process that will choke off the money being funneled to terrorist organizations all over the world. He especially wants to stop the flow of U.S. Dollars to countries that support terrorism. Our job will be to find the sources of money that fund any terrorist organization. With the information we give the President, the U.S. government will bring economic sanctions against those nations. He will disclose our evidence to the world at the United Nations, and America will freeze all of their assets and strongly encourage other nations to do the same."

Omid asked, "Mr. Ridley…"

"Omid, let me stop you right there. We are a team and from now on all of you please, now this is an order, call me Mike. Understood?" All shook their heads in agreement and Hadar smiled because she was the first to be given the order. Mike continued, "Omid, your question please."

"Mike, we are less than six months to the general election. Everybody believes that Jordan will be the Republican nominee and the Democrats are likely to select Wild. So my question is: what happens if President Jordan is not reelected?"

"Omid, I raised that question with the President in my meeting and he said we are to work as long as he is President. If he is not reelected President, then the new President will be informed of our mission and he has the power to continue the program or not. The President told me his belief that he doesn't think it is possible to find and trace the money very quickly. He confided in me that we may not accomplish our mission even in his second term, but stopping the funding for terrorist has to be the highest priority for the nation."

Baker asked. "With the primary less than three weeks away, what do you think we can accomplish between then and now, and what could be accomplished before the election?"

All team members are waiting for Ridley's answer to this tough question. "Ted, as difficult as it is to say it, not much. I seriously doubt that we can find out enough information to be helpful to the President's reelection. I know that disappoints some or all of you, but I want to be a realist. I'm not the type of person that overpromises and under delivers. In all my years of working for the government, I have tried to set realistic goals for my boss and myself.

"I have had some experience infiltrating some of these organizations and it just takes time. We will have to worm our way into organizations and governments. I do believe that if we can take down the big funders, then the smaller ones will stop funding organizations too."

John asked, "Have you any thoughts as to how we can 'follow the money?'"

"John, my thoughts are not cast in stone. I want a great deal of feedback from all of you, but it seems to me the best way to find out how the money flows is to be a competing source of funding."

"Are you saying that our group will fund terrorist organizations to attack America?"

"The President has placed no limits on our activities. He has left it up to Frank Williams and me, along with all of you to develop the plans and then put them in place. So, to directly answer your question, John, yes. We may well be in a position to fund future attacks against the United States." Heads are spinning at the thought of America funding attacks against America.

Omid thought, *I didn't sign on to potentially kill Americans.* He spoke up, "Mike, I didn't sign on to kill Americans and while I don't know for sure, I don't think my fellow team members signed on to kill Americans either. There has to be a better way."

"Let me be very clear, we have been charged by the President to break the flow of money and identify to the world those who are laundering the money. If all of you feel the same as Omid, then I have misjudged you. We have an opportunity to change the world and if we succeed, we just may make the world a safer place, at least for a while. Placing limits on what we can do to achieve our goal will surely limit our success. The successful hunter is the one who has the most arrows in his quiver. If you are not ready to use every option to achieve success, then I can't have you on my team. Ladies and gentlemen, I need to know right now if you are fully committed. I want to go into this battle with as much ammunition as possible. Omid are you in or out?"

Chapter 89

MORDECAI TEXTS HADAR

It is less than three weeks until the election primary and the Brotherhood has been planning their exit from the United States. Mordecai has not yet responded to Hadar's text. He has been looking for an opportunity to go to the penthouse and respond to Hadar. The days have been warm in Houston and the air conditioning in the condo is not working well, so at night, many of the members' head to the rooftop to cool off.

Ishtar has been working very hard to coordinate their departure and he has most of the travel plans worked out. He asked Sargon to meet with him, "I want to tell the Brotherhood where we are going. We'll need Oleg to contact his uncle and start wiring money into our bank accounts. He will set up the accounts for us and have them funded before we leave. When we arrive, we will go to the bank, show our passports and give the president of the bank our account numbers."

Sargon asked him to rehearse the details. "How will the housing work?"

Ishtar responded, "Viktor will sign a long-term lease on the compound through one of his companies so none of our names will be listed on the lease agreement. His oil company will make the lease payments through a series of banks making it very difficult, if not impossible, to trace the source of the money."

"How will we get to the pickup point?"

Ishtar responded, "I have sent Michael to buy two cars. We will drive them to the pickup point and abandon the cars. Once we are aboard the mother ship, I will call my operative and tell him where to pick up the cars."

Sargon responded, "So, nobody will know where we left the country until we are gone. Excellent plan. Let's give the members the general outline at tonight's meeting. I believe it's okay to tell them where we are going."

Sargon called the meeting and asked Ishtar to tell the Brotherhood the overview of the plan. Ishtar spoke to the Brotherhood. "My brothers, the time is fast approaching for our departure to our new home. The American primary is two and one half weeks away. We will leave Houston in the early afternoon of Election Day in two cars and drive to our pickup point about two hours from here. A boat will land and pick us up and take us to our transport ship that will take us to our new home on the island of Saba in the Caribbean. I encourage you to spend some time tonight on the Internet looking up the island and all that it has to offer. I think you will find it a beautiful place with nice restaurants, beautiful beaches and beautiful women. We will meet again tomorrow, and I will do my best to answer your questions, but for tonight look at your new home."

★★★

Almost 1200 miles away as the dinner meeting is breaking up, Hadar's phone buzzed. She stepped outside, not to take a call but to remotely check on Mordecai to see if the ID bracelet is still working. The bracelet is the only way the Brotherhood can be tracked. She left a text message on Mordecai's phone that she was en route and could not talk until about nine in the morning Houston time.

★★★

Mordecai has seen the excitement on the Brotherhood's faces about their new home and said to Sargon, "I can tell it may be a while before I get to a computer. I'm going to the penthouse for some cool air and perhaps after my return I will get a chance at one of our computers to look at my new home. Have you looked at Saba Island? What do you think of it as a place to start over?"

Sargon responded, "I have spent a considerable amount of time looking at the island, albeit on the Internet. I think we will be happy and we can be safe and prosper."

Mordecai thanked Sargon for his thoughts and headed for the stairs. The Brotherhood has lived in this building for a while, and with no service to keep it clean, it has become dirty and has a stale smell. As Mordecai walked up the steps, he couldn't think about Saba, but only of Hadar and the last time he held her. He wondered, *could I convince her to come to Saba and live with me? What would it take to get her to come? I don't think it's money, but I will have a great deal of that. Perhaps I can find some need on the island that she can come and try to solve. Isn't that why she is going to Africa; to teach the natives how to build better housing? I need to see about poverty on Saba when I return.*

He reached into his pocket pulled out his cell phone and is ready to dial her number when he remembers she is on a plane and can't get cell phone calls. *I'll leave her a text and tell her I'll look forward to her call in the morning.* Mordecai thought about what he could say to convey his interest in her and at the same entice her. He paced back and forth on the sun deck; then the message came to him. The sun porch has no lights so when he opened his phone the light of the dial illuminated the deck; he pushed the keys in a text message and pushed Send.

In an instant, over 1200 miles away, Hadar's phone buzzed. She had started back to the meeting room in the restaurant and was somewhat startled by the text vibration. She stopped on the walk, opened the phone and read the message from Mordecai. Hadar said out loud but in a soft voice, "Oh. My. God." She closed the phone and hurried into the meeting room. Handing the phone to Mike Ridley, she said, "Open it and read the message from Mordecai."

Mike opened the phone and the screen illuminated with the message, "Come to Saba and live with me. M" Mike asked, "Does anybody know anything about a place called Saba?"

Chapter 90

FRANK WILLIAMS CALLS THE PRESIDENT

"Mr. President, we know where the Brotherhood is headed; they will be going to the island Saba in the Caribbean. Based on the best intelligence we have, we think they will make the move on primary day."

"Frank, do we know if the ID bracelet GPS is still working?"

"Mr. President, to the best of my knowledge it is; we checked the signal about thirty minutes ago. If it is still working, we should be able to track them all the way out of the country and to Saba. We'll find out in a few weeks whether it's with them or they left it behind. We have a team in Houston that has them under surveillance. When they move out, if we see no location change, then we'll know they left it behind.

"I have several backup teams that will follow them all the way to the escape point. In addition, I have already dispatched a team to Saba to get as close as possible to their compound."

The President responded to Williams, "Excellent work, keep me informed. I'll pass your information on to the Cabinet; I'm sure they will be pleased. Frank, one other question, how are the meetings going with Mike Ridley?"

"Mr. President, we had a rocky start, but I think Mike is coming around to the idea that he has a great team to work with him. It will take time, but I think they will come together. This assignment will take a long time to complete; I don't think the U.S. government has ever undertaken this level of espionage.

"We all think your idea may in fact bring a greater level of peace that has not existed in many decades."

"Your team may be the best hope for world peace."

Frank did not react to the President's statement but thought to himself; *I can't lay the idea of saving the world on my team. While it is a lofty idea, our people must build one block at a time, and it will take time before the wall has any shape.*

Mike told the team members, "Be back at Jacaranda at 8:00 AM sharp and be prepared for a full day of orientation; enjoy the rest of your evening."

John looked at his watch and noticed is close to the time when Anna is supposed to get off work, so he left the meeting room to look for her. In the meantime, Omid asked Megan, "Would you like to go for a walk on the beach?"

Megan responded, "Yes, but not a long one; you see I need to get to bed soon." She looked up into Omid's eyes and saw the change on his face. He understands what she means when she says she needs to get to bed.

Omid, looking back into her eyes said, "We will make it a short walk; I don't want to keep you out too late. I need to get to bed myself." The two of them headed to the beach for a quick stroll in the moonlight.

The sky is clear and the moon is bright and very large. Omid looked at Megan; she appeared soft in the glow of the moonlight and as she turned her body the bright moon highlighted her shape. Omid looks at her and thinks, *what a beautiful woman. How is it possible for me?*

Megan looked at Omid and asked, "What are you thinking?"

Omid stopped, turned and took Megan in his arms and then said to her quietly, "I'm the luckiest man in the world; you have changed me forever." The two of them gently kissed and then walked for a few more feet when Omid said, "Bedtime."

Chapter 91

JOHN FINDS ANNA...NOW WHAT?

John has been looking for Anna and can't find her. Finally in desperation, he asked one of the waiters, "Do you know were Anna is? I need to talk with her?"

"I saw her just a moment ago; let me see if I can find her, who shall I say is looking for her?"

"Tell her it's John from this evening."

The waiter disappeared and seemed to be gone for some time. When the waiter returned he said to John, "I think she left, I don't see her anywhere."

John said, "Thank you," and started toward the front door, somewhat disappointed. As he walked through the door, he saw Anna sitting on the bench people use when they are waiting to be called for seating.

John asked, "How long have you been sitting here?"

"Not long; I saw your meeting was still going on, so I decided to wait out here for a while hoping you would come through the door before I fell asleep or gave up and went home."

John asked, "May I sit with you?"

"Of course." She slid over to make room for him, but just enough so that he had to sit close to her. "How did your meeting go?"

John responded, "It started out a little rough, but I think we all have a better understanding of our mission."

Anna asked, "What was your meeting about?"

John thought, *what can I tell her that will not give away any information about what we are doing and yet will be believable and allow me to continue to see her while I'm here.* "Let me answer your question this way: You know when Apple Computer is working on a new product and they do their best to keep it secret until they are ready to tell the world what they have?"

"You mean like when they introduced the iPhone?"

"Exactly. We are working on a product that we need to keep secret until we are ready to release it to the public, so I can't really tell you anything, is that okay?"

"I wouldn't want you to break a confidence. Do you think you will be able release your product soon?"

"Unfortunately, tonight was the first planning secession and none of us have any idea how long it will take. On a happier note, I'm going to be around Sanibel for some time and I want to spend more time with you."

Anna responded, "I might like that."

John asked, "Is there anything you would like to do tonight? It looks like they have already rolled up the sidewalks."

Anna asked, "Have you ever had a Sanibel Sand Dollar?"

"I have never heard of a Sanibel Sand Dollar, what is it?"

"My car is over here I'll show you; hop in." They got into the car and Anna turned the car to the right out of the Jacaranda parking lot. They headed toward the lighthouse on Periwinkle, through the big intersection and continued toward the lighthouse. About a mile and a half from the four-way intersection, Anna turned into a lighted parking lot and John saw a sign that said Pinocchio's.

John looked at the line out the door and down the steps. "Is this an ice cream store?"

Anna responded, "This is an experience like no other. When we get inside you'll see. When you are asked, no matter what you see in all the cases, you want a Sanibel Sand Dollar, got it?"

"Yes, Ma'am." It took almost 20 minutes to get inside. John looked at all the flavors and in the corner of the storage case, he saw a sign that said Sanibel Sand Dollar.

John turned to Anna and she said, "You promised."

John ordered two scoops of Sanibel Sand Dollar in a waffle cone. The server scooped out the ice cream and turned his back to John. When he turned around to hand John his ice cream he saw that the server has put two animal crackers in the top of the ice cream. Anna got her cone and they went outside and sat on a bench and enjoyed their ice cream. John said to Anna, "I have never had anything like this before, can we get more?"

"Let's save some for the rest of the people. Next time we come, I'll let you try a different flavor; perhaps watermelon sorbet."

John thought, *then there just might be a next time.*

Anna turned to John and with a smile on her face she says, "I like the way you lick."

John thinks, *what does that mean?*

Chapter 92

NEXT MORNING

It's 7:30 AM and the team is assembled in the lobby. They got in the cars and head to Jacaranda. Ted asks the team, "Did you sleep well?" Megan and Omid looked at each other knowing they were up most of the night making love and got very little sleep, but they answered, "Fine." Hadar replied "Not enough; I had a lot on my mind." And John replied, "I never realized how milk just before you go to bed makes you sleep."

The rest of the way, the car was silent and when they pull into the parking lot Hadar said, "I'm starving. I hope they have some good stuff to eat." They all broke up laughing. She bolted from the team and headed for the back room and the food. The rest of the team joined her along with Mike and Frank, but this time Ellen and Mary are not in the room. Everybody got a plateful of food, and sat at the tables arranged in a horse-shoe shape with a small table in the open end for Mike.

When they finished their food and have their second cup of coffee, Mike called them to order. When the room quieted, Mike began, "Hadar received a reply to her message to Mordecai and she needs to respond this morning. For now, we must focus on what she wants to say in her text."

Frank told the team that he had updated the President on the potential location of the Brotherhood and by now a surveillance team is on its way to Saba. "We have another team outside of the apartment in Houston that is monitoring the Brotherhood's movements. They will be able to track the GPS in the ID bracelet if Mordecai takes it with him."

Ted spoke up to add, "We will have several teams follow them on primary day but from a significant distance just to make sure they all leave."

Mike spoke, "Thanks for the update; now let's move on to Hadar's reply. What are your thoughts?"

Ted suggested, "It appears to me that Mordecai is much more confident than the last contact. My guess is that he feels secure in the plan to get away and where they are headed; that is why he has asked Hadar to join him on the island."

John added, "Based on the physical abuse Hadar had to endure in Houston at their last meeting, it seems he still has the hots for her and he wants her in Saba to find out how great the sex can be for both of them."

Mike turned to Hadar and Megan for their thoughts. "Ladies, what do you think?"

Hadar was the first to reply. "I agree with John. He wants me in bed and that is all he wants. I don't think he is interested in me helping anybody but Mordecai. My concern is that if we postpone my visit, will he lose interest in me?"

Megan looked at Hadar and the rest of the team before she responded. All were wondering what the other woman on the team would have to say. "I have listened to all of your suggestions and I for one am not interested in sending my sister to Saba to be a sex slave to a terrorist. I see this differently than you do. In my forensics work, I have always tried to get to the facts. Let's review some of the facts: any man in the world, and some women, would be attracted to Hadar. She came here to help us, and we all understood it was her assets that attracted Mordecai to her. We decided, with her consent, to use her assets to try to catch the Brotherhood. We now know where they are and we have an ID bracelet on Mordecai so we can track him, all because of Hadar. We now know where they are headed for safety and we can track them. My guess is that once Mordecai gets to Saba, he will focus his sexual desires on a local girl. Because they never found out what the sex would be like, Mordecai will always be vulnerable to Hadar, at least for some time. I would respond that I just arrived in Africa and I have a lot of work to do and the people are expecting me to help them. I would very much like to come and be with you, but I don't think I can come for at least six months. The reality is we have no reason at the moment to put her at risk and we may never have a reason to put her at risk. We need to use the possibility of sex as a lure to keep attracting Mordecai."

After the team has had a chance to digest the comments from Megan, Mike spoke, "One of the traits of a great leader is an understanding of when to put teammates in harm's way. Can you as a leader find an alternative way to attack the problem? Megan, I think your idea is excellent and I wholeheartedly endorse it. I would like to take a recess so that Megan and Hadar can work out the details of the message, and when they are done we can talk about our mission."

After Megan and Hadar left the room, Hadar stopped Megan in the hallway and asked if they could talk for just a moment. "Megan I want you to understand that if the team wanted me to go to Saba and give myself to Mordecai, I would have done it. I would have not been happy, but I was willing to do it. Your action saved me and I will forever be grateful for protecting me. My guess is that you will not be able to protect me forever."

Chapter 93

OLEG CALLS HIS UNCLE

It is two weeks before their departure, and Sargon has asked Oleg to contact his uncle in Russia just to verify things are in place before the Brotherhood leaves for Saba. The time difference is nine hours, so at noon in Texas it's 9 PM in Moscow. Viktor Antipova is never in his office at nine o'clock in the evening, but the phone number that Oleg Barbolio was given goes directly to his cell phone, which Viktor always carries with him.

Oleg decided to make the call around eight in the morning to his uncle. He climbed the stairs to the penthouse to make his call. The DHS team was watching the sun deck, and saw Oleg walking out on the deck with his cell phone. The team turned on its electronic ear that can hear everything. Because of the range, they can hear the beeps as Oleg dials the phone. They now have the phone number and they can figure out who he is calling later. They heard the phone ring, and as soon as Oleg started speaking they knew it was Russian.

The DHS team has a Russian interpreter on the team and he is already listening in to Oleg's side of the conversation. "What they are talking about is confirming the bank accounts are set up and the house and cars are rented." The conversation changed, and Oleg asks if his uncle has seen the news on all the things America is doing to deal with the crisis. The interpreter does the best he can, but only hearing one side of the conversation he can only guess at the response.

The conversation went long enough that they picked up the frequency of Oleg's cell phone, so they were able to record the rest of the conversation. Oleg thanked his uncle and said he hoped to see him on Saba in about three weeks. Oleg told him he is looking forward to his visit. Oleg hung up and spent a little more time on the sun deck, and then made his way down the stairs. When he arrived at the apartment Sargon met him at the door and asked, "Everything still on track?"

Oleg responded, "We are ready to depart. Tomorrow I will check with the boat crew, but I don't anticipate any problems with our transportation."

The DHS team sent the tape of the conversation and the Russian interpreter back to the command post located in a Federal Building in downtown Houston at the U.S. Marshall's office located at 515 Rusk Street. Here they can come and go as they like and not be detected as DHS agents. Special agent Bagrov is a natural-born American from a Russian family that immigrated to the United States shortly after the Cold War began.

Agent Bagrov had been listening to the tape in the car on his way to the command center and is confused about what he is hearing on the tape. He told Commander Lewis, "There is something on the tape that doesn't make sense. I want to get another colleague to listen to the tape and see if he can figure out what is being said."

"Can you reach him quickly?"

"Yes. On the way over I sent him a text to see if he was available, and he said he was so I will need a quiet room, the smaller the better. I'll need a speaker phone, so I can make the call."

Lewis replied, "Give me a few minutes and I'll see what I can do for you." Bagrov plays the conversation over and over as he waits to hear from Lewis.

About fifteen minutes later, Commander Lewis appeared and said to Bagrov, "Follow me." They walked down the hallway and the commander opened a small room not much larger than a broom closet. Bagrov walked in and saw that the room has been soundproofed; perhaps for recording messages. The commander tells Bagrov that this was a studio that was used to broadcast messages to Mexico to try and convince Mexicans to stay at home. "There is a phone on the desk for you to make your call; I will stand guard until you are done."

The Brotherhood of the Red Nile

The commander closed the door and Bagrov made his call to his friend at CIA whose name is Zimin. The phone rang and Zimin answered. Bagrov tells him he wants to play a tape and get his opinion on what is being said. Zimin asked Bagrov to play it again and then again; in total he has played the tape twelve times. Finally he asks Zimin, "What did you hear?"

"I can't be sure, but he seems to say they own a Senator who will help them stop the progress America is making."

"Can you understand the Senator's name?"

"I think it's …"

Bagrov opened the door and has asked Commander Lewis to step in the room. He wants the commander to hear Zimin's translation of the phone call. Zimin repeated what he told Bagrov.

The commander was in shock when he heard what was said. He spoke to both of them. "This is a matter for the Attorney General." The commander took the recording and advised both men, "You cannot say anything to anyone except with the permission of the Attorney General. Do you both understand? Do you have any duplicates?"

They responded, "We understand, and no, this is the only copy."

Lewis told Bagrov to return to his unit and say nothing. As Bagrov left, Lewis thought about what he has to do. *I have to contact somebody; should it be Williams of DHS or should I go directly to Attorney General Clinton? Why would Clinton take my call? If I speak with Williams, I risk something leaking out. I will have to try the Attorney General and hope that he will talk with me, and I'll let him call Williams.*

Lewis decided to call the Attorney General. He looked in the Federal Directory and got the phone number for the AG office. He knows it's not the office of the AG, but perhaps he can get them to transfer his call. Lewis dialed the number and it rang several times. Someone answered the phone, "Justice Department. May I help you?"

"Yes. I'm Commander Lewis of the U.S. Marshals office in Houston, Texas, and I'm part of the observation team that is covering the terrorists, the Brotherhood of the Red Nile. I just received information of national security and I need to speak with the Attorney General immediately."

"Please hold." The operator comes back on the line, "I will transfer you to someone that can help you." At that moment his heart sank because he believes that he is going to be transferred to an assistant and he can only risk telling so much.

He heard the line click, "This is Attorney General Clinton, is this Commander Lewis?"

"Yes, sir, it is."

"Are you on a secure line, Commander?"

"Yes, sir." Lewis proceeded to tell Clinton his story and when he got to the name of the Senator, Clinton interrupted, "There must be a mistake; are you sure?"

"Sir, I had another translator double check and he agrees."

Clinton asked, "Who has the tape?"

"I do, sir."

"Other than the other translator, who knows the content on the tape?"

"Nobody, sir."

"I'm going to send a Treasury Department plane directly to Houston and I want you and the tape on the plane. You are to say nothing about it. When asked where you are going, you will respond that you're taking a few day's rest. Go home and pack a bag. I'll need your cell phone number so we can call you and give you the arrival time of the plane. Remember, say nothing to anybody."

"Yes, sir. May I ask you a question?"

"Of course. I'll do my best to try and answer it for you."

"Is it possible…?"

"Stop, do not ask the question; we'll discuss that when you arrive."

Chapter 94

THE MEETING ROOM AND
THE ASSIGNMENT

Hadar has sent the agreed upon message. Both Hadar and Megan return to the meeting room and Mike Ridley calls them to order. "Let's talk about the mission and the degree of difficulty that faces us. The President wants us to gather evidence on how the money flows from individuals or nations to fund terrorist groups. We are to find out who is sending the money and how it is processed. Once we can prove the path from sender to receiver, we will report to the President all the parties involved, and I mean everybody.

"Once we have the trail and we can prove it beyond the shadow of a doubt, we deliver it to the President. It's his prerogative to release the information to the press and Treasury Departments in the countries involved. Right now we have no idea of the magnitude of the money being funneled to these organizations. I think there are several types of organizations that we will need to identify, and then trace their source of money.

"We have the groups like the Brotherhood of the Red Nile who are concerned with interruption and destruction of the global capital markets. Then we have the groups that are infiltrating countries around the world trying to gain a foothold in the lives of people and eventually taking control of the government and turning these nations into Islamic nations."

Omid interrupted, "Mike, I'm sorry for interrupting, but I must ask a question. Do you really believe that Islam wants to control the world?"

"Let's establish a second ground rule of how we are going to work together; if you have a question, then ask it while it's on your mind. There are no dumb questions and a question left unasked is a danger to all of us. If we don't have a free flow of information from all of you, we leave ourselves very exposed.

"So, back to your question, Omid. Yes, I do believe that Islam wants to control the world; I believe that they feel they are right and the rest of the people of the world are wrong and it's up to the followers of Islam to change the world or die trying. Let me give you three examples of countries that have seen the rise of Islam and how it is changing those nation states. England, Ireland, and France are nations that have allowed an influx of people from predominantly Middle Eastern nations. They are changing the culture of these nations and will attempt to replace their laws with Sharia law. The creation of the European Union opened the borders to a virtually unlimited number of Muslims into these and many other nations. You can read in the papers how the citizens are concerned that they are losing their identity as Irish, French, or English.

"The European Union was established in 1993, just over twenty years ago. The migration of Muslims to the member nations is part of their plan to convert as many nations as possible to Islam. If they have come this far in 20 years, imagine what it will be like in another 20 years. Currently the Muslim population in Europe is in excess of 43 million or 6% of the population in the EU. It is estimated that in 17 years that the Muslim population in France will be at 40%.

"Let me use one more example right here in the United States. The Muslims wanted to build a mosque next to ground zero in Manhattan - the site of the September 11 attack and were outraged when people objected. We have a world that is worried about political correctness, and because we don't want to offend people, the Muslims use this against us. It was very important to them to have a mosque near ground zero because they knew that thousands of people would come to visit the site. They would see the mosque near the memorial and people would think the Muslims were also a peaceful people. They intended to use the mosque to reach out to the people of the neighborhood to help those in need and to enlighten them as to the ways of Islam. The mission of these mosques is more deadly than bombing buildings. In America, as of the end of the year 2000, we had just over 1,200 mosques, but by the end of 2010, just 10 years later, they had grown by 74% to 2,106. The population of Muslims in the United States has grown at the same rate as the mosques.

"It is possible that not all Muslims are out to conquer the world, but I think the vast majority would agree that Islam should rule the world."

Baker asked a question, "Mike, there are, by your count, 2,106 mosques in the United States. You have four people and yourself; how is it possible to even look at those 2,106 to find out if they are sending money to support terrorists?"

"Ted, good question. We need manpower, a lot of manpower, to collect data and send it to us. Let's just start with DHS and all the units under its control. We go through the Secretary of Homeland Security and order any data captured on any mosque where we think they are trying to influence by both legal and illegal means. We will first and for a long time just collect data; as we get more data, we look for patterns. For example, is a large percentage of the cash taken in by the mosque sent someplace else?

"These mosques don't just write a check to the Brotherhood; it has to be scrubbed by moving it through financial institutions. If we can find a pattern of the banks consistently involved, then we have a transfer point. I believe they use many transfer points in laundering the money. It is possible that some banks don't know they are scrubbing the money. If we can slow down the flow of money by identifying banks to the public, then we can interdict the funding for terrorists and other activities."

Megan asked, "Mike, where do we start?"

"Let's start with a map of the world and look at all the countries that have exploding Muslim populations. Let's pinpoint the mosques in that country and then see what we can find out by talking to people in the government or local community. In France, the people are starting to get angry with the Muslims taking over the country. The people who are upset will be an excellent source of information. One word of caution, if we want to talk to a government official, we need to do a background check to see if they are Muslim first. We will probably alert some leaders that we are collecting data, but hopefully we can keep our real mission secret for a long time."

Mike turned around and flipped on an overhead and said, "Here is where they are and this is where we start. These are the areas of the world with growing Muslim populations." The slide shows the concentration of Muslims around the world.

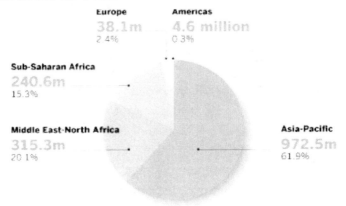

Europe
38.1m
2.4%

Americas
4.6 million
0.3%

Sub-Saharan Africa
240.6m
15.3%

Middle East-North Africa
315.3m
20.1%

Asia-Pacific
972.5m
61.9%

This chart from Pew Research shows that Asia has the highest number of Muslims. I don't want to dismiss Asia as a source of possible funding, but I think we need to focus our attention on the Middle East/North Africa, Sub-Saharan Africa, and Europe and America. Out of all of these, I think we should start with the Middle East and Europe.

"As we gather information, we may start to make some people very nervous and when we make people nervous, our lives may well be in danger. We will move to our new quarters this afternoon and begin to set up shop. I do not know where this assignment will take us nor do I know if we will be successful, but I do believe that as we release information to the President and he challenges people and governments, our lives will be in serious danger."

Chapter 95

PRIMARY DAY AND MOVING DAY

The Internet voting in primaries started at 12:01 AM on the East Coast. The voting will start at 12:01 AM in every time zone across the country, and then just as it opened, it will close at midnight in each time zone. Once all the polls have closed, the Federal Election Commission will announce the winning candidates for their party's nomination for President, Senators and Congressmen. After the FEC reports, then the states will report their outcomes.

It is about 9:00 AM in Houston. The voting has been going on for two and one-half hours. The Brotherhood has been up and packed since 6 AM. They have had their breakfast and were sitting in the living room waiting for Ishtar to tell them the activities of the day. Sargon addressed them, "My brothers, today is a great day, for we are leaving this wretched country of infidels and going to new place to continue our lives and the mission of Allah by bringing down America. We are headed to our new home that is beautiful and peaceful. We will build a mosque where we will pray and use our resources to support brothers who continue the mission. Ishtar, tell us please our route to paradise."

"My brothers, as you know, America is distracted by voting. The curfew has been lifted until midnight; it is under the veil of darkness that we will board our shuttle boat and be taken to international waters where we will be transferred to the mother ship that will take us to Saba. We want to be at the pickup point at the end of Jitney Road on the estuary of Sabine Lake by dusk. It should take us about two hours from here to the drop point. I do not want to spend more than ten minutes waiting for the pickup. We will stop at the beginning of Jitney Road and I will radio the shuttle boat our location and time to the pick us up at the pickup point. When they tell me they are twenty minutes away, we will start down Jitney Road with our running lights on for security. As we get closer to the pickup point, we will look for the incoming shuttle. My goal is to hit the pickup point just about the same time the shuttle arrives. I want us to grab our gear and proceed quickly to the boat. I want the whole transfer to take less than three minutes. We will all go below decks and wait until we have been told that we have cleared United States waters. We must be watchful of helicopters patrolling the coastline. Any questions?"

Cyrus asked, "How long do you think it will take once we are picked up to make it to Saba?"

"Depending on weather, it could take three days."

Michael asked, "If we are seen by a Coast Guard helicopter, what do we do?"

"We will have a SAM on the shuttle. If the Coast Guard gets close and asks us to go dead in the water so they can land and board, we may have to shoot them out of the sky." Ishtar's answer seemed to startle the rest of the Brotherhood.

Sargon could see the reaction on their faces. "Let me say that I have had a conversation with Ishtar and shooting the air ship out of the sky is a matter of last resort."

Ishtar responded, "The travel lane we are taking is not a major shipping lane; it should be clear at night and we will not use any running lights until we are in international waters. If the Coast Guard spots us, we will continue on. As a precaution, we will change the numbers on the boat so if the Coast Guard signals ahead with our old number they will think we are a different boat."

★★★

Every indication is that millions of people, perhaps for whatever reason, have been voting. William Wild knows that a lot of people are not able to vote because of the restrictions. Depending on the number of votes for him versus the President, he may have to find a way for more people to vote in the general election. All he can do at the moment is wait for the results; he is assuming that no challenger will gather enough votes to contest his nomination at the electronic convention. As the day progressed, the vote was going relatively smoothly for the first Internet election. Wild received some reports of servers crashing because of so many votes to process, but the standby servers rapidly brought the voting back on line. Wild was concerned about the ability of the computers at the Social Security server farm to keep up with the voter identification. Under his plan, they will not need the server farm at all.

Wild is concerned that if the vote in the primary is close, he will have to move quickly to change the rules. He decided that it could not be discussed at the convention. He needs a Judas goat to work on his behalf; he has decided that it will be the ACLU.

Chapter 96

TIME TO GO

The Brotherhood had their last dinner in America and were waiting for the signal from Ishtar that it's time to go. Ishtar looked at his watch; it's 9 PM. He said to the rest of the Brotherhood, "Time to go." They picked up their bags and headed downstairs to the cars; Ishtar has an intercom between the cars so they can stay in contact. In the first car are Sargon, Oleg, and Cyrus; in the second car are Mordecai, Ishtar, and Michael. Before they got in the car Ishtar, changed his mind and said, "Michael, you switch with Cyrus and drive; that way Michael and Mordecai both have American drivers licenses. If something goes wrong and we get pulled over, the cops will not be suspicious."

Across the street the observation post is scrambling with radio squelches, "They are on the move; let's get ready to roll."

A voice comes over the radio, "Do we have signal for the ID brace-let GPS?'"

"That's a roger, and strong too."

The command comes over the radio, "Let them leave and wait ten minutes before you depart."

"Roger."

"Is the silent bird in the air, and do you see them?"

"Bright as day." The commandos had been watching them along with the rest of the team. When Michael and Mordecai went out to fill the gas tanks for their trip, the commandos posed as window washers. So, at the traffic light outside the hotel, they washed and wiped the windows with a chemical that cannot be seen except with special night vision glasses.

One of the commandos riding in the silent helicopter is several miles behind the two cars and with his night scope he could easily follow them. The marking chemical was all over the hood on both cars. Right on time ten minutes later, the chase cars left to follow the terrorists. They would get updates from the chopper and would maintain distance and make the necessary turns. Everything was going well until they got off of Interstate 10 and headed to Port Author. They had to pick up route 87 South out of Port Author. Very quickly they realized there was no cover for them- just barren land. As they worked their way south on First Avenue, the chase cars decided to stop at the Coast Guard station and let the surveillance helicopter follow them to the drop point.

The team turned into the Coast Guard Station and Commander Lewis asked to speak with the base commander. Lewis explained with the least amount of detail what was going on and he needed to know if he had any aircraft in the sky locally. The base commander looked at his flight board and he saw that he did have one rescue unit on routine patrol.

Lewis asked, "When are they due back and how will they approach the base?"

The commander responded to Lewis's question, "The normal flight pattern is to fly across the Sabine Pass channel and then follow Jitney Road right into the landing pad."

Lewis asked, "What time are they due in?"

"About 11:45 PM. Why is that so important?"

"How far is the flying time from the start of Jitney Road to the base?"

"Well, depending on winds, about fifteen to twenty minutes." The pickup is due at 11:30; just about the time the chopper is crossing on to Jitney Road.

"Commander, you need to get on the radio and tell the chopper to come in from the north and do it now."

"Why should I take orders from you?"

"Commander, I'm speaking to you on behalf of the President of the United States and I'm ordering you to call that chopper and divert its approach."

"I have no order to tell me to make the change." Commander Lewis pulls out his side arm and points it at the base commander's head, "Do it now or I will blow your head off and make the call on my own; you have to the count of three. One, two…"

"Okay, I'll do it." He walked over to the radio and called the chopper. "Tango Zulu 45, please come in, over."

No response. Lewis looked at his watch and it read 11:23. "Call again."

"Tango Zulu 45, please come in, over." Still no answer; it is now 11:26.

Lewis, now panicking, said, "Call again!"

"Tango Zulu 45, please come in, over." No response.

Lewis called his helicopter. "How far out are you from the drop point?"

"We are about – oh My God!"

Lewis yelled, "What happened?"

"I just saw a huge fireball like something exploding in the air."

Lewis knew what it was and turned to the base commander and said, "Sorry about your loss."

The shuttle boat took on its passengers and sped off to international waters. Mordecai looked at Ishtar and said, "You just blew that helicopter out of the sky."

"I had to because they were a threat to our exit. I think we will be safe now." This is the second killing for Ishtar, and Mordecai wonders how many more?

Chapter 97

EARLY MORNING AT THE WHITE HOUSE

It is three thirty in the morning and Karen wakes Nathan, "The returns will be in shortly, put on your robe and join me in the living room." Karen had on a dark blue silk dressing gown with a gold sash; as she turned away to go to the living room, Nathan reached out and grabbed the gold sash and pulled on it. The tug untied the sash and the gown flew open to reveal the front of Karen's naked body. Jordan continued to pull on the sash and the gown came off her left shoulder. It happened so quickly that Karen didn't initially realize she was so exposed. Once she realized what was going on, she quickly grabbed the gown and pulled it back around her. She realized the President of the United States would rather play with her than watch election returns. And come to think of it, she would choose playing with Jordan over election returns anytime.

Karen climbed into bed and straddled the President who was still under the sheets; she opened the gown and let it flow down the sides of her naked body onto the sheets. Karen looked into Nathan's eyes and leaned down to kiss him on the lips. As she came down her breasts pressed on the sheets. She could feel that the President wanted her and she desperately wanted him, too. After a slow twenty minutes of lovemaking, Karen said, "Let's go see who won."

Karen got up and tied her robe. The President got up and put on a black silk robe with the Presidential seal on it. They both brushed their teeth and their hair and walked hand in hand down to the living room. Because of the rules set by the Federal Election Commission, no results could be reported until twelve thirty Pacific Time. Nathan had no doubt that he won the Republican nomination, for he was unopposed. He wasn't as sure of the outcome on the Democratic side, but he will just wait and see. At twelve forty five the results were released on C-SPAN; William Wild will face Nathan Jordan for the Presidency of the United States in November.

Now that the outcome is official, the networks start to discuss the statistics on who voted and why. The major unknown was how Internet voting would affect the number of people voting. The country had never before had Internet voting, and the outcome of the primary might have an impact as to how the candidates would conduct the fall campaign.

The news anchor for NBC Election News reported that the voter turnout was unimaginable. In Nathan's first election as President, the turnout was 48% of the eligible voters. In this primary, 68% of eligible voters participated in the Presidential primary. The reporter went on to say that in many states, the turnout for state and local officials was almost 70%.

Jordan was most interested in the total vote count for him in the primary; he believed that Wild would be just as interested. The numbers were almost dead even for both men. These numbers would mean that even though a lot more people voted, neither candidate outdrew the other. Jordan said, "This will be a very close election in November." At the same time, William Wild decided it was time to make a call to see if he could affect the outcome in his favor.

Wild knew that being the front-runner and a virtual shoo-in to win the nomination he was under Secret Service protection; including monitoring his phone calls, which he believed was illegal, but justified in the end. However, Attorney General Clinton had instructed the Secret Service to notify him immediately if Wild made any calls to the organizations on the list he gave them.

At three thirty in the morning, William Wild dialed 202-457-0800; then he punched in the extension number 453. The phone rang three times and a voice said, "I saw the result; when do you want to meet?"

Wild responded, "After the convention next month, but you could start working on your brief now?"

The Secret Service Special Agent Mitchell who was in charge saw the phone number on the computer log that was dialed from Wild's personal cell phone. It matched a number on the Attorney General's list. "Should I contact the office of the Attorney General now or wait until morning? I think I will wait and notify him in the morning; how important could it be anyway?"

Chapter 98

ON THE WAY TO THE MOTHER SHIP

All of the Brotherhood was in shock after Ishtar used a SAM to bring down the Coast Guard rescue helicopter. They went below right after they boarded the shuttle; all except Ishtar. Nothing was said about anything for almost twenty minutes, but to Cyrus it seemed much longer. It was total silence. Sargon finally spoke, "I, like you, did not expect that we would have to shoot down the Coast Guard helicopter, but the hard cold reality is that it was right on top of us. They could have sent our position to the base and brought in more support. We could well have been captured; I don't think we had any choice."

The shuttle made its way out into the Gulf, still several hours away from the mother ship. Back on Sanibel, Hadar checked the signal on the ID bracelet. It has tracked Mordecai's movements and shows him heading east and south from the inlet where the Brotherhood were picked up. Frank Williams' phone rang and he was told about the downed Coast Guard helicopter at the pickup point.

Frank responded, "Any survivors?"

The response came back, "No."

"Are we tracking them by plane or satellite?"

The response was, "Sir, we are using both."

"How low does the plane have to fly?"

"Sir, are you asking is the plane in range of a SAM?"

"Yes, I am."

"Then the answer is we are using a Coast Guard Search and Rescue plane which was retro-fitted to track the signal. It does not have to fly that low, but it could be seen from the ocean at night because of its running lights."

Williams commanded, "I can track it with a satellite; have the plane return to base immediately. Please confirm that it has broken off pursuit."

There was a long pause, and Frank could hear conversations in the background. The voice returned and said, "Message received and the plane is returning to base."

Frank walked to Mike's house and knocked on the door. While he waited for Mike to answer the door, he thought, *those young men who were in the business of saving lives just gave their lives for our country. The aircraft was unarmed. It was going in to help people and those same people took their lives.*

Mike opened the door and saw Frank. "Something happen?"

Frank told Mike about the downed Coast Guard aircraft at the pickup site.

"I assume by the look on your face there were no survivors?"

"None."

"Frank, please come in for a moment and let's talk."

Frank walked in and Mike offered him a drink, "Just a beer, please."

"Frank, I have been in this spy business for a long time and I have seen good people get killed because they were in the wrong place at the wrong time. I hope that you or I never get a phone call from somebody to tell us that we lost one of our team. As dangerous as this mission is, I fully expect that I will lose at least one, before it is over. The more information we find, the more exposed we will be to attack. I think I want to go to the President and get a disappearing agreement for each of the Pathfinders much like the one I had with President Carter. If they survive, then they need to be taken care of and protected."

Frank responded, "You mean the way the Logistics Office sheltered and protected you?"

"Exactly. I will call the White House and arrange a meeting with the President as soon as possible."

Frank's mood brightened because he felt that Mike could get the President to issue the orders and he could tell the team what was in store when the mission was complete. He said to Mike, "We have to do everything possible to protect the team members' identities."

Mike responded, "I agree." But he thought, *these people would be going after bad guys who place no value on life; if you get in the way, they will blow you away just like those pilots tonight.*

Chapter 99

CLINTON AND THE PHONE
CALL FROM WILD

Attorney General Clinton arrived at his office late because he wanted to watch the returns. When he arrived, he saw that his private line was blinking; he picked it up and dialed in his security code to retrieve the message. Clinton heard, "Sir, this is FBI Special Agent Mitchell assigned to Senator William Wild. You left a note that if Mr. Wild made a phone call to a phone number on your list you wanted to be notified. Around three forty five this morning, I saw the phone in Mr. Wild's home dial one of those numbers. While I could not see who was making the call, I know that the phone called one of your numbers. Please advise what you want me to do with the information? You can reach me at the VIP security center." Mitchell left a return phone number and Clinton wrote it down.

Clinton walked over to his safe, dialed the combination and took out the transcript of Oleg's conversation with his uncle Viktor in Moscow. He read the part where Viktor said, "We have an American Senator on our side and in our pocket; his name is William Wild." Clinton walked back to his desk and sat down and began to think about what is in front of him. *Is it possible that Senator Wild, the Democratic nominee for President of the United States is working for and with terrorists? Does he want to be President so badly that he would sell his soul to terrorists to become President?*

What do I do with this information? I need to get the phone number from Agent Mitchell to see who was being called last night. I will go to the security center and

*get the number. Nobody needs to know any of this; when the time is right, I will
have to decide if I'm going to confront him, or will I have the President contact him.
No, I can't involve the President. He has to be out of the loop. It will have to be me,
one-on-one with Wild. He has to know that if he doesn't quit the race, I will surely
find a way to release the information to the press.*

*I need more evidence. I will call and get an appointment with Judge Thomas
Taylor, chief judge of the FISA court. I will ask Judge Taylor to give me a wiretap
order for Senator Wild's phones. He will want to know why and I will only tell him
that we suspect that someone connected with Wild may be a spy for the Russian
government. Now that he is the nominee for the Democratic Party, he will get classified briefings. We need to do our best to make sure that classified material doesn't
get into Russian hands.*

*How do I control the information we hear in the wiretap? The greater the
number of people involved, the greater the chance that we have a leak. I'm going
to have to talk with Frank Williams and see what he recommends and whom he
thinks can handle the job and keep it secret. My guess is that Wild will not make a
move until after the Democratic Convention, so I have three weeks to get this set up.
First, Judge Taylor, and at the same time Frank Williams. Now I have to go to the
Security Center.*

Clinton asked his assistant to have the car brought around and told her,
"I will be gone most of the day. If you need to reach me, call my cell
phone." Clinton took the elevator down to the ground floor and got in the
car. "We are going to the mobile security command center at 9 Q Street
NW; will you close the partition, please." Clinton waited until the privacy
partition is in place; then he called Judge Taylor.

The phone rang several times and a woman answered the phone, "Judge
Taylor's office; may I help you?"

Clinton responded, "This is Attorney General Drew Clinton. Is Judge
Taylor available?"

"I'll check for you sir... I'm sorry, Mr. Attorney General, but Judge
Taylor is in a hearing at the moment and asks if he can call you in about
an hour?"

Clinton replied. "That will be fine. Here is the number where he can
reach me - oh, will you tell Judge Taylor it's very important and I need to
speak with him in private."

"I will get the message to him."

Just as Clinton hung up with Judge Taylor's office, the car turned the corner on Q Street; he could see the trailer up ahead. "Please pull in behind the trailer and wait for me."

"Yes, sir."

Clinton knocked on the door and it opened. A rather young-looking, extremely well-fit man inquired who he is and what he wants. When Clinton told him, the young man snapped to attention.

Clinton told the young man, "Relax, I'm looking for FBI Special Agent Mitchell; is he around?"

"Sir, I'll check the duty roster. Sir, he had the night shift, so he is off duty now."

"Do you know where I can reach him?"

"Sir, I can try and reach him on the phone for you if you would like."

"Please try to locate him."

The agent checked the duty roster and found a contact number and dialed it. The phone rang and rang and a groggy voice answered "Mitchell."

"Agent Mitchell, I have the Attorney General here in the headquarters looking for you."

"Put him on the phone."

"Sir, I didn't know you were coming or I would have stayed."

"Not a problem; do you know where the phone records are from last night?"

"Yes, sir. I have them with me. I don't live far from the command center; if you give me ten minutes I can meet you there."

"That will be fine. I will be in the Black SUV behind the command center; when you arrive, knock on the door."

"Yes, sir. Oh sir, after I left you that message, a second number appeared from your list."

"Do you remember the number?"

"No, but I have it here." He gave the number to Clinton and said, "I will be there in ten or less."

Clinton had written down the phone number 202-298-5700. He dialed the number and the voice said "The Embassy of the Russian Federation" and Clinton pushed the end button on his phone.

Chapter 100

TED AND HADAR FINALLY TALK, AND?

It has been over two weeks since Ted and Hadar had their interlude on the steps at the Tween Waters Inn. It would have been easy to take her upstairs and have sex with her, but he needed to find out where their relationship was going. As much as he wanted her, he wasn't interested in a one-night stand. They agreed to discuss and figure it out, but the meeting has not taken place and Hadar is getting really upset. They have barely spoken to each other; there has been very little eye contact and no sexual flirting. Hadar has had enough, and she has decided that she is going to make the first move with maximum force.

She is in her room planning her attack; first she has to decide what to wear and then what to say. She knows that each room has a peephole in the door and she guesses that Ted will look out to see who is there after he hears the knock on the door. Hadar walked over to her door and visually measured where the peephole came on her body. She saw that the hole in the door is just above her chin. She figured if she stood back about two feet Ted would see her breasts.

She looked through her clothes and found a very skimpy two-piece string bikini. She put it on and said as she looked in the mirror, "Perfect." If she pulled the top down under her breasts, it adds some support but she doesn't need support; the movement is more for effect. She turned her attention to the words she needed to say to get Ted to open the door. "Ted,

322

we need to talk, and I'm prepared to stand out in front of your door naked and yell to the world until you let me in."

She grabbed a white sheer beach cover-up, except it doesn't cover much. So, she had to walk with her arms over her chest. Ted's room is in the back of the complex. It has a small water garden with a bench where they could sit and talk. Hadar walked to Ted's door and took a deep breath. She knocked on the door and took a step back to wait for Ted to answer the door. She opened the cover up and slid the top under her breasts; no response from Ted. She knocked again and no answer. She is sure Ted is in his room. The light is on, why doesn't he answer the door?

She heard a voice to her left, and it is Ted leaning against the wall. Hadar had to make a quick decision. *Do I cover up before I turn to him or do I face him naked?* Hadar turned to Ted naked and said, "Are we going to talk?"

"You know, this is the second time I have seen those and I'm just as impressed. They are beautiful; you are beautiful."

"So, I'm not asking you to have sex, although that might be nice. No, that would be fantastic. All I'm asking is for us to figure out where we are going, but if we don't ever talk about it, how will we ever figure it out?"

Ted asks, "Are you cold? You have been exposed to the night air for a while and with the amount of skin surface area I'm concerned…"

Whack.

"You know," he said with a smile on his face, "I missed those. I need to be smacked around now and then."

"My pleasure; so are we going to talk tonight?"

"Let's go in so you can warm up, but could you please put them away, at least for a while?"

Hadar reached under her breasts and pulled up the top to cover her breasts. She could tell by the look on Ted's face that she needs to use the cover-up.

Ted's room has a couch and a chair. Hadar sat in the middle of the couch and Ted starts toward the chair, but Hadar pointed to the couch telling Ted, "Sit here next to me."

Ted reluctantly sat down next to Hadar; she turned to her left and brushed Ted with her left breast. She realized that Ted tried to slip away so she says, "I'm sorry. Sometimes I am not aware how close I am to someone and I rub them the wrong way. That didn't come out right," and they both laugh.

Hadar says, "It felt good to laugh with you; I have missed that. Ted, what is wrong with me?"

"Hadar the problem is not you; the problem is me. You see I was married once and I thought I was in love with my wife and I guess I was for some time. But I got a promotion and I was spending more and more time working and I had less time for her, so finally she asked me to choose – find a different job or wife. I chose the job.

"I'm very attracted to you. In fact, who wouldn't be, but I don't want to make the decision to choose again, and I'm afraid that if we go to bed together, I will be forced to choose all over again."

Hadar has been listening to Ted and has some tears in her eyes as she tries to understand his pain and his dilemma. "Ted, thank you for sharing your issues and concerns with me, but I must react to what you are concerned about. We are going to be working on this project until at least the end of the year and perhaps a great deal longer depending on the outcome of the election. I have already asked you to help me become an American, and I do want to stay here and help in any way I can. I can't say that I don't love you, but I can't say that I do either. I feel a powerful attraction stronger than I have ever felt for anyone before. I don't want to lose this opportunity. If I have found my soul mate, if it is you… you may be my once in a lifetime lover, friend, and husband.

"I have a suggestion. Let's try it out until we find out if this assignment is going to be extended. Mike has told us that this assignment could take years to complete and we will all be at high risk. If something should happen to you and we had never made love, I would shrivel up and die. Somebody once said, 'It is better to have loved and lost then to have never loved at all.'"

Ted responded, "I think it was Tennyson who made that statement on love. If we go to bed tonight, we may well be setting ourselves up for a loss in many ways."

Hadar responded, "I believe we will be forever changed; only time will tell how much."

Hadar slowly stood up and reached back for Ted's hand. He took hers and stood up next to her. He took off Hadar's wrap and let it fall to the floor. As they walked to the bed Ted asked, "Are you going to hurt me?"

With a very serious look on her face she said, "How could I hurt you?"

"You could smother me."

Whack! They both fell on the bed and laughed and...

Chapter 101

CLINTON AND JUDGE TAYLOR

Drew Clinton is in his car waiting for Special Agent Mitchell to bring him the record of the calls from Senator Wild's house this morning. While he is waiting, he got a phone call from Judge Thomas Taylor of the FISA Court. The FISA court is a special court that was set up after the September 11th attack that issues special orders including wire taps in cases of national security. The Judge returned the call himself. "Drew, how are you and how can I help?"

"I'm fine, Judge Taylor, but I need to speak with you on a matter of national security as soon as possible."

"If you can hold for a moment, I'll check my calendar."

"Go right ahead."

Judge Taylor came back on the line. "I can meet with you at four this afternoon in my office, will that work for you?"

Clinton responded, "I'll be there at four. If I'm going to be more than a few minutes late, I'll call you." Just as he hung up, someone knocked on his window. Clinton asked his driver to identify the person knocking. The driver exited the car and checked the identification; it is Special Agent Mitchell.

Mitchell opened the door and got in the car and sat opposite from Clinton. He reached in his pocket and pulled out the telephone log that shows all the calls in and out of Wild's house, from 12 AM to 6 AM today. Clinton recognized one of the numbers from his list. It is the DC office of the ACLU; he double-checked the other number, and it matches the phone number he called a while ago.

Clinton asked, "Where is this log kept and who is in charge of securing it?"

Mitchell responded, "Sir, the phone log is kept by computer and we print out the information on paper. That is where this came from. At the end of the day, the digital log is downloaded to a CD and is sent to the Hoover building where it is cataloged and then sent into storage; probably offsite somewhere. I don't know for sure."

"What happens to the information on the computer after the download?"

"Sir, it is my understanding that the data is erased from the hard drive at the end of every download."

"Is it possible that the data could be retrieved even if the hard drive is erased?"

"Sir, this is not my field, but I have been told that what we do is reformat the storage disk, and that makes it almost impossible to recapture data."

Clinton said to Mitchell, "Have you spoken to anyone about this?"

"No, sir, no one."

"Special Agent Mitchell, I'm going to have you reassigned to me for a special mission; I will be in touch. You are to tell no one about this, am I clear?"

"Yes, sir."

"I'll be in touch soon."

"Yes, sir." Mitchell left the car.

Clinton told the driver, "I want to go to the Old Post Office Building at Pennsylvania and 12th and I want you to wait away from the building, and I will call you when I'm ready."

It took about twenty minutes to get there. At about three thirty, he walked into the lobby and he realized that he had not had any lunch. He spotted the Georgetown Deli in the lobby and a few tables outside the deli. He walked in and ordered a turkey sandwich on whole wheat with Swiss and lettuce, tomato, bacon, and mayo. Then he asked for a Diet Coke and a bag of salty chips. Clinton sat at a small table. It is late in the afternoon and there are not many people around. It will start getting busy at four thirty when the first shift is letting out. He took his time enjoying the sandwich. Finally, he looked at his watch and saw that it was five to four. Clinton got up, finished his soda with a burp, and threw everything in the trashcan. He headed for the elevator.

Clinton reached to push the up button, but the door opened. He stepped in and pushed the eleventh floor; the doors closed and he was alone. He thought to himself, *I wonder if they chose the eleventh floor because they were established due to the terrorist attack on September the eleventh.* The door opened. As he stepped out he looked at the directory on the wall; all he saw were names. He looked for Taylor, in 1106. The sign directed him to turn right. Clinton walked down the hall and saw office 1106, turned the knob and walked in.

The receptionist greeted him and said, "May I help you?"

"Yes, I have a four o'clock appointment with Judge Taylor."

"And your name, sir?"

"I'm Drew Clinton."

"I'll let Judge Taylor know you are here; please be seated."

Clinton sat down and noticed he is the only person in the waiting room. He looked at his watch and it is exactly four o'clock. Thomas walked out a door with his hand extended welcoming Clinton. "Please follow me, Mr. Attorney General." The receptionist is shocked that the Attorney General of the United States was in her reception room.

Taylor led Clinton down a hallway to an office that has Taylor's name on it. They walk in and Taylor asked, "Drew, can I get you something to drink, coffee, tea, soda, water?"

"No thank you; I'm fine."

"Then if I can't get you something to drink, what can I do for you?"

"Thomas, I must ask that this conversation, for national security reasons, be kept totally confidential; you must assure me that you will not discuss what we are about to talk about with anyone. Is that clear?"

"Yes, sir."

"Excellent."

"Judge Taylor, I would like the FISA court to order a wiretap for a U.S. Senator who may be working either directly or indirectly with the Brotherhood of the Red Nile."

"Isn't that the group that bombed Texas and Louisiana?"

"The same one. We also believe he will try to subvert the Presidential election in the fall. Furthermore, we have some evidence that he is being paid off by the Russian government, or at the least a very wealthy Russian by the name of Viktor Antipova."

"How do you know the connections?"

Clinton shared all the information he has with Taylor, holding nothing back.

"If I'm going to approve the wiretap, what restrictions would you place on it?"

"I will have two Special Agents assigned to me. They will record all the phone calls in and out of his home or office and all of his cell phone calls. These two agents will report directly to me. They will edit and destroy any conversation not pertinent to the investigation. When and if we have enough information to warrant an arrest, we will come and ask for a warrant for an arrest with charges of treason."

"Drew, so far you have not given me a name, and until I get a name, I can't issue an order for a wiretap. Who is the person under investigation for treason?"

"Thomas, it is very difficult to tell you because it is so hard to believe that a U.S. Senator would betray his country to win higher office, but the person's name on the wiretap order is Senator William Wild."

"Is that the same Wild running for President?"

"Judge Thomas, I'm afraid so."

"I just can't believe it - a sitting U.S. Senator would commit treason to win the Presidency."

"Judge Taylor, I have reviewed the FISA rules, and I understand you can give me the order and then seal it so only the two of us for the moment would know. If we do not find the supporting material, then you can destroy the order. On the other hand, should we find sufficient evidence, then I would come to you asking for a federal grand jury to investigate the charges."

"I will draft the order later today and hand-deliver it to you in the morning at Justice; is that soon enough? And per your request, I will seal the order… what has our nation become?"

Chapter 102

NEW HOME FOR THE BROTHERHOOD

After a long and at times a stormy journey, the Brotherhood has reached their new home on Saba. They are still trying to get over the downing of the helicopter at the pickup point, but the more they discuss it, they understand why it had to be done. The have timed their arrival on Saba after midnight. They are met at the dock at Wells Beach by two of Ishtar's operatives with cars. The Brotherhood gets into the cars and they are swiftly driven to the compound where they will live in fantastic luxury. All are very tired, as the rough seas didn't allow for much sleep. When they walk into their houses in the gated compound, they are only interested in going to bed.

After a good night's sleep, Ishtar spoke to Sargon. "We need to go to the RBC Bank at Windwardside to sign up for our accounts. I will have U.S. Passports for each of us to present to the bank. In the case of Michael and Mordecai, I will exchange their old U.S. Passports for new ones with a different street address and town. After we go to the bank, we will want to go to the Big Rock Market and see what they have to eat. When we return, we will send the servants shopping to stock the kitchens. If we want something different, we can ask at the market. If they cannot get what we want, we could contact one of the hotels and find out where they get their provisions. If we fill our brothers' bellies, they will feel better."

Sargon asked, "Will we have TV in our houses?"

"I have arranged for our own satellite dish, so we can watch whatever we want."

"Will we have American networks on the service?"

"Yes, sir, we will, and I have also arranged for backup generators to be installed at each house. I will have a supply of gasoline to power the generators in case we lose power during the hurricane season."

Sargon called for a Brotherhood meeting in his house in fifteen minutes.

Back in Sanibel, Hadar checked the signal on the ID bracelet GPS and pinpointed Mordecai's location. Hadar passed the coordinates to Frank who relayed them to the surveillance team on Saba.

The team leader informed Williams, "We've got them."

Williams thought, *as long as he wears the ID bracelet, we can track them anywhere in the world. The challenge will be if Mordecai finds another woman that will not want him to wear a bracelet with Hadar's name on it; how likely is it that he will take it off?*

The Brotherhood has assembled. Sargon told them, "I have seen nothing on the American media that has said anything about the helicopter crashing. We have to assume that the government didn't know anything about who or why the aircraft was shot down. The spot we chose to leave from did not have boat traffic, so it is possible that the helicopter thought we were smugglers bringing in drugs. Moving on, each of you will have satellite TV in your house as soon as we can get them installed. Until then, feel free to come to my house and use the TV.

"In a few moments, we will get in the cars and be taken to the RBC Bank to verify our deposit accounts. Each of you will receive a new American passport including Michael and Mordecai. I will want you to give me the old ones and I will keep them in a safe here in my house."

Cyrus asked, "What if I want to go back to Iran?"

Oleg asked, "What if I want to go back to Russia?"

Ishtar turned to Michael and whispered in his ear, "Fat chance of that ever happening."

Sargon knew he had to respond to the questions and wonders, *do I tell them the truth - that none of us will ever be able to go home? The U.S. government put a $25 million bounty on Osama and it still took them ten years to find and kill him for killing 2,700 people and knocking down two buildings. How much bounty will be on **our** heads and how long do we have?* "I want to be truthful. I think, it may be a long time before we can ever go to our home countries. Since I do not know if it is a day or a lifetime, we must enjoy this beautiful island for as long as we can.

"I do want to talk about your bank accounts. Each of you is responsible for managing your money. You cannot under any circumstances have an account in the United States. The account opening disclosure will create an opportunity for the U.S. government to find us. We cannot give them the tools to find us. No money can be sent to the United States regardless of how many times you scrub it. No mail can go to the U.S. from here. If you leave Saba and go to a different place, you can send mail to the U.S. from that country, but no return address in Saba can be used. The last thing is a visitor from off-island. You must present somebody you want to invite to the island before the entire Brotherhood for vetting and approval. If they are not approved, then they cannot under any circumstances come."

Mordecai has been listening to what Sargon is saying, but he looked at his ID bracelet from Hadar and thought, *she is not from America; she is in Africa, so maybe I can get her approved to come to Saba. He ran his finger across Hadar's name and remembered their contact in Houston. Do I really need to ask for permission to bring her to the island?*

Chapter 103

WILD PREPARES FOR
DEMOCRAT CONVENTION

The rules from the Federal Election Commission state that the winner of the majority of the votes in the primary is the party nominee. William Wild has the vast majority of votes in the Democratic primary, so he will be the Democratic Party nominee. Wild has chosen Fred Tulu as his Vice-President. The webcast Convention will begin in two hours on C-SPAN to conduct business and give acceptance speeches. The Convention will run from 7-9 PM Central Time. The speeches will be uploaded to YouTube so they can be viewed by anybody who wants to see them. These speeches will be on YouTube until the day before the general election. They will be shut down on Election Day and then made available forever after that.

It is three weeks until Wild's Convention speech and he has been working diligently with his speechwriters on what he wants to say to America. "I'm really only going to have about twenty minutes under the rules, so I have to be crisp and to the point. I must point out the differences between us; there must be a clear separation between us."

Grady, one of Wild's speechwriters asked a question. "Sir, wouldn't it be better to more closely align yourself with the President; the more distance you have, the easier it is to vote for the incumbent? If you're both on the same side of finding the terrorists, then it is a matter of how you might go after them that is important to the American people?"

"No, they just want to get them."

"So, what you are saying is, I should agree with Jordan on the substance of the issues but differ on the tactics? Do you really think the American people at this stage of the crisis are concerned about nuts and bolts? They want hope and they want to believe that their President wants the best for them and will do his best to give them what they want. That is what they want to hear. I can't go on that stage and say in my acceptance speech that I agree in principal with what Nathan Jordan plans to do. You may be right that it's what I should do for the good of the country, but let's face it, that wouldn't be good for William Wild." Then, in a voice that is loud and angry Wild addressed his team. **"I want to be President of the United States and I'll do anything to make it happen, is that understood?**

"Here are the points I need to make in the speech for now, not necessarily in this order:

Jordan is a failed president, he is responsible for the safety of the country and was responsible when 60,000 Americans were killed;

He has used the Executive Order to the point that he has become a dictator taking your rights away;

Jordan keeps you locked in your houses with curfews and Martial Law;

He is spending trillions of dollars of your tax money on pipelines to nowhere;

He keeps you from getting your money out of your bank;

He has isolated us from the rest of the world;

What will I do for you as your President?

First, I will suspend the curfew and Martial Law. America is a free country, and its people need to be free to seek the opportunities of this great country.

Second, you need money to spend and we have the ability to give you money. I want to reopen the banks and supply them with enough cash to give people who need their money to pay bills and feed their families.

Third, I want to put people to work all over the country; not just in one region of the nation. We have to repair bridges and highways and hire more teachers so we can improve the quality of education for future generations.

Four, our energy resources may have been destroyed, so I want to have a spending program much like the ones used to put a man on the moon to develop alternative energy, green energy jobs for America, good paying jobs for Americans.

Last, I want America to be great again. We need to be members of the world community. We cannot devolve into an isolationist nation; we must rejoin and take our membership position alongside the other nations of the world. It is my hope that working together with other nations, we can find the people who brought this terrible destruction and loss of life to America to justice."

"This is what I want to say, so I charge you to go polish this and make it the best it can be for me to deliver to the American people."

Grady has been sitting quietly making notes of what Wild is saying. He can't believe what he has heard. He wants to give everything away with no accountability. *The terrorists have won. If Wild is elected President, then the terrorists have castrated this once great nation. I have to resign and go see...*

Chapter 104

CLINTON AND MITCHELL
PLAN SURVEILLANCE

Drew Clinton has called FBI Special Agent Mitchell and asked him to come to his office at 9 AM sharp. It's five minutes to nine now, and Mitchell is sitting in the outer lobby of the Office of the Attorney General of the United States. He is very nervous as he waits for Clinton to ask for him. Promptly at 9 AM, the Attorney General opens the door to his office and signals for Mitchell to come in. As Mitchell walks through the door, he is struck at being in the office occupied by so many famous people in American history.

Clinton invited him to sit down. "By the way, Agent Mitchell, do you have a first name?"

"Yes, sir. Bill, but most of my friends call me Billy; you see I was named after the famous flyer."

"Do you mind if I call you Billy?"

"It would be an honor, sir." Mitchell is thinking, *what do I call him?*

"Billy, I'm sure you are wondering if we are going to be working closely together what you should call me. I think the best answer is sir; it just takes too much time to call me Mr. Attorney General."

"Sir is fine with me."

"Billy, I have an order from the FISA court for a legal wiretap on all of the subject's communications and I want you to help me with that tap. We have to tap all the phones in his house and office and we need to tap into his cell phone."

"Well, sir, on the surface that doesn't seem like a problem. We have the technology to do that. Is there anything special about the location or the person we are taping?"

Clinton thought about that implication. "I think we are going to need two additional people for monitoring communications to and from his home and office. I need you to tell me the names of two people that you think can keep a secret forever and would give their life for you working on this assignment."

"Sir, I need to think about that for a minute; can you tell me nature of the wiretaps?"

Clinton stopped for a moment to think before he answered. *This wiretap is a matter of national security and right now only Judge Taylor and I know who it is… but Billy will figure it out as soon as he knows where he is going to set up the tap.* "Billy I want you to look at the order and tell me if you recognize the name on the order."

Clinton handed Billy the order; he read the name and then he read it again, and then looked at Clinton. "This is the Democratic nominee for President of the United States, sir."

"Yes, that is true. You are probably wondering why this tap was ordered and what you need to listen for."

Clinton took the tape recorder out of his desk and played the agents reviewing and translating the Russian and the identification of Senator Wild as the one receiving money from Viktor Antipova.

"Who is he?"

"He is one of the wealthiest men in the world and the richest person in Russia. We also believe that he was the source of funding for the Brotherhood of the Red Nile attack on America."

"Sir, if you're right, then he has betrayed the country and committed treason."

"I believe he has, and there is more."

"MORE?"

"I believe that he is going to go to the Ninth Circuit Court in San Francisco to get the Court to declare the provision in the election rule requiring a Social Security number to vote as a violation of the voter protection law, and that a simple statement attesting the right to vote should be sufficient."

"Sir, that would leave the election open to many illegal people voting and probably swing the election to Wild."

"I agree."

"So, Billy, what are the challenges to this wiretap?"

"Sir, the first challenge is that he is or will shortly be a legitimate candidate for President. He is entitled to Secret Service protection and national security briefings. My God, he could be feeding information to the Russians. I'm sorry, sir, for my outburst."

"Not a problem. I feel the same way."

"Sir, his Secret Service detail will scan his home and Senate office for eavesdropping devices. They will do the same in his office and possibly his cell phone. They will be looking for planted devices, so we have to find a way to intercept and listen to the conversations without a bug in the room.

"In actuality, the cell phone is easier than a hardwired phone. All we have to do is the same thing they did in Houston; find the radio frequency of his phone, then we can hear both sides if we are within about three hundred feet. The toughest challenge is his office phone."

Clinton asks, "Why is the office such a challenge?"

"Sir, with his position as a leader in the Senate, he may have twenty lines in his office and he may share some of lines with his staff. He may have a couple of strictly private lines, but he could talk on any line."

"Billy, that may be true, but if he is going to make one of those special calls, my guess is that he makes it on one of his private lines."

"I agree sir, but he could still make a call outside the office and then the best we can do is just get his side of the story."

"Well, that's better than nothing."

"I agree. Sir, we are going to need more than two men if we are going to cover him when he is out and about. They have to be equipped with listening devices to record his side of the conversation."

Clinton thought about expanding the team, but is concerned about too many people and possible leaks. "Billy, I'm concerned that if we expand the team, we risk the possibility of a leak. Any other alternatives?"

"I just might have an idea. Each day when a Secret Service agent signs in, he retrieves his communication equipment that has been charged overnight. You have seen agents talking into their jacket sleeve and they have that curled wire out of the neck of their shirts."

"Yes, I have, so how does that help?"

"It doesn't directly, but we are going to change the equipment we issue to the Secret Service, or at least the ones guarding Wild. We are going to issue them a 050-AUD-PENBK."

"What is that? I have never heard of it before."

"Sir, it is a fully functioning pen, but it is also a four point five gigabyte recorder that can record voices for up to 256 hours. We give the pens to the agents who are going to be assigned to Wild. We will instruct them that the pen transmits a signal. The agents will be told that whenever they are with the Senator out of his house, car or office, they need to push the button."

"What a great device; are they expensive?"

"No, about $80 bucks on the Web. We do have a challenge with the hardwired phones and the sweeping of the home and the office."

"Well, Mr. Wizard, any ideas?"

"I think the standard protocol is to sweep the phones and the rooms; things like pictures on the walls, planters, lamps etc., but hardwired phones send a signal over copper wire to a switching station. What if we could capture the signal as it leaves the house on the way to switching station?"

Clinton replies, "That could work."

"The big challenge is his Senate office. We will have to trace the wires and find a place in the line to capture the signal."

Clinton asks, "How soon can we start?"

"How about now? I'll identify two other people to work on the team; I can order the pens online today and you will need to get me into the Capital to look at the wiring for the Senator's office."

"I'll make the call to the head of security immediately."

"Sir, may I ask you a question?"

"Go ahead, Billy."

"Are you sure?"

Chapter 105

PRESIDENT PLANS HIS SPEECH

Nathan Jordan is meeting with the First Lady and the writing team that has been helping him with his weekly radio address. The team has just over a month to prepare the speech for the President's input and final revisions. The team, along with the President, is meeting in Karen's conference room and has been talking over some ideas. The President's cell phone rings and everybody stops so the President can take the call, "This is Jordan. Hello, Drew. That's excellent! Thank you."

Karen turned to the President, "Is everything okay?"

"Everything is fine, and I think I just got great news from Drew Clinton."

Karen asked, "So what is the good news?"

"I'll get into it in a minute; let's talk about the speech content."

"I want to start out with recognition of the contribution that has been made by all Americans. I believe this has been the greatest challenge for the American people and I want to tell them how proud of them I am. Together we have already accomplished a lot; but even with what we have already done, we have much more to do to restore America to greatness. We must decide what type of America we will be? Will we continue to be dependent on foreign governments for the bulk of our energy? Should we spend our money on true Americans first? Clearly the people who attacked us came through our borders illegally. Should we protect our borders? Let me be perfectly clear: protecting and securing our borders doesn't mean closing our borders."

As Karen and the team sat, they are mesmerized by what Jordan is saying. Jordan looked down and saw that no notes are being taken and he says, "Is anybody taking notes?"

Karen responded, "Not to worry, this session is being legally recorded so keep going; you're on a roll."

"We have to become energy independent. If you reelect me as President, I promise to cut our import of foreign energy by 50% from the level on my inauguration to the end of my second term and I promise that we will be on a trajectory to full energy independence by the end of the next President's first term.

"Putting people to work making a good wage is the path to prosperity. I realize that the devastation caused by these vicious attacks has put millions of people out of work. People are now going back to work because of all the recovery work that needs to be done. Before this disaster, almost fifty percent of Americans were being paid by the government and not working.

"It is important that the government help support those of us who are sick or disabled or elderly, but if the government is going to pay, then nobody else can pay. There will be no more double dipping. We need a government that is smaller and more efficient and one that works closely with the private sector to help it become more productive.

"One of the most important things I can do, if you reelect me as your President, is to work to destroy terrorism and terrorists and to identify with indisputable proof those individuals and nation states that are responsible for this attack - those that fund terrorism.

Every supporter of terrorists and terrorism be warned, we are coming to get you and you will be exposed to the whole world for what you are. We will take your money and we will take your power. Then we will take you to jail."

Karen responded, "Unbelievable. I would not change a thing. I will get it typed up and have it for you in the morning. What do the rest of you think? Anything to add?"

The team responded in unison, "Nothing."

Jordan said, "I'm so glad you like it. Now I can tell you about that phone call I just had with the Attorney General.

"I was reviewing the rules and limitations on my convention acceptance speech and I thought I found a loophole, but I needed Drew to confirm it for me with the Federal Election Commission. I could be wrong, but my guess is Senator Wild will make his speech from his office all alone. We will see the family pictures; the American flag and his tone will be somewhat somber. We know that he will attack me for all that I have done for what he thinks is a violation of the Constitution. My point is, it will be just him."

Karen asked, "So, what is your idea?"

"Drew confirmed that only one camera can be used and that while it can fade in and out, its primary focus has to be me."

"So, we knew that?"

"Yes, we did, but the rules do not state where I can broadcast from."

"Why wouldn't you want to broadcast from the Oval Office?"

The President responds, "One word."

"Okay, I give up. What is the one word?" Karen responded, a little put out with Nathan.

"People. If I give my speech from the Oval Office, there will not be people in the office to outwardly react to what I'm saying." The President continued, "If I was making the speech at a different time, it would have been in a convention hall and you could see and hear the crowd is pleased with my speech. We can't move the camera, but America can still hear the reaction of a crowd."

"What a great idea! Have you thought of a place in Washington? We can't drive them to the site, because it would use some of our gas quota."

"My dear First Lady, I have found the perfect place. It is a place that will hold a small crowd of about 660 people near the Metro line, and people who live downtown can walk to the place... and it has historical significance."

"You know this is killing me; you have me all excited and I'm bursting to know the name of the place, so can you please tell us."

The President paused. Karen and the team are sitting on the edge of their chairs as the President speaks, "The name of the venue is..."

Chapter 106

CLINTON HAS A PLAN

So far the wiretaps have produced no traffic to the ACLU or the Russians. Clinton thinks he needs a plan that will change the behavior of Wild should he go astray. *I have to come up with a way to control Wild's actions without him knowing who it is.* Mitchell *suggests that he will go to Wal-Mart and buy a disposable cell phone for me to use. I will have to develop some messages that I can send to Wild that will cause him to stop what he plans to do. I need to do it in such a way that the message will be clear to him, but mean little to most people.*

The one thing Wild can do that has the greatest potential to harm Jordan's chances and increasing Wild's is changing the voter registration. I know from the records that he has already made an initial call to the ACLU the morning he saw the primary results. It is most likely they will do his bidding and file the suit. Now that Wild has given his acceptance speech, he will most likely make his first move soon. I need to get a message to him in the next twenty-four hours as a preemptive strike, but what do I say? It has to be enough to shock him into making a call, but not to the ACLU. He needs to call Viktor; that is the phone call I need on tape. If I can catch him with the Russian, I will own him and he will hesitate to deal with the ACLU. What can I say; what is the message that will strike fear in Wild's heart?

Clinton picked up several newspapers on his desk that reviewed Wild's acceptance speech the night before. Even the normally left-leaning papers have some harsh words for Wild's presentation. Quotes like, "His delivery lacked emotion." Another paper suggested that, "His message was stale and dated." One of the few conservative papers suggested, "The same old out-dated playbook that didn't play well in Peoria."

I'm sure Wild has spent the morning with his campaign staff trying to figure out how he can recover. Most of the time, candidates get a bounce in the polls after their Convention, but this time he actually lost ground. One paper reported a rumor that one of Wild's senior speechwriters left the campaign. I wonder if he is the one who wrote last night's acceptance speech.

My guess is that Wild will have a hard time with the press today, and for the next few days. It is three weeks until Jordan's turn and he is a better speaker than Wild, but this new format may be difficult for him as well. If Nathan doesn't do any better than Wild, the race will draw closer. If Wild thinks he is way behind, he may become desperate and try anything. He will have to be careful, because if he is desperate and acts desperate, he will lose his base. He will put pressure on his surrogates to attack Jordan on his behalf. If Wild feels like he is behind, I would expect that he would come out swinging in the first debate.

If I can come up with the right messages he will have to choose between being exposed as a traitor, or in effect giving up the race. What is the word? Clinton is becoming more and more frustrated, so he calls Billy Mitchell into his office to see if he has an idea. "Billy, I need you to send the first message to Wild; do you have the disposable phones I asked for?"

"Yes, sir, I do. Once I send a message, I will take the battery out of the phone and toss it in a trashcan and in another part of town I will smash the phone. There will be no way to trace the message."

"Billy, I'm not very good at this spy stuff, so I'm having difficulty find a single word to scare Wild? What is one word that could strike fear in his heart?"

"Sir, are you open for a suggestion?"

"Absolutely, Billy. I'm all ears."

Billy stood up and went to a white board and wrote a word on the board. "Sir, how about this, combined with Internet slang like TINAG, which stands for 'This Is Not A Game'? Does it work for you, sir?"

"Perfect, Billy. Send it now to his cell phone; do you know where he is right now?"

"Let me check. Sir, he is in his office."

"I wonder how long it will take him to react."

"We'll know shortly if he makes a call to Russia." Billy took out one of the disposable cell phones and typed in 'T R E A S O N, TINAG' and pushed the Send button.

Chapter 107

A PIPELINE FOR THE PRESIDENT

The President has been working on his acceptance speech, but has scheduled a break to meet with the Secretary of Energy, Mike Findley, for an update on all the pipeline projects. Mary buzzes the President and tells him Mr. Findley is here for his ten o'clock appointment. "Mary, please show him in, and see if he wants something to drink."

"Right away, sir."

The door to the Oval Office opened and Mary escorted Mr. Findley to a seat on the couch; after he sat down, she brought him a black coffee. "Mr. President, how are you?"

"I'm fine, how goes the pipeline business?"

"Mr. President, it goes very well, and you have to make a decision."

"Mr. Secretary, a decision on what?"

"Sir, we are at a point on both pipeline projects where I think we are well ahead of schedule. We could throw a switch to turn on the pumps and compressors and open the valves any day you want after November 1st. Once you throw the switch, we will begin to push the contaminated oil out of the pipeline into the temporary pipeline to store it in the strategic petroleum reserve caves in the Gulf of Mexico. And my guess is that within a few days of the opening the Texas pipeline, we will be able to open the natural gas pipeline in the north and then open the connections to our 4,500 test wells and begin sending billions of cubic feet across America every day.

"Sir, if I may, I would like to suggest a plan for your consideration."

"Go right ahead; be my guest."

"Sir, if at any time during what I have to say that you are offended, then just tell me to stop and I will go no further."

What could he have in mind that might be offensive? "Mike, I agree, but I want to hear you out and then if I have a problem I'll let you know; is that okay?"

"Yes, sir. Moving the contaminated energy out of the ground in Texas will give you a big boost not only with the people of Texas, but you will have made America safer and the vast majority of Americans will be proud of what you accomplished. In addition, opening the natural gas pipeline and bringing a new source, an American source of clean energy, will immediately reduce our dependence on imported energy. If it were me, I would consider two times to throw the switches; the determining date would be the outcome of the general election."

Mike knows the next part will be difficult for him and perhaps the President may be somewhat uncomfortable. "Mr. President I have two scenarios. The first is that you lose the election. I would have a ceremony similar to the Christmas tree lighting on the mall. You might even think of Thanksgiving eve as a day to throw the switches. It will be a great accomplishment, and it would be soon enough after the election, but well in advance of the January 20th inauguration to add to your legacy."

The President responded, "Then the second is, if I keep my job, we wait till January 20th and throw the switches from the Capital during my speech."

"That is correct, Mr. President."

"Let me ask you a question. No, perhaps more than one."

"Go right ahead, Mr. President. I'll do my best to answer."

"If the projects are going so well, how do you slow them down without alerting somebody who's not favorable to us?"

"I thought you might ask that question; I do have an answer. We have crews working twenty-four seven. I'd have to figure out how much time off we need to give the crews to slow their progress. If you win, I'll keep them humming to make sure we are closing down and testing everything starting January first. If, on the other hand you should lose, I think we can get it done by the day before Thanksgiving. We may be able to complete all the testing, so throwing the switch will be mostly ceremonial, but it will be done before you leave office, I can promise you that."

"I think I would like to wait on the decision until after my acceptance speech and perhaps the first debate which is on domestic policy and see what the reaction is to what I have to say. You keep working full speed just as you are. I do have one question for you."

"I'll do my best, sir."

"We had 4,500 so-called test wells drilled on government land to see if there was natural gas there. Are they all done?"

"Sir, based on the drilling schedule, they should all be done by the first of November."

"How many are connected to the main pipeline?"

"Sir, we've had about a 70% hit rate, so if this holds up we should have about 3,000 wells to connect to the new pipeline as they are completed."

"Will these three thousand wells make a difference?"

"Sir, more of a feeling that we are doing something; we are heading toward a goal. If we continue to drill all over the country, we could very quickly begin to liquefy natural gas and ship it to nations dependent on imported energy. If we make it less expensive, those nations will buy more and more from us instead of the OPEC nations, and that would begin to impact the flow of money to terrorists."

This has been one of my ideas for a long time and if I'm reelected, I can make it happen with the help of Mike Ridley and his Pathfinders.

"Mike, great job, and I was not offended by anything you said. It was bold and innovative on your part, but I know some people who will be hopping mad."

Chapter 108

CLINTON'S NEXT MESSAGE

Drew Clinton called Billy Mitchell, his special assistant, to see if he has heard anything about Wild after his text message. "Billy, we sent the text during his morning meeting; have you heard anything from Secret Service about any unusual reaction on the part of the Senator?"

Billy responded, "Sir, the only thing I saw on the reporting screen was that he seemed a little agitated, but we don't know if it is from the reviews of his speech last night or the text message we sent."

"Billy, I think it's time to send another text to Senator Wild; what do you think the message should be?"

"Sir, I think we still have to shock him. We have to, as they say, push over the apple cart and watch how he reacts. How about his Russian contact's first name and FE for fatal error, so the message would be: Viktor FE."

Clinton responded, "I like it a lot; send it, and you know the drill with the phones."

"Sir, I have been thinking about the frequency of the messages we send. Sir, how frequently should we send the messages to the Senator? If we keep sending messages and he does nothing, then what do we do?"

"My guess, Billy, is that Jordan will do a much better job tomorrow night on his acceptance speech than Wild did on his, and he will start to panic about his chances. My guess is if the ratings and reviews are good, on Wednesday morning, he picks up the phone to call the ACLU. We need to be thinking about what to say in the message about ACLU."

"Sir, it seems to me the FE concept works as well with ACLU as it did with Viktor, so FE ACLU could be our next message."

"Billy, I need to think about that. Call me if you hear anything based on our second message."

"Yes, sir."

After Clinton hung up he sat back in his chair and wondered, *if Wild calls the Russian, what will he say to him about what is going on? Will he tell Viktor that somebody knows what is going on and is trying to get him to throw the election to Jordan? My guess is he has taken a lot of money both personally and in his campaign and can't pay it back. Even if he had the money, he went past the point of no return when he took the money from the Russians.*

If he took money from the Russians, it has to be reported on his campaign, or at least it should have been reported. In the case of his personal finances it would be reported as income, but doesn't necessarily have to be reported with the Russian oilman as the source. The FEC will have his campaign finance reporting; I need to look at that. I believe he chose to make his tax returns public for the last five years. So, if he has been taking money and hasn't reported it, then he could have possible charges of money laundering and tax fraud, just to start.

Wild will have to walk a very fine line to prove to the Russians that he is trying to do the best he can, and at the same time not trying so hard as to have his secret revealed. Can he resign? Ross Perot was not a major party candidate, but he withdraw in 1992. If Wild withdrew before the election, would the country still have an election? Would the Vice President automatically become the Presidential nominee? Would we have a new primary? Wow, a lot of questions that I don't know the answers to, and I don't think I want to call anybody and ask for answers.

Clinton now faces the hard question – should he tell the President what he is doing? The President is not only the leader of the nation, he is the leader of the Republican Party, and as such, does he have a right to know what is going on?

Clinton asked himself, *does the President of the United States need to know that the person he is running against for the most powerful job in the world has potentially committed treason?*

Chapter 109

THE PRESIDENT REVEALS THE LOCATION

The President made his decision where to broadcast his convention acceptance speech and he has instructed everybody in the White House that is working to pull it off not to reveal the location to anyone, including the First Lady. He wants to surprise her, Senator Wild, and his campaign staff. Nathan hopes the C-SPAN producers will not leak the location; all the secrecy is adding to the drama and Jordan loves it. Nathan chose this spot for its historical significance to him and to the nation. The entire nation will know the place when the camera is turned on outside and reveals where they are.

It is three hours to broadcast, and he knows the First Lady thinks that the broadcast will be in the Oval Office, because she has seen camera crews going in and out all day. This has all been a hoax to fool Karen. "Mary, call the First Lady and have her meet me on the Truman Balcony in about ten minutes."

"Yes, Mr. President."

Karen is sitting at her favorite table; the geraniums are the deepest red of the season. She is dutifully sitting in the chair waiting for Nathan. About two minutes later, Nathan came strolling onto the porch. He saw Karen and walked over and gave her a big passionate kiss. Karen responded with an equally passionate one and after they separate she asks. "What was that for?"

"My dear, today is one of the greatest days in my life."

Karen asked, "Why?"

Jordan responded, "Two reasons: first, later tonight I'm going to make love to the First Lady of the United States and nobody else gets to do that."

"And the second reason, Mr. President?"

"I'm going to make my acceptance speech in the most fitting place in the nation."

Karen responded, "The Oval Office?"

"No. We are leaving in about one hour and we are going to Ford's Theater where I will deliver my speech."

"What a wonderful idea, can you do that?"

"Yes, ma'am. I had the Attorney General himself go to the Federal Election commission to get their approval. We will only have one camera that can pan in and out, but what is great is I will have at least 660 people around me to react to what I say; I hope they will be supporters. If they are, the nation will hear people excited about my reelection. In Wild's speech he was alone in his office, so no reaction."

"I chose Ford's because of the historical significance, not because Lincoln was shot there, but because after four long years the President and the nation could see the end of the war. Everybody knew that the repair of the nation's wounds would take a long time. Lincoln in Ford's was a turning point in American history, and this is the turning point in our American history. More people died in a few seconds in Texas City than died in any single day in the Civil War over 160 years ago. I want Americans to remember their past and remember those people who died in Texas and join me in building a better and safer America and a better and safer world."

Karen jumped up, puts her arms around Jordan, kissed him, and told him she has goose bumps for two reasons: his speech and the lovemaking later tonight.

"Come and help me pick out the suit, and tie to wear tonight; I want to look my best." The two of them left the balcony and headed to the family quarters and the President's bedroom to pick out his clothes.

As they walked through the door, the President looked at his watch, took Karen's hand, and led her over to the bed and said, "I think we have time if you are up for it?" Karen reaches out to touch Nathan's leg and says with a coy smile on her face, "It feels like you're up for it, so if you're game, I'm game."

Across town, Billy Mitchell has sent a new text message to Wild, IKWUD, which means, "I Know What You Did." If that is not bad enough, Wild has just heard from a Washington Post reporter wanting to know if he had any thoughts about the President making his acceptance speech at Ford's Theater. At that moment, Wild is less concerned about where the President is speaking, and more concerned that somebody knows what he has done with the Russian.

All of a sudden, he is becoming very concerned; perhaps even afraid because he is beginning to think that the source of the text messages is…

Chapter 110

FORD'S THEATER

The President and the First Lady finished their lovemaking with time enough for a joint shower a back and front scrub for the First Lady. They were dressed and ready to go with half an hour to spare. The two of them were in the back seat of the Presidential limo, with the partition window up, and Karen, who has her arm intertwined with Nathan's, leaned over to whisper something in his ear. He leaned down in all seriousness to hear what the First Lady has to say; Karen then stuck her tongue in his ear and laughed. The President is a little perturbed, but then he laughed, and Karen said, "The first part of tonight was wonderful; I doubt you can top that with the speech. If you deliver it with the passion you did in my office, the crowd will be on its feet applauding. One thing you must be diligent to watch is your time; you have exactly 20 minutes, the same as Wild. If you go over, they will cut you off even though you are the President of the United States. If they let you run longer, Senator Wild's team will be all over them for being biased. If I may, I would like to make a suggestion?"

"I'm all ears... well, maybe one wet one doesn't count as a full ear." They both laughed. "Go ahead; what is your idea."

"You know that the crowd for the most part will be biased towards you and they will look for opportunities to applaud, yell, and whistle. You must raise your hands and say to the crowd, 'Thank you very much, but even the President of the United States is on a time clock, and I think some of the American people will want to hear what I have to say.'"

"Excellent idea, the audience will calm down and want to hear all I have to say."

By the time the car reached Ford's, there was a line to get into the theater. As Karen and the President exited the limo, they could hear the crowd yelling support, "Go Mr. President!", and "We're behind you Mr. President!"

As they got closer to the stage door, reporters crowded around the President and the Secret Service gently moved them back so the President and Karen have some breathing room. The President said to the reporters, "I'll take a few questions and then we have to go talk to the American people."

William Wild is watching on a TV in his office, the very office where he made his speech, to the same American people, and he is not happy. The President and the First Lady look happy.

"Mr. President, why did you choose Ford's Theater for your acceptance speech?"

"I wanted to use this historic place because it reminds me, no - it reminds all Americans of the outcome when we struggle against each other. Lincoln died trying to keep the nation together. He succeeded, but he knew there was a long struggle ahead to heal the wounds. Our America was attacked by people who hate us and would see us dead if we do not accept their rules and laws. We must fight to protect our freedom, and let me assure you we are going to fight. I'm sorry, but I must go in and talk to all Americans."

The two of them stepped past the reporters and into the theater. They walked up on the stage and looked onto the Lincoln box with great respect. The President's advance team had set up the podium so that when the camera pulled out it would see the bunting and the picture of George Washington in front of Lincoln's box. Karen had Nathan step up to the podium and she stepped behind the camera.

She looked at the President and then mouthed to him the word. "Perfect."

Wild received another text message as he got up to leave the office. In his mind, everything is crashing down on him and he sees his hopes for the Presidency diminishing rapidly unless he does something right away. *I have to level the playing field; it is real simple. If I'm going to win, I have to get more votes than him. I have to increase the voter pool by getting the restrictions lifted by the court. If I can get the waver of the Social Security identification, I can bring in many more voters. I need to ask the ACLU to file the lawsuit. Regardless of the threats from whomever, I'm going to fight this to win.*

The next morning the reviews are in and Jordan hit a home run; even the leftist papers had to admit, "Ford's Theater was a stroke of genius."

The Post said, "Hard to recover when you have been hit by Lincoln."

The Wall Street Journal said, "Jordan's charisma has clearly gotten better with age."

Wild has been reading the headlines; he picked up the phone on his desk to call the DC office of ACLU; he asked for extension 32. After the phone rang several times, Wild said, "I need to speak with Walter Thomas."

"May I tell him who is calling?"

"Tell him it is Senator William Wild."

"One moment, please."

Billy rang Clinton and told him, "Wild is on the phone with ACLU now. Do I send a message, and if so what?"

They both thought for a moment. Clinton said. "Now is not the time for subtlety; send a simple straightforward message. Billy sends this, 'Talking to ACLU may cost you and your family more than the election, hang up now and never call again, we are watching and listening.'"

Billy pushes Send.

After Clinton gave Billy the order to send the most threatening message so far, he thought to himself. *Have I crossed the line? Am I no better than the people that have compromised Wild? Is the Attorney General of the United States a blackmailer? Have I rationalized my behavior because I think I'm protecting America? I have kept this information from the President; will it look bad for him if what we are doing gets out?*

Chapter 111

WILD IN A PANIC

Wild disconnected his call with the ACLU when he saw the threatening text message because this one scared him more than any of the others. No special text phrases, just plain English and to the point. He asked everybody to leave. He knew by the expressions on their faces that the President, based on last night's performance, is almost unbeatable and he agrees with them. Wild knows he can't take the message to the Secret Service because it will lead to consequences of his betrayal of his country – conviction and death for him and humiliating disgrace for his family. Telling anybody what he has done is not an option. Wild has a thought, not a pleasant one, but at least it's an option. *I need to call Viktor to try and find out if he is the source of the messages. I don't want to spook him into doing something that I might regret later, especially if it isn't him.*

Wild looked at his watch and there is eight hours difference, so it is deep into the night. *I will call first thing in the morning; for now I must think about the three debates and see if I can find a way to trip Jordan. He is very confident based on his performance last night, so he might be just a little cocky. If I can turn the tide in the first debate I might have a chance. It might be wishful thinking, but I need to do something positive at least until I can speak to Viktor in the morning.* Wild called his staff to meet him in the big conference room immediately.

All the staff filed in slowly with no energy. Wild saw their faces and he knew he had to turn them around or at least try, if for no other reason than to buy time through the election. "Ladies and gentlemen I have a question.

Which would be more fun and exciting, working for a candidate that looks like a shoo-in or one that has no chance in hell to win?"

The staff starts looking at each other and is wondering where he is going.

Wild then asked, "How about this question, which is easier to market, a charismatic couple or an old dog like me?"

Some of the staff chuckles at that question.

"I have one more question and it is the most important one: where do we learn the most important life lessons, in our successes or our failures? We may not win, but we must try our best even in failure."

Wild knows that he has no chance, but if he quits he is in serious trouble. "We may be mad at what happened last night. The President got one on us because he was thinking outside the box. We got our butt smacked last night because of me, not you. I believe in you and we owe the American people the best and most challenging campaign ever. We need to take this election directly to the President, we need to make him the best he can be and if the American people choose Jordan, it is because we made him better. I know I have a reputation of being an angry old man; I can't change the old, but I can change the angry. I promise you that I will try to look and act more Presidential. So, are you ready to fight as an underdog or do you want to quit?"

Based on the reaction Wild saw on their faces and their body language, they do want to try and fight. He said to them, "So let's start with preparation for the first debate, Getting America Back to Greatness. Wild wrote the words on the board and said to the room, "What does that mean to you and then tell me what it means to the American People? Single words only please, no speeches. That's my job," and the room laughs.

"Better schools, better roads, green energy, more police and firemen."

Wild is furiously writing and is happy that his team is engaged; they are following his acceptance speech. "Any more?"

Jobs, higher minimum wage, more benefits, better and free healthcare.
"More?"

"Longer day care, extend unemployment, more job training, lower college cost." The one person in the room not engaged is Grady. While working on Wild's acceptance speech, he gave serious thought about resigning and going to the Jordan camp. He didn't do it, but as he hears the same ideas that were in the acceptance speech, he knows this is not going to work, and the people who are Wild supporters will be very disappointed. Some traditional big government Democrats will be excited until they see the polling data after the first debate; then they will sit on their hands and more important, they will sit on their money. The meeting ended, and the people left the conference room with excitement in the air. Grady stayed behind and asked Wild if he could have a moment. Wild invited him in and Grady closed the door. "Senator, I listened to the meeting this morning and I just don't think working for you fits me right now, so I have to leave."

"Are you coming back?"

"I don't know. I just don't know, sir."

Chapter 112

THE PRESIDENT AND HIS TEAM
HAVE A SECRET WEAPON

It is later that same day when Grady calls the White House Press Office and tells them he was with the Wild camp and just resigned this morning and he would like to help the Jordan campaign. Grady is asked to hold and the call is switched to Karen's Chief of Staff, Maggie Brown. The Press Office tells her who is on the call and what it is about, and Maggie tells the staffer to transfer the call.

She answered the phone, "This is Maggie Brown; how can I help you?"

Grady told Maggie what he would like to do and why. She listened very carefully; especially to some of the details of the morning session and then asked, "Could you come to the Press Office later today so we could talk in person?"

"What time do you want me there?"

"Can you be here at four thirty?"

"Not a problem."

"I'll arrange for a pass at the White House security office at the end of G Street. I'll meet you there."

Maggie hung up and walked as quickly as possible without running, because running in the White House is a sign of danger and sets off all sorts of alarms. Maggie headed for the Office of the First Lady. As she made a sharp turn around a corner to another hallway, she plowed into somebody and for a moment she doesn't see whom she has almost knocked down. All she hears is a voice that says, "What is your hurry?"

She looked up in horror to see the President and said, "Oh, Mr. President. I'm truly sorry; have I hurt you? Should I call for a doctor?"

Jordan said, "Just slow down; I'm fine. I'm a lot bigger than you. Are you okay?"

"I'm fine, sir. Are you sure you don't need a doctor or something?"

The President put his hand on Maggie's shoulders and said, "What is the rush all about?"

"Sir, I just got off the phone and was headed to the First Lady's office to tell her the good news; at least I hope it is good news."

"How about we both go see the First Lady and you can tell us both, but let's just walk okay?"

"Yes, sir." They have a short walk to Karen's office and the President holds the door for Maggie.

"No, sir, you first."

"Go on in. I have the door; it will be fine."

Jordan walked over to Karen who is standing and gave her a nice kiss on the lips.

Karen asked. "What is all the commotion?"

Jordan answered, "It appears our Maggie has found us a spy in the Wild camp."

"Well, not exactly ma'am; one of his senior staffers resigned today and wants to talk to us about coming to our side."

Karen responded, "How do we know that he is in fact not a spy for the Wild camp to find out our plans?"

"Ma'am, I don't know, but he will be here at four thirty and I will question him."

"Maggie, why don't you bring him here and we will both question him."

The President interjected, "Can I come too and ask some questions?"

Karen looked at Nathan directly and with all the compassion in the world she said, "NO!"

Maggie said to both of them, "If he is for real, then we will have first-hand knowledge of what Wild is planning to do in the first debate."

Then Karen added, "We could get the jump on Wild."

Maggie asked, "Ma'am, do you think it's a good idea to bring him to your office? Perhaps my office would be less intimidating."

"I like that. We don't want to spook him on his first visit. When you call security see what information they can get on Grady. By the way, is Grady his first or last name?"

"Grady is his first name; his last name is Wild."

The Brotherhood of the Red Nile

Chapter 113

SHOULD I RESIGN?

Drew Clinton is having serious second thoughts concerning what he is doing to William Wild; especially the last message that was a threat against his life. He had vetted Mike Ridley and the Pathfinders' top-secret contracts with the government. During the process, Jordan has told Clinton that Mike and his team will be jointly reporting to Jordan as necessary, and Williams on a day-to-day basis. Clinton decides that he needs to talk with Williams about what is going on with Wild and what help Williams' Pathfinders can be to him.

Clinton called Williams' office, and got his assistant on the line. She told Clinton, "Mr. Williams is in Sanibel; can I have him call you?"

"Yes, it is important that I speak to him right away. Could you have him call me on my secure cell phone?"

"Does Mr. Williams have your number?"

"I believe so, but why don't you take it down just in case? Please call him right away."

"I'm not sure where he is at the moment, but I will do my best to find him as quickly as possible."

"Thank you very much for your help."

As soon as Clinton hung up, Marie dialed the hotel and asks for Mr. Williams' room. The operator rang the room and no one answered. It went to voice mail and she left a message. Next, she tried his cell phone and again no answer, but she left a message saying she has also left a voice message at the hotel. "Please call the Attorney General as soon as possible. He says it's urgent."

Frank Williams had his cell phone with him, but turned off, because he is taking Ellen to one of the most famous places on Captiva to eat. They are going to the Bubble Room. Not only is the décor outrageous, the food is very good. It's not as good as Jacaranda, but their desserts are over the top. At least this is what Frank has heard from a lot of people. The restaurant is a short drive from the Tween Waters Inn; they arrived in less than ten minutes, and when they got out of the car, the bright sun cast a golden light on Ellen - and Frank just had to stop and look.

They have been on the island much longer than anticipated, so Ellen had to buy new clothes. Frank really likes the dress she has on today. It is full length with slits on each side up to her knees. It is very thin, almost transparent, so as to give the appearance of being strapless. The upper part fits firmly around her torso and she more than fills the top. The pale yellow with white edging look very tropical; she is just stunning.

They walked in, arm and arm and were greeted by a receptionist, "Welcome to the Bubble Room. Do you have a reservation?"

"Yes, the name is Williams."

"Excellent. I see here you never been to the Bubble Room before?"

"No."

"I think you'll enjoy it, and by the way, Miss, I love your dress."

Frank responded, "Me too."

Just as they sat down the waiter came over and asked, "Excuse me. Are you Mr. Frank Williams, staying at the Tween Waters?"

"Yes, why?"

"Sir, I have a message for you from your office."

The waiter handed Frank the note. He sees that is from Marie. "Call me ASAP, very important."

"Ellen, it's from Marie. I need to step outside and return her call."

"I understand; come back as quickly as you can."

"Please order me a Corona, no lime. I'll be back as soon as I can." Frank walked out to his car and dialed his office. Marie picked up on the second ring. He asked, "How did you find me?"

"Just dumb luck; I called your hotel and left a message. Then I called your cell, called the hotel back and asked for the front desk, and then I asked if they had seen you and he said yes and that you asked for directions to the Bubble Room."

"So, what is so important?"

"The Attorney General called and needs to speak with you right away. He says it's very important."

"Put me on hold and call his office and see if we can talk in two hours, at three thirty."

Marie put Frank on hold and called Clinton's office to ask if Williams could call him at three thirty? She returned to Frank and told him, "That is fine. Do you have his secure cell phone number?"

"Let me check." He went to his contact file. He looked up Clinton's name and repeated the cell number to Marie.

Marie responded, "That's the one."

"Thanks, Marie."

"Sorry for interrupting you at the Bubble Room. It's a crazy place, and by the way, sir, try the Red Velvet Cake."

"I'll tell Ellen you recommend it."

Frank returned and sat next to Ellen. "Drew Clinton needs to talk. It must be something important, and Marie says we must try the Red Velvet Cake; it's to die for."

They spent most of their time looking at all the stuff in the restaurant. The walls and ceilings have decorations everywhere, but the restaurant gets its name from all of the old-fashioned bubble lights on almost everything. They finished their cake and the waiter brought the check and said, "Don't forget our gift shop on the other side of the parking lot."

As they walk out to the car Frank looked at his watch. "We'll have to come to the gift shop another time."

Ellen agrees, "We should come back." As they drove back to the hotel, Ellen said to Frank, "I had a nice time."

"Me, too."

As they pulled into the parking lot, Ellen got out of the car and told Frank, "Come and get me when you're done with your call."

"I'll look forward to that." Frank watched her walk away and says to himself, *what a gorgeous woman and she is all mine.*

Frank dialed Drew's private number just ahead of three thirty and got Drew on the second ring. "Drew, Frank Williams. How can I help?"

"Frank, I…" He paused.

Frank asked again, "Drew, are you there?"

"Yes, I'm here."

"What is wrong Drew?"

"I think I have to resign."

Chapter 114

YOUNG MR. WILD COMES A CALLING

At four o'clock sharp, Grady Wild is at the G Street White House security office for his appointment. He signs in the logbook and notes that Maggie Brown expects him and he is to meet her in the Press Office. The security guard looked up Maggie Brown's phone number and called her to tell her that Mr. Wild is here to see her.

She confirmed he is there to see her. "Please process Mr. Wild. When you are done with him, please escort him to the Press Office where I'll be waiting for him." Maggie called the First Lady and told her that Wild has arrived, and she will bring him to her office at about five o'clock.

Maggie is in the Press Office a little before four thirty and she can see the security guard bring Grady in the door. She walked over to greet him, "Welcome to the White House and thank you for coming on such short notice; please follow me. I have a small room where we can sit and talk. Around five, I want to take you to meet a very special person."

After they entered the meeting room, he said to Maggie, "This is very nice."

Maggie responded with a smile on her face, "Were you expecting an interrogation room?"

Grady said, "I don't know what I expected."

"Please have a seat. Would you like something to drink water, tea, cold soda?"

"Do you have a Diet Coke?"

"Do you want it with ice?"

"Yes, please."

"I think I'll have one myself." They both sat down and take a sip of their soda.

"So, Mr. Grady Wild, what can I do for you?"

"I'm not really sure. Maybe just listen for a moment or two and then we can see where it goes."

"I'm fine with that. Why don't you start by telling me what happened that caused you to make the call this morning?"

"Things didn't just happen this morning; they have been building over the last few months. I was really scared and upset by what happened in Texas and Louisiana. I still can't believe that happened. My dad, Senator Wild; he was very angry and I thought he was going to try and do something about it. So, when he announced to our family that he was going to run for President to try and fix things, I was very proud and wanted to help. I asked my dad if I could work on his Presidential campaign, and he said he would be proud to have me.

"I had the opportunity to sit in on many meetings and I noticed that my dad changed. He seemed nervous almost as if he was being watched. Anyway, the team started talking about strategy and messages. They were all wrong."

"What was all wrong?"

"The themes or talking points. It was if he was avoiding the real issues; he was using the old Democrat playbook for other times and trying to make it fit.

"I felt we shouldn't be talking about building roads and repaving bridges and hiring more teachers and police and fireman; I just couldn't figure out where he was coming from. Anytime somebody would bring up expansion of our own energy, he would dismiss it and focus on green energy. He kept avoiding the real problems of today.

"All of us worked real hard on developing a bold acceptance speech addressing the needs of the people, but he never used it. The reaction after his speech wasn't a surprise; we all knew what he did was trash. We were meeting this morning about the first debate and the same old stuff kept coming up and he was encouraging it. After the meeting, I went into his office and I told him I couldn't do this anymore. I have to move on to something else. He asked me what I was going to do and I guess I lied when I said I didn't know."

"Do you know what you want to do?"

"I think I would like to work for the reelection of President Jordan."

"I want you to walk with me; I will take you on a small tour of the White House. Have you ever been here?"

"Once when I was small; I don't really remember."

"Well, when we go out this door, if we were to turn left, we could work our way to the Oval Office. But don't be nervous; we are not headed there. We are going to walk all the way across the White House to my area, the East Wing." After about a ten minute walk, they neared Maggie's office, but they didn't stop there. They kept going.

"I thought we were going to your office. Wasn't that it back there; I saw your name on the door."

"We are going there in a moment, but I told you I wanted you to meet someone at five o'clock. Here we are." Maggie knocked on the door and a female voice answers,

"Come in." They walked through the door and Grady found himself looking at the First Lady Karen Jordan. "Please come in." She extended her hand. Grady slowly extended his hand and gently shook Karen's. She invited Grady to sit down. He couldn't take his eyes off of Karen. She always looked beautiful on the TV, but in person she is so striking, she almost takes your breath away.

"So, Grady, I'm sure Maggie has asked you a lot of questions. I would like to start with one question. Are you interested in working on my husband's campaign?"

Grady thought for a moment and responded, "Yes, ma'am, I think so."

"Then I have just one other question and I hope you'll understand why I have to ask it."

"I'll do my best to answer it."

"My question is, how do I know that I can trust you to be on our side?"

Chapter 115

CLINTON RESIGNING, NEVER

Frank Williams has just started his phone conversation with Drew Clinton and Drew has told Frank, "I think I have to resign."

Shocked, Frank asked, "Why do you think you have to resign?"

Drew responded by telling Frank what he did with the messages that he ordered sent to Wild, and Frank knows that he isn't getting the whole story.

"Drew, I understand what you have told me so far, so tell me the rest of the story. Why did you send the messages in the first place?"

Drew told Frank about the phone call one of Frank's men recorded in Houston and the verified translation, that it was in Russian and that one of the Brotherhood members made the call. Next Drew told Frank about the previous call to the ACLU and the one after Wild's acceptance speech reviews. "We have some intelligence that the Democrats are going to try and get the 9th Circuit Court to overturn the Social Security number requirements for voter identification. We think that Wild will use the ACLU to file the suit; this is the Democrats attempt to rig the election through voter fraud."

Frank is upset that he didn't come to him to tell him about the recorded phone call. "Drew, I don't understand why my man went to you instead of coming to me."

"As best I can tell, the commander of the U.S. Marshal's office in Houston witnessed the transcription of the tape and told your man that the tape and transcript were under the jurisdiction of Justice Department. The commander thought Justice also had jurisdiction, assuming the possibility of treason. I'm head of the Justice Department and given this involves a sitting U.S. Senator along with the sensitive nature of the possible crime, it made sense to him, and I can't disagree."

As Frank listened he calmed down. He asked, "Drew, why do you think you should resign?

"I'm concerned that I went too far as they say; I made a mistake and I crossed the line. If you make a mistake and break the law you must pay?"

"Drew, you are the lawyer, not me. I don't see what law you broke; I don't see the mistake. You went to the FISA court, presented your case to the judge, and he granted you the secret wiretap order. You used the order to try and collect more evidence to support your case. You have evidence of a relationship with a Russian named Viktor based on the taped phone call in Texas.

"Drew, I can't come up with even a small reason why you should consider resigning."

"So, you don't think the last message was a threat of harm to him and or his family?"

"I absolutely think there was a threat, but you can't actually carry it out. You were using the words to provoke him to call Viktor and let him know what is going on. Has he called Viktor before?"

"Not to the best of my knowledge, but we are monitoring to see if he does call."

"So, you did not drive him to make the call. He will make the call when and if he needs to make the call."

"Do you think he knows who is watching and listening?"

"Not at the moment. I don't think he is sure; he might be thinking it's the Russians checking up on him."

"Frank, I have one other issue that I need to bring to your attention."

"Go ahead tell me, but have we put the resignation issue to bed?"

"I think so, except for the fact that I have shared none of this with the President."

"Why, what was your reason?"

"My logic was that if I told the President, he may order me to notify the Secret Service and the FBI to investigate the allegations. The more people involved, the greater the risk of it leaking that Senator Wild is a traitor, and when the press asks the President when did he know and why didn't he say something, the President would have to admit that he has known for some time and didn't disclose it. It would make the President look really bad and people would wonder what else does he know that he hasn't told us? I felt my job was to protect the President, and not telling him was the best way to protect him from harm. I'm willing take the bullet for the President."

"I understand your feelings of guilt and of possible wrongdoing, but I just don't see it in your case. You will be more help to the country if you keep the pressure on Wild and serve the President."

"Frank, I need to ask you something else related to our discussion. The report from the agent said that one of the Brotherhood members made the call to Moscow and all he could get was that he was talking to somebody whose first or last name was Viktor. Your Pathfinders' know more about all the Brotherhood of the Red Nile than anyone; could you ask Mike and the team if any of them knows the name of the Russian in the Brotherhood and if they know anybody name Viktor? Let me know as soon as you can."

"Will do, Drew."

Frank hung up the phone; he knows the answers to all of Drew's questions about the Brotherhood. He thought, *I want to run it by Mike first and see what he wants to do.*

Frank returns to Ellen at the table and says, "Something serious has happened and I need to speak with Mike." They finished their meal and drove back to their hotel. He dropped off Ellen and parked the car.

Frank climbed the stairs to his room knowing that the love of his life is on the other side of the door at this moment, probably waiting for him to come in and make love with her. Frank has to choose between delaying Ellen and getting back in the car and going to talk with Mike about Drew's requests. Ellen can hear the sound of a car leaving the parking lot and…

Chapter 116

MEETING WITH KAREN

Karen has just been introduced to Grady Wild, the son of William Wild, the Democratic candidate for President. Grady is stunned how different she looks in person. Karen has just asked Grady a very serious question; one that he was not prepared to get especially from the First Lady. Her questioning was soft and very polite, but she is firm and he can tell she wants a serious answer.

"Should I address you as Mrs. First Lady, ma'am, or what?"

Karen responded, "Ma'am will be fine for now."

"Ma'am, I don't want to take up a lot of your time; I know you're a very busy person."

"Grady, I have time and the whole story will be very important to me to help me understand why you are here."

"Ma'am, I don't know how much you know about my father, but he started out as a city councilman back in our home town."

"Where are you from?"

"My father was raised in Appleton, Wisconsin and lived there all of his life. He was on the city council for a few years and did a great job. People encouraged him to run for Congress, so he talked it over with my mom and they decided he should try. He won and was re-elected seven times and then he stepped up and ran for the Senate and won again. He has served three plus terms as the Senator from Wisconsin. He held various leadership positions and eventually became the Majority Leader in the Senate."

Karen has been very patient listening to his father's life story and when she sees an opening she asks the pointed question, "How is the relationship between you and your father?" Karen can tell that this was an uncomfortable question for Grady, but he has to answer.

"Well, ma'am, it has never been what you would call great. You see, he was always gone from home and when he went to the Senate things got worse between my mom and him, and then with me."

Karen asked, "If your relationship was so strained, why did you get involved with his campaign?"

"Well, ma'am, it's kind of understood that if your father is running for President, the children need to get involved and support their dad. Were your children involved in the Presidents first campaign?"

Karen had to stop and think about Nathan's first Presidential campaign. She concluded, "The kids had a small role because Nathan and I wanted it that way." Her mind flashed to the Obama Grant Park speech where he kissed his wife and kids and sent them back stage and he was the only one on the stage. "Nathan wanted everybody around. We like to have our children with us, but we didn't push them to participate. They had their own lives and we respected that. So, should I think by your answer you didn't want to be involved with your father's campaign, regardless of the fact he was running for President?"

"I think my father had to make a choice, politics or his family, and he chose politics."

"You think he chose politics over you?"

"Yes. I decided that I was his son and I should help; it was a guilt trip for the most part."

"What changed your mind?"

"I was never into politics. I guess I was turned off by the way my father treated me. Not that he was abusive; he just ignored us. When I saw what happened to those people in Texas and Louisiana, I just felt I needed to help. When my father announced he was seeking the nomination I was, for a while, very proud of him."

Karen says, "But."

"But, when I started getting involved, I didn't see how what his party was proposing was going to really help those millions of people, and the more I heard them talk, the madder and more disillusioned I became. His acceptance speech was the straw the broke my will to want to help my father. Ma'am, I don't know if I can work for the President or not; I'm not even sure that I have the will to even try. But I do know somebody has to try."

Karen just looked at Grady for what seems like a long while. Then slowly she stood and walked over to the chair next to Grady. She sat down and placed her right hand gently on his shoulder and said to him, "Grady you are confused and unsure what you want to do. I think you have been very honest, in fact, brutally honest, with me and I believe you can be trusted but I'm not sure you are ready to go to work on my husband's campaign. I want you to go home, back to Appleton, and think about what it would be like working in a campaign that wants to defeat your father. If we win and your father is crushed, how will that affect your relationship with him? Most importantly, can you live with yourself? If you can, here is my card. You call me if you want to come and work with us; I know we would love to have you."

Maggie took the cue from the First Lady and told Grady, "It's time to go."

Grady stood, extended his hand to the First Lady and said, "Thank you, ma'am. It was a pleasure meeting you."

"Thank you, Grady, and have a safe trip home." Karen returned to her desk and sat thinking for a moment, *I'm sure he could have given us some of Wild's playbook, but this was not the time to ask. He needs to heal.*

In about fifteen minutes, Maggie came back to Karen's office and said, "You did a great job."

Karen replied, "He is a troubled young man; I hope he finds direction."

Maggie has had her hands behind her back. She pulled her right hand out and in it is a large brown envelop. "What is this?"

"Grady told me on the way out to give it to you."

"So, what is it?"

"I don't know; open it and see."

Karen opened the envelope and slid out the contents. Maggie asked, "What is it?"

Karen replied, "OH! It is this morning's meeting notes for the first debate for Senator Wild."

Chapter 117

THE FIRST DEBATE

C-SPAN is using a split screen and each candidate can see each other even though they are not standing next to each other. When a candidate is talking, his image will be the only image on the screen. When it comes time for questions, each candidate will see the question on their screen. The candidate will have a maximum of three minutes to respond and there will be no rebuttal. On the camera in front of each candidate, there will be three lights: one green, one yellow, and one red. The green light will be on until the candidate gets to one minute left in their turn and then the yellow light comes on. When there is twenty seconds left, the yellow light starts flashing and when the red light comes on, the other candidate will have his turn.

Nathan has been practicing the time and light sequence so as not to be cut off. Karen and her team have been working with the President in every spare moment so he has the procedure cold. The team has solicited questions from all over the country trying to make sure there are no surprises.

As the President walked into the Press Briefing room in the White House, he saw the room full of people, reporters, and friends. He said to the head of security, "We have to clear the room of all but the First Lady and my support team. It would be unfair to have audience reaction on my side and none on Senator Wild's."

The head of security told the people they must leave, but after the debate they would be allowed in to ask questions.

The head of each team was at a coin toss earlier in the day and the President won the toss and decided to go second. Under the rules, Senator Wild will go first in the second debate and then there will be a coin toss for the last debate. About fifteen minutes before the debate began, Karen and Nathan were sitting in the chairs in the front row. Jordan noticed that the White House name would be seen on the wall behind him and asked, "Can that sign be taken down?"

Karen responded, "Don't worry we have cleared it with the FEC."

Karen took Nathan's right hand with her left and placed the President's hand on her heart. She looked him in the eyes and said, "This is going to be fun; enjoy it, and then we can enjoy each other later. I love you and I'm proud of what you stand for and what you are trying to do for the country. Now, go show the world what a competent man you are and that you are good for this country."

With that said, she leaned over gave him a slight kiss on the lips and he kissed her back. "Mr. President, it is time to go."

Karen went to the back of the room so the President wouldn't see her, but he knows she is there.

The President took his place. In front of him he can see Senator Wild and asked him, "Senator, can you hear me?"

"Yes, Mr. President, I can, and can you hear me?"

"Yes, Senator, I can. I just wanted to wish you the best tonight." Wild, very surprised, stumbled to say the same thing to the President.

Wild had the opening forty-five minutes and the tone and pace made it seem like three hours. He continued the same rhetoric from the convention speech; nothing new. Wild finished early and didn't seem to know what to do with his extra time. The President is very concerned that half the audience has already left. Wild's time is up and it's Jordan's time. He began by answering the question up front, Getting America back to Greatness. "My fellow Americans, for far too long we as a government and a people have taken our eye off the ball. We have been more focused on helping other nations and we have lost our compassion for Americans. Many of you out there listening pay taxes, and we as the government are charged with the responsibility of spending your money wisely. Should we be spending your money to buy tanks, aircraft for other nations? I tell you this has to stop. America has always been a generous country, and in many cases to a fault.

It is time we spend our resources to put people to work so they can feed their families instead of the government feeding them." The rest of the President's time was spent answering the question. He saw his yellow light flashing and he ended on the second.

Then came the time for the questions from Federal Election Commission. The first went to Senator Wild. "How will you put people back to work?"

Wild answered, "If we are going to grow our economy we need educated people. Those people with advanced degrees will get higher paying jobs because the economy will need these people. So, in order to get better-educated people, we have to hire more teachers at all levels. We need to repair our roads and bridges; construction jobs are good paying jobs and if the rich will give just a little bit more, we will have the money to create those jobs."

"Mr. President, your response."

"My fellow Americans, you be the judge and see if you think my idea is better than my opponent's. The private sector has to create the jobs. If the private sector hires people they pay taxes. The more people working, then the more revenue the government receives. The number of people needing help from the government diminishes, so the less the government has to provide. Here is one idea that we as a country talk about every time the price of gas goes up over four dollars a gallon. We still import sixty-five percent of our energy. Do you realize that what we pay for foreign oil is equal to one hundred percent of the Department of Defense budget for a year? How about another example; that the value of the money we send out of the country for energy is equal to the annual Social Security budget?

"We need to develop all of our energy resources, and we need a new national policy that we will be exporters of energy in less than ten years. By making America the low cost provider of energy in the world, we will make America a strong economic power. Companies will want to come to America and build plants and hire millions of Americans to good paying jobs."

Karen is so excited at Jordan's response she wants to stand up and cheer, but she knows she can't; she will cheer later in private.

Each question has the same outcome. Wild tries his best to have energy and enthusiasm, but he just can't compete with Jordan. Wild sees what

Jordan is doing and he just can't keep up. Before the night is over, he knows he has lost not only tonight, but also the election. He will continue through to the end, but he is reminded of the story that went around Washington when Jimmy Carter was running for reelection. On his last visit to California, he was told by his Chief of Staff the election is lost.

After the debate was over, Wild said to himself, "If Jimmy Carter can do it, then so can I and to hell with the Russians."

Chapter 118

FRANK TALKS TO MIKE ABOUT DREW'S PROBLEM, OR IS IT?

As Frank drove away from the hotel on his way to Mike's house he began thinking about the last few weeks on Sanibel and how good it has been for both of them. *Ellen is like a lovesick newlywed who can't get enough lovemaking and I can't say I mind. I have rediscovered the beauty of my wife and when we are alone I have no inhibitions with her. The sex has helped her appreciate what a wonderful and desirable person she is and has rebuilt her confidence. I have re-discovered my soul mate and my lover once again. I hope there is carryover when we head back to DC. Perhaps we will have to look at coming to Sanibel more often and if the banks ever get back in business, we could buy something for her as a getaway and a place to retire; I think she would like that.*

Frank reached the entrance of Mike's condo and pushed the call button. Then he realized that he was so caught up thinking about Ellen he went to the wrong place. Frank backed up the car and headed to the compound. As he approached the gate he was greeted by what appeared to a retired gentlemen who asks, "Identify yourself and the nature of your business."

"My name is Frank Williams and I'm the boss of all the people in the compound. Will you please call Mr. Ridley and let me pass." Frank is a little upset with having to wait, but the guard opens the gate and lets Frank pass.

The guard said, "They are meeting in bungalow number three."

Frank pulled the car around to number three and got out. Mike met him at the door. "I'm sorry about the delay; we are still working things out. Please come in to the meeting."

"Mike, I need to talk to you about an important issue that might involve you and your team, but I would like to meet with you alone first."

Mike said, "Look, Frank. My team and I are one, so if you think you might have an assignment for us then you need to talk to all of us. These are your people; don't you trust them?"

"Of course I trust them I just think that the protocol would be for me to talk with you and..."

"Never mind, Frank. Come in and talk with us."

Omid, Megan, Hadar, John, and Ted Baker are in the room around a dining room table and Mike and Frank join them. Mike begins by telling the group, "Frank might have our first assignment; go ahead Frank."

The story unfolds and everybody on the team started writing and then stopped at the point Frank tells the team that Wild might be a traitor. Baker was the first to respond, "How can you run for the Presidency knowing you're a traitor to your country?"

Everybody in the room, including Hadar knew the seriousness of what Ted had just said.

Omid said, "I'm no lawyer, but it would seem to me that the Attorney General is trying to catch a traitor and to me everything every trick, lie, every misrepresentation is on the table."

Frank could clearly sense anger in the room. Based on the reactions of the team members, his team was working with their emotions. Mike stepped in and said, "Frank, I think we need to disband this entire unit and look for replacements."

Frank along with everybody else in the room was in shock but he said to Mike, "Do you mind telling me why you want me to fire all these people. I'm sure they all want to know the answer to that question?"

Mike responded in a dominating voice, "Not one of you asked the boss, "what do you want us to do?" You all went directly to your emotions and reacted to what was said. We can't be effective if we let our emotions get control of us. This was the boss coming to us with a problem that involved the Attorney General of the United States, one of Frank's friends. But more important than that, he is a contemporary of Drew Clinton. His friend and working partner came to him for help, so do you want to look for new jobs, or are we going to try and help our boss and his friend – and, oh by the way, America?"

John Seacrest spoke up and asked, "Mr. Williams, sir, can I ask what facts do you know?"

Frank went through all the detail he could remember and all the team members are writing furiously.

When John heard the name, Viktor he asked, "Sir, would it be possible to get a copy of the recorded phone call?"

Williams asked with somewhat of smart reply. "What good would it do you? You don't speak Russian do you?"

"In fact, sir, I do fluently, so if I could listen to the tape I might be able to pick up some information that the others perhaps missed in their translation. You see, sir, one of the members of the Brotherhood of the Red Nile is in fact a Russian petroleum engineer who studied at Stanford. His uncle, whom we believe is behind the funding of the Brotherhood is one of the richest men in Russia and he made his fortune in buying, selling, and drilling for oil, and by the way, sir, the uncle's first name is Viktor."

The rest of the Pathfinders kept their heads down and listened.

Mike responded, "Excellent work, John. Frank we will build a profile for you on Viktor, last name unknown, and get it to you so you can give it to the Attorney General."

John listened to Mike's commitments to Frank, but he was thinking, *Viktor's last name is Antipova and I know right where he is.*

Chapter 119

FRANK RETURNS TO A WAITING ELLEN

Frank said, "Goodbye" to the team and asked Mike to join him outside. As they walked through the front door of the bungalow he said to Mike, "I think we came together in there today and I really appreciate your help with my problem. Anything that you can develop that will help the Attorney General will be greatly appreciated. We need him to be strong and healthy to prosecute the bad guys that you find for us.

"I think the Pathfinders can be a force for good in the government and I see many opportunities down the road if Jordan is reelected President. This project will be a test of your team's capabilities. I have to tell you that Washington wants me back, so Ellen and I will be leaving Sanibel the day after tomorrow. Ellen and I have come to really love this place and we will hate to leave. Perhaps coming back to check on the progress the team is making will give both of us a chance to enjoy Sanibel again. Mike, call me as soon as you have more details on Viktor. I really want to help Drew."

Frank got in his car and went out the gate waving to the guard and headed north on Periwinkle toward Tween Waters Inn and the beautiful Ellen. He called the room to tell Ellen he is on his way and he should be there in about fifteen minutes. Ellen responds, "I'll be waiting."

On his way to the room he wondered, *what can I do special tomorrow night for Ellen on our last night on Sanibel? I'm not very good at the romantic stuff; I guess I'll have to talk to the front desk and see if they have any ideas.* Frank pulled into the parking lot and started walking up the stairs toward his room when he saw a few rose petals on the floor. He thought it was strange but didn't give it another thought. The wind must have carried them here. His thoughts changed when he walked into the room.

Just inside the door he first looked at the floor and the trail of rose petals leading his eyes to the bed. As he looked in the middle of the bed he saw a nearly naked Ellen who was partially covered in rose petals. She had petals outlining her whole body. She has used more petals along her sides to help outline her hips. Because her breasts are so full, firm, and round the petals won't stay in place and they keep sliding off. Frank watched as she tries to put more petals on her breast but she finally gives up and said, "The heck with it; they are what they are."

Frank just stood at the edge of the bed looking at Ellen. The contrasts are incredible. The white sheets, the red roses, the dark tan lines from Ellen's bathing suit and the red rose petals on the whiteness of her middle torso. The red rose petals on her very white breast make an inviting contrast.

Ellen looked up and said, "Do you want to pick some petals?" Within a few moments, Frank was undressed standing at the side of the bed wondering what he should do next.

Frank picked most of the petals off Ellen. Together they made love over the scent of the roses being crushed by their bodies and the perfume smell enhancing their stimulation. When the climax is over, the two of them lay together naked, sweating from the intensity of the lovemaking, rose petals stuck to their bodies. They are both silent for the longest time and then Frank finally broke the silence. Frank kissed Ellen on the forehead while he is holding one of her breasts.

"Ellen, we have to go back to DC the day after tomorrow."

Ellen responded pouting, "Do we have to?"

"I can't think of any trip we have ever taken that I, and I hope you, have enjoyed as much as our time on Sanibel. I feel like I rediscovered you and all that you can do for me, including some of the most incredible sex we have ever had."

Ellen quickly jumped in, "I have never had as much fun, play fun, sexy fun, with you in all our married life. We have to come back and see if the magic can happen again."

Frank responded, "I agree."

Ellen asked, "How soon?"

"Finding out who wins the election will have a big impact when we can come back and why we would come back to Sanibel."

"So, if Jordan wins we might come back?"

"Most definitely."

"Is he going to win?"

"I don't know; voters can be quirky. It really depends on what happens in the next two debates and if there are no further attacks."

"Do you think there will be another attack before the election?"

"Ellen, we have seen there are a lot of strange and misguided people in the world, so anything could happen."

Chapter 120

THE SECOND DEBATE

The campaign momentum is like the Dickens story, The Tale of Two Cities; Jordan's camp is seeing a ground swell of support nationally, while Wild's poor performance in the first debate has seen his support slipping. The New York Times in an above the fold headline said, "Wild has to win big tonight, or go home." The second debate subject is, "What Should America's Role be in the World?" The camps are divided. One believes we are the Sheriff to the world and the other believes that we need to take care of ourselves first.

The rules are the same as the first debate so Wild will go first, "In three, two, one."

"Good evening and welcome to the second debate between myself and Mr. Jordan. The subject for this debate is, 'What should be America's role in the world?' I think we are the last bastions of hope for freedom, and as such we need to defend all nations that are being attacked by those who want to overthrow a free and elected government. We must be ready to intervene to protect innocent women and children. We must make those hard decisions sometime at the expense of our own people's needs. If we don't do it, then who will? No other nation has the power of right on their side the way the United Sates does. We are a nation of immigrants and we need to bring more qualified immigrants to America. We must grant citizenship for undocumented people in the United States." Wild fills all of his time this debate, but he has left himself wide open to criticism from Jordan.

When Jordan's turn came he said to the people watching, "We must provide for the American people first and foremost. We do not have the resources to be the World Sheriff any longer. We have no more right to tell another government what it should do to and for their people than another government should tell us what to do to and for our people. Yes, it is true, at least for now; we have the military power to punish other nations who do not conform to our wishes and standards. We have seen in our own country the rebellion of individuals who think that they have a better way and they set off nuclear bombs that killed almost 60,000 Americans. There is a lesson to be learned about our role. I'm not saying that we should lead from behind as some of my predecessors have practiced, what I'm saying is it is no longer our way or the high way.

"What Mr. Wild is proposing, it seems to me, lacks vision. On too many occasions America has acted on either a foreign or domestic policy where the leadership in Congress and the White House has not spent enough time thinking about what might be the consequences of our actions. I believe gone are the days when we ruled the world as the sole superpower and where we could impose our will on the world. It seems to me that we have to continue the fight against terrorism, and I will speak more about that in the next debate. We as a nation need to take care of our own first. The idea that we would even consider spending billions of your dollars to impose our will on other nations has passed. As your President, should you reelect me, I promise I will not choose between feeding our people and bombing another nation because we don't like what they are doing. America no longer needs to be feared, but I do want it respected for what it is trying to do for its people."

Question one from the Web: "With all the turmoil in Egypt, Syria, Iraq, and Iran, should America be involved in the problems of these countries?"

Wild responded, "We have to do everything we can to promote stability in the Middle East and if at times we have to conduct air strikes to protect populations, then we must do it."

Jordan responded, "The people of the Middle East have their own culture, religion, and value system. We should not try to force our value system on them. I have no doubt that if the roles were reversed, we would be just as angry. If we don't like what they are doing, we will never be able to change their ways by endless bombing runs."

Question two: "Should we be trying to win these people over with guns and money in foreign aid; an outdated idea?"

Wild responded, "Providing money to governments for food to feed their people and weapons to protect them from other nations who might attack is an excellent way to build positive relations with the people and the government."

Jordan responded, "I cannot justify the spending billions of Americans tax dollars on foreign aid when we have people in need right here in America. If we can get our economy growing and the Federal cash register overflowing, let's pay down the debt and then we can offer loans, not free gifts."

Question three, to President Jordan. "If we stop paying foreign aid, won't other countries like the Russians or the Chinese consider taking our place, and they will want more for their money? Aren't they likely to turn their beneficiaries into puppet states?"

Jordan knows that this question has come from one of Wild supporters, and depending upon how he answers the question, it could turn the tide for the campaign and re-energize Wild and his people.

Jordan responded. "Excellent question, history might be a good place to look for your answer. The Russians invaded Afghanistan and stayed for ten years and finally left. They had spent billions of dollars, lost thousands of soldier's lives and what did they gain? Nothing. Millions of Americans after the Iraq and Afghanistan wars felt like the Russian people felt after their involvement in Afghanistan. They were war-weary and questioned what they achieved. It is the same answer as before, nothing but more debt and dead soldiers. I have concerns about this. What do Americans get from bombing nations we just don't understand? Nothing."

Chapter 121

NATHAN MEETS WITH HIS SECRET TEAM

It is the day after the second debate and President Jordan is in his office reading the newspaper reviews of his and Senator Wild's performances last night. Mary called him to tell him his ten o'clock appointments have arrived, and Jordan tells Mary to show them to the small conference room. The President stops just before he is ready to get up and go to the conference room. As he sits back down in his chair, he is beginning to think, *there is a possibility that he could be reelected and if so, what will he want to do in his second term? The list goes on and on, but I have to focus on a few bold initiatives that will ring with the people, get them excited and let the world know where we stand as a nation. Energy, Security, grow the economy, and lastly putting people to work are the big concerns of the people. The rest may be important in the long run, but will mean very little to the people in the here and now. I have to manage people's expectations; I don't want to overpromise and under deliver.*

The President stood and left the Oval Office and headed to the conference room and his team. In the room are the Secretaries of Energy, Defense, Homeland Security and the National Security Advisor. "Thank you all for coming. We are getting down to the wire, the last debate and election day, soon all this will either be over or in place for another four years. What I want today is to talk with you about what a second term might involve. Now, I don't want to go into fine detail, just some simple thoughts." Jordan explained to those assembled what he has been thinking about and solicited their input.

Mike Findley is in charge of energy. "Sir, I agree with you that we must become energy independent. I'm not saying this because I'm the person in charge of energy, but I believe we have to solve the energy problem to create the second Great American Revolution. We are slaves to the whims of the OPEC nations and their desire to control the world. People who we have thought were our friends, in many cases, have really been our enemies."

"Mike, I really like the concept of the second Great American Revolution. How are the pipelines coming?"

"Sir, ahead of schedule. But if I may, sir, another issue is what to do about the shut-in wells in the Gulf?"

"We are going to need that oil if we want the country to grow."

"I agree, sir, but the process we are now using only allows a trickle of the potential out there.

"Then we have to find a solution soon."

"Yes, sir."

"Bob Hamilton, what is the condition of the military?"

"Sir, we're stretched helping with the curfew and assisting with the coverage in Martial Law. If we could get some relief, we could be ready in case of another attack."

"Bob, any indication that somebody will try an attack similar to the one by the Brotherhood?"

"Mr. President, our sources tell us there is still a great deal of chatter about the two attacks, and there is an indication that Iran has at least three more converted weapons like those used against us for sale. We also understand that the price of these weapons has tripled and could go much higher. We think it is important to work with the resources of Homeland Security to find and perhaps destroy these bombs.

"Sir, in our last meeting we talked about securing our borders as a matter of defense. We have no idea how many terrorist organizations already have people in the United States, nor do we know who they are, and we have no clue where they are. Sir, you could have a terrorist cell living across the street from the White House."

"Mr. Simons, we have not heard from Homeland Security."

The Brotherhood of the Red Nile

"Mr. President, I agree with Bob that our borders are like a sieve. The Brotherhood came in undetected and left almost undetected. We must address this issue right away. I think it is a matter of National Security."

Fred Markel, the National Security Advisor, responded to Bill Simons comment, "Borders are a challenge, but so is the number of illegals in the country. We have to fix both of these security problems."

"Gentlemen, we have addressed all the issues except for economic growth, and with that, more jobs. What do we do there?"

Findley is the first to respond, "Sir, I have mentioned the need to get the oil out of the Gulf. If we can find a way to get it flowing, we will put millions back to work. In each area of the nation on private and government land, we need to look for oil and natural gas. We hired a vast number of people to build the two pipelines and we are going to have to build a new pipeline structure to get the oil and natural gas in the ground in Texas and the Gulf flowing again. The lost refineries in Texas have to be replaced, meaning more building and more jobs. Once we figure out a way to secure the border, we will need to build that protection. That too will create millions of good paying jobs."

Bob followed up, "Sir, we are going to have to become a new and different nation. The American people will hear your dream. Should you be reelected, the new America will be more concerned about itself and less concerned about the world. Some of your detractors will not like what you say and will call it isolationism. I'm not suggesting that we ignore the rest of the world, but I want everybody thinking about what is best for America."

Jordan thanked them for their reinforcement of his thoughts, and closed the meeting by saying, "I want to thank all of you for your service. Keep your fingers crossed that America truly shares our vision and will accept the difficult road ahead."

Chapter 122

ONE WEEK TO GO, THIRD DEBATE

Jordan knows that in this debate with the subject "Keeping America Safe", he is the most exposed to criticism. In the last election, he told the American people that terrorists would not attack on his watch - but they did and more Americans died than any single battle in the Civil War.

Wild goes first.

"My fellow Americans, the subject for tonight's debate is keeping America safe. Four years ago my opponent ran on a platform that America would not be attacked on his watch. Over 60,000 of your loved ones, friends, and neighbors were killed in the most vicious attack on America in history. My fellow Americans, we have a country that has a dusk to dawn curfew and Martial Law in every state. Does that make you feel safe now? It has taken a huge percentage of the American military to enforce the curfew and Martial law that means they can't find and destroy the bad guys. Does that make you feel safe?

"Not too far down the road from where I'm speaking is the National Archives, and in this building we have the Constitution and the Bill of Rights. These sacred documents spell out how the government should be set up and they create certain specific checks and balances to ensure your freedoms. Your President has suspended your rights and ignored the Congress and he has used the executive order one hundred and twenty three times; in one of those orders he took the land and houses of millions of Texans. Does that make you feel safe? Your President, by ignoring these sacred documents, has made himself a dictator. Does that make you feel safe? Your President has locked up your money in the banks, shut down the capital markets and brought chaos to the rest of the world. Does that make you feel safe?

"My fellow Americans, the choice is clear. You can reelect Nathan Jordan as the first American dictator or you can vote for William Wild for President. The choice is clear. We are at different ends of the spectrum. This is not a case as in many past elections where both candidates were close to the center, not right or left leaning, but open to ideas and solutions. Next Tuesday the differences are clear. I ask for your support for an America that is free again; I ask for your vote."

Nathan Jordan responds,

"My Fellow Americans, I agree with Senator Wild that our country is at a crossroads. I believe we are on the verge of the Second American Revolution. A Second Revolution that wants to put people back to work. A Second Revolution that makes America energy independent. A Second Revolution that makes America the largest oil and natural gas exporting country in the world. A Second Revolution that uses the profits from energy not to fund terrorists, but to make life better for all Americans.

"I want a Second American Revolution with a smaller federal government, a government that spends its resources on America first. We have to secure our borders and just like the outcome of the first American Revolution, I want a new wave of legal immigrants who want to come to America to work, grow, with prosperity for them, their children, and grandchildren, not to go on public support.

"I know that I have failed you on my campaign promise of four years ago; America will not be attacked on my watch. I'm truly sorry at having failed, I'm sorry for the lives that were lost but I have learned more and grown as a person from my mistakes than my successes. I have tried to be honest with you, as we have worked our way through this crisis. The challenges ahead of us are many and some will be very difficult causing some sacrifice for many Americans but I believe the spirit of '76 can lead us again to glory.

"I want to respond to some of the allegations of my opponent. I have reached out to the leadership in the Congress, including Senator Wild, asking Congress to review all of my executive orders when they have enough members for a quorum.

"You just heard my opponent tell you that I have had total disregard for the sacred documents that founded our great nation. I took a great deal of time and involved many lawyers just because I wanted to protect your rights. Now to his last point that I'm a dictator. On my watch, I tried to make the right decisions for America and I knew that many would not be popular with my opposition and many Americans. I have told you the truth, as I knew it at the time I spoke to you, and if I had bad information I corrected it.

"So, my fellow revolutionaries, next Tuesday you will have a say in the future of America. Do you want a Second American Revolution or do you want what my opponent has to offer? As you reach for the lever, think about what he has offered to you. If you know what he wants to do and you agree, pull the lever for him. However, if you want to join the Second American Revolution, then pull the lever for me."

Karen came over to Nathan hugged and kissed him and said, "You will never have to do that again; win or lose it's done. It is now up to the people and we will know in a week what they think. I think the people will know that you spoke from the heart. You didn't sugarcoat it. You were magnificent; I'm proud to be an American, I'm proud of my country, and most of all, I'm so proud of you."

Chapter 123

ELECTION DAY

It was a crisp November morning when the President and Mrs. Jordan awoke. The President had a very light schedule of appointments, so he enjoyed just lying in bed with Karen. Nathan said to Karen, "You know it would be a lot more fun if we were naked under the sheets."

Karen responded, "If I get naked, how do I know that you won't attack me and take advantage of my nakedness?"

"Let me make this very clear: if you get naked I am going to make love to you and if we are both lucky maybe more than once."

Karen responds, "I'll race you."

After several sessions of lovemaking they both lay back on the pillow exhausted. With Jordan's arms around Karen, they are lying next to each other like spoons in a drawer. Nathan said, "As much as I would love to lay here and hold your rich and sensuous body, I'm hungry and I have to vote and meet a few people."

This is going to be a long day, as they will not know if Nathan has been reelected until after three thirty AM tomorrow morning.

They both got up and went into the President's bathroom and into the large shower. Nathan washed Karen's back. With a warm soapy washcloth Nathan washed Karen's butt and then turned her around and seductively washed her breasts.

Karen said to Nathan, "I think they are clean enough; you're done."

Jordan responded. "Are you giving orders to the President of the United States?"

"You bet! What are you going to do about it?"

"Find something else to wash." And they both laughed.

Once they were dressed, they went to the Truman Balcony to have brunch. When they finished Jordan got up from the table, walked over to Karen and bent over to give her a kiss good bye. While Karen raised her head Nathan slowly brought his hand up and gently caressed Karen's left breast. She had an initial start and then intensified the return kiss. Their lips parted. Jordan started to release his hand, but Karen quickly reached up and placed her hand over his and said softly, "I love you, regardless of the outcome."

Jordan responded, "Me too."

The President walked down the steps with a clear spring in his step and walked into Mary's office and asked, "Have you voted yet?"

"Yes, sir."

"Did you vote for me?"

"I don't have to answer that question," She said with a smile on her face.

"Who do I have today?"

"Mr. President, you have a meeting coming up in about twenty minutes with Attorney General Clinton and Frank Williams from Homeland Security."

"Do we know what the meeting is about?"

"Mr. President, I was told that the topic is National Security."

The President walked into the Oval Office, went to his desk and saw a selection of newspapers from across the nation and some print outs of the major bloggers. All seem to suggest that the President is a shoo-in to win; the question is just by how much. The buzzer rang and Mary told Jordan, "Sir, your eleven o'clock is here."

"I'll be right out."

Jordan walked out and greeted Drew and Frank and escorted them inside his office. "So, I understand the two of you want to talk about a National Security issue."

Clinton, because of his senior position spoke first. "Mr. President, it has come to our attention through several sources that an elected official has been compromised by a foreign power."

Jordan responded, "Do we know what if any information this person has traded to the foreign government? Is there any evidence that the person has received any compensation?"

"No, sir. We have a recorded telephone call from one of the terrorists of the Brotherhood of the Red Nile speaking to a counterpart in Russia, and in that phone call he mentioned the name of the person."

The President spoke. "What are you doing to find out if this person is in fact a traitor?"

"We have wiretaps on all his phones and he is being shadowed by a team of secret Service agents."

The President spoke. "You said that the recorded message mentions a name."

"Yes, sir, it does."

"Who is it?"

Both men swallowed hard and Drew said, "William Wild."

"I can't believe it. William Wild is not a traitor."

"Mr. President, I would like to think the same, but the issue is if he is elected President what responsibility do you have to release the information? We are still working on the data and I know my Pathfinders will not gather enough information before tomorrow morning. But if he is elected, you will have to do something before you leave office, because if we find out he is a Russian puppet, our country is in serious trouble."

"Can you get me a transcript of the phone call today?"

"Yes, sir. Today."

"I can't believe that Bill Wild is a traitor."

Chapter 124

THE WINNER IS: AMERICA

The news networks did not get any of the voter information for the primaries. They have gotten a little smarter. Because the election is being held on the Internet, they can send emails to try to solicit voters' to respond to their questions. Every indication is that the percentage of votes casting ballots in the Presidential election may approach ninety percent of the eligible voters, the highest of all time. Because of the lateness of the hour in reporting the Presidential outcome, the broadcasts focus on the state and local elections. One clear pattern is developing; those Senators running for reelection or for an open seat who support Jordan are crushing their Wild supporting opponents. The whole House of Representatives is up for election, and again the man rather than the party seems to be the deciding factor. Those supporting Jordan, regardless of party, are winning big time.

Nathan went upstairs to the family quarters and Karen greeted him with a warm kiss. All of their children, their spouses and their children are there and they will try to stay awake until the result will be announced about three or four in the morning. The whole gang sat down to a wonderful dinner, and after dinner the grandchildren are finally put to bed. The adults found places to take a nap, knowing they can't stay awake all night.

Karen and Nathan were sitting alone in the sitting room just off the President's bedroom. Jordan turned to Karen, who was nearly asleep. "I learned something today."

Karen could tell that what he was about to tell her was very important.

"I had a visit this morning from Drew Clinton and Frank Williams; they told me that there is some evidence that an elected official was possibly a traitor working for the Russians.

Karen replied, "How is that possible? Do you know who they suspect?"

"Yes, and that's why it is so difficult. If he is elected, I might have to have him arrested before I leave Office."

"I don't understand, what do you mean before you leave office?"

"Karen, the person under suspicion is William Wild."

"That can't be - Bill Wild a traitor?"

"I listened to the recording between one of the members of the Brotherhood talking to Moscow and Senator Wild is mentioned on the tape as owing them a lot. So, if he wins tonight with my term up January 20, the country could be without an elected President. I know there is a succession plan, but still, at a time when America is trying to recover from a massive terrorist attack, I'm not sure the country could handle the shock that their new President is involved with terrorists.

"Nathan, I'm sure you will be elected, so what do you do with Wild?"

"Karen, I don't know. I'll have to cross that bridge when I come to it, but for now let me hold you and pray that we win."

Karen has fallen asleep in Nathan's arms, but Nathan could not. His eyes would shift to the clock on the wall; the time was moving very slowly. He passed the time by reviewing his last four years; all the good and the bad things he had done and those he had failed to do. He hoped that historians would think he did a good job and that his handling of the attack will bode well for his legacy.

Nathan didn't realize that he had fallen asleep, and he awoke with Karen still asleep in his arms. All of his children came running into his room and yelled, "Dad, you won, and it was the greatest landslide in the history of the nation."

Nathan leaned down and kissed Karen on the cheek and said to her, "Wake up, new First Lady."

Karen opened her eyes and in a groggy voice said, "We won?"

Nathan looked at her; she looked into his eyes and she saw the tears of joy. Karen sat up and said, "I must look frightful."

Nathan replied, "My dear wife, you look marvelous!!"

The kids broke out laughing at the way their father spoke to their mother.

Nathan said, "Now scoot along. Your mother and I have to get ready to meet the press, and I want all of you with me so you need to spruce up a little for the cameras."

The kids are gone and Jordan said to Karen, "We did it, we won. America has made a clear choice. They want to be part of the Second American Revolution. You and your staff made all of this possible; I can't thank you enough for your support and encouragement."

Karen said, "Thank you, my love, but there is one thing you can do for me."

"Name it and if I can do it then it's yours."

"Could you wash my back?"

"Absolutely, and I'll throw in the front for free."

They both laughed as they walked down the hallway with clothing falling to the floor; when they reached his shower they were both naked. Nathan stopped, took Karen in his arms and said to her, "I am truly the luckiest man in the world."

Karen responded, "Yes, you are. We need to get in the shower. I'm cold."

At eleven AM the entire Jordan family was at the podium in the Press Room. The President stepped to the microphone and said, "I know that many of you were up all night waiting for the results and you are tired, so I will make this short. Thank you, America, for choosing the Second American Revolution. There are thousands of people that need thanking and you know who you are, but one person was the most significant contributor to the success of this campaign. She is standing right next to me, the First Lady of the United States."

The room filled with applause for Karen. She waved and said, "Thank you. I want to thank the American people for their loyalty to and confidence in my husband." She stopped waving and stepped back. She said to the kids, "We need to move off the platform because the press wants to ask the President some questions. We'll just step off, but we can watch."

Jordan spoke, "I will take a few questions, but I want to spend some time with my family."

Reporter John Duffy from the New York Times, "Mr. President, are you aware of the magnitude of your victory?"

"John, I have not had a chance to look at the results; can you tell me how it went?"

"Well, Mr. President, you won by the largest number of electoral votes ever, five-hundred and twenty for you, and eighteen for Senator Wild. In the 1964 election, Lyndon Johnson got 61% and for this election you won 81% of the popular vote - unheard of. What do you think?"

"John, I'm overwhelmed. I don't know what to say."

Rupert Smith, Washington Post: "Mr. President, what are the issues that you think your second administration will have to face?"

"Rupert, I will address that question in my inaugural address but not now. This is a time to celebrate a new beginning for America.

"I do have one last comment before I leave to be with my family. To all the people who voted for me and those who voted for Senator Wild, we both thank you for participating in this important and historic election. I promise I will do my best to make America better for all Americans. I cannot achieve a new America alone. I will need your help and support, whether you be Republican, Democrat, or Independent. Be assured that our journey will be difficult and sometimes seemingly impossible, but together we will prevail. May Our God Bless America."

Epilogue

January 20th Inauguration Day

Nathan and Karen were dressed and ready to go about thirty minutes early and were sitting in the Blue Room waiting to leave. All the children have left for the Capital, and it is just Karen and Nathan. A White House security officer knocked on the door and the President said, "Come in."

The door opened and the security officer said, "It's time to go, Mr. President."

They followed the guard to the front portico of the White House where the presidential limousine was waiting. The two of them got in and sped off to the Capital. In about ten minutes, the car pulled up to the Capital and they got out and went inside. The sun was shining and not a cloud was in the sky. Karen was escorted to her seat and at eleven fifty, the President walked out on the stage to the podium. The Chief Justice of the Supreme Court stood at the podium and handed the family Bible to Karen. It is open to one of their favorite passages, the twenty-third Psalm verse four:

"Even though I walk through the darkest valley, I will fear no evil, for You are with me; Your rod and Your staff, they comfort me."

Nathan repeated the oath from the Chief Justice: "I, Nathan Wallis Jordan, do solemnly swear, that I will faithfully execute the Office of President of the United States, and will, to the best of my ability, preserve, protect and defend the Constitution of the United States, so help me God."

A massive crowd rained down thunderous applause on the President. The President used his hands to try and quiet the crowd, but they resist. The applause finally died down, and everyone on the platform sat. When all was quiet, the President addressed the crowd, the nation, and the world. One man is watching and listening on the other side of the world with great interest.

"My fellow Revolutionaries, as we embark on the Second American Revolution we have many challenges. Some of the challenges are similar to ones our Founding Fathers faced and many are new. We are untested and we must find out if we can change. We must determine whether we can change, or if we are so far away from the principals of our Constitution that we can never recover. I believe the will of America is strong, its values can be rejuvenated, and we can again be a great, but different nation. I offer to you a roadmap of things I want to accomplish over the next four years that will begin to make America and Americans great.

"Over sixty years ago a great leader for change, Dr. Martin Luther King Jr., stood on the steps of the Lincoln Memorial just down the Mall from here and said the famous words, 'I have a dream.' I too have a dream; that in the next four years America will provide a job, a good paying job, for every person regardless of age, sex, or national origin that wants to work. If we put people to work, then wealth will grow, people will buy houses and second homes, cars, and all manner of goods and services, employing more and more people.

"Second, America must become energy independent."

At that moment the President stopped and pulled some bunting off a section of the platform that revealed two large switches. The President said to everyone, "I want America and I want the OPEC nations to watch what I'm about to do. By throwing this switch, I'm activating thousands of pumps and compressors." The President threw the switch. "I have just activated the biggest natural gas pipeline in the world, built for America by Americans. For every unit of natural gas we pump out of the ground, we can stop importing eight gallons of oil from nations that believe they control our destiny... NO MORE.

"This second switch activates a 360-mile pipeline, again built by Americans for America that will drain the contaminated oil, natural gas, and refined product from the pipelines in Texas, beginning the restoration of the land in Texas and someday allowing Texans to return to Texas.

"We will employ millions of people all over the country to work in developing all the energy resources America has and building whatever needs to be built to make us independent. We must meet the goal of energy independence within ten years. My goal by the end of my second term is to have reduced our oil imports by fifty percent.

"We must secure our borders, so for a time we will be restricting all immigration. Some will say that we are a nation of immigrants and that is true, but we have a very large population of undocumented immigrants in the country. We must find out who is in this country legally and who is here illegally. We must do this for our own protection. I will instruct the Justice Department and Homeland Security to work with the states to develop a Red, White, and Blue, New America identification card that will be available at all government offices. They will be able to issue the card to everybody, including the First Lady and myself, and anybody who has proof they are in America legally. Everybody will have one year to get the card; after that if you do not have proof of citizenship or legal entry, you will be arrested and deported." You can hear a murmur in the crowd and then a wave of applause comes in support of the President.

"One of our sacred trusts is that your government will protect you. People no longer wear white hats or black hats so we can tell who the good and the bad guys are; we need to know. If you come here to go to school, you better go to school or you're going home." The crowd applauds again.

"One last thing and this is very important. What good does it do us to try and rebuild America when people can bring atomic bombs to try to destroy us? We have to stop terrorism, and the way to stop it is to take away the money the nations send to terrorist groups to attack us and other free nations in the world. I pledge to you that after we develop our energy resource I want to export energy around the world to drive down the price of energy and put the funders of terrorism out of business.

"Most of you don't know that when we were trying to stop the flow of contaminated energy from Texas there was a saying that helped to keep everybody focused on the goal and it was 'Stop the Damn Oil.' I want a new slogan to lead us in the fight against terrorism: 'Stop the Oil, Stop the Terrorists.' In closing, this is very important: to the terrorist, the governments and the people that support them, be warned that we are coming to get you, wherever you are. We will take your money, and we will take your weapons, and if you resist us we will take your lives." The President chants from the podium, "Stop the Oil, Stop the Terrorists" and the whole crowd joins in the chant. After a few moment of chanting, the President signals the crowd to be quiet and then he finishes.

"May Our God Bless America."

Coming soon a new series from Dan Perkins

Ted Baker
TERRORIST GOLD

Chapter One

WE'RE COMING TO GET YOU

Viktor Antipova is sitting in the media room of his twenty thousand square foot penthouse on top of his twenty five-story office building across from Red Square. The massive penthouse takes the entire top floor of the building and may well be the largest in Moscow. It has its own elevator, so Viktor can come and go when he pleases. The main room has fifteen-foot high ceilings and on one inside wall, there is a walk-in Russian limestone fireplace with a roaring fire being fed by his private gas well under the building. The wall opposite the fireplace has ten-foot high windows that run the length of the room, over seventy-five feet.

Tonight, in late January, the snow is blowing so hard you cannot see the Palaces across Red Square even though they are beautifully illuminated. But tonight, Viktor is not interested in the views outside of the grand windows. He is more interested in what is on his new eighty-inch big screen TV. He is standing and pacing as he listens and watches the address by President Jordan. The image of the President is almost life size and when he addresses the issue of destroying terrorism by stopping the flow of money generated by oil profits, Viktor's anger is so strong that he kicks the footstool narrowly missing the TV screen.

When the President got to the part about attacking terrorist he said, "And to the terrorists, keep this in mind that we are coming to get you, wherever you are. We will take your money, we will take your weapons, and if we have to we will take your lives."

Viktor thought to himself, *no other leader has ever threatened to do what the President of the United Sates has just told the world that he intends to do. My question is, will he? I know he has the resources, but will he have the stomach and the tenacity to dig us out of our holes, whether in the ground or in palaces? We have trillions of dollars at stake and we will not give up without a serious fight.* Viktor walked over to his desk and turned on the computer screen to see how the oil markets are reacting to the President's threats. He noticed that the near futures are unchanged, but the further out in maturity you go, say three to five years, the price is dropping and dropping fast.

If America is truly headed down a path of not only energy independence, but also becoming the low cost provider to the world, then trillions of dollars will be lost. On the other side of the world, almost six thousand miles from Moscow is Sanibel, Florida. For now, it is the home of Mike Ridley and the Pathfinders. They too are assembled in their meetinghouse and they, like Viktor, have been watching the President's speech and they are excited. With President Jordan's reelection, they know they will have four years to attack terrorists. The President has told them they will have the vast resources of the U.S. government to find the source of the money funding the terrorist groups. Once they have found the true path of the money, they will document it to the President and await his order on taking their money, taking their weapons and capturing them for trial. The Pathfinders will have the right to defend themselves and if necessary they will have the power to take terrorists' lives if they are attacked.

Mike Ridley and the Pathfinders are sitting in the living room of one of the houses in their compound on Sanibel Island. Sanibel is located six miles out in the Gulf of Mexico off the coast of Southwest Florida near Ft. Myers. The compound on Sanibel will be the staging area for the missions the Pathfinders will undertake. They have been watching the President's address and they are so excited that he has laid down the gauntlet and he is committed to their work. They know it will be dangerous work, but with Mike to guide them, they believe they will succeed.

After the President, finished Mike walked over and turned off the TV. The Pathfinders were disappointed, because they wanted to watch the parade. "I'll set the DVR to record and if we have time later, we can look at the tape. For now, we have work to do. As Mr. Williams was leaving here to go back to Washington, he had a conversation with me. He has our first mission that I think is really three. Let me state, as a ground rule going forward, we will be the only people who know the names of our targets. I do not want anybody else other than Mr. Williams and the President to know what we are doing; any questions?

"Mr. Williams told me a shocking story that was told to him by the Attorney General of the United States. He said that the AG has evidence that a Russian oil billionaire has somehow corrupted a United States Senator and that the Russian is connected to one of the members of the Brotherhood of the Red Nile. Williams thinks that the Russian oilman is the source of funding for the Brotherhood. Our job is to try and figure out how our Russian corrupted Senator William Wild."

Ted interrupted, "Is this the same Senator Wild that was running for President?"

Mike responded, "Yes."

Ted continued, "If he had won the election, we would have had the President being blackmailed by the Russians. Man, did America dodge a bullet!"

"We have to build a plan to find out if Wild directly or indirectly got or is getting money from the Russian, and at the same time we need to find out if Viktor Antipova was the source of funding for the Brotherhood of the Red Nile. If we can prove it, all of us, along with some help, will pay a visit to Saba in the Caribbean and have a chat with the Brotherhood. Hadar will see Mordecai one more time as we lead them off the island to trial and perhaps death. John, I need you to reach out to your contacts at Interpol and see what they have on Viktor Antipova. Ted, I need you to talk to Mr. Williams and tell him we need a contact at the Comptroller of the Currency to talk about Senator Wild's personal and campaign bank accounts."

Ted asked, "What will they do for us?"

"We will want to look at all the bank records of the Wild family and extended family and campaign organization to see if we can determine whether money is coming from the Russian. As a candidate for the Presidency, he has to file a series of financial reports showing income and expenditures."

Ted said, "My guess is that he has no money left."

"Ted, under the campaign rules, at the end of a campaign after the candidate has paid all the bills, any money that is left can go to the candidate. So, if Wild's income were greater than his expenses, he pockets the money. Almost all campaigns run in the red, so if Wild's runs in the black, we know something is wrong."

Ted responded, "What a great way to launder money."

Mike said, "Exactly, and we have to follow the flow of the money because foreigners like our Russian friends are limited as to how much they can contribute to a campaign. If we are lucky, our path will lead directly to Viktor Antipova and we could have our first success.

"If we can build the evidence that Viktor was behind the funding of the Brotherhood, then we or the Russian government will take his money and his assets. We will be sending a very important message to those who provide the money and those who take the money and carry out attacks across the globe. I believe we will have to find and destroy more than one terrorist group to put the fear of Allah and us into them."

Testimonials

Other books by Dan Perkins
The Brotherhood of the Red Nile,
A Terrorist Perspective

5.0 out of 5 stars **Surprise!**

By

Beverly Pack-

This review is for The Brotherhood of the Red Nile: A
Terrorist Perspective: A Terrorist Perspective (Kindle Edition)

I wasn't sure how I would feel about a book written about terrorism, especially one written from the terrorist perspective. I usually
enjoy "warm and fuzzy" books with happy endings or "who done
it" mysteries. I was surprised at how much I enjoyed this book!
Dan has definitely hit a grand slam home run! Dan did a master-
ful job of pulling all of the threads of the story together, while
keeping the action exciting. The personalities of the characters
jump off of the page and are very believable. The conversations
of the terrorists gave insight into how some of the world views
the USA. I was chilled by the reality of how vulnerable our
country is and it reminded me of the importance of prayer for
our country. I can't wait to start reading America Rebuilds! Thank
you, Dan, for such a well-researched and well-written book!

5.0 out of 5 stars **Talk about a cliffhanger!**

By

Denise McKee

This review is from: The Brotherhood of the
Red Nile: A Terrorist Perspective (Paperback)

Great book! A book that really makes you think long after you've finished the book. Can't wait to read the next in series!

5.0 out of 5 stars This book is harder to put down than any of the Jack Reacher Books,
This review is from: The Brotherhood of the Red Nile: A Terrorist Perspective: A Terrorist Perspective (Kindle Edition)

Reading this book may make you worry that your reading yesterday's paper and not a work of fiction.

Carl Sandquist
5.0 out of 5 stars Is it real? It's certainly realistic!
By
Bill Rinderknecht
This review is from: The Brotherhood of the Red Nile: A Terrorist Perspective: A Terrorist Perspective (Kindle Edition)

As I finished Brotherhood of the Red Nile: A Terrorist Perspective, asked myself, "Could this happen here in the U.S.?" Dan Perkins first venture into writing is a hit. He has captured the mentality of the diverse group of attackers, the agents whose mission was to stop the attack, and the collateral personalities. It was so engaging I kept pressing to get to the next chapter so I could find out what happened to the characters I left two chapters ago. The book's organization, flow and tempo really kept my interest; I was caught up in the personal, regional, and national perspectives in this thriller... and the best thing is, it just sets the stage for Dan's next book!

5.0 out of 5 stars The Hit Book for 2014
By
Robert Nickell (California)
This review is from: The Brotherhood of the Red Nile: A Terrorist Perspective: A Terrorist Perspective (Kindle Edition)

I read Tom Clancy, Dan Brown, David Baldacci, Michael Connely etc. and now I read Dan Perkins!! He is brilliant. I discovered he was a first time writer, so there are some writing skill issues that must be 100% overlooked, as the story line is incredible. Once I broke through 50% of book one, I was hooked; I had down the characters and the concept. The plot and story will keep you reading chapter after chapter until you fall asleep. I finished book one, and downloaded book two within 5 minutes.

I highly recommend buying this book today, and start reading tonight. It will also scare you. It is so close to reality that it will really make you think about our safety in the USA and other parts of the world.

5.0 out of 5 stars **Great, riveting book**
By
John – See all my reviews
This review is from: The Brotherhood of the
Red Nile: A Terrorist Perspective (Paperback)

Having spent 30 years in law enforcement, I long thought this would be the best way to seriously harm the country. The current Iranian negotiations would not prevent this terrorist act from occurring. Dan's book is riveting. It is politically current. I have recommended it to several people. Keep them coming, Dan.

The Brotherhood of the Red Nile, America Rebuilds
5.0 out of 5 stars **Scary Good Thriller With a Well Thought Out Terrorist Attack**,
By
Amazon Customer (Reno, NV)
This review is from: The Brotherhood of the Red Nile: America Rebuilds (Kindle Edition)

This story starts with a nuclear bomb being detonated in one of the main oil refineries in Texas. If course you have the basic destruction of things being blow up, people being killed, and high levels of radiation. But the mastermind behind this plan, all of the contaminated oil is still being pumped through the various pipelines for the country.

This oil is only a couple miles away from the main hubs where the pressure is going to blast all that oil through out the whole country contaminating everything within a couple miles of each line. The real problem is there is no way to for sure stop that flow of oil, no main kill switch. And even if they could stop the flow of oil, what are we supposed to do without oil and the by-products.

I have not read the first book but that has not affected this review at all. This book is amazing! Just the concept of such a planned out attack, I never even would have thought about that as something that we faced. There is so much detail about what is happening that you just get sucked into the story. And if that wasn't enough, at the end of each short chapter you learn how far the oil has to go before getting to each major point in the pipeline.

This book is scary good. You have to read it!

5.0 out of 5 stars **America Rebuilds continues the ride from book one of Dan ...**, May 3, 2014
By
Mare - See all my reviews
This review is from: The Brotherhood of the Red Nile: America Rebuilds (Paperback)

America Rebuilds continues the ride from book one of Dan Perkin's trilogy with the pages seeming to turn even faster. Dan makes us face the fact that a devastating attack could happen here and forces us to ask the question - could we survive. Looking forward to the publication of book three!

5.0 out of 5 stars **wonderful suspense...Greta story...super imagination. This is TODAY NEWS!**
By
Robert W Rohl (Aberdeen, SD United States) - See all my reviews
This review is from: The Brotherhood of the Red Nile: America Rebuilds (Hardcover)

"America Rebuilds" is a wonderful follow up to book 1 in the trilogy........AND.. I hope there is a movie because I want to see

Who would get to play" Hadar" in the movie....Dan Perkins....I like your taste and I like your books. Knock us over with book #3.

5.0 out of 5 stars Don't miss the Brotherhood Trilogy,
By
Prefer anonymity - See all my reviews
This review is from: The Brotherhood of the
Red Nile: America Rebuilds (Hardcover)

Book One is a psychological thriller that is intriguing and believable. Instead of a novel, it could be the headlines of tomorrow's news. Book Two - America Rebuilds creates a different, but equally compelling, reader experience. Dan Perkins gives the reader a never-ending overdose of adrenaline as the aftermath of the terrorist attack builds to heights that are frightening to imagine. He keeps you at the edge of your seat while you turn pages in your compulsion to learn how far the devastation will spread and how many more Americans will die. As you read, you begin to recognize that life, as we know it will never be the same. America Rebuilds is the nightmare scenario that we have all been dreading since 9-11. I can't wait for Book Three, hoping that America has a reason to cheer again.

5.0 out of 5 stars so realistic it's scary,
By
Lakefront Muse (Quebec, Canada) - See all my reviews
This review is from: The Brotherhood of the
Red Nile: America Rebuilds (Hardcover)

In this fast-paced page-turning thriller, I kept shaking my head over and over at how realistic everything was. As someone who worked briefly (four years) on intelligence issues, I was impressed with the detail and depth of every scenario in this novel. Anyone reading this will feel like an insider at the White House and privy to the top-secret briefings of the president and senior members of Cabinet. And, if you've never been out to a Gulf oil platform area, you'll feel the breeze on your face in these pages. I can't wait to see this made into a movie. It would be a blockbuster!

5.0 out of 5 stars **Book by Dan Perkins**,
By
Robert Nickell (California) – See all my reviews
This review is from: The Brotherhood of the Red Nile: America Rebuilds (Kindle Edition)

Wow!! I read book two in three nights, and I cannot wait to read book three. Dan is a great writer, and storyteller. I highly recommend reading both books ASAP. This will be the trilogy everyone is talking about by summer of this year. It is so on target it is scary.

Go buy it now!!!

5.0 out of 5 stars **A Gripping Book**, March 28, 2014
By
Elizabeth C – See all my reviews
This review is from: The Brotherhood of the Red Nile: America Rebuilds (Paperback)

I thoroughly enjoyed reading America Rebuilds as it kept me so engaged I felt it was in real-time. I felt my pulse racing and feeling the fear. The characters are vivid to the point that I can visualize them. I'm looking forward to the THIRD book